The Last Voyage

'Dearest, I'll have to be in Belfast for a week or ten days. She really is a beautiful vessel. I'll be sorry to see her go.'

'You'll still have the other ones, won't you?'

'The *Titanic* next.' Clive nodded. 'Bigger and better. The wrights at Harland and Wolff are frightfully proud of their luxury liners. Can't say I blame them.'

'Will you sail with her when she's fitted out?'

'The *Olympic*? I doubt it. I don't want to leave you and the children. Let's hang on until *Titanic* makes her maiden voyage and we'll all go out together.'

'It won't come cheap.'

'Nothing worthwhile ever does,' Clive said. 'Must say, I like the idea of a two-man show in a New York gallery . . .'

JESSICA STIRLING

The Last Voyage

HODDER

First published in Great Britain in 2011 by Hodder & Stoughton
An Hachette UK company

First published in paperback in 2012

1

Copyright © Jessica Stirling 2011

A CIP catalogue record for this title is available from the British Library

Paperback ISBN 978 1 444 71640 5
Ebook ISBN 978 1 444 71639 9

Typeset in Plantin Light by Palimpsest Book Production Limited,
Falkirk, Stirlingshire

Printed and bound by CPI Group (UK) Ltd, Croydon, CR0 4YY

Hodder & Stoughton policy is to use papers that are natural, renewable
and recyclable products and made from wood grown in sustainable
forests. The logging and manufacturing processes are expected to
conform to the environmental regulations of the country of origin.

Hodder & Stoughton Ltd
338 Euston Road
London NW1 3BH

www.hodder.co.uk

PART ONE

Artists in Love
1907

I

The moor drowsed under a hot August sun, as shabby and tawny as the flanks of an old lion. The wavering haze suggested that it stretched to an infinite horizon but Julie knew that if she climbed the half-mile to Bishop's Tor the green and golden pastures of the river valley would open before her, pricked by the landmark tower of Widecombe church. It was far too warm to go exploring, however, and she had seen the view before.

'Has he gone?'

'No, you can still see his dust,' her sister answered.

'He has a cheek, you know, leaving us here.'

'He's bored, that's all,' Anna said.

'He's not the only one who's bored,' said Julie.

Sitting up, she caught a last glimpse of the pony-trap heading for the inn at Storr where Papa would down a pint or two and, if luck was on his side, find some male company to engage in conversation.

She unbuttoned her blouse, fanned air on to her breasts, then, hitching herself round on her bottom, opened her knees to catch any hint of breeze that might stray up from the valley.

Anna looked away. 'I wish you wouldn't do that.'

'Do what?'

'Expose yourself.'

'Oh, don't be such a prude.'

'It isn't decent.'

'A glimpse of my frillies is hardly going to frighten the horses.'

'What horses? I don't see any horses.'

'Must you be so literal, Anna? Why don't you get on with your work?'

'Work!' Anna said scathingly. 'I wish Papa would admit that we haven't an iota of talent between us. He pats our heads and says, "Very good, very good," when even a blind man can see how awful it is. I mean, look!' She lifted her sketch book from the grass and held it up as if she were holding a rat by the tail. 'Four years of lessons with Mr Rodale and this is the best I can do. And don't look so smug. You're no better at drawing than I am.'

'I'd be the last to deny it,' Julie conceded.

Only Uncle Otto, her mother's brother, had ever confronted Papa with the truth. 'Put them into service, Stanley,' he'd said. 'Sign them on at the pickle factory but for heaven's sake stop trying to turn them into something they're not. They're no more artists than I am,' then, pinching Julie's cheek, had added, 'No offence, my dear, no offence.'

Papa had persisted in dragging them round London's picture galleries and had stubbornly enrolled them for lessons with Mr Rodale, who advertised himself as a master of the art of drawing. And as if that wasn't enough 'art' to be going on with they were forever being subjected to the stuff, good and bad, that poured through the shop in

Ledbetter Street where the Martindales had operated a picture framing business for going on half a century.

Pampered by nannies, spoiled by a succession of cooks and housekeepers, Stanley's little darlings had sailed through day school and had returned home each evening to tea, toast and seed cake and as warm a welcome as any girl without a mother could wish for. The only fly in the ointment was Papa's determination that they would become artists in their own right and make the name of Martindale famous for something other than mounts and mouldings.

Anna tossed aside the sketch book and rolled on to her stomach.

'I suppose we'd better do something before Papa comes back.'

'Like what?' said Julie.

'We could draw each other.'

'Oh, no,' Julie said. 'Please, no, not again.'

She propped herself on an elbow and looked down at her sister who, at seventeen, was threatening to blossom into a beauty. Dark eyes and a pouting rosebud mouth had already ignited the interest of young men in the workshop, not to mention the gentlemen who bobbed in and out of the front shop – the gallery, as Papa called it – to discuss how best their latest acquisition might be displayed. There had even been offers, politely put, from several ageing disciples of Rossetti to have Anna model for them. Papa, of course, would have none of it.

Anna raised her head. 'Listen.'

'What is it?'

'Someone's coming. Cover yourself, Julie. Please cover yourself.'

Julie smoothed her skirts and fumbled with the buttons of her blouse.

She could hear voices now and – was it her imagination? – smell cigar smoke.

A small boy, no more than six years old, dashed out of the bushes. He was naked to the waist, barefoot and bare-legged, and had a feather stuck in his hair. He skidded to a halt, eyes round and mouth open.

'Squaws,' he said at length. 'I found squaws.'

A man appeared from behind the gorse bushes and gave the girls the eye.

'They're not squaws, Toby,' he said. 'I do believe they're Martindales.'

Anna was embarrassed by the tray of pastels, the water bottle, the satchel of pencils and the bone-handled penknife that Uncle Otto had given her for her seventeenth birthday, all the paraphernalia of an amateur dabbler that the great Edgar Banbury could hardly fail to notice.

In a light falsetto at odds with his burly frame, he said, 'What are you doing alone in the wilds of Dartmoor? Where's your father? No, don't tell me. He's sloped off to the pub in search of grog? Am I not right?'

'You are, Mr Banbury,' said Julie. 'And you, sir? Are you lodged nearby?'

They had first encountered Edgar Banbury at last winter's Royal Academy exhibition when he'd broken away from a crowd of acolytes to chat with Papa and Uncle Otto and, more particularly perhaps, with the flame-haired girl who'd been Uncle Otto's companion for the evening.

'We're camped over at Foxhailes,' Mr Banbury said. 'We've been sketching too. Haven't we, Toby?'

'I made a painting with Pappy's big brush,' the boy informed them.

'And a very fine painting it was,' Mr Banbury said. 'Now why don't you pop back uphill, Toby, and find the rest of our expedition? Will you do that for me?'

'Yes, I will,' Toby said obligingly and shot off around the bush.

Edgar Banbury blew out his cheeks. 'I fear I've reached an age when coping with young children is well nigh impossible. May I sit?'

'Please do,' said Julie.

Anna watched her sister plant herself on the turf close to the artist's big brown boots. Everything about him was brown, brown and hairy. In spite of the heat he wore a heavy Norfolk jacket over a woollen cardigan and the sort of shirt you only saw on woodsmen. With his long legs drawn up and the stump of a cigar smouldering between his fingers he looked a deal less dashing than he did in the famous self-portrait in the Millbank gallery.

'On holiday?' he asked.

'Yes,' Julie answered. 'A week in my uncle's rustic retreat.'

'Otto? Is he with you?'

'No, he's in London attending to business,' said Julie. 'It's a very small cottage. There really isn't room for all of us.'

'You must forgive me.' Edgar Banbury blew smoke. 'I've rather forgotten your names.'

'Julie.' Julie touched a finger to her chest. 'And Anna.'

'We met,' said Anna, 'at the winter exhibition.'

'That much I do recall,' said Edgar Banbury. 'While I

may have forgotten your name I certainly haven't forgotten you, Miss Martindale.' He hoisted up a knee and cupped a hand over it. 'Has anyone ever told you that you're the image of your mother?'

'My mother?' said Anna. 'I hadn't realised you were . . .'

'So old?' said Edgar Banbury. 'Well, I am – of an age with your uncle, in fact. Your mother was a very lovely woman. We were all struck with her beauty but she, unfortunately, didn't think much of us.'

Toby reappeared. He was accompanied by a young man in a collarless shirt, cotton trousers and a straw hat that looked if it had been chewed by cattle. Slung across the young man's shoulder was a little girl of three or four, her face pressed shyly into his neck.

'Is she asleep?' Edgar Banbury said.

'No such luck,' the young man said. 'She's sulking. Too much sun, I think.'

'Here, let me take her.'

Edgar Banbury detached the child from the young man's arms.

The little girl looked up. 'Where's Howdard?'

'Yes,' Edgar Banbury said. 'Where is Howard?'

'He's coming,' Toby said. 'He wouldn't let me help him.'

'Wise fellow,' Edgar Banbury said. 'By the by, Clive, these charming young ladies are Stanley Martindale's daughters. Allow me to introduce you.'

'Allow me to introduce myself.' Stepping past Anna, he shook Julie's hand. 'Clive Cavendish. Perhaps you've heard of me?'

'I can't say I have,' said Julie.

'He's far too modest,' Edgar Banbury said. 'He's the chap

who painted *The Best of Friends* which created a minor sensation at Maule's last summer.'

'I certainly recall the painting,' Julie said. 'A very nice dog, if I may say so.'

'The dog gave me a great deal of trouble,' Clive Cavendish admitted.

'If you insist on painting huge shaggy Newfoundlands,' Edgar Banbury said, 'what do you expect?'

'They sat well enough for Landseer,' Clive reminded him.

'Not with naked girls perched on their backs.' Edgar Banbury looked round. 'Ah-hah! Stirring in the undergrowth. Could this be our Howard at last?'

'Howdard.' The little girl dropped to the grass and threw herself on the newcomer. 'You found us.'

He was, Anna thought, less than charitable towards the child but she could hardly blame him for being brusque. He was burdened with two bulging canvas satchels, two stiff cardboard folders and a wooden easel and juggling the equipment required his full attention.

'Good man,' Clive Cavendish said. 'Now we can be on our way.'

'Come along, ladies,' said Edgar Banbury. 'Pack your kit and join us for tea. We'll pick up your father from the pub en route.'

'I'm not sure we should impose on your hospitality, Mr Banbury,' Julie said.

'Impose on me then, Miss Martindale,' Clive Cavendish said. He swung the little girl on to his shoulders and called out, 'All set?'

'All set,' Toby shouted and scampered off downhill.

2

The massive feather-hoofed mare had a bell on her collar and wild flowers in her mane, flowers, Anna guessed, that the child, Phoebe, had put there.

At the field gate at the bottom of the hill, Mr Banbury harnessed the mare to the shafts of a farm cart with the skill of a born countryman which, Anna knew, he most emphatically was not. He was the third son of a builders' merchant from Manchester who had run off to London and so impressed the powers that be with his precocious, not to say ferocious talent that he'd been granted a scholarship at the recently established Slade School of Fine Art; an honour that even his strait-laced father had been unable to ignore.

According to Uncle Otto, a fount of salacious gossip, Edgar Banbury had been among the first of the school's rapscallions, disciplined in the classroom, disordered without and with a string of female conquests longer than the Palace Pier. His marriage to the daughter of a humble greengrocer from St Albans had broken many a heart. Driving a farm cart with his son on his knee, he didn't look much like a heart-breaker, Anna thought, nor like the noble figure at the centre of his gigantic ink and watercolour study, *Caesar Entering Rome*, that hung in the New English Art Club.

'And what do *you* do, Mr . . .'

Howard stared at the dusty road and pointedly ignored her. Anna had no clue what position he held in the great man's entourage, for no one had seen fit to introduce him. Behind her Julie reclined on a bale of sweet-smelling hay, Mr Cavendish's arm hovering about her shoulders, the little girl curled on her lap.

'I said' – Anna raised her voice by half an octave – 'what do you—'

'Buskin.'

'Oh, you perform for money in the street, do you?'

'My name: Buskin.'

'Like Shakespeare's shoe?'

'That's bodkin.'

'No, it's not. I do happen to know the difference between a sharp-pointed implement and a boot worn by tragic actors.'

'Good for you,' Howard Buskin said. 'You're right, of course.'

He wore stained grey flannels, a shirt with a soft collar and rolled-up sleeves; no waistcoat, hat or cap. His dark hair was already beginning to recede which made him look older than he probably was. He had a square face, grey eyes, and a mouth not so much pugnacious as petulant. He continued to stare down at the white dust of the country road, as if, Anna thought, he's afraid to look at me.

'Are you a painter, too, Mr Buskin?'

'I paint,' he admitted reluctantly, 'on occasion.'

'Do you exhibit?'

'No.'

'Why is that?' Anna said. 'Don't all painters long to be hung?'

He turned on her abruptly. 'Look here, Miss Martindale, you're under no obligation to make conversation. You're Edgar's friend, not mine.'

At least he knows my name, Anna told herself; that's something.

She said, 'Very well. If you prefer silence, so be it.'

Huffily, she folded her arms but when the cart lurched and Mr Buskin stuck out a hand to steady her she did not draw away.

'Careful,' he said. 'Be careful,' then, a moment later, 'Anna, is it?'

'Yes, Anna.'

'You may call me Howard if you wish.'

The inn at Storr was small and shabby and, at that hour of the afternoon, deserted. There was no light within the building; no sign of life save for a few hens clucking on the step. The pony was tethered to a rail and Papa sat disconsolately, all alone, on a bench by the inn door. He was bent over like a man with stomach ache, a tankard clasped in both hands. His hat was tipped over his eyes and his nose – quite a prominent nose – had already begun to peel.

The farm cart was almost upon him before he looked up.

'Banbury! What the devil are you doing here?'

'I might ask the same of you, Mr Martindale.'

'As you see' – Papa waved the tankard – 'I'm partaking of refreshment.'

'While your poor daughters languish on the moor.'

'Ah, I see you found them.'

'I did,' Mr Banbury said, 'and it's not my intention to release them until they've been stuffed with bread and butter and bathed in tea.'

Julie clapped her hands. 'Please say we can, Papa.'

'Can what?'

'Go to Mr Banbury's camp for tea.'

'Camp?' Papa stepped forward. 'Where is this camp?'

'Foxhailes,' Edgar Banbury told him. 'Are you coming, or not?'

'Am I invited?' Papa said.

'Of course you are, man, of course you are,' Mr Banbury said and, flicking the reins, set the cart in motion, leaving Stanley to settle his bill and follow on behind.

There was no lodge, no park and no long view to take the breath away. You turned off a back road between two stone gateposts and there it was in all its glory – Foxhailes House, a huge picturesque mock-Tudor villa bristling with brick chimneys. Behind the house the moor reared up like a tidal wave. It reminded Julie of a Doré engraving in one of the books in Uncle Otto's library and even bathed in sunlight retained an aura of windy nights and scudding cloud.

'Welcome,' Clive Cavendish said as if he'd read her mind, 'to Baskerville Hall,' and let out a soft little howl that tingled in her ear and made her shiver. 'Have no fear, Miss Martindale, the only hound in these 'ere parts be Howard, and we keep him locked up after nightfall. B'ain't that right, Howard?'

'Very funny,' Howard said sourly.

The cart drew to a halt on the rutted gravel. Clive lowered the little girl to the ground and offered Julie his hand.

'Whose house is it?' she asked.

'It belongs to Verity Millar,' Clive told her. 'Howard's mother.'

Phoebe trotted off into the ornate porch from which, at that moment, a woman emerged, her arms spread wide in welcome.

'Talk of the devil,' said Clive.

It was typical of the hoi polloi to assume that Verity Millar was a lady by disposition if not title but no one who worked at Foxhailes suffered from that illusion. Even loyal Mr Moss, her steward, considered his employer 'showy', which was really no more than you might expect from a woman who had married an American thirty years her senior who'd made his pile by striking gold in the Klondike.

The Klondike story was nonsense, of course, as a little elementary arithmetic would have shown. Clarence Millar had been no nearer the Yukon than Ohio where he'd earned a fortune quarrying vast quantities of sandstone to build the cities of the plains. Some months short of the financial crisis of '93, and recently widowed, Clarence had sold his stone pits and had shipped out for England in search of cultural enlightenment. What he'd wound up with was a spirited new wife, a moody stepson, a town house in London, a modest estate in Devon and more cultural enlightenment than his ticker could cope with.

After five years of marriage to Verity, he'd keeled over late one night in the arms of his sweetheart and was dead before sunrise. The fact that the sweetheart was a buxom young thing he'd met in the Rising Sun and that the keeling over had occurred in a basement in Paddington had somewhat assuaged Verity's grief, that and a fat packet of gilt-edged investments which, there being no other heirs that the lawyers could unearth, fell uncontested into her lap.

Howard Buskin was not overjoyed at his mother's good fortune.

Nothing, it seemed, brought Howard joy. He'd always been dour and solitary even when they'd lived in rowdy Hoxton and his mother had eked out a living modelling at the Fulham Polytechnic and singing bawdy songs in a velvet dress at the Empress Variety Theatre when the management were light on programme fillers. From whom Howard had inherited his incredible skill with pencil and brush was a mystery, one to which Verity, in that wonderfully vague way of hers, refused to furnish an answer.

'He was no one, Howard,' she'd say. 'No one of any consequence.'

'His name. For God's sake, Mama, at least tell me his name.'

'Do you know, I don't think I even knew his name?'

'Liar, you liar!'

'Jim – yes, that was it. Jim somebody. You can't expect me to remember everything that happened thirty years ago.'

'What about my grandfather; your father? Surely you remember him?'

'Dead these many years.'

'But who was he? Who the devil was he?'

'He sold boots and shoes.'

'What? From a stall?'

'In Halifax.'

'Halifax!'

'Hush now, darling. Don't excite yourself. It's all water under the bridge.'

If Howard had been more of a reader and less of a brooder he might have fancied himself the offspring of a convict or perhaps a peer of the realm. But Howard had never acquired the reading habit and preferred to visualise his father as lean, bearded and effete, like Zurbaran's painting of St Francis, and his grandfather sad-eyed and dignified, like Whistler's portrait of Carlyle.

Three years back, in an attempt to bring her son out of his shell, Verity had paid her friend Banbury to accompany Howard to Paris, ostensibly to look at the Rembrandts in the Louvre but mainly to introduce him to sights of a more intimate nature in those big dark houses in the heart of the Ile where the most beautiful young immigrant girls were to be found.

The trip had turned into a disaster when in the house of a certain madam well used to the English and their ways, Howard had punched a pretty little Jewish girl in the face and had broken her nose; a fit of something more than pique that had cost Edgar every sou in his wallet.

Whatever happened in Paris had put Howard off women for ever.

Verity was therefore astonished to see her son seated on the tailgate of Edgar's hired cart with his arm around a pretty, dark-haired girl and, before she could help herself, rushed out into the sunlight to bid the little charmer a very warm welcome. 'And who's this, darling? Who is this lovely creature?'

'Oh, God!' Clive said. 'She's doing it again.'

'Doing what?' said Julie.

'Scaring off the competition.'

He led Julie across the lawn where a lad was vainly

attempting to erect a wooden table while another struggled with poles and a canvas awning. A maid, not much older than a child, darted out of a side entrance with a huge teapot in both hands and, catching sight of Mr Cavendish, squealed and vanished indoors again.

Clive groaned. 'Rustics, you can never really train them, can you?' He looked down at Julie. 'You'll find the cloakroom at the end of the corridor, left of the door.'

'The cloakroom?'

'The closet.'

'Oh, yes, thank you.' Julie made no move towards the house. 'Why did you refer to my sister as the competition?'

'Edgar's convinced that Mother Millar is desperately seeking a wife for her son. I'm a little more sceptical. I think she wants to keep him to herself,' Clive said. 'Of course, I'm only a simple-minded painter of pictures and know nothing of female psychology. Edgar has much more experience in these matters than I have.'

'So I've heard,' said Julie. 'Does he not also have a wife?'

'Clara, yes, but she's in a delicate condition again and has been packed off to spend the final few weeks of her confinement with her mother in St Albans.'

'And you, Mr Cavendish, do you have a wife?'

'No,' Clive answered, with a lift of the eyebrow. 'No wife. Would you like to see the rose garden, such as it is?'

'Indeed,' said Julie, 'I would.'

Shadows were lengthening before the awning was erected, the table made steady and tea brought out. An elderly countryman with side whiskers drove the horse and cart away and returned to fetch Papa's hired pony and lead it off to be watered. It was still very hot, so hot that sandwiches curled at the edges and the icing on the little sponge cakes melted, neither of which disasters seemed to bother the hostess who, throwing up her arms, announced that she had done her best and if they didn't like it they could lump it.

She dumped herself on a wicker chair in the middle of the lawn and summoned Anna to sit by her. Howard served them tea and sandwiches, then, to Anna's surprise, drifted off to join Mr Banbury and her father who, shaded by the awning, were stuffing food into their mouths while the little boy, Toby, and his sister played beneath the trestle.

The tea was too strong and the sandwiches – boiled ham – rather salty. Anna juggled plate and cup while Mrs Millar stroked the back of her neck as if she were a cat who might be persuaded to purr. 'So,' the woman said, 'you're Otto Goldstein's niece, are you? I wonder why he hasn't brought you to visit.'

'We haven't been in Devon much since we were children,' Anna replied.

'You're hardly more than a child now, my dear. How old are you?'

'Seventeen.'

'Howard is twenty-nine.'

'Really?' said Anna.

'I think,' the woman said, 'Otto deliberately kept you from us.'

'Why would he do that?'

'My reputation for one thing.'

Putting down her cup, Anna glanced round in search of Julie who, together with Mr Cavendish, seemed to have disappeared.

'Why, Mrs Millar, I didn't know you had a reputation.'

'Has Otto never mentioned me?'

'No, actually, he hasn't.'

'How remiss of him.' Verity kicked her heels as if confessing gave her pleasure. 'Howard is my secret shame, you see. He was born out of wedlock. It's best you hear it from me and not some scandalmonger if Howard's going to be your friend.'

'Is Howard going to be my friend?'

Verity ignored the question. 'How is your uncle? Does he still have that marvellous moustache?'

'Yes.'

'Does he have a lover? Of course he has a lover. Several, I expect.'

'I – I really couldn't say.'

Embarrassed, Anna scanned the lawn once more but saw no sign of her sister or Mr Cavendish. She wondered if they had gone into the house and if Julie was locked in the handsome painter's arms, kissing and being kissed. She had never been kissed by a grown man and wasn't entirely sure she wanted to be.

'You see,' said Verity Millar, 'he can't take his eyes off you.'

'Beg pardon?'

'Howard: he's been staring at you ever since we sat down.'

'Why would he stare at me?' said Anna.

'He's admiring you from afar. That's his way.'

Anna resisted the temptation to turn her head.

'Howard tells me he's a painter,' she said.

'Oh, he is. Quite brilliant. Even Edgar says so.'

'But he doesn't exhibit.'

'No. He says he won't inflict his work on the public until he's learned how to put the bloom on the peach – whatever that means.'

It was on the tip of Anna's tongue to tell the woman what it meant but she thought better of it. Knuckles touched her neck again and a finger brushed the coil of hair that stuck out from under her bonnet, a gesture far too intimate for short acquaintance.

'Howard's father,' Anna said, 'was he a painter too?'

'He was nothing,' Verity Millar said, 'but a ship that passed in the night. Oh, look, I think your papa is making ready to leave. I've so enjoyed our conversation, Miss Martindale. I hope we'll meet again soon.'

'I hope so too,' Anna lied politely.

The cottage in the lane just outside Brampton was very small and very clean. The stone walls were whitewashed every spring and the wooden floors regularly scrubbed by a woman from the village who also made the beds and prepared an evening meal when Otto or his guests were in residence.

There were two small rooms on the ground floor and a single bedroom tucked under the sloping roof. It was all very quaint, Julie said, but just a little too cramped to be cosy. Papa had the bedroom downstairs next to the parlour and Anna and she shared the wooden bed upstairs; all very different from Ledbetter Street with its spacious apartments, tall curtained windows and the growl of London traffic to send you to sleep.

'Did he kiss you?' Anna asked.

'Of course he didn't kiss me,' Julie answered. 'Mr Cavendish may be an artist but he's also a gentleman.'

'He's a protégé of Mr Banbury and we all know what he's like.'

'Mr Cavendish wants me to pose for him.'

'I thought as much,' said Anna. 'Does he want you to take off your clothes and sit astride a big black dog?'

'He's moved on since he painted that picture.'

'What is it now? Tigers?'

'Why, I do believe you're jealous,' Julie said.

'Not me,' said Anna. 'In any case, Papa won't let you sit for anyone.'

'I'll bet he'd let me sit for Edgar Banbury.'

'You have to be careful of Mr Banbury,' Anna said. 'He's a little too fond of young girls.'

'I'm not as young as all that,' said Julie. 'Besides, it isn't hairy old Edgar who's asked me to pose for him.'

Anna was propped up in bed. In the light of the oil lamp her hair looked like a huge black ink stain on the pillow. Her breasts filled the front of her nightdress and lacy frills couldn't quite hide the swell of her nipples; a sight, however familiar, that never failed to rouse a pang of envy in Julie. She had no chest to speak of and her nipples were as flat as carpet tacks.

Seated on the ledge by the open window, she brought her knees up to her chest and cupped her shins. She had long, slender legs – which was more than could be said for Anna – and perfectly formed feet; mythical feet, Uncle Otto called them, like those of a Botticelli Venus.

The bed was large enough to accommodate two in comfort but the mattress was lumpy and the blankets heavy. Anna was a restless sleeper, forever twitching and flailing, as if she were drowning in her dreams. It was bad enough having to share a room with her sister at home, Julie thought, but sharing a bed and calling it a holiday was really too much.

'Are you going to sit there all night?' Anna said.

'Put out the lamp if it bothers you.'

'What bothers me is you perched at the window where anyone can see you.'

'Anyone?' said Julie. 'Like who?'

'He's not down there, is he?'

'Who?'

'Your Mr Cavendish.'

'Do not be ridiculous. Besides, he isn't *my* Mr Cavendish.'

'I think,' said Anna, 'you rather wish he was.'

There was no breeze to speak of and the trees that surrounded the cottage were motionless. You could hear nothing, not even the cry of a fox or the squeal of a rabbit or any of the sinister country noises that had kept Julie awake when she'd first come to Uncle Otto's house as a child. Uncle Otto's house: Uncle Otto's little cottage, purchased in spite of Papa's protests that property in Devon would never accrue in value. Julie had been sixteen before it had dawned on her that the cottage on the edge of Dartmoor wasn't an investment but a love nest to which her uncle slipped away for trysts with ladies who were too well known to billet within a twenty-mile radius of Charing Cross.

'He's here to paint Mrs Millar's portrait,' she said.

'Mr Cavendish?'

'No, Mr Banbury.'

'If he's working on a commission,' Anna said, 'why bring the children?'

'His wife's expecting again. She's gone off to stay with her mother.'

'Did Mr Cavendish tell you all this?'

Julie nodded. 'Yes.'

'Did he also happen to mention that Howard Buskin has no father?'

'No, he didn't,' Julie said. 'Are you sure?'

'Absolutely. Mother Millar told me,' Anna said. 'She called him "my secret shame", like something out of a trashy novel. She said it would be better to hear it from her lips than anyone else's.'

'Can't say I much care for Mother Millar,' Julie said.

'She knows Uncle Otto from the old days.'

'Everyone knows Uncle Otto from the old days.'

'I wonder if they were – you know.'

'Lovers?' said Julie. 'Well, I wouldn't be surprised. Everyone seems to have been in love with everyone else back then.'

'Except Mama.'

'Yes, except Mama.'

'And Papa.'

'That goes without saying,' said Julie. 'Shall I close the window?'

'I wish you would,' said Anna. 'You know how I hate moths.'

Reaching out, Julie found the metal rod, drew the little lead-paned window tight to the frame and clipped the rod to the bolt.

'Thank you,' Anna said. 'Now the lamp.'

Julie snuffed the wick and eased herself into bed by Anna's side.

There was still no sound outside, nothing but the all-encompassing August night, as dense and silent as the depths of the sea.

She felt her sister stir, heard her sigh.

'Do you believe in love at first sight?' Anna asked.

'No,' Julie answered. 'I don't.'

'No more do I,' said Anna and, giving the pillow a thump, turned on her side to sleep.

3

Mr Cavendish wasn't the sort of fellow to let the grass grow under his feet. He arrived at the garden gate before Papa had raked the grate let alone cooked breakfast.

Julie laced her bodice, struggled into her skirt and, opening the little window as wide as it would go, leaned out and peered, blinking, at the foreshortened figures on the path below. Her bladder was uncomfortably full but the water closet was downstairs behind the kitchen and she was far too demure to make use of the chamber pot that nestled beneath the bed. She hopped on one foot, applied her sunniest smile and called out, 'Good morning, Mr Cavendish.'

Faces tipped up: Papa scowling, Mr Cavendish grinning.

He had spruced himself up for the visit. His striped shirt was spotless and his chewed straw boater had been replaced by a round hat that reminded Julie of a pith helmet. He was clean-shaven, had combed his chestnut curls and in the early morning light looked, she thought, positively scrumptious.

She said, 'I didn't hear the cart.'

'I came on Shanks's pony.'

'You walked?'

'People do, you know.'

'Julie,' her father barked, 'put on some clothes, if you please.'

'It's only arms, Papa. I'm sure Mr Cavendish has seen bare arms before.'

Clearly disconcerted at being caught in nightshirt and trousers with his braces hanging down his back like a monkey's tail, her father was even grumpier than usual at this hour of the morning.

'Why are you here?' she enquired. 'Have you come for breakfast?'

'A splash of tea would be very welcome,' Clive Cavendish admitted.

'Don't they feed you at Foxhailes?'

'*Julie!*'

'Yes, Papa, yes.' Then to Mr Cavendish, 'Down in a tick. Don't go away.'

'Fat chance of that,' said Anna from the bed. 'Three miles on foot before breakfast. By gum, he's keen. Is Mr Buskin with him?'

'It doesn't look like it.'

Anna stretched her arms above her head and yawned. 'I suppose I'd better make myself presentable and put in an appearance before he whisks you off.'

'I doubt if Mr Cavendish will be whisking me anywhere, not if Papa has anything to do with it,' Julie said. 'Have you seen my Russian blouse?'

Anna rolled from the bed and planted her feet on the floor.

'Third drawer down in the chest, I think,' she said.

Julie fished out the blouse, snatched up Anna's hairbrush and the toffee tin filled with hairpins and, before her sister could protest, headed off to the water closet downstairs.

★

If he painted with as much fervour as he ate, Anna thought, Mr Cavendish would soon be rich and famous. It didn't seem to matter that the sausages were burned and the eggs rubbery or that the bread that Papa had fried was four days old. Mr Cavendish was out to impress and if he'd been presented with a plate of raw entrails would probably have tucked in with just as much relish.

They were seated at the parlour table upon which Julie had tossed a none-too-clean cloth and set out napkins, cruet and cutlery while Papa dressed. He was still unshaven, though, and with a day's stubble on his chin looked scruffy compared to their guest. He was very smooth and cool, was Mr Cavendish, even while forking food into his mouth.

'A little more bread, Mr Cavendish?'

'If there is some, sir, please.'

'Another sausage?'

'By all means.'

'Julie.'

Julie rose dutifully from the table and headed for the kitchen where the frying pan was still spitting on the stove. Anna noted how Mr Cavendish swivelled his eyes to follow her sister out of the room; noted too how Julie added sway to her hips and made her skinny little bottom dance under her plain brown skirt.

'Bristol?' her father said.

'Uh?' said Mr Cavendish. 'Oh, yes, Bristol.'

'And what does your father do there?'

'He's a lawyer.'

'Successful?' Papa said.

'Moderately. My brother partners the firm.'

'Ah, you have a brother?' Papa said as if that fact surprised him.

'And two sisters, both married.'

An inquisition was inevitable, Anna supposed. There had been suitors before, nervous young men keen to marry into the business, none of whom had interested Julie in the slightest and none of whom had survived Papa's interrogations.

'Do you live at home?' Papa said.

'Good heavens, no!' Mr Cavendish said. 'I'm the black sheep of the family. Well, no, to be fair that's not strictly true. My father doesn't disapprove of what I do. Indeed, I think he's rather proud of my accomplishments.'

'Which are?' said Anna.

'I had a small show of my watercolours in Maule's last year.'

'Yes,' Papa said, without inflexion. 'Sold out, I believe.'

Mr Cavendish looked modestly down at his plate. 'I count myself fortunate that some people like my work.'

'We mounted one of your copperplates recently: *Lily of the Valley*.' Papa paused and added tactfully, 'Very accomplished.'

'I'm not awfully fond of the needle,' Mr Cavendish confessed. 'Etching's not something I intend to pursue. I simply don't have time.'

'Why is that?' Papa asked.

An unassuming shrug: 'Commissions.'

'Is that why you're here on Dartmoor?' Papa said. 'To sketch ponies?'

'Ponies?'

'I thought perhaps you fancied a change from dogs,' Papa said.

For an instant Mr Cavendish's mouth opened like that of a fish, then he laughed. 'Oh, that's good, sir,' he said, 'that's very good.'

Julie returned from the kitchen, plate in hand. 'What's good?'

'Papa made a joke,' Anna told her.

'Really?' Julie said. 'He'll be playing his ukulele next.'

'Oh, do you play the ukulele, sir?'

'Of course I don't,' Papa said. 'She's teasing you, Mr Cavendish.'

'No, Papa, I'm teasing *you*.' Julie planted a kiss on the crown of her father's head and seated herself at the table. 'Eat, Mr Cavendish, eat and don't be shy.'

One more slice of greasy bread and he would throw up all over the tablecloth. He chopped up a sausage, speared two pieces on the fork, shoved them into his mouth and chewed again, manfully.

'Fresh air has obviously sharpened your appetite,' the girl, Anna, said.

'Um,' he said. 'Um, yes, it has rather but I admit I'm almost stuffed.'

He had sacrificed several hours of sleep and walked three miles from Foxhailes for Howard's sake but he was damned if he'd ruin his digestion just to please the irksome little twerp. Tramping cross country to Brampton at the crack of dawn had not been an entirely selfless act, however. The elder Martindale was not without her charms. She was certainly attractive, more so than her sister who, at seventeen, had that moist dewy look that lascivious old-school scoundrels like Edgar found irresistible.

He demolished the remainder of the sausage and pushed the plate away.

The Martindales watched apprehensively as if they expected him to break wind. He brought out his cigarette case, clicked it open and offered it round.

'Turkish,' he said, 'or American?'

Anna shook her head.

'Turkish, if I may,' said Julie.

The old man clearly didn't approve of women smoking but he was incapable of stopping his strong-willed daughter doing what she wished. It might prove amusing to find out just how far Julie Martindale's rebellious streak could be stretched, Clive thought, as she plucked a cigarette from his case.

He said, 'I believe you're heading back to London tomorrow.'

'Yes,' the old man said. 'Holiday over.'

'I, for one, shan't be sorry,' Julie said.

'I thought you came to Brampton to paint,' Clive said. 'A week hardly seems long enough. Doesn't Dartmoor inspire you?'

'I'm not a country girl at heart,' said Julie. 'Nor am I a painter.'

'I've done my best,' the old man said. 'I've given them every opportunity.'

'It's not your fault, Papa,' Anna said. 'We're just not cut out for it.'

'I assume,' Clive said carefully, 'you've taken lessons?'

'The best money could buy,' the old man said. 'Four years of instruction and nothing to show for it.'

'Who's your teacher?' Clive asked.

'Mr Rodale,' Anna told him.

Although he'd never heard of Mr Rodale he nodded as if he had. 'In that case – I mean, if you're leaving tomorrow, it seems I've arrived in the nick of time.'

'For what?' Papa Martindale said.

'To invite you to a picnic.'

'At Foxhailes?' said Anna.

'On the moor,' Clive said. 'Bishop's Brook. Do you know it?'

'Yes,' Julie said. 'We used to paddle there with Uncle Otto years ago.'

'Bring your books and do a little sketching if you wish, though Edgar will no doubt frown on anything resembling effort.'

'Who'll be at this picnic?' the old man said suspiciously.

'Everyone.'

'Including Mr Buskin?' Anna asked.

'Without doubt,' Clive answered and, rather to his surprise, saw her blush.

4

The pencil was no thicker than a straw and had a fine hard point, the sort of point that pricked your thumb if you were careless. Anna watched the bird materialise on a blank page of the notebook: wings and tail, head and beak and then the eye – three tiny arcing strokes and a single dot pressed firmly into the paper.

'What is it?' she asked.

'Pied wagtail,' Clive answered.

'Where?'

'There,' he said. 'See.'

The black and white bird perched on a stone by the edge of the pool before, conscious of Anna's scrutiny, it flew away.

Bored by Verity Millar's aimless prattle, Clive had left the others lounging on the bank of the stream and had wandered off a little way on his own. He supported the notebook with his left hand and drew with his right, quick, flicking strokes of the pencil, casual-seeming yet wholly assured.

Anna was glad she'd left her pastels at home.

She said, 'What else have you done?'

He turned the leaves of the notebook and she, with a hand

on his shoulder, leaned forward to admire the thumbnail sketches. Eight tiny vignettes had been rendered in as many minutes: Verity slouched on her camp chair, featureless but unmistakable; Papa drinking bottled beer, bowler hat tipped back; Edgar Banbury sprawling, long-legged, boot heel propped on boot toe; Howard hugging his knees, sullen as a granite outcrop. Anna envied Mr Cavendish his eye, the artist's eye that saw things that she would never see.

He turned the page with his fingertip.

'Your sister,' he said. 'Isn't she pretty?'

Julie paddling with the children in the brook, skirt hoisted to her knees, hands on her hips; Clive had replaced her plain skirt with a floral dress caught up like a cockle-gatherer's in the manner of a Reynolds or a Millais.

'Is that really how you see her?' Anna asked.

'I do take liberties now and then.'

'I wonder how you see me.'

He laughed and turned the page once more.

Anna felt a little throb of disappointment. He'd drawn her at the instant she'd turned to look for him, arm raised to shield her eyes, bonnet against her chest, her hair, three or four hasty scribbles, framing a vacuous face.

'May I have it?' she said.

'No, you may not.'

'Why not?'

'It's nothing,' Clive said. 'A doodle doesn't do you justice.' He rested his head against her skirt and looked up. 'You're far too beautiful to capture on a scrap of paper. Edgar could do it, perhaps, but I'm not Edgar.'

'You're placating me, aren't you?'

'No, I'm—'

'What's going on here?' said a voice behind her.

'Not a thing, old chap,' said Clive. 'I thought you were asleep.'

'Well, I'm not,' Howard Buskin said. 'Have you been working?'

'Just keeping my hand in.' Clive slipped the pencil into its sheath, closed the notebook and popped it into a pocket of his shirt. He got nimbly to his feet. 'Can't think why you didn't bring your materials, Howard, now we have two pretty young ladies to model for us.'

Howard Buskin stuck out his hand. 'Let me see.'

'Certainly not,' Clive said.

'Are you ashamed of what you've done?'

'You're a fine one to talk,' Clive said. 'I've never so much as glimpsed one of your drawings. You lock yourself away in that studio of yours like a monk in a cell.'

'How I choose to work is my business.'

'And my casual doodles are mine,' said Clive.

Howard turned on Anna. 'Have you seen it?'

'Yes, it's – it's lovely.'

'Ah!' Howard said. 'Ah-hah!'

'What's that supposed to mean?' said Clive.

'Syrup,' Howard said. 'Sugar and syrup. You're nothing but a sentimentalist, Cavendish; a flatterer.'

'One would be hard pushed not to flatter Miss Martindale.'

'It's only a little drawing,' Anna put in. 'He drew a bird too, a wagtail.'

'Oh, yes, a wagtail,' Howard said. 'He's very good with wagtails.'

'I'm also very good at giving black eyes,' Clive reminded him.

Howard inhaled noisily through his nostrils. 'We'll be packing up soon,' he said. 'Mama has a headache. If you want another slice of cake you'd better have it before it goes into the basket.'

Clive bowed. 'Thank you, Howard.'

He waited, scowling, for Anna to detach herself from Cavendish and return to the remnants of the picnic over which a cloud of insects hovered now. Julie was dressing the little girl, Phoebe, who, with her brother, had scampered in and out of the shallow water all afternoon clad only in knickers and a cotton vest.

'Miss Martindale,' Howard said stiffly, 'are you coming?'

'In a moment, Mr Buskin,' Anna said. 'In a moment.'

He turned and clomped away just as he'd done at Foxhailes yesterday afternoon; a fit of pique that Anna – quite wrongly – mistook for jealousy.

A little after eight, stuffed with green pea soup, beef olives and boiled potatoes, Papa fell asleep in Uncle Otto's armchair. A brisk little breeze had sprung up and the trees around the cottage whispered uneasily as if they sensed the beginning of the end of summer. As soon as the woman from the village had gone home Julie draped Papa's cardigan over her shoulders and Anna and she went outside to hold an inquest on the day's events.

'I don't know what to make of him,' Anna began. 'One moment he seems to be blowing hot – well, at least lukewarm – and the next he ignores me. Clive says he's not comfortable with women.'

'Perhaps,' Julie said, 'it's just you.'

'Me?'

'You do tend to have that effect on men.'

'Don't be ridiculous,' Anna said. 'I'm not at all sure I even like him.'

'He follows you around with his eyes, you know, looking doleful.'

'Clive says—'

'You seem to get on well with Clive.'

'He's a jolly sight more approachable than Mr Buskin,' said Anna. 'Besides, I was curious to see his drawings.'

'Are they any good?'

'Lovely,' Anna said. 'Quite lovely – for thumbnails, that is.'

'He drew me, didn't he?'

Anna paused. 'Yes, he did – while you were paddling.'

'I thought as much.' Julie reached into a pocket in her skirt and produced two crushed cigarettes and a box of kitchen matches.

'Turkish,' she said, deep-voiced, 'or American?'

Anna giggled and watched her sister light up. She accepted one of the cigarettes, held it at arm's length and poked the air with it in the hope of making a smoke ring. 'You have to suck first,' Julie said. 'It's just like kissing.'

'What do you know about kissing?'

'Not much,' Julie said. 'But I'm eager to learn.'

'Julie!'

'There's nothing shocking about that,' Julie said. 'Do stop pretending you're a little innocent, Anna. You must know by now that you – we – that we're ripe for the picking.'

'What a horrible thing to say.'

'It's true, though. You know it, I know it, and even Papa knows it.'

'He doesn't like artists.'

'He doesn't like amateurs,' said Julie. 'Clive Cavendish is different.'

Anna stuck the cigarette in her mouth and inhaled. She coughed, coughed again and patted her bosom with the flat of her hand.

'Takes practice,' said Julie. 'Like everything else.'

The wind gathered in the trees and rushed off down the lane bowling a few early autumn leaves before it. Julie leaned on the gate and sighed.

'What's wrong?' Anna said.

'I'm just wondering if we'll ever see Mr Cavendish again.'

'I'll be very surprised if we don't,' said Anna.

The wind rattled the windows of the billiard room and made the light flicker. It had been Clarence Millar's idea to have the house equipped with a new-fangled electrical generator but the job had been done by local tradesmen who had proved less than competent at reading diagrams. It was bad enough in summer, Howard complained, but when the winter gales swept over Dartmoor the place would suddenly be plunged into darkness and some poor soul would have to rush out to the shed behind the kitchens to crank the infernal machine.

'He had to be different, you see,' Howard said. 'He had to be a step ahead of everyone else. Fat lot of good it did him. Left this place in a terrible shambles when he died. He never did understand that England is not America and progress here comes treading slow.'

The bulb flickered again and the fire in the hearth at the end of the long room flared in the wind that strode off the moor, heralding, Clive thought, an end to the hot spell.

He must go home soon, back to his studio in Chelsea. He had work to do, studio work, and a commission to lay out, for, unlike Edgar Banbury, whose laziness was legendary, he didn't paint by fits and starts.

'It won't last, you know,' Howard said.

'What won't last?'

'The light – not with a storm coming.'

'Is there a storm coming?' Clive said.

'Oh, yes,' Howard said gravely. 'Can't you feel it?'

'I'm surprised you can feel anything, the amount of that stuff you've consumed.'

Howard crouched on the couch by the fire and sloshed the liquid in his glass.

'Whisky,' he said. 'Nothing quite like it for drowning one's sorrows.'

'Sorrows? What sorrows? Who do you think you are – young Werther?'

'I have no idea,' Howard said, 'what you're talking about.'

'It's a novel, a famous German novel by—'

Howard sat bolt upright. 'Are you patronising me?'

'For God's sake, Howard, don't be so touchy. If you'd give Miss Martindale half a chance and stop growling like a bear with a bellyache I'm sure she'd find you more interesting.'

'I don't care if she finds me interesting,' Howard said. 'She's only a stupid female with nothing in her head but—'

'Mating,' Clive suggested.

'Mating?'

'I mean marriage.'

Howard emptied his glass. 'I know what you mean by "mating". I'm not as green as all that. As for marriage, as for sharing one's bed with a woman, I can think of few things more disagreeable.'

'Have you ever shared a bed with a woman?'

Howard rose from the couch, crossed to the cabinet under the cue rack and poured whisky from a decanter. He held the heavy siphon under one arm and fired a jet of soda water into his glass.

'Did Mama put you up to this?' he asked.

'Up to what?' said Clive.

'Asking stupid questions,' Howard said. 'Mama only wants to marry me off in order to be rid of me.'

'That,' Clive said, 'I doubt. She just wants you to be happy.'

'Then why doesn't she leave me alone?'

'She wants grandchildren, preferably a whole squad of them,' Clive said. 'Your mama requires a family, Howard, don't you see?'

'She has a family. She has me.'

'I mean heirs, a line of succession.'

'She isn't bloody royalty, though she may think she is,' Howard said. 'I'm not going to marry just to please my mama. It's high time she realised I'm wedded to my art.'

'Aren't we all, old son, aren't we all,' Clive said. 'Now, time for bed, don't you think? It's fast approaching midnight.'

'Where – where is everyone?'

'All sound asleep, I imagine.'

'I – I'd better say goodnight to Mama.'

'Probably not a good idea,' said Clive.

'She may need help with her corset.'

'Doesn't the maid – doesn't Emily do that?'

'Not if it's late, no. I do it.'

'Really!' Clive said. 'Well, one lives and one learns.'

'Wedded' – Howard emptied his glass – 'to my art.' He rested his brow on Clive's shoulder. 'She is lovely, though, isn't she?'

'And you, my lad, are blotto,' Clive said.

He propped Howard against the cue rack and reached out to the electrical light switch which administered a tiny shock when he touched it.

'Clive?' Howard said shrilly. 'Where are you?'

'I'm here, Howard. I'm here,' Clive said and steered him out of the billiard room before he could start droning on again about his mother's stays or the lovely Anna Martindale who, in the great cruel scheme of things, Howard reckoned he would never see again.

5

No sooner had August given way to September than the weather broke. Rain poured out of leaden skies and the streets of London were soon awash. Otto Goldstein didn't mind the rain. What irked him was the paucity of daylight, for, like many craftsmen, he preferred to work in natural light.

He spent the morning at the bench sanding and sizing the battered frame of the Earl of Hayford's latest acquisition, a massive, storm-tossed seascape ascribed – wrongly in Otto's opinion – to Willem van de Velde the Younger. He would have pushed on with applying gold leaf but that delicate task required not only light but patience. With a half past noon appointment looming over him, he propped the frame carefully against the wall and took himself upstairs to bathe, shave and change into his second-best lounge suit which was all the trimming that a luncheon in the grill room of the Hyde Park Hotel required.

The girls were playing Parcheesi in the drawing room and to judge by the racket might soon be hurling the pieces at each other. Anna had told him about Julie's flirtation with the painter, Clive Cavendish. Julie had told him about Howard Buskin's limping pursuit of Anna and, as if that wasn't enough, Stanley had chewed his ear about

Mrs Millar. Otto had listened attentively, had nodded when appropriate, frowned when disapproval was called for and, for once, had kept his mouth shut. He had no intention of answering the girls' probing questions about Cavendish, Banbury or his erstwhile acquaintance with Verity Buskin Millar.

He combed his moustache, applied pomade to his thinning locks, buttoned his waistcoat and, not a moment too soon, left his bedroom and hurried across the hall to say goodbye to the girls.

'No, Anna,' he barked from the doorway. 'Put the dice cup down.'

'It's not her turn. It's my turn.'

'Nothing of the sort,' Julie piped up. 'I threw a doublet.'

'Stop it,' Otto said. 'Both of you.'

'You smell funny,' Julie said. 'Is that pomade?'

'Size, I expect,' Otto told her.

'You look very spiffy for a weekday,' Anna said. 'Where are you off to?'

'Albert Gate.'

'Does Papa know?' said Julie.

'I don't require your papa's permission to go out to lunch.'

Julie nodded sagely. 'It's a woman, isn't it?'

'Anyone we know?' said Anna.

'I doubt it,' Otto fibbed.

'Won't you at least tell us her name?'

'Esmeralda.'

'Is she a model?' Julie asked.

'Only of rectitude,' Otto answered, and headed post haste for the hall.

*

Huge hats ornamented with feathers were the height of fashion but wet weather had taken a toll on the millinery and there were some sorry sights on view in the grill room that afternoon.

The last time Otto had been in the Hyde Park Hotel he'd danced with Lisa Goodman, heiress to the Goodman upholstery fortune, in the luxurious Louis XVI ballroom upstairs. Lisa's mother had considered him rather a catch but, unfortunately, Lisa had had other ideas. The grill room wasn't quite as grand as the ballroom. It had a beamed ceiling, panelled walls and an open-fronted servery that released waves of steam like the engine room of an ocean liner.

Otto looked round for the largest hat in the room and, finding it, summoned a waiter to escort him to the table in the corner where the widow Millar, waving a glove to attract his attention, waited.

Twelve years since last he'd clapped eyes on Verity Buskin Millar, ten on top of that since they'd wrestled in a lumpy bed in a garret in Hoxton where Verity had been living at the time. He was no longer the lithe young immigrant and she no longer the vivacious, green-eyed waif whom Edgar Banbury had once described as the most energetic harlot in London.

Otto bowed and touched his lips to her ungloved hand.

'Verity,' he lied softly, 'you've hardly changed at all.'

'Nature has not been kind to me, I fear,' Verity said. 'You, however, are just as divinely handsome as you always were.'

The waiter pulled out a chair. Otto seated himself.

He couldn't quite believe the damage that the passage of years had laid upon Verity; an expensive frock of royal-blue cloth with braid and velvet trimmings couldn't disguise it. The cost of becoming a lady had obviously been too high for poor Verity to bear without blemish.

'I'm rich now, you know,' she said.

'I'd heard that, yes.'

'You never met Clarence, did you?'

'I never had the pleasure.'

'American,' she said. 'Not your type.'

'I've nothing against Americans,' Otto said.

'They have no class,' said Verity. 'Not like you, Otto.'

She had always been too forthright even for the unruly clan Edgar Banbury had gathered round him back in the '80s. Otto had never really been part of it. He was a mere artisan with money in his pocket and a willingness to lend – but the women had liked him, which may have been the reason he'd hung around so long.

The waiter brought the menu. Otto ordered a bottle of dry champagne and waited for Verity to make the running.

'A cottage in Brampton,' she said, 'not three miles from my house, yet you never deigned to call. Would it be presumptuous to ask why?'

'As a happily married woman,' Otto said, 'you wouldn't have welcomed a visit from an old flame.'

'Clarence wouldn't have minded. He knew I was no angel when we met.'

The waiter poured champagne and politely offered the menu card again.

Otto shook his head and waved him away.

'Aren't we going to eat?' said Verity.

'Shortly,' Otto told her. 'First you must tell me what you want with me.'

'To renew our old acquaintance, my dear.'

Otto smiled. 'If it's another husband you're after, Verity, I may as well tell you I'm a confirmed bachelor, totally set in my ways.'

'Is that what you think? What conceit!'

'Conceit was always my strong suit,' Otto said. 'Come now, out with it. Why after all these many moons have you decided to invite me to lunch? I assume you're no longer in need of a free meal. It's the girls, isn't it?'

'Meeting them reminded me how fond we once were of—'

'Verity, Verity,' Otto chided. 'Enough of the twaddle. Out with it.'

'Oh, very well,' Verity Millar said. 'I'm not fishing for a husband, if you must know; I'm fishing for a wife.'

'A wife?'

'For my son, Howard.'

'I see.' Otto paused. 'Which of my nieces has taken his fancy?'

'Anna.'

'She's very young.'

'She's almost eighteen; that's old enough.'

'For what?' said Otto.

'Marriage, of course,' said Verity.

'Can't you do better than a frame-maker's daughter?'

'I think he's in love with her.'

'Infatuation,' Otto said. 'A summer romance.'

'Howard isn't given to impulse. He's very – very shy.'

'How old is Howard now?' Otto said. 'Twenty-seven, twenty-eight?'

'Twenty-nine.'

'And you, Verity, what are you worth these days?'

'Beg pardon?'

'The size of your fortune; round figures will do.'

'I honestly don't know. Quite substantial.'

'So,' Otto said evenly, 'what's wrong with him?'

'With Howard? Nothing. He's a fine upstanding young man.'

'Who can't find a wife for himself?' Otto said. 'He's a painter, isn't he?'

'Anna told you, I suppose. What else did she tell you?'

'I'm only her uncle, Verity, not her confidant. I can tell you, however, that several young gentlemen have already expressed an interest.'

Verity covered his hand with hers. 'Don't tell me she's engaged.'

'Not,' Otto said cautiously, 'to my knowledge, no.'

'Thank God for that,' Verity said and, sitting back, summoned a waiter so that Otto might order lunch.

The Martindale Gallery of Frames and Mounts – Stanley's shop in other words – had only a single small window looking out into Ledbetter Street. It was flanked by a shop that sold rods and guns and one that sold nothing but fitted dressing cases which, in Stanley's view, was a specialisation too far. At the bottom of the street on one corner of the Strand was a seafood restaurant that catered exclusively to the carriage trade. On the other was a musical emporium that displayed pianos and harps in its broad bay window and offered first-floor rehearsal rooms for budding divas so that once out of the traffic's roar you might well be treated to a faint snatch of *Don Quichotte* or a few bars from *Rigoletto*.

There was no sound from the rehearsal rooms that forenoon, however, or if there was Stanley, seated at a mahogany desk diligently entering delivery dates in the order log, was deaf to it.

The day was so gloomy he'd turned up the gaslight which, reflected in glass and gilt display frames, lent the shop a glitter it didn't deserve. From the workshop came the rasp of a saw and someone – the new apprentice, most like – whistling a music-hall tune. Stanley was on the point of throwing down his fountain pen and diving into the workshop to tell the boy off when the front door opened and a man stepped out of the rain.

He was clad in one of the voluminous waterproof capes that bicycling fanatics wore on weekend excursions. Rainwater dripped from the hem of the cape and puddled the polished floor.

'Sir?' Stanley rose like a jack-in-the-box. 'What can I do for you?'

There was a great deal of fumbling beneath the cape. Hands appeared and lowered a portfolio to the floor. The hands moved up, spilling water from the folds, and untied the hood of the cape.

'Cavendish!' Stanley exclaimed, then, with a little more civility, 'I didn't expect to see you again so soon. What brings you to this part of town?'

'Business,' Clive said, adding, 'mainly.'

'I think,' Stanley said, 'it might be as well if you removed that garment.'

Clive laughed. 'Yes, you're probably right.'

He struggled out of the cape and gave it to Stanley who, holding it at arm's length, carried it into the workshop where it might drip to its heart's content.

When he turned he was surprised to find Cavendish at

his heels. Peering inquisitively into the workshop, the painter said, 'You've a thriving business going on here, Mr Martindale, haven't you?'

Stanley hastily closed the workshop door. 'We tick over, thank you.'

'How many men do you employ?' Cavendish asked.

'Five.'

'Does that include your brother?'

'Brother-in-law,' Stanley corrected. 'Yes.'

'And you all' – Cavendish glanced at the ceiling – 'live upstairs?'

'We do.'

'Are the Miss Martindales at home by any chance?'

'I believe they might be. Why?'

'I thought since I'm here I may as well pay my respects.'

'It's not business at all, Cavendish, is it? You've come to see my daughters.'

'Quite honestly, sir, yes.' Clive hoisted up the portfolio. 'But I do have some work for you if you care to give me an estimate.'

'Hmm.' Stanley nodded. 'What's in the folder?'

'Four watercolours.'

'Put them on the desk,' Stanley said, 'and I'll calculate a price.'

'Oh!' Clive hid his disappointment. 'Yes, of course.'

'It's not something I care to rush, pricing,' Stanley said. 'Perhaps you'd prefer to wait upstairs while I do it.'

'Most kind, Mr Martindale, most kind,' Clive Cavendish said and, abandoning the watercolours to their fate, followed Stanley down the narrow corridor that led to the domestic stairs.

*

Otto had forgotten that Verity had a sweet tooth. The speed with which she demolished a peach melba, however, brought it all flooding back: the bon-bons, the chocolates, late night cups of cocoa laced with sugar, jams and jellies and syrupy sponge puddings that should by rights have piled on pounds. Perhaps, he thought, her restless temperament had saved her from a portly middle age, or perhaps she had simply gone hungry too often to be anything other than immune to the effect of sweet things.

He smoked a cigarette, sipped coffee and watched little grains of spun sugar adhere to her upper lip. He had no right to mock Verity. By any measure she had done well for herself, in and out of the marriage bed. He waited politely until the spoon scraped the bottom of the dish before he returned to the topic on hand.

'Am I to understand that you wish me to act as a matchmaker?'

'I wouldn't put it quite like that,' Verity said. 'I'm just inviting your help to bring my son and your niece together so that nature might take its course.'

'And what if nature doesn't take its course?'

'At least we'll have tried.'

'Not so much of the "we", Verity, if you please,' Otto said. 'I'm somewhat disinclined to be incorporated into conspiring on behalf of my brother-in-law's child. I mean, I haven't even met your son.'

'Ah, but you have.'

'What? Yes, once or twice – when he was scarcely out of frocks.'

'Seven, Otto. He was seven. Don't you remember him at all?'

'I'm sorry, Verity, but I'm afraid I don't.'

'Well, he remembers you. For a little while – before I convinced him otherwise – he thought you might be his father.'

'Doesn't he know who his father is?'

'Howard's pedigree is of no consequence.'

'Personally I don't give a hoot about your shady past, Verity,' Otto said, 'though I suspect my brother-in-law might.'

Verity paused. 'I don't think your brother-in-law likes me.'

'Stanley doesn't like anyone much,' said Otto. 'He's disposed, by nature, to be unsociable. Where is your son, by the way? Is he still in Devon?'

'He's helping Edgar amuse the children while I'm in town.'

'What's Banbury doing in wildest Dartmoor when his wife's in labour?'

'She's not in labour just yet,' said Verity. 'You seem frightfully well informed about what's going on.'

'You can't be a celebrated eccentric – pardon me, artist – like Banbury and expect to have a private life. Is he painting your portrait?'

'He is.'

'And taking for ever to do it.'

'Edgar's always thorough when it comes to portraits.'

'Yes,' said Otto. 'He gets to know his female subjects inside as well as out – or so one is led to believe.'

'You're a fine one to talk,' said Verity. 'Last I heard you were going to marry the Goodman girl.'

'She wouldn't have me,' Otto said.

'Why ever not?'

'She had her mind set on marrying a gentile.'

'But isn't she a Jew?'

'Absolutely,' said Otto.

'I don't understand.'

'I wouldn't expect you to,' said Otto. 'However, if it's any consolation, my dear Mrs Millar, my niece is not Jewish, though my sister, her mother, was. Anna has a strain of the Hebrew in her that can't be totally discounted, of course, but otherwise she's as pure an English rose as you'll find anywhere.'

'I don't think it would matter to Howard if she were a Hottentot,' said Verity. 'And it certainly doesn't matter to me.'

'Why are you so desperate to find Howard a wife?'

'I have money,' Verity said, 'and money makes its own demands on one. Some day all too soon Howard will be a wealthy young man and prey to every gold-digger in London. I've no wish to see my fortune – Clarence's fortune – squandered on some trollop. It's a wife Howard needs, a sensible young woman from a respectable family who'll provide a home and children and give his life purpose.'

'A tall order for a girl of seventeen,' Otto said.

'Courtship and a long engagement will take care of that.'

'But why my niece? Why Anna?'

'Because she's the first girl Howard's ever shown much – any – interest in. Would you object to your niece marrying my son?'

'In principle, no.'

'He's very talented.'

'And wealthy?' Otto said. 'Or will be in time.'

'Quite!' said Verity. 'What more could your niece want in a husband?'

'I've no idea,' said Otto. 'Perhaps she might like to be loved.'

'Loved?' said Verity as if she'd never heard of the word.

Otto stubbed out his cigarette. 'The best I can do is put Anna and your son together and see what transpires.'

'Where?' said Verity eagerly.

'Maule's Gallery in St James's – do you know it?'

'Of course I know it,' said Verity.

'They're previewing their winter show in October. Will you make sure Howard turns up for the opening?'

'If I have to drag him along by the hair,' said Verity.

Stanley Martindale's assertion that business was 'ticking over' was somewhat shy of the truth. Business had never been better. Annual turnover had increased tenfold since Stanley's father, J.D. Martindale, had signed over the firm and stalked off in high dudgeon, dragging Stanley's mother and spinster sister, Edith, into early retirement in a dreary seaside town in North Wales.

It remained a mystery to Stanley why his father had abruptly surrendered everything he cared about to support a prejudice he didn't really care about at all. He was just that sort of man, Stanley supposed, so stubborn, opinionated and unyielding that he'd refused to attend the baptism of his granddaughters or the funeral of his daughter-in-law and for over twenty years had remained locked away in a Welsh backwater playing golf or, for all Stanley knew, just sitting on the beach with Mama and Edith waiting for the sun to shine.

Stanley met his mother and sister when they came up to town to shop or consult some quack doctor in search of a cure for Edith's 'nerves'. Edith refused to visit Ledbetter Street in case she bumped into 'that man' – by which she meant Otto – and the uneasy meetings took place by the pavilion in Regent's Park or in Fortnum's tearoom. Stanley had long since stopped taking the girls along, for as they grew older their aunt's malicious asides raised questions that neither he nor Otto was prepared to answer.

The girls' bedroom occupied what Uncle Otto jocularly referred to as the east wing which wasn't, of course, a wing at all but simply one more apartment in the higgledy-piggledy dwelling. The 'great hall' – another of Otto's fancies – had more entrances than Lambeth Palace. A short corridor led from it to the kitchens, a staircase, going down, gave access to the shop and another staircase, going up, took you to the servants' quarters. Public rooms and all three bedrooms opened on to the hall and when you added in a bathroom, fully plumbed, and a nook in lieu of a cloakroom it wasn't surprising that traffic across the hall was considerable.

On that particular evening the sisters had retired early to discuss Clive Cavendish's unexpected appearance.

'Why didn't he stay for dinner?' Anna asked.

'He's too polite to impose himself.'

'He had a cheek coming round without sending his card first.'

'He brought watercolours for Papa to frame,' said Julie.

'An excuse to see you, that's all.'

'I thought they were rather good watercolours,' said Julie.

'Oh, his technique's excellent,' Anna said, 'but they do have a certain – I don't know – fatal conformity. Perhaps he's only inspired by the female form.' She paused. 'It was really quite disgusting the way he eyed you up and down while supping his oxtail soup.'

Seated on the side of her bed, Julie lifted a pillow and made as if to throw it but there was no temper in her response and Anna continued to ply her hairbrush at the dressing table unperturbed.

Hugging the pillow, Julie said, 'I really do think he likes me.'

'I'm absolutely sure he likes you,' Anna said. 'The question you must ask yourself, dearest, is why he likes you. Did he say anything that might give you a clue – by which I mean did he kiss you?'

'You certainly provided him with a perfect opportunity,' said Julie. 'I don't know what he thought of you, scuttling off and leaving us alone.'

'I went to tell Mrs Sims to set an extra place for lunch,' Anna said. '*Did* he try to kiss you?'

'No, but he gave me the address of his studio in Chelsea,' Julie said. 'He's invited me to drop by tomorrow afternoon.'

'Well,' said Anna, sitting very still, 'that might be rather fun.'

'He wants me to go alone.'

'But you won't, will you? I mean, you won't leave me behind?'

'Do you know,' said Julie, 'I think I probably will.'

6

The building was four storeys high, squeezed between gaunt dwelling houses. Clive's was not the only open window in the Trafalgar studios. As she stepped from the cab Julie glimpsed a bare-breasted woman and a shock-haired young man with a pipe in his mouth and a mallet in his hand hammering away at a piece of marble. The air was ripe with smells of cooking. Smoke from the soaring chimneys of the Lots Road generating station off to the west hung in a pall over the rooftops.

'Yes,' Clive greeted her on the stair. 'I know it's a dump but it's cheap and it suits my purpose. How long do we have?'

'I promised my sister I'd meet her at four.'

'At Harrods?'

'How did you know?'

'Where else would you deposit a sister who assumes you're going to embrace a fate worse than death?'

'I don't follow your reasoning, I'm afraid.'

'Don't try. Come along, step inside and let's have a look at you.'

Clive hung her hat and coat behind the door, steered her directly to a velour-covered armchair and posed her as carefully as if she were made of glass.

The armchair, a decrepit leather couch, a divan uphol-stered in blood-red silk and a gibbet-like easel furnished the top-floor room. Beneath the window was a boot rack in which paints, brushes and other tools of the artist's trade were laid out and on a shelf above the empty fireplace was a strange array of painted vases and pretty little figurines which, when Julie looked closer, were not pretty at all but primitive and shockingly explicit.

Clive took his place on a stool behind a drawing board freighted with weights, cranks and chains, like an instrument of torture. A sheet of tinted paper was already pinned to the centre of the board. Clive took a stick of charcoal from a box on a ledge out of Julie's sight, then, jumping up, came to her again, pressed a finger to her cheek and directed her head a little to the right.

'Beautiful,' he said softly. 'Absolutely beautiful,' and returned to the stool.

Julie said, 'May I speak?'

'You may.'

'Do you always work at a draughtsman's board?'

'Not always, no.'

'I thought you were a painter?'

'I am,' Clive said. 'I'm also an illustrator.'

'Are you really?' said Julie.

'Jack of all trades, that's me,' Clive said. 'Keep your head still.'

'I'm sorry.'

'Don't be,' Clive said. 'Holding a pose isn't easy. Even professional models grumble about it sometimes.'

'Do you use' – Julie hesitated – 'professionals?'

'Of course.'

'What do they charge?'

'It varies a great deal. Why, are you thinking of taking it up?'

'I might,' Julie said. 'Would a shilling an hour be unreasonable?'

'Far from it.'

'One and six for ninety minutes, say?'

He looked up. 'Please don't move.'

She said, 'Sorry.'

He said, 'Cab fare, I suppose?'

Julie said, 'Yes.'

'What if I told you I'm broke?'

'You're not, are you?'

'Actually, no, I'm not.'

'Well, will you pay me?' Julie said.

'Will I get value for money?'

'That's for you to say.'

'If I didn't know you better I'd say you were baiting me.'

'Better doesn't enter into it,' Julie said. 'You don't know me at all.'

'That's true,' he said. 'However, you're not the first young woman to wander into the depths of Chelsea in search of excitement.'

'Is that what I'm doing?' said Julie.

'Women are fascinated by artists.' His hand glided over the paper, head dipping and rising. 'I think it's because we spend a great deal of time studying the female form. If there's one thing a woman likes more than anything else it's to be the sole focus of a man's attention.'

'Who gave you this insight into female psychology? Was it Mr Banbury, by any chance?'

'Edgar? No, he's basically afraid of women. He can't stop falling in love with them and that puts him off his stroke for weeks.'

'Until he has them, you mean?'

'More or less,' Clive agreed.

Julie stared out at the drab sky, at seagulls perched on the chimneypots and pigeons on the tiles. In one soot-stained window she caught sight of a woman, a servant most like, folding sheets and in another an elderly man in vest and braces shaving at a basin.

'Do you want to have me?' she said.

'I already have you,' Clive said, 'right where I want you.'

'I meant—'

'Julie,' he said, 'you're fidgeting again. Please stop.'

She arrived a few minutes after four to find Anna pacing back and forth in front of the plate-glass windows. When Julie alighted from the cab Anna hurried to the pavement's edge and caught her by the arm.

'A hansom? I hope he paid for it.'

'I'm dying for a cup of tea,' Julie said. 'Shall we give the Ritz a try?'

'The Ritz! How much *did* he pay you?'

'I'm joking,' Julie said. 'I can run to a pastry in Eglinton's but only if you have the tram fare.'

Eglinton's tearoom was crowded at that hour in the afternoon. Anna was obliged to contain her impatience until a table at the rear fell vacant and Julie and she were seated.

'Why did he give you money?' was Anna's first question.

'I asked for a fee.'

'You kissed him, didn't you? I mean, you let him take liberties?'

'Chance,' Julie said, 'would be a fine thing. The only clothes I took off were my hat and coat. It's a head and shoulders study in charcoal, fifteen inches by twenty. It isn't quite finished but it is rather gorgeous.'

'Gorgeous?' said Anna. 'What does that mean?'

'I didn't know I looked like that.'

'You probably don't,' said Anna tartly.

'I am, apparently, a very good subject. Clive wants to use me again.'

'Of course he does,' said Anna. 'What's his studio like?'

'Quite spacious.'

'Does he live there?'

'Yes, there's a tiny room at the back with a bed in it. He cooks on a paraffin stove in an alcove with a sink. The water closet doesn't flush properly but otherwise it's quite habitable.'

'In other words Mr Cavendish is a pauper,' said Anna.

'By no means,' said Julie. 'He receives a monthly allowance from his father and earns extra cash by drawing for the newspapers.'

'How did he meet Edgar Banbury?'

'Mr Banbury taught at the Fulham for a couple of years. That's also where Clive met Howard Buskin.'

'The Fulham?' said Anna. 'I thought he studied at the Slade.'

'If you mean Howard, he did,' Julie said, 'but he walked out after one term.'

'What else did Mr Cavendish say about Howard?'

'Nothing. We were far too busy discussing our next meeting.'

'Oh, my goodness,' said Anna. 'Are you going to sit for him again?'

'As often as I possibly can,' said Julie.

Before her fourth visit to the Trafalgar studios Julie sewed lace frills to her petticoat and purchased a satin-silk girdle with four straps that ruched up the petticoat and revealed through the frills a tantalising glimpse of loose silk drawers.

She spent half of Friday morning locked in the bathroom studying herself in the mirror above the washbasin. She regretted that her breasts were small and her belly flat and wondered what Clive would think of that wispy part of her, framed by cloth suspenders, that polite society insisted did not exist while nature, and hygiene, said otherwise.

Sunlight flitted across the Chelsea rooftops and a brisk wind, running counter to the tide, had sent the seagulls off, squealing, in the direction of the river. In an open window below Clive's studio a young woman in a dressing gown smoked a cigar and when Julie alighted from the hansom called out a cheery greeting. Julie waved then hurried through the door and up the narrow staircase to the landing where Clive was waiting. She could smell soap and a faint undertow of shellac as he ushered her into the studio. The drawing board had been pushed against the wall, the armchair relegated to a corner, the divan brought into the centre of the room and the easel rolled forward.

Clive took off her hat and tossed it on to the divan. He unbuttoned her coat and threw it open. With an arm across her stomach, he worked one-handed on the little buttons of her blouse.

'Were the watercolours delivered to Maule's?' he asked.

'Yes, yesterday.'

'With the invoice?'

'I believe so,' Julie said. 'You've thirty days to pay.'

'Or what?'

'I – I don't know.'

He tugged down the sleeves of her coat and pinned her arms behind her. He kissed her, lightly at first, and ran the tip of his tongue across her lips. She opened her mouth and let his tongue find hers. He loosened her bodice and cupped her breasts. She felt herself swell and grow moist.

'What are you doing?' she said.

'What do you think I'm doing?' he said. 'Do you want me to stop?'

'No,' she said, and then again, 'No,' and ten minutes later gave herself up to him on the bed in the little back room.

7

'What,' Howard Buskin said, 'is that?'

'What does it look like?'

'It looks like Julie Martindale.'

'Spot on,' Clive said.

'Do you mean to say she sat for you?'

'Well, I didn't do it from memory, Howard. What do you think of it?'

Howard crossed to the window and studied the drawing in fading daylight.

'Fair,' he said, at length. 'A fair likeness.'

'Praise indeed coming from you,' said Clive.

'Where did you do it?'

'Do what?'

'Where was the sitting?'

'Here, right here,' Clive said. 'She planted her dainty little bottom in that very armchair, good as gold.'

'Her sister came with her, I assume.'

'No, she came alone.'

'I'm amazed – astonished that her father gave permission.'

'Her father knows nothing about it,' Clive said.

'So what are you going to do with it?' Howard said.

'Under the circumstances you can't possibly offer it for sale.'

'I've no intention of offering it for sale.' Clive retrieved the drawing and put it carefully away between tissues in a folder. 'As a matter of fact, I'm keeping it as a memento.'

'You had her, didn't you?' Howard said.

Grinning, Clive held up both hands.

'What a callous swine you are,' Howard said. 'You haven't had the sister, too, have you?'

'Anna? No, not my type.'

'They're Jews, Clive, Jews.'

'No, they're not. In any case, it makes no difference to me.'

Howard opened his mouth to say something then changed his mind. He crossed the room and confronted the huge canvas upon which Clive had laid down the outline of a composition.

Peering, Howard said, 'Is this another of your erotic fantasies?'

'Not my erotic anything,' said Clive. 'It's a nude in classic pose reclining on a divan. Ingres, Titian, Goya, Velasquez – take your pick: *une grande odalisque.*'

'It's certainly *grande* enough. It's bloody enormous.'

'It probably needs to be to cover the damp patches on Wedmore's wall.'

'Wedmore? Sir Magnus Wedmore? Surely not?'

'Why not? His money's as good as anyone's. Besides, the finished piece will vanish into Maggie's fortress in Hyde Park Gate and never be seen again.'

'When did he commission you?' Howard asked.

'He purchased *The Best of Friends* from Maule's last

summer and he's been at me ever since to do him a full study – a proper nude, he calls it.'

'Dear God, Cavendish, have you no integrity?'

'Of course I do, Howard: fifty guineas worth of integrity.'

Howard whistled. 'If Wedmore's been chasing you for a painting why has it taken you so long to get around to it?'

'I've been waiting for the right girl to come along.'

'Don't tell me you're giving Wedmore Julie Martindale on a plate?'

'On a divan, actually,' Clive said.

'How many sittings will it take?'

'Fifteen, twenty – what does it matter?'

'How will she find time?'

'Love,' Clive said, 'will find a way. By the by, what are you doing in London, apart from impugning my reputation and taking me out to dinner?'

'Edgar's wife's due this week. My mother packed him off home.'

'I thought perhaps you'd come up for Maule's winter exhibition?'

'Are you showing anything?' Howard said.

'Four watercolours, that's all.'

'The ones you did in Devon?'

'Blue skies and rolling hills will always find buyers.'

Howard snorted and with a last lingering glance at the canvas buttoned his overcoat and put on his hat. 'Where are we going to eat? Regent Street?'

'How about Pagani's for a change – if you're paying, that is.'

'Don't I always?' Howard paused. 'Cavendish?'

'What?'

'Did she cry?'

'No, Howard,' Clive answered softly. 'She didn't cry.'

The still life was arranged on a sewing box that had once belonged to her mother; a relic, so Otto said, of the days when a young girl was expected to be proficient with a needle as part of her domestic training. On top of the box was a jade-green ginger jar, a fluted crystal wine glass and one rather battered orange. Anna had tackled the subject before and, as might be expected, had completely failed to capture the harmony of the objects.

'Ah, there you are,' said Otto. 'I wondered where you were hiding.'

'I'm not hiding. I'm drawing.'

'An exercise for Mr Rodale, I take it.'

'We're not going back to Mr Rodale's.'

'Really! Does Stanley know that?'

'He will soon enough.'

The sketch book lay flat on the morning room table, Anna hunched over it.

Otto pulled out a chair, spun it around and rested his arms on the back.

He watched his niece slash angrily at the drawing which was already so overworked that all relevance to the objects on the sewing box was lost in a mass of cross-hatching.

'Anna,' he said at length, 'what's wrong?'

'I can't do it.' She threw down the pencil. 'I just can't do it.'

And then she began to cry.

Otto drew her to him. 'Now, now, dearest,' he said. 'It's only a silly drawing; nothing to get upset about. It *is* only a silly drawing, isn't it? I mean, it wouldn't have anything to do with Julie, would it? You've hardly spoken to her all week.' He cupped her chin and lifted her head to look into her eyes. 'Would it, by any chance, have something to do with a boy?'

'A boy? What boy?'

'These trips to Harrods – are you meeting someone at Harrods?'

She answered without hesitation. 'No.'

'Is Julie?'

'No.'

'If it's something that can be fixed,' Otto said, 'then fix it I will.'

'No,' Anna said. 'It's too late,' and rushed off, sobbing, to her room.

Anna's underclothes were draped on a bedpost and she'd kicked off her shoes with such force than one had landed on the dressing table where it lay, dusted with powder, like a prop from last year's pantomime.

When Julie slipped into the room Anna rose up in bed and in a thin, gnarly whisper, cried, 'I won't lie for you again, Julie.'

'Did you tell Uncle Otto?'

'No.'

'I mean about me,' said Julie.

'That you're not – that you've been – I don't know how to say it.'

'Clive calls it making love.'

Anna tightened her grip on the bed sheet. 'Does it hurt?'

'Only a little at first.' Julie began to undress. 'In any case, you won't have to tell lies on my behalf again.'

'Oh, my goodness! You told Papa.'

'Of course I didn't tell Papa,' Julie said. 'At least I didn't put it in so many words. I simply pointed out that I'm quite old enough to do what I want to do.'

'What did he say to that?'

'He wasn't pleased.'

'We're not going back to old Rodale's, are we?'

'No,' Julie said. 'Papa can nurse that disappointment for a while.'

'Well,' Anna said, 'at least some good's come out of it.'

Julie folded her skirt and placed it on a wooden hanger. She undid the clasps that held up her stockings, aware that Anna was watching her.

'There's nothing to see, Anna,' she said. 'Everything's just as it was before.'

'I wasn't – I mean . . .' Anna said. 'Does he – does he kiss you?'

'Yes, he kisses me,' Julie said. 'He kisses me everywhere.'

'Even down there?'

'Especially down there,' said Julie.

'Oh, my goodness!' Anna said and pulled the sheet up over her head.

Stooped over the fender, Stanley gazed bleakly into the embers of the fire. Add a muffler and a bonnet, Otto thought, and he'd fit perfectly into one of those melancholy Scottish paintings of a shepherd whose dog has just died.

'There's nothing to be gained from moping, Stanley,' Otto said. 'Julie's always been headstrong but I'm quite sure she won't do anything foolish.'

'What did Anna tell you?'

'Not a blessed thing,' said Otto. 'Well, nothing definite.'

Stanley looked up. 'We could beat it out of her.'

'Don't be an idiot,' said Otto. 'You've never taken the cane to either of the girls; I doubt if you're going to start now. What has you so hot and bothered? Is it the fact that Cavendish is an artist, that he's a friend of Edgar Banbury's or simply that you can't stand the idea of losing a daughter?'

'It was bound to happen sooner or later, I suppose.'

'The first sensible thing you've said all evening.' Otto placed a hand on his brother-in-law's shoulder. 'Women aren't impervious to the clamour of nature that drove us to do silly things when we were their age.'

'I never did a silly thing in my life.'

'Stanley! Stanley!'

'Be that as it may,' Papa Martindale said, 'what's your point?'

'In my opinion there's only one thing you can do now.'

'Which is?'

'Let nature take its course,' said Otto.

8

The digging up of the Mall to accommodate a memorial to the late Queen Victoria had covered St James's in a layer of dust that, coupled with the hammering of drills and pickaxes, drove the members of the innumerable clubs in the vicinity to distraction. The directors of the famous auction house of Christie & Manson took precautions against damage to valuable lots by laying fibre mats at every entrance and draping the windows of the public rooms with fine mesh curtains.

Samuel Maule and his brothers, not to be outdone, soon followed suit and, according to Edgar Banbury, entering the little gallery these days was like stepping into a fever ward.

'Now that, Verity, is what I call a hat.' Edgar tweaked the feather that jutted from Verity's chapeau. 'My God, you might knock out a fellow's eye with it if you're not careful.'

'Mrs Millar certainly knocks my eye out.' Young Mr John squeezed past the widow and gave her a friendly nudge. 'Are we all well?'

'We are, Gus,' said Edgar, 'or were until you arrived.'

'Heard you've added to your brood again, Banbury. True?'

'Bouncing boy. Thomas by name, grouchy by nature.'

'Both fit?' said Mr John, already moving on. 'Clara too, I trust?'

'Bright as a button.'

'Good, good,' and with half a dozen adoring young women trailing in his wake, Gus vanished into the crowd.

'Quite a crush for a private viewing.' Otto defended his wine glass with both hands. 'What's the big attraction, Banbury?'

'Calvetti's bust of Lucy Gaynor, I imagine.'

'Really?' said Otto. 'Marble?'

'Bronze. You may order a copy if you wish.'

'I think Otto would prefer to get his hands on the original,' said Verity.

'Of course I would,' Otto said. 'Lucy Gaynor's bust is not a thing to be sneezed at.' He glanced down at his niece. 'I'm sorry, Anna. I'm afraid these reprobates bring out the worst in me.'

Clive craned his neck. 'Is Lucy Gaynor actually here?'

'Alas, no,' said Edgar Banbury. 'She's on tour with *Major Barbara* and in Manchester this week.'

'You're remarkably well informed, old boy,' said Otto.

'Shaw happened to mention it in passing.'

'Shaw?' Julie said. 'G.B. Shaw?'

'Edgar's being coy,' said Verity. 'Wyndham's are on the verge of commissioning a portrait of the Irishman and our dear Edgar's well in the running.'

'Is that why you're up in London?' Clive said.

'In truth,' said Edgar, 'I'm up in London to escape the odour of babies.'

'You should be with your wife at this time, you know,' Howard said.

'Well,' said Edgar, 'one does have to earn a crust.'

Howard said, 'My mother's paid for a portrait you've so far failed to deliver. I wager you won't be so lax when it comes to dealing with Wyndham.'

'You're right, of course,' Edgar said. 'In my defence, may I point out that your mother is a much more rewarding subject than Bernard Shaw.'

'Rewarding?' said Verity. 'Am I really?'

'There's character in your face, Verity, character as well as beauty,' Edgar answered, 'which is more than can be said for a conceited Irishman with little more to offer than a beard and eyebrows. Nevertheless, for someone who's never delivered a painting in his life, Howard, you're not entitled to criticise. You may be a dab hand with a brush but until you start showing the world what you're capable of you're really no better than an amateur.'

'That,' Howard said through his teeth, 'is unfair.'

'It isn't enough to have talent flowing from your fingertips,' Edgar went on. 'You need nerve as well, the courage to show your work in public. Until you've suffered the taunts of reviewers who can't tell a masterpiece from a mantelpiece, you've no leg to stand on – and no right to castigate me. By the by, my portrait of your mother is as near finished as makes no matter and, with your permission, Verity, will be the star attraction of next summer's Academy exhibition. Now, if you'll excuse me, I'm going off to consort with my friends.'

'Edgar, please don't go,' Verity cried. 'Howard didn't mean it.'

'Oh, but I did, Mama,' Howard said. 'He should be thoroughly ashamed of himself cavorting round London when his wife, poor woman, has need of him.'

'You're being very righteous all of a sudden, Howard,' said Clive, 'and just a little priggish.'

'Mr Cavendish,' Julie intervened, 'where are your exhibits?'

'In another room.'

'Will you take me through, please?'

'Are you going to purchase one of my watercolours, Miss Martindale?'

'No,' said Julie, taking his arm. 'I just want to look at the frames.'

It took Anna several minutes to find a niche that contained nothing more suggestive than a pair of floral paintings by Gerald Sheepshank, one of her father's regular customers. She felt quite safe with Gerald's nasturtiums looking over her shoulder, for he was a painter of the old school who wouldn't dream of turning a bowl of flowers into an exercise in sexual allusion.

Howard trailed her through the crowd carrying a glass of wine in each hand.

'Typical of the Maules to do things on the cheap,' he groused. 'Profits they make from us artists you'd think they could run to a decent Chardonnay instead of this gnat's pi— I mean, this watery stuff.'

'Don't you deal with the Maules?'

'No.' Howard paused. 'I don't have a dealer.'

'Won't Clive put in a good word for you?'

'I don't need Cavendish to put in a word for me,' Howard said. 'When the time's ripe I'll find a dealer for myself.'

'And when,' said Anna, 'will the time be ripe?'

Howard moved a half step closer. 'Just what's your game, Miss Martindale?'

'My game? I don't know what you mean.'

'What are we doing alone in this quiet corner?'

'I was under the impression we were seeking respite from the crowd. However, if you find my company disagreeable . . .'

'No,' Howard said hastily. 'It isn't that.'

'What is it then?'

'Don't you realise that my mother and your uncle are conspiring to throw us together?' he said. 'I rather thought you might be in on it.'

'If you're concerned about the supper party my uncle's arranged for us after the show, have no fear, he's merely being kind.'

'To whom?'

They were very close now, almost as if they were about to embrace. She could smell wine, sweet and slightly sickly, on Howard's breath. 'Julie and Clive,' she said. 'My uncle's a hopeless romantic. He knows what's going on.'

'I'll wager he doesn't,' Howard said.

'If he doesn't,' Anna said, 'I do.' She brought her mouth close to his ear. 'My question to you, Howard, is what Clive Cavendish intends to do when he's finished with her?'

Howard flushed and looked away. 'I don't think it's quite right for us to be talking this way behind Clive's back.'

'Oh!' said Anna. 'It's all right for your friend to make love to my sister, but not all right for me to question his intentions.'

'What about your sister's intentions?'

'She's in love with him.'

'And believes he'll marry her?'

'Yes.'

'Well, I tell you he won't.'

'Would you, Howard?' said Anna.

'Would I what?'

'Marry a woman with whom you'd already been intimate?'

'Stupid question!'

'Is it?' said Anna. 'Why?'

'Because I've never – I mean, I'm not like Clive.'

'That's what I thought,' said Anna. 'Now about this supper party at Jules, I take it you will accompany me?'

'I suppose I'll have to now.'

'And be pleasant?'

'Yes,' Howard said grudgingly. 'And be pleasant.'

Anna kicked off her shoes and fell back on the bed.

'Oh, my goodness,' she said. 'I do believe I'm tipsy.'

'It's just as well Papa didn't wait up for us,' Julie said.

'What time is it?'

'After one.'

Anna giggled. 'What day is it?'

'Oh, come now, you're not that bad,' Julie said. 'It's Thursday.'

Anna rolled on to her stomach and paddled her legs.

'Thursday,' she said. 'Thursday already. Hooray!'

'What's so special about Thursday?' said Julie.

'It's almost next door to Saturday.'

Julie wasn't entirely sober either, for Uncle Otto had insisted on ordering exotic and expensive liqueurs to round off the meal. The boys, Howard as well as Clive, had taken great delight in tasting each strange potion while reminiscing about gay Paree and the bars as well as the galleries they'd visited in the city of light.

She wriggled into her nightdress, pulled down the sheet and dropped into bed. She had a slightly queasy feeling in the pit of her stomach that wouldn't go away. She lay back against the pillows and drew the quilt up to her throat.

Anna remained on top of the bed, legs and arms spread out as if she were swimming in a sea of dreams.

'What was that lovely stuff called?' she said. 'Almanac?'

'Armagnac,' Julie told her.

'Armagnac, Armagnac, wherefore art thou Armagnac?'

'Pull yourself together,' Julie said, 'and get undressed. If you fall asleep with your clothes on you'll feel seedy in the morning.'

'Why must you always be so sensible?'

'Sensible?' said Julie. 'I'm not in the least sensible.'

'No, you're not, are you?' Anna groped for the floor with her feet and, swaying slightly, began to undress. 'I wish I could be more like you. I mean, I wish I could ignore pro – pro –'

'Priety,' Julie suggested.

'Yes, that's it.' Anna fumbled with buttons and tapes. 'If only I could throw caution to the winds and just do as I want.'

'And what do you want?'

'I want someone to paint *me*,' Anna said.

'Meaning Mr Buskin?'

'Anyone, anyone at all,' Anna said. 'Do you think Clive would like to paint me once he's finished with you?'

'I doubt it,' Julie said curtly, and switched off the lamp.

9

It hadn't occurred to Julie that lovemaking would be so exhausting. She had imagined it as an unpleasant adjunct to marriage, a price to be paid for acquiring a husband. She'd pictured bridal gowns, rose petals and a charming old vicar bestowing blessings, Anna and Mrs Sims weeping as she floated up the aisle on the arm of a faceless gentleman who was just as ignorant as she was about that aspect of wedlock and who would do his duty on their wedding night with fumbling apology. She was greatly surprised, therefore, to discover that lovemaking need not be brief or furtive and that decorum had no part in it.

Sated and sleepy, she shed her kimono and lay down on the divan, which, it seemed, was exactly how Clive, the artist, wanted her after Clive, the man, had spent an hour on top of her in the small back room. She watched him climb into a baggy pair of trousers and a paint-stained shirt and set about arranging the tubes and brushes on the table that served as a palette.

Clive might dress like a tramp when he worked but in all other respects he was as meticulous as a surgeon preparing to operate on a difficult patient. He believed in painting to the scale of vision which was why the canvas was so large and why, as her image emerged upon it, she could not ignore how well it captured her languid sensuality. He had also chosen to paint her 'wet on wet', a technique, Clive informed her, that Whistler had perfected for covering a canvas in a single sitting but one that he hadn't quite mastered yet – which was why, after each brief session, the canvas was scrubbed down and he would start again.

'I don't believe a word of it,' Julie told him. 'I think you just want to keep me coming here as long as possible so that we can – can be together.'

'Devious I may be, darling, but not when it comes to painting.'

'Do you always work at such a snail's pace?'

'If I did,' Clive said, 'I'd have starved to death years ago. I'm lightning fast as a rule and very prolific, unlike our friend Howard, who'll labour over a single canvas for months.'

'I'll bet it didn't take you months to paint that blonde girl astride that blessed dog – unless, of course, you were having your way with her too.'

'Stop fishing, Julie. I did not have my way with Myrtle – or with the dog,' Clive said. 'I'll let you into a secret: great swathes of *The Best of Friends* were painted in a rush from memory. It was a relief when Wedmore bought the thing and removed it from public view.'

'It was popular, though, was it not? I mean, it made your name.'

'You've been talking to Buskin, haven't you? Howard thinks I'm a cheapjack just because I dash things off.'

'Well, you're not dashing me off, are you?' Julie said.

'Under the circumstances I'm obligated to do you justice.'

'And give Sir Magnus Wedmore value for his money?' Julie said.

'That, too,' Clive agreed. 'Now, if you'd be good enough to lift your knee a little higher and adjust the position of your right arm across your – yes, that's it. You're becoming rather good at this, you know.'

'At what precisely?'

He laughed, charged a long-handled brush with paint and laid down ground in a series of big floppy strokes that Julie thought wouldn't have shamed a paper-hanger. The whisper of the brush strokes blended pleasantly with the familiar sounds from the street.

Her eyelids drooped.

'Don't fall asleep,' Clive said.

'Sorry,' she murmured. 'What time is it?'

'A little after three.'

'Oh, dear: we only have an hour.'

'No, we don't,' said Clive. 'We have until six.'

'Six? But Anna—'

'Is being taken care of,' said Clive from behind the easel.

'Taken care of? By whom?'

'Mr Buskin, of course.'

'He's not taking her to his studio, is he?'

'He never takes anyone to his studio,' Clive assured her.

'Anna said not a word to me.'

'I expect she wanted to surprise you.'

'Six?' said Julie. 'Six is too late. Papa—'

'Your uncle, wily old chap, put the plan together,' Clive said. 'There's a group show at the Fine Art Society – been running for months – and you and Anna just happened to trip along to see it and, lo and behold!, bumped into Howard

Buskin and my good self and were invited to tea, which is why you'll be late home for supper.'

'My father will have a fit if we're late.'

'Your father isn't your keeper, Julie,' Clive said.

She wasn't in the least sleepy now. She stared at the back of the canvas and endeavoured to calculate who would benefit most from Uncle Otto's plan.

At length she said, 'Is Howard Buskin courting my sister?'

'I rather think he might be.'

She paused again. 'Are you courting me, Clive?'

His head appeared. 'Actually, I'm trying to paint you.'

'Is that all?'

'At this moment,' Clive said, 'yes, that's all.'

'I don't suppose you even like me, do you?'

'Don't be ridiculous,' said Clive, invisible again. 'Of course, I do.'

Hyde Park in mild October weather was no bad place to spend a Saturday afternoon and, as it turned out, Howard Buskin no bad companion to spend it with. He'd been lurking close to Harrods front entrance but didn't show himself until Julie had driven off in a cab, and then, with a little cry of 'Anna,' he'd appeared out of the crowd of elegant ladies and top-hatted gentlemen, had taken her arm and steered her along Knightsbridge into the park.

'Do you mind telling me where we're going?' said Anna.

'If you've no objection I thought we might pay our respects to Prince Albert before we have tea,' Howard said.

'I've no objection at all,' said Anna, 'but I didn't think mock Gothic monuments would be to your taste.'

'I like the camel,' Howard said. 'Don't you like camels?'

'I've never given it much thought.'

'They spit, you know.'

'Yes,' said Anna, still frowning. 'I believe I knew that.'

'If they don't like the look of you they spit.' He watched a group of lady bicyclists wobble past in the distance. 'Not the stone ones, of course. The stone ones just bark at you – like dogs.'

'You're teasing me, aren't you?'

'I'm not much use at small talk.'

'Then' – Anna tightened her grip on his arm – 'I'll do the talking for both of us.'

'That,' he said, 'seems like an ideal solution.'

'Shall I begin?'

'Please do.'

The house that Clarence Millar had purchased in a cul-de-sac off Holland Park Avenue had six public rooms, two bathrooms and, high among the clouds, a spacious studio used at one time by the late Sir Terence Gomer, one of the Royal Academy's favourite sons.

True to form, Howard loathed the place from the first and complained vehemently that the lofty studio room was nothing but a monument to the fortune that might be made by feeding sentimental pap to a philistine public. Gomer's version of pap was a string of huge paintings, fine in detail and high in finish, illustrating scenes from the life of Our Lord who, as the critic Walter Pater had shrewdly pointed out, bore more than a passing resemblance to Sir Terence's comely young wife.

In protest at being forced to reside in such a poisoned pile, Howard had retired to one tiny attic room in which he worked, ate and slept like a hermit or a monk. Soon after Clarence had passed away, however, he'd moved his materials into Gomer's grand studio and, to Verity's relief, slept in a proper bed and turned up in the dining room for meals. He didn't throw open the doors of his studio, though, and would go quite wild if an inexperienced servant girl took it upon herself to pop in to set the fire or sweep the floor.

At half past three o'clock on Saturday afternoon Otto presented himself at the door of the Millar residence. The butler, a portly autocrat with a mouth like a fish hook, relieved Otto of his hat, coat and gloves which he passed to a rake-thin housekeeper who, in turn, passed them on to a young girl in maid's uniform who lugged them off to the cloakroom while the butler escorted Otto across the hall and ushered him into the drawing room.

'That will be all, thank you, Percy,' Verity said in a polished voice and waited, motionless, for the butler to depart before she rushed forward, planted a kiss on Otto's cheek and drew him to a chintz-covered settee.

'Some digs!' said Otto. 'Quite a change from the old days.'

The drawing room, painted white, was pleasantly airy and uncluttered. Patterns were confined to a wall frieze and loose covers on the armchairs. One painting hung over the fireplace, a fine early Banbury, depicting, *à la* Degas, the chorus line backstage at the Gaiety.

'Did he meet her as arranged?' Verity asked.

'How would I know?' said Otto. 'I didn't follow them.'

'I wonder where he's taken her?'

'The park, probably.'

'Is that what you'd do if you were Howard?'

'If I were Howard . . .' Otto began and then thought better

of it. 'On the off chance that all does not go well with our star-crossed lovers and Howard comes trailing home early perhaps we'd better do what has to be done without more ado.'

'Do I make you nervous?' said Verity. 'Does sitting close to me—'

'Verity,' said Otto firmly, 'the paintings.'

Four flights of stairs left Otto breathless. It occurred to him during the ascent of the last steep stretch that Terence Gomer might have added ten years to his life if he'd had the sense to work at ground level. Wheezing like a barrel-organ, he rested on the landing before the double doors while Verity paused, a hand on the lock.

'Well,' Otto said, 'do we, or don't we? Make up your mind.'

'Yes,' Verity said, 'we do,' and threw open the doors.

The studio was the size of a ballroom and filled with light from huge skylights and north-facing windows. There was little by way of furniture: an easel, an oval table, a few chairs and footstools and a platform on castors upon which a model might pose. It wasn't the light that made Otto blink but the sight of Verity and himself reflected in a cheval glass at the end of the room and Howard Buskin's visage staring at them accusingly from the easel.

'Yes,' Verity said, behind him. 'You see.'

In the course of his life Otto had inspected hundreds of self-portraits but he had never seen anything quite like Howard Buskin's interpretation of Howard Buskin. Head tilted, eyes shaded, a sinister half-smile hinted at some secret drama being enacted in paint, a drama of which only the sitter was aware. The background was plain blue-tinted canvas, the colour repeated in the dark blue of the subject's jacket and again on the flesh of the brow. There were no strong lines to spoil the form which, as far as Otto could make out, had been rendered entirely by subtle brushwork.

'What do you think of it?' said Verity anxiously.

'I think it's brilliant,' Otto said. 'Brilliant but disturbing.'

'There are lots of others,' Verity said. 'Dozens of them.'

'Where?'

Verity dug into a pocket in her dress and brought out a key. She held it up between finger and thumb and asked, 'Do you think it's deceitful of me to go behind Howard's back?'

'I think,' Otto answered, 'that as we've come this far it would be criminal not to go the whole hog.'

Verity nodded. 'Quite right,' she said. 'Stand back.'

She unlocked the door of a wall cupboard and opened it cautiously. Two rolls of raw canvas slid out, followed by a stretcher, a couple of maulsticks and a single small painting, unframed. Otto stooped and retrieved the painting, a still life with fruit and wine bottles, an earthenware pitcher and a swathe of patterned silk that looped and twined sinuously between the objects.

'Good God!' Otto said.

'Oh, there are dozens like that,' said Verity.

She opened the cupboard door wider. Otto saw more canvases stuffed into the recess under shelves laden with a conglomeration of crusted pots and jars. Kneeling, he pulled out another painting, a bleak, empty landscape of moorland cowering under a blue-black sky. Otto turned the canvas around: no date, no signature. He handed it back to Verity who returned it to the cupboard and closed and locked the door.

'I'm not finished,' said Otto. 'I want to see more.'

'And so you shall,' said Verity. 'And so, my dear, you shall.'

Theatres were buzzing as curtain time approached and not far along the Strand the entrance to the Savoy was cluttered with cabs, horse-drawn and motorised, as the upper crust came rolling out to play. Pubs and restaurants were doing a roaring trade and the hoarse din of omnibus traffic hung over Ledbetter Street.

Stanley paced the pavement restlessly, stepping back into the shop doorway when a cab flew by or a group of Saturday night revellers, heading for the Crown or the Eagle, pushed past him. It was closing in on supper time and sensibly he should go upstairs before Mrs Sims lost her temper but he couldn't bring himself to abandon his vigil. To do so would be like abandoning his daughters who, for all he knew, were lost in the bustling city and at the mercy of some cad or confidence man whose wiles had stolen their wits away.

'Papa!'

They breezed around the corner by the seafood restaurant, Cavendish and Julie, Anna and Buskin, looking so secure and happy that his anxiety drained away at once.

Julie kissed his cheek. 'Were you worried?'

'A little, yes, just a little.'

'Howard and I must share the blame,' Cavendish said. 'Chance encounter at the Fine Art show. Too good an opportunity to miss. Carried the ladies off for tea. Lost all track, sir. Sure you'll understand. No disrespect intended.'

'None,' said Stanley, 'taken.'

Anna put an arm about his waist. 'Poor Papa. Did you think we'd been kidnapped? Well, now you know we're safe may we have your permission to trot round to Gatti's for a bite of supper?'

'Mrs Sims . . .' Stanley began.

'Will understand,' said Julie.

'Home by eleven,' Anna put in. 'Howard will see to it. Won't you, Howard?'

'My word on it, sir,' Howard said.

Stanley sighed. He was giddy with relief that his children were safe and, at the same time, sad to realise that they were children no longer.

'Eleven it is,' he said. 'Enjoy yourselves,' and, a moment later, locked up the shop and went upstairs to eat alone.

IO

It was close to the end of October before Otto caught up with Edgar Banbury who, with wife and children tucked away in St Albans, had slipped over to Paris for a week or two and had only recently returned.

Edgar was apparently still smarting over Howard's censure and wasn't answering Verity's letters which, Howard said, was simply Edgar's way of avoiding an explanation as to why Mama's portrait remained unfinished. The Wyndham's commission was also in abeyance, for Shaw, it seemed, was pressing for a bust rather than a painting to show off his noble dome to best advantage.

There was no sign of Shaw or any of the Café Royal's genuine celebrities in the first-floor wine bar when Otto sauntered in. In tweeds and woollen muffler, Banbury wasn't hard to spot. He was sipping wine at a marble-topped table in the company of two pretty young women whom Otto recognised as the 'Scotch' sisters, Morven and Sheonah, whose fresh, blue-eyed beauty had been captured in a remarkable studio portrait by no less a light than John Singer Sargent.

What the young ladies were doing in London Otto had no notion but if Banbury had hopes of making a conquest,

Otto thought, the old reprobate would surely be disappointed. The Scotch sisters were far too shrewd to fall for Edgar's hairy charm and looked thoroughly, if politely, bored.

'Goldstein.' Edgar glanced up, annoyed. 'What do you want?'

Otto bowed to the girls who responded with relieved smiles.

'A brief word with you, Edgar, if I may.'

'Can't it wait, man?' Edgar growled. 'Can't you see I have guests?'

One sister – Sheonah – shot to her feet. She was a little older now than when Sargent had painted her but no less striking. 'We'll be leaving you to it, Mr Banbury,' she said, giving her sister, Morven, a nudge. 'It's been a pleasure to meet you but we're dining shortly with another gentleman and had better be on our way.'

'What other gentleman?' said Edgar.

'Mr Augustus John,' Morven said. 'Do you know him?'

'Oh, yes, I know him,' Edgar said and, gazing after the girls as they retreated towards the stairs, muttered, 'Bloody Gus! Bloody upstart!'

'Aren't they a little too young even for you, Edgar?' Otto said. 'Besides, after one has had one's daughters painted by Sargent it's unlikely a commission is going to come *your* way.' He removed his hat, pulled out a chair and tapped the empty claret bottle. 'Another of the same? My treat.'

'It had better be,' Edgar said. 'I am, shall we say, in a state of temporary financial embarrassment.' He waggled his fingers to attract the attention of a waiter and, as the empty bottle and glasses were removed, studied Otto warily.

'Verity sent you, I suppose.'

'No,' said Otto. 'Verity did not send me.'

'The damned thing's almost finished. If I could just find some decent studio space in London she could have it in a month.' He straightened. 'Here, she doesn't want her fee back, does she?'

'I'm not here to talk about Verity. I'm interested in what you make of Howard.' Otto leaned forward. 'I've just seen his paintings.'

'Surely Howard didn't show them to you?'

'No,' Otto answered. 'Verity did.'

'What did she drag out?'

'Pretty well the lot, I think.'

'The landscapes, the still lifes . . .'

'And the self-portraits,' said Otto. 'They're good, aren't they?'

'Good?' said Edgar. 'They're magnificent. I could have them on the rail in the Salon d'Automne tomorrow if only the little beggar would let me. Did Verity show you the small study in which he appears to be climbing out of the canvas?'

'Yes,' Otto said. 'Very disturbing.'

'Why are you so interested in Howard Buskin all of a sudden?'

'Verity seems keen to marry him off to my niece.'

'Did Verity ever tell you what happened in Paris?'

'Paris? No, not a word about Paris. What *did* happen in Paris?'

'I can't tell you,' Edgar said. 'Verity swore me to secrecy. Let's just say it wasn't pleasant. If you really want my advice . . .'

'I do.'

'If Anna Martindale was my daughter I wouldn't let her marry Howard.'

'Really?' said Otto. 'Why not?'

'Because he'll destroy her,' Edgar said. 'Piece by piece, he will destroy her.'

'Edgar, are you sure?'

'Yes, my friend,' said Edgar Banbury. 'I'm sure.'

Money being no object, Howard had taken a box for the first production of the Royal Opera's winter season. It obviously hadn't dawned on him that two lonely souls in a box for six would attract comment. It also hadn't occurred to him that, having been composed by a German, *Tannhäuser* might actually be sung in German. Within minutes of the curtain rising, and already cringing at the attention Anna and he had received, Howard sank into a foetal crouch which he maintained throughout the whole of the first long act.

When the curtain descended and the audience broke into incomprehensible applause, he muttered, 'God, I need a drink,' and catching Anna by the arm yanked her out into the passageway in search of the Circle bar.

One stiff whisky later, with a little colour in his cheeks and the glaze gone from his eyes, he found his voice. 'How long does this thing last?'

'Aren't you enjoying it?' Anna said.

'Are you?'

'Oh, yes. It's wonderful. So moving.'

'Moving?' said Howard. 'What's moving about it?'

'The struggle between sacred and profane love.'

'I didn't know you spoke German. It is German, isn't it?'

'It is, and I don't', said Anna. 'One doesn't have to understand the language to be caught up by the music. Aren't you even a little bit moved, Howard?'

'Well,' he lied, 'perhaps just a little.'

'The second act is even better, believe me.'

'Longer, too, I imagine?'

'If you're not enjoying it, we'll leave.'

'No, no, I wouldn't dream of it,' Howard said bravely. 'Another glass?'

'I think not,' said Anna; then, 'Howard, may I ask you a question?'

'Of course.'

'Do you really want to be here with me or did Clive put you up to it?'

Practice made lying easier. 'Clive had nothing to do with it. We're here because I know how much you enjoy opera. No other reason.'

'Where are they? Clive and Julie, I mean.'

'At the studio, I expect.'

'Is Clive serious about my sister?'

'I imagine he must be.'

'Howard, are you serious about me?'

'I – what's that noise?'

'The five minute bell,' said Anna.

'Well,' Howard said, 'in that case we'd better hurry.' He offered his arm. 'Wouldn't want to miss a note, now would we?'

Clive lugged two buckets of coal from the communal cellar, broke up an orange box to provide kindling and, while Julie slept in his bed in the little back room, built a roaring fire in the grate. It was the first of the winter fires and he loved the dancing shadows that the flames painted on the studio walls and even the occasional belch of smoke that escaped from the iron hood. If he'd been of a more scientific turn of mind he might have pondered the effect of carbon molecules on oil paint but he was far too fond of comfort to fret about that.

Clad in nothing but a grubby pair of Aertex drawers, he knelt before the grate and studied his day's work. He had abandoned his attempt to paint like Jamie Whistler and had reverted to the tried and true technique of laying wet paint on dry which, much to Julie's relief, had fairly pushed the work along. His one regret was that his masterpiece would vanish into Magnus Wedmore's mansion and that he and Julie might be dead and gone before it turned up in Christie's to enhance his reputation and make him rich.

Squatting by the fireplace, he pictured an opulent house in Hampstead or Grove Hill, a house with a long garden and Julie in pale blue muslin cutting flowers, Julie in rose pink playing with a child, Julie in a scarlet travelling gown and fur-fringed cap posing in the patchwork snow of early spring.

My God, he thought, I'm falling in love with Julie Martindale.

What the devil am I going to do now?

'Marry her?' Howard Buskin said. 'Why do you want to marry her when you've already slept with her? Wedmore's painting – is it finished?'

'Almost. Two sittings, three at most.'

'And then you'll be paid?'

'I certainly hope so,' Clive said.

'Once you've a nice piece of chink in your pocket I'm sure you'll come to your senses,' Howard said. 'Unless you think she's worth it financially.'

'I don't see what money has to do with it.'

'Her papa's bound to settle something on her.'

'Martindale's in trade, Howard. He's not that rich.'

'He doesn't just make frames for galleries, you know. He supplies ready-mades in fifteen assorted sizes to print shops all over the south of England which, according to Mama, really brings home the bacon. And talking of bacon,' Howard said, 'if you do have a fit of conscience and actually marry the girl how in God's name are you going to keep her? You can't expect her to live in this hovel.'

'I'll take on more work.'

'If you can find it,' said Howard.

'Oh, I can find it,' Clive said. 'I'm not fussy. I'll take anything I can get.'

'And perjure your talent in the process.'

'According to you I don't have any talent.'

Howard dabbed a forefinger to a corner of the canvas and, frowning, inspected it. 'Dry,' he said, then, almost as an afterthought, glanced up at the painting. 'It's not bad, I suppose, if you like that sort of thing.'

'What sort of thing?' said Clive.

'Titillation disguised as art.'

'Keep this up, Howard, and I will throw you down the stairs,' Clive said. 'I had rather thought you'd be pleased for me.'

'Why would your foolishness please me?'

'Because it'll bring you closer to Anna.'

'Spare me the preaching of the newly converted.' Howard dug his fists into his coat pockets and hunched his shoulders. 'It's bloody freezing in here, Clive. Why don't you light the fire?'

'I'm saving my coals for my lady love.'

'Pish!' said Howard. 'Utter pish!'

Clive took his overcoat from the peg behind the door and put it on. He crammed a cloth cap on to his head, twined a scarf about his throat and then, as if the act of dressing had wearied him, slumped on the edge of the divan.

'You're right,' he said. 'I do have to be practical. First thing, I'll slip down to Bristol and drop a hint to my parents that marriage is on my mind. Dad will be so relieved it's not some tart I've fallen for he might even top up my allowance.'

'Here,' said Howard suddenly, 'Julie's not with child, is she?'

'No, she's not with child – or if she is she's keeping it secret.'

'You really have it bad, don't you?'

'Yes, Howard, I do. And, believe me, I'm just as surprised as you are.'

'Have you asked her yet?'

'Asked her what?' said Clive.

'To marry you.'

'No, not yet.'

'What if she turns you down?'

'Dear God!' Clive sat bolt upright. 'I never even thought of that.'

Uncle Otto had taken an early breakfast and had gone down to the workshop to supervise a delivery of wood from a mill in Bermondsey. He was very scrupulous when it came to timber and would go over every pre-cut length with a magnifying glass to check for splitting. Papa been summoned by the curator of the Dulwich Picture Gallery to inspect the frames of two Flemish paintings that were beginning to warp and might require to be replaced and had left the apartment before the girls were out of bed.

It was after ten before Julie emerged from the bathroom and joined Anna in the breakfast room. Quite used to the indolent ways of her charges, Mrs Sims had put eggs and bacon on warming-plates on the sideboard and left it to the nervous little day maid to deliver coffee and toast.

'You look terrible,' said Anna, through a mouthful of scrambled egg. 'This game you're playing is obviously taking its toll.'

'It isn't a game.' Julie poured coffee. 'Whatever you may think, Anna, posing for hours on end is hard work. In any case, Clive will finish it soon.'

'And then what?'

'He'll show the painting to Sir Magnus and if it meets with the old man's approval he'll have it framed.'

'Framed?' said Anna, startled. 'By whom?'

'Not,' said Julie, 'by Martindale's, that's for sure.'

'I should hope not,' said Anna. 'Am I on duty this afternoon?'

'No, Clive's gone off to Bristol to visit his parents.'

'Really?' said Anna. 'How long will he be gone?'

'Two or three days.'

'Howard said nothing to me.'

'Aren't you meeting him for lunch, or something?'

'One o'clock at Baker Street tube station. I think we're going to Tussauds.'

'Tussauds? Why, for heaven's sake?'

'We have to go somewhere, don't we?' Anna said. 'I'll be jolly glad when Clive's masterpiece is finished and we can give up this tedious pretence.'

'I thought you rather liked it.'

Anna scratched butter on to a piece of toast. 'If you think lolling on a couch all afternoon is hard work, try squiring Howard Buskin round town.'

'The opera . . .'

'A disaster. Howard has no ear for music. I only go out with him for your sake, Julie, for you and for Clive.' Anna reached for the coffee pot. 'Aren't you going to eat something?'

'I'm not hungry,' Julie answered.

'You're not sick, are you?'

'Just a little bit nauseous, that's all.'

'Oh, my goodness! You're not—'

'Late?' Julie shook her head. 'Quite the opposite, in fact.'

'Oh, poor you,' said Anna sympathetically. 'Poor old you.'

For all his lack of social graces Howard Buskin was never less than punctual. He was already loitering by the news vendor's stall at the mouth of Baker Street Underground when Anna emerged. She held on to her skirts with one hand and her hat with the other as a brisk wind from the direction of Regent's Park practically blew her into Howard's arms.

'Oufff,' she said. 'It certainly is fresh today.'

Howard was wrapped in a long, fly-fronted Chesterfield overcoat and had exchanged his bowler for a trilby. She took his arm.

'Lunch or waxworks?' she said. 'Which comes first?'

'Neither,' said Howard.

He stepped to the kerb and flagged down a motorised taxicab before it turned into Euston Road. The cab squealed to a halt at the pavement's edge. Howard tugged open the door and bundled Anna inside.

'Where are we going?' said Anna breathlessly.

'Chelsea,' Howard instructed the driver. 'Vine Street, Chelsea.'

'If we're going to Clive's place,' Anna said, 'I should warn you that Clive won't be there. He's in Bristol.'

'Um,' Howard said. 'I know.'

Anna had always thought of Chelsea as home to Holbein, Turner and Rossetti and her favourite of all authors, George Eliot. The area around Vine Street was a far cry from red-brick Queen Anne mansions and flowery walks, however, and the Trafalgar building was anything but picturesque.

She followed Howard up a dank staircase to a top landing, watched him fiddle with an old-fashioned latch and push open the door.

'Doesn't Clive lock it?' she asked.

'Why would he? He has nothing to hide. Besides,' Howard said, 'it's an artists' building and artists are as honest as the day is long. Coming?'

She clung to the belt of Howard's overcoat and peeped into the wash of light. She was aware of windows, huge windows, to her left and a shadowy doorway far to her right. Giving Howard a little shove, she said, 'Well, where is it?'

'Oh, you're keen,' Howard said. 'It's there on the easel.'

The painting was as large as a Venetian waterscape. It

represented intimacy on a grand scale, every nook and cranny of her sister's slender body exposed to view.

'Well, what do you think of it?' Howard said.

'It's disgusting.'

'Actually, it's better than one would expect from Cavendish. If he resists the temptation to over-egg the pudding I imagine Wedmore will be delighted. It has everything one might want in a nude, including pubic hair.'

'How can you say that about my sister?'

'It isn't your sister, it's art.' Howard paused. 'Do you still want me to pry out all your little secrets with my brush?'

'No,' Anna murmured. 'No, I do not. I want to go now.'

'Does it frighten you?'

'No, it – I . . .'

'Does it excite you?'

'Excite me? No!'

'Then why are you trembling?'

'I'm cold, that's all.'

Howard put an arm about her as if to share his warmth. Instead he steered her away from the easel to a shadowy doorway at the rear of the room.

'Where are you taking me?'

'There's something else I want you to see.'

He nudged the door with his knee and swung her round before him. Light from a tiny window outlined a few pots and pans, a sink and a paraffin stove in a narrow passageway. Before her, pale in the gloom, was a truckle bed with rumpled sheets and scattered pillows.

'That's where they do it,' Howard said.

Turning, Anna struck his chest with her fist.

'Stop it,' she said. 'Stop it. Stop it.'

'He lies there on top of her and puts it into her,' Howard said. 'Would you like me to do that to you?'

Before she could answer he trapped her arm between his stomach and her belly. His knuckles dug into her through her skirts. He put a hand between her legs and kissed her. She lifted herself on tiptoe to escape his groping fingers, then, yielding, sank down and, for an instant, seemed to be riding on his arm.

'Do you want me to do it?' he said.

'No.'

'We could do it here, where they do it. No one would ever know.'

She opened her eyes as wide as they would go. The panic inside her gave way to inexplicable longing, not for clumsy Howard Buskin but for Clive, her sister's lover, who would surely have taken her without a qualm.

'No, Howard,' she heard herself say. 'Not here. Not anywhere.'

His hand trailed from her thigh. He reached up and tweaked the brim of his trilby, setting it square on his head.

'Are we still on for lunch?'

'Under the circumstances, I think I prefer to go home,' Anna said and, giving him a little shove, headed swiftly for the stairs.

PART TWO

Fun and Games
1908

II

Julie opened her eyes, stared at the soot-blackened cornices high above the bed and, turning on her hip, rolled into the hollow that Clive's bottom had left in the mattress. She slept naked, shamelessly naked. There was something deliciously liberating about throwing away her nightgown – 'dispensing with the flannel,' Clive called it – and relying on her husband to keep her warm on cold winter nights.

Winter, though, was almost over. For the first time in weeks there was no ice on the window pane. Julie snuggled under the blankets to wait for Clive to finish his bath, bound upstairs and pop into bed again, all clean and smelling of soap. Then they would lie together listening to wagons clanking in the railway sidings, horse traffic clattering out of the coal yards and Pickford's motorised vans grinding gears from the direction of Regent's Park Road.

Julie had gradually grown used to Faversham Garden. It was quite different from the flat off the Strand, what with the niff of gasworks, sludgy smells from the canal and the faint 'fragrance' of the lavatories behind the rented end terrace house of which they had sole occupancy and which, thank God, had an indoor water closet. Unfortunately, there was no longer a garden. It had been lost a half-century ago when the railway had brought industry if not prosperity to Camden Town.

The marriage was working out well but the wedding had been something of a disaster. Aunt Edith and Julie's grandparents had declined Papa's invitation to attend and the gathering in St Stephen's had been top-heavy with Clive's relations. The haste with which the wedding had been arranged had caused a certain amount of unpleasantness but in the end Clive's folks had returned to Bristol cheered by Otto's assurances that he would keep an eye on the happy couple and see to it that they didn't starve.

By that time Julie and Clive were in bed in a rain-lashed hotel in Dieppe, intent on determining whether lovemaking within marriage was different from lovemaking without benefit of clergy, an experiment that continued long after they'd returned to London and had settled into the terraced house in Faversham Garden that Uncle Otto had found for them.

There were four small rooms, a kitchen, a garret and a basement in which Clive had temporarily set up his drawing board. The garret was occupied by the Cavendish's one and only servant, Maisie, a skinny sixteen year old Barnardo's girl whose prime tasks were to keep dirt at bay and help with the cooking. The kitchen had two gas rings and an iron stove upon which Julie experimented with a selection of plain fare dishes, though Clive did not consider it beneath his dignity to whip up an omelette or a rarebit now and then. Maisie ate in the kitchen with her employers except on those occasions when Uncle Otto came to dinner, Uncle Otto *sans* Anna and Stanley who were both, it seemed, sulking.

The sale of 'The Red Divan' to a delighted Sir Marcus had given the newly-weds financial breathing space but a dingy basement was not an ideal place in which to work and Clive was restricted to dashing off illustrations for newspapers and magazines using Julie and Maisie, in various guises, as models. By the standards of many men and women the Cavendishes lived a life of ease, if not luxury. They lay in bed long after the rest of Camden had gone trudging off to work and made love in the cold light of mid-morning while Maisie emptied the big tin bath and mopped up the puddles that Clive had left on the kitchen floor in the wake of his daily ablution.

As a rule Clive arrived in the bedroom with a towel about his loins and a sheet slung, toga-wise, over his shoulder, a form of dress designed not only to spare Maisie's blushes but to display his broad shoulders and strong thighs to his wife who, sitting up in bed, would pander to his vanity by crossing her eyes and sticking out her tongue. But not this morning. This morning Clive appeared in the bedroom clad in shirt and trousers, his hair, still wet, curling across his brow.

'What?' Julie sat up. 'What's wrong?'

Clive waved a letter the air. 'Not a thing, darling. In fact, it looks like our ship's come in.' He held the letter out to her. 'Offer of a commission. Six posters for the Midland Railway to advertise the forthcoming Olympiad.'

Julie squinted at the typewritten page. 'The what?'

'The Games, the International Games,' Clive said. 'Never for a moment did I imagine I'd get a Midland contract. Thought it would go to Lavery or Jimmy Pryde. But with the games kicking off at the end of April the Midland need the work done quickly and someone – Emslie of the *Graphic* perhaps – recommended me. By the time I've finished milking this commission I'll be the toast of London. Sports and pageantry are sure-fire winners for an artist like me. Muscular young men throwing things and sleek young women in bathing costumes. Flags and bands. Kings, princes and prelates saluting in the stands while the crowds throw their hats in the air. Oh, I will do justice to every last flounce and flourish and to every noble Corinthian.'

He kissed her hastily, and leapt to his feet.

'Clive, where are you going?'

'To the Midland offices to squeeze some cash out of them for materials.'

'Will you be home for lunch?'

'Lunch?' Clive laughed. 'No, no lunch today, sweetheart,' and, five minutes later, went sprinting down the High Street in search of an omnibus.

At school Anna had been compelled to play tennis and lacrosse but being neither muscular nor well-coordinated had shown no aptitude for either. She had never learned to swim, ride a horse or a bicycle, to skate on ice or throw anything much heavier than a pillow, and when it came to running – well, a ten-yard dash to beat her sister to the bathroom of a morning was her limit.

She was, of course, aware – who wasn't? – that London was playing host to the nations in Olympic competition and that a great new stadium was being built north of Shepherd's Bush, cheek by jowl with the fantastic pavilions that, come summer, would house the Franco-British Exhibition, news of whose progress already filled the corners of the press that weren't taken up with murder, Irish Home Rule or bloody boring sport.

It wasn't just sport that Anna found boring these days. It was all she could do not to bite Papa's head off when he suggested that she might resume drawing lessons. Her response to that proposal was to gather up all her materials, stuff them into the bottom of the glory-hole at the back of the hall cupboard and cover them with a moth-eaten travelling rug.

She shopped listlessly, mooched round the galleries and drank tea, alone, in the Corner House. Between solitary outings she played endless hands of Patience in the morning room or lurked in her bedroom and brushed her hair, plucked her eyebrows and applied so much powder that Uncle Otto was moved to ask if she was appearing in *The Mikado*.

In mid-January she wrote to Julie to suggest meeting for afternoon tea. Julie wrote back promptly setting a date and a time. The meeting wasn't as friendly as Anna had hoped, for something had been lost between them, a bond broken. They agreed, albeit tacitly, not to meet again too soon.

'What are you doing?' Anna asked.

Uncle Otto looked up from the workbench. 'Marbling.'

'Is it difficult?'

'It does take a certain amount of experience.'

'It doesn't actually look like marble, you know.'

'It's not meant to,' Otto said. 'It's just a pattern that suits some tastes.'

'Is this frame for anyone in particular?'

'No,' Otto said. 'It's part of a general order for Jeavon's of Southampton. They're photographers not art suppliers.'

Anna watched him paint veins on to the gazed surface with short, flicking strokes of the brush. 'I could do that,' she said.

'I expect you could,' said Otto, 'with a bit of practice.'

'Let me try.'

He hesitated, then, nodding, gave her the little brush which she held as tightly as if she intended to punch holes in the black glaze. Otto settled the handle of the brush into the cradle of her thumb and forefinger. He'd done it so often he'd forgotten how difficult it could be to keep the wrist firm. He let her dribble rivulets of pale green paint over the horizontal and then, dipping the brush again, attack the left-hand vertical. It would take him ten minutes to repair the damage but a little time lost was a fair exchange for seeing Anna smile.

'Oh,' she said, 'this is easy.' She looked up. 'Aren't I good?'

'Perhaps just a tiny bit too eager,' Otto told her. 'Shorter strokes, please.'

'Like this?'

'Yes, that's better,' he said – which it wasn't.

She painted away, tongue stuck out like a kitten's. She was still so young, so incredibly innocent that Otto hesitated to put the question.

'Have you seen anything of Howard Buskin lately?'

'Why do you ask?'

'Well,' Otto said, 'you saw quite a lot of him before Christmas.'

'Not out of choice,' Anna said. 'I was chaperoning Julie, if you must know.'

'Were you now?' Otto took the brush, wiped it on a pinch of newspaper and offered it back to her. She shook her head. Otto went on, 'I was rather under the impression you were providing Clive and Julie with an alibi.'

'What if I was? He married her, didn't he? She got what she wanted.'

'What about you, Anna? What do you want?'

'Not,' she said, 'to be pursued by Howard Buskin.'

'Did you ever sit for Howard?'

'No one sits for Howard. He's afraid of women. No,' Anna corrected herself, 'he's afraid of his mama.' She snatched a sheet of newspaper from the bench and wiped her hands. 'You expected me to marry Howard, didn't you?'

'No. We just thought . . .' Otto hesitated. 'Something happened, didn't it? Did he molest you?'

'Molest me? You make me sound like a policeman who's had his helmet knocked off by a drunk,' Anna said. 'To answer your question – both your questions – Howard did not molest me. And no, I haven't seen him since the wedding. I don't care if he's rich. I don't care if Edgar Banbury says he's the best painter since Da Vinci, I'm simply not interested.'

'Good,' Otto said. 'That's good.'

'What's good about it?'

'He was never the right man for you.'

'Isn't that for me to decide? I'm not like Julie. I'm not . . .'

'Not what?'

'In love,' Anna snapped, then, spinning on her heel, headed out of the workshop before Otto could invite her to explain.

Night drifted down over Camden. Water vapour absorbed soot and dust and transformed them into a granular mist that made the eyes smart and the throat ache. Stallholders packed away their wares, pubs and eating places turned up the gas and the streets were flooded with men and women tramping home after a hard day's labour. Dusk was Julie's least favourite time. For a melancholy half-hour she would hanker after the comforts of Ledbetter Street and the bright lights of the Strand. At this hour, as a rule, she would coax her husband away from his drawing board to sit with her in the kitchen while Maisie prepared the evening meal or, now and then, to snuggle by the fire in the dingy parlour, sip a glass of sherry and pretend that they were gentlefolk.

On that February evening, however, dusk thickened, night fell and the topping on the shepherd's pie that Maisie had put in the oven turned from brown to black. At eight o'clock, Julie instructed Maisie to take the pie from the oven, scrape off the burned bits and put the remains on to three plates, one of which she would reheat when Clive finally elected to come home.

She knew he had business to attend to but had no idea what 'business' entailed or why it was taking him so long. In the back of her mind was a fear that Clive had tired of marital routine and had gone off on a lark with his artist friends, a fear that took no account of the fact that Clive had no artist friends apart from Edgar Banbury and Howard Buskin, neither of whom was liable to be trolling the pubs in Camden or, for that matter, drinking champagne and flirting with the girls in the bar of the Café Royal.

It was half past nine before the street door thudded and a familiar voice called out, 'Darling, I'm home,' a banal greeting that sent Julie rushing upstairs. She might have thrown herself into his arms if his arms hadn't been full of packages that he unloaded on to the hall stand.

'What a day!' Clive shucked off his overcoat. 'You've no idea how fussy the Midland can be when it comes to getting it right.'

'Did you find a suitable model?'

'A model?'

'At the Café Royal perhaps?'

'Ah!' he said. 'I see. You think I've been out enjoying myself. Fact is, I have been enjoying myself – but not in the way you suppose.'

She wasn't quite ready to forgive him. 'Supper's ruined.'

'I'll make do with a poached egg.' He paused. 'Where's Maisie?'

'Downstairs. Why?'

'I'd like a hand to lug this tackle down to the basement.'

Julie sniffed. 'I'll do it.'

'Will you?' He seemed genuinely grateful. 'Will you really?'

And because he looked so handsome and so contrite and was, after all, her husband, she gave him a little punch on the chest and said, 'Of course, I will.'

Maisie said, 'I could be a runner for you, Mr Cavendish.'

She was seated on a stool in her special corner with a plate of charred remains on her lap and a spoon in her hand. She had very dainty manners for an East End orphan. She picked out fragments of meat and slipped them into her mouth from the tip of the spoon while giving Clive an eager-to-please look that in another phase of his life might have had him speculating on how he could persuade her to pose for something more risqué than illustrations for the *Ladies Journal*.

'No, Maisie,' he told her. 'Somehow I don't think you'd fill the bill.'

'Get me a bow an' arrer an' I could be one o' them harchers.'

'Don't be silly,' Julie said. 'You're far too small.'

'Or you could toss me up in the air then like one o' them Dames.'

'Dames?' said Julie.

Clive propped his stocking feet on the cool end of the stove and leaned back in his chair. 'I think she means the Danish gymnasts who gave a demonstration in Hyde Park a couple of years ago. Is that right, Maisie?'

'Saw them, I did, on a houting.'

'You're remarkably well up in sporting matters, Maisie,' Julie said.

'Read all the papers, I do. I *can* read, you know.'

'Yes, Maisie,' Clive said, not unkindly. 'You've told us often enough.'

'If you ain't gonner draw me, Mr Cavendish, who are you gonner draw?'

'I'm not sure yet,' Clive said. 'The Midland require pilot sketches for approval in three weeks and finished work by mid-April. They've supplied me with addresses for various sporting organisations which should make things easier. The only thing they absolutely insist upon is one poster illustrating the Great Stadium in all its glory, something, I fancy, like the Roman Coliseum.'

'Wiff lions, Mr Cavendish?' said Maisie.

'Probably not,' said Clive.

'Do you even know what this stadium looks like?' Julie asked.

'No, but give me three days without rain, darling, and I'll be more familiar with its every aspect than the architects who designed it.'

'How much is all this hard work going to bring in?' Julie said.

'Thirty pounds the poster, plus a small – a very small – royalty.'

'Ooooo,' said Maisie. 'That'll keep us in treacle pud for a while.'

'You,' said Julie, 'have too much to say for yourself. Finish that pie, wash up and get off to bed.'

Obediently, Maisie carried her plate to the sink, scraped the scraps into a tin bucket and moved to the table to clear away the teacups. She leaned her elbows on the table top, chin on hand. 'Wrestlers,' she said. 'Can't go wrong wiff wrestlers.'

'You might have a point there, Maisie,' Clive conceded.

'Or Jock Halswelle in his shorts.'

'Who's he when he's at home?' said Julie

'Britain's best athlete,' Clive said. 'He won two medals in Athens.'

'And all the sprints at the Powderhall,' Maisie added.

'Well, *I've* never heard of him,' said Julie.

Clive and his maidservant groaned in unison.

12

Dartmoor in February wasn't Verity's idea of a winter retreat particularly now she could afford to chase the sun to Italy or the south of France. She would, in fact, have settled for wintering in her town house in Holland Park which at least had the benefit of being warm. It was also convenient for calling on the doctor in Wimpole Street whose injections gave her some relief from the rattling cough that made her days a misery and kept her awake at nights. What had brought her to Foxhailes just before Christmas and what kept her there deep into the New Year was not anxiety about her health but anxiety about her future, that empty space on the map of life that Howard alone could fill.

In Howard's view, a cook, a lady's maid – Emily – and the locals whom Mr Moss had rounded up were all the staff Mama required to keep her comfortable while the wind howled over the moor, the lights flickered and the water pipes froze. But comfort, such as it was, was not enough for Verity. Trapped in Foxhailes, she had nothing with which to occupy herself save nursing her cough and fretting about the welfare of her son who, in the wake of Julie Martindale's wedding to Clive Cavendish, had sunk into a state of morbid self-absorption that seemed, at least to Verity, to hint at mental disorder.

'I'm not going mad, Mother,' Howard assured her. 'I'm painting.'

That much was true. Day after day, in all weathers, he'd tramp out with a bundle of painter's tools strapped to his back and return late in the afternoon, soaked to the skin and so numb that it was all he could do to tote his oilskin-wrapped canvas into the stable where he'd set up a studio. Verity's only consolation in those dreary wintry weeks was that Howard no longer hid his work from her and when, muffled in furs like an Arctic explorer, she ventured across the lawn to the stable he did not chase her away.

Three smelly oil lamps shed light on the easel canvas. All around the stable were canvases of identical size and shape, each bearing the rudiments of a moorland scene. After nightfall, by lamplight, Howard laboured patiently over the crude oil sketches, refining and enhancing them so that the finished pictures were far from mere impressions. It seemed odd to Verity that Howard preferred to paint in a bitterly cold outbuilding when the house offered a choice of umpteen rooms.

She watched him labour over a tiny corner of the canvas and wondered, not for the first time, where her son's talent had come from. Howard's father, a Yorkshire black-smith, had had not one drop of artistic blood in him. He could hardly believe his luck when she'd tumbled, half tipsy, into his bed one summer's afternoon when his wife and daughters were at market. He'd taken her in a wordless frenzy of lust and hadn't even had the courtesy to offer a ride back to the railway halt afterwards. She hadn't clapped eyes on him since, yet here he was, resurrected in her broad-browed son who, in his thirtieth year, was the spitting image of the dour Yorkshire blacksmith who'd sired him.

'Howard?'

'Uh?'

'Don't you think it's time we went home?'

The brush hovered over the canvas. 'This is our home now, Mama. Let it go.'

'Let what go?'

'London,' Howard said. 'Her?'

'Her?'

'I don't need a wife. I don't want a wife.'

'Oh!' Verity said. 'Is that what we're doing in Devon? We're escaping from Anna Martindale, are we?' She took a pace forward and removed the brush from his fingers. He made no attempt to stop her. 'Why are you so against the poor girl, Howard? Are you afraid you might fall for her?'

'I'm not afraid. I just don't want to be distracted.'

'In that case,' said Verity, 'why don't I go home to Holland Park and leave you here with cook and a couple of servants?'

'No,' Howard said. 'I want you to stay.'

She took no satisfaction in Howard's dependence. Down deep behind her breastbone, where her cough had its murky origins, she experienced a welling of pity for her troubled son. 'I'm touched,' she said truthfully, 'but I think it's time you learned to stand on your own feet. After all, I will not be with you for ever.'

'Don't say that, please,' Howard said. 'You should be in bed. Come, I'll help you over to the house.' He offered his arm. Verity ignored it.

'Then what?' she said. 'Will you scuttle back here to pretend that painting makes you happy?'

'But it does, Mama. It's the only thing that makes me happy.' He offered his arm again. 'Come on. We'll eat dinner together and then I'll tuck you up in bed.'

'I wish Edgar were here. He'd know what to do.'

'Edgar?' Howard allowed his arm to drop. 'Edgar can barely look after himself, let alone look after you. In any case, he's in Italy – Florence, I believe – with Clara and the children.'

'What's he doing in Florence?'

'Spending the money you paid him for your portrait and, I assume, finding excuses to do very little else. He has a young nanny in tow, a maid who probably won't remain a maid for long. Is that what you want for me? Or would you rather I abandoned the one thing I enjoy and like that fool, Cavendish, prise open the legs of some dim-witted girl who I'll then feel obliged to marry? No, Mama. No. I'm not going to be dictated to by my penis.'

'I can't bear to hear you talk like that.'

'You've heard worse in your time, I'm sure.'

Verity coughed, hand to mouth, and shivered inside her furs.

'You really are unwell, aren't you?' Howard said. 'I'll send for a doctor first thing tomorrow.'

'It's nothing,' Verity told him. 'I don't need a doctor. I need – I need . . .'

'What?'

'A family,' she blurted out. 'A family to call my own.'

'Well, that,' Howard said, 'is something I can't provide.'

'Or won't,' said Verity and stumbled out of the stable and went back to the warmth of the house.

A half-hour later, washed, shaved and respectably dressed, Howard joined her in the dining room and, an hour after that, solicitously escorted her upstairs to help Emily put her to bed.

There was no scarcity of artists packed into cluttered Camden. They were a sociable bunch and Clive was on nodding terms with most of them. He'd no wish to be corralled into joining any of the groups that flourished in the borough, however, or in having his work displayed in cooperative galleries or signing on to aesthetic manifestos that would be out of fashion before spring turned to summer.

He was not averse to pulling the odd string, though, and within forty-eight hours of signing the Midland contract had secured a cheap middle-floor studio only ten minutes' walk from home.

The studio was not as lofty as the Trafalgar but had good light, a gas fire and more than enough space to accommodate his board and easel. The one disadvantage was that Roger Manfred had a studio above him and Charlie Moore one below. The pair were forever pestering him to join them for Sunday breakfast or trot along to 'At Homes' where a crowd of up-and-comings discussed professional matters and, Clive had no doubt, knocked back the booze and squabbled.

He hired a cart and two men to transport his equipment from the basement in Faversham Garden and, with time pressing, had his materials installed in the studio by half past eight in the morning, leaving Julie and Maisie, deprived of routine, stumbling about back home.

'He's gorn, Mrs Cavendish. He's gorn,' Maisie said plaintively, as if her master had lit out for Australia. 'He didn't even stop for 'is bath.'

Somewhat dazed at being up so early, Julie slumped at the kitchen table and contemplated the inordinate length of day that stretched ahead. In a remarkably short time she had become dependent on Clive, not only to warm her bed but just to be there, present if unseen.

'Market's open,' Maisie suggested. 'We could do a shop.'

'Perhaps,' Julie said. 'What's happening with my eggs?'

'Shan't be a tick,' Maisie promised. 'You want them turned?'

'Did Mr Cavendish eat anything before he went out?'

'Toast, that's all. He'll be starved by dinner time. Could fetch 'im round a pork pie or a 'am sandwich 'bout noon, if you like,' Maisie suggested. 'He might be glad of a bit o' company by then.'

And then again, Julie thought, he might not.

She listened to the eggs spitting in the pan and said nothing.

''Course,' Maisie went on, 'like as not Mr Cavendish won't be there.'

Julie looked up. 'Why do you say that?'

'Got a appointment at Stamford Bridge.'

'Doing what?'

'Meetin' folk from the London Athletic Club.'

'He said nothing to me about it.'

'Maybe you wasn't interested.' Maisie slithered two fried eggs on to a plate and placed the plate on the table by Julie's elbow. 'Or maybe 'e just forgot.'

*

The weather that February forenoon was crisp and cloudless and the first-floor bedroom in which his mother lay was dappled with sunlight. He instructed Emily to leave the curtains open and, in spite of his mother's mewling protest, despatched a boy to Brampton to round up a doctor.

The doctor was an elderly gent with mutton-chop whiskers and a weary air of having seen it all before. He arrived in a jaunting cart and, ignoring Howard's anxious questions, followed Emily upstairs. Verity, it seemed, had found sufficient strength to have the sheets changed, wash her face, brush her hair, apply a touch of rouge and be helped into a clean nightgown and a satin bed-jacket and, sitting up in bed, looked less like a patient than an ageing bride.

'Good morning, Mrs Millar. I'm Dr Ogilvy.'

'Good morning,' said Verity.

Dr Ogilvy handed his black bag to Emily and approached the bed.

'Now,' he said, 'tell me what ails you.'

Howard retreated to the landing where he paced back and forth until, a quarter of an hour later, the doctor emerged.

He looked, Howard thought, very grim.

'Are you Mrs Millar's only child?'

'I am,' Howard said. 'Why? What's wrong with her?'

'I'm afraid,' the doctor said, 'it's not good news.'

Clive entered the Stamford Bridge ground shortly after eleven o'clock. His letter to the London Athletic Club's secretary had elicited an invitation to a meeting not at the Great Stadium in Shepherd's Bush or one of the elite clubs in which the organisers of sport in England held court but, rather oddly, in Fulham.

Clive was familiar with Stamford Bridge. In his student days, he'd joined thousands of fans here to cheer the heroes of the track. He was somewhat disgruntled to find goal posts planted on the grass in the centre of the oval to remind him that the recently formed Chelsea Football Club now shared the ground with athletes. Out on the pitch two men with sickles were trimming the scant winter grass while on the track six runners in shorts and vests were straining every sinew to be first to break the tape. Clive barely noticed the gentlemen in top hats and bowlers at first and only became aware of them when cheering broke out.

He headed across the grass to introduce himself. By that time the runners were stooped over, collecting breath, or bouncing up and down and flapping their arms to indicate that they were still full of vim, while their trainers attempted to cover them with blankets as if they were racehorses.

Clive tugged a notebook from his pocket, tapped out the tiny pencil and, out of habit, began to record the athletes' poses in swift thumbnail sketches.

'Oy?' said one of the trainers. 'What you think you're doing?'

'Making a few notes,' said Clive.

'You one o' them bookmakers?'

The trainer was small in stature, wiry as a whippet and, Clive guessed, about sixty years old. His bowler sat on top of a shock of pure white hair and his features were gnarled like the bark of an old oak. In five or six lightning strokes Clive captured his likeness.

'I'm here by invitation,' Clive said.

'Whose invitation?'

'Mr Cook's invitation.'

'Oh!' said the trainer, chastened. 'Righto.'

A gentleman in well-cut tweeds stepped on to the track and offered his hand.

'Cavendish, is it?' he said. 'I'm Theodore Cook.'

Cook had been a leading light in the fencing team that had brought medals back from Paris and Athens and was currently a member of the British Olympic Committee. He was also the son of Jane Cook, a well-known artist and illustrator. In addition to being an art critic for the *Daily Telegraph*, he had written several books on painting and sculpture. Clive began to suspect that there might be more to his contract with the Midland than first met the eye.

'I'm exceedingly pleased to meet you at last, Mr Cavendish.'

'And I you, sir,' Clive heard himself say. 'Is your mother well?'

'My mother is blooming,' Theo Cook replied.

'Still painting?'

'Like a demon,' Theo Cook said. 'And you, Mr Cavendish, are you prepared to do justice to our Olympians?'

'Indeed, sir, I'm only too eager to get started.'

'You have a studio, I take it?'

'I do, but I prefer to sketch on the spot, if that isn't inconvenient.'

'Not at all,' Theo Cook said. 'Do you see who we have here this morning? Bannerman, for a start, Telfer Scully and, of course, our white hope for medals, Jock Halswelle. Any one of them will be honoured to pose for you. First, however, I'd like to introduce you to Lord Desborough who, as you're no doubt aware, is President of our Games.'

A tall middle-aged man with a moustache detached himself from the time-keepers. William Grenfell, Lord Desborough, had rowed for Oxford, fenced for Great Britain, stroked an eight across the Channel, swum Niagara twice and climbed the Matterhorn by three different routes. He'd also shot tigers in India, bears in the Rockies and scoured the seas off Florida of tarpon and, by way of a hobby, perhaps, had become a member of parliament at the tender age of twenty-five and now, in his fifties, sat in the Upper House.

Clive's father had followed Willie Desborough's exploits in the press for many years. Clive wondered what his father would say if he were here to see his son being greeted by the great man. He wondered too if Julie would be impressed or if she would simply write Desborough off as just another upper-crust sportsman with more money than sense. He knew what little Maisie would say.

'A toff,' she'd say, round-eyed. 'Oooo, ain't 'e a dish of fish.'

'I'm a great admirer of your work, Cavendish,' Desborough said, 'the Wedmore pictures in particular. What can we do to assist you?'

And for the first time, though not the last, Clive shook hands with an aristocrat.

13

On a cold, calm, grey morning Howard accompanied his mother across Lambeth Bridge to St Thomas's Hospital where Sir Robert Templar-Agnew, a nurse in a starched apron and four young doctors in training carried her off into the bowels of the building and left Howard to cool his heels in a small private waiting room that smelled not of medicine but of pipe smoke.

Verity had not been fazed by the Brampton doctor's gloomy diagnosis. In fact, she appeared to regard being ill as a fair swop for a return to London. She hadn't objected when Howard had called in Templar-Agnew and had meekly consented to lug herself over to St Thomas's and subject her chest to rays from a new device by which Sir Robert set great store.

If he'd been better versed in modern medicine Howard might have put his foot down, but by that time he, like Verity, was no more than a piece of flotsam bobbing on a sea of physiological ignorance. Now, alone in the little waiting room, leafing through copies of the *Field*, he was tormented by an irrational fear that he might never see his mother again.

After what seemed like hours, Verity was ushered back

into the waiting room and a few minutes later Sir Robert delivered his verdict.

'Chronic pneumonia would be my guess.'

'Your *guess*?' Howard said. 'Didn't the machine tell you anything?'

'Not as much as we'd hoped,' the doctor admitted. 'The bronchial tree remains cloudy.'

'Cloudy?' Howard said. 'Is my mother going to die?'

'Not immediately.'

'Dear God!' Howard shouted. 'What does "not immediately" mean?'

Sir Robert raised himself on tiptoe which, Howard thought, did nothing to add to his stature. 'The symptoms of chronic pneumonia,' he explained, 'are often obscure in the early stages. It's not uncommon to meet with advanced fibrosis of long standing which, as far as one can make out, may not be the case here. Prolongation of some of the phenomena of the original disease usually indicates the supervention of pulmonary fibrosis, but in Mrs Millar's case it appears that fibrosis is not fully established and the prognosis—'

'Wait,' said Howard. 'What do you mean by the original disease?'

'Pleurisy, perhaps, or . . .' Sir Robert had the decency to hesitate.

'Or what?' said Howard.

'Syphilis,' the doctor said. 'Yes, most likely syphilis.'

Little Maisie Fellowes was a cheerful soul, if a bit too chatty for Julie's taste. The Barnardo's girl was no substitute for a confidante, however, and as February crept into March Julie found herself missing Anna. If she hadn't been quite so obstinate she might have taken herself across town to Ledbetter Street to make peace with her sister but that course of action smacked of defeat, a signal that her impulsive marriage to a dashing young artist was veering toward the rocks.

She wasn't appeased by Clive's assurances that the Midland contract would provide a stepping stone to bigger and better things, nor was she amused by the boyish glee with which her husband recounted how he'd shared a pint with big Con O'Kelly, the heavyweight wrestler, and how, to everyone's amusement, he'd ruined his shoes by throwing his weight into the rope with the London City Police tug-of-war team during a practice in Finsbury Park.

When she enquired about 'lady competitors' Clive laughed and told her that snobs in long skirts with feathers in their hats lacked pictorial dynamic. Maisie giggled and, throwing back her narrow shoulders, mimed the shooting of an arrow from a bow, an invisible arrow that narrowly missed Julie's ear.

'Who'd you draw today, Mr Cavendish?' Maisie asked.

'Telfer Scully.'

'What's he like?'

'Oh, you'd love him, Maisie. He's just your type.'

'What's my type then, Mr Cavendish?'

'He's built like a gorilla and he'd eat you like a ripe banana.'

'Ooooo!' said Maisie. 'How lovely!'

'What about me, Clive?' Julie said.

'What about you?'

'Don't you have a man for me to admire?'

'You have me, sweetheart,' Clive told her. 'Am I not man enough for you?'

But Julie, trapped in a bitter mood, was no longer sure that he was.

'I think,' Uncle Otto said, wiping soup from his moustache, 'you're making too much of it, Julie. If Clive was an insurance clerk or, heaven forbid, a docker you'd see even less of him. It's something men have to do – work, I mean – and artists are no different in that respect from other mortals.'

'If Clive was a docker,' Julie said, 'at least he'd be home for supper.'

'Well, yes,' Otto conceded, 'but, by the sound of it, Clive has snared some important clients. Naturally, he's keen to do his best by them.'

'What about me?' said Julie. 'Shouldn't he be doing his best by me? He knows perfectly well you were invited to eat with us tonight and he doesn't even have the courtesy to turn up on time. I've half a mind to send Maisie round to that blasted studio just to see if he's there.'

'Have you been in the new studio yet?' Otto said.

'I'm still waiting to be asked.'

Dolled up for the occasion in a clean apron and frilly cap, Maisie removed the soup plates. She paused at the door of the dining room.

'Shall I be serving the entry now, madam?'

'Is the beef ready?' said Julie.

'Will be in a tick, madam.'

'Serve it.'

'What about Mr Cavendish?'

'Serve it,' Julie said again. ' Damn it, just serve it.'

The dining room had a musty smell that a coal fire did little to dispel. The electrical light bulb that hung above the table was visible through the frayed tassels of a parchment shade. The table was set with good china, though, elegant water glasses and fine Irish linen, wedding gifts brought out only when Otto came to visit.

Julie took a cigarette from her uncle's case and let him light it for her.

She blew smoke and studied the light bulb above her head.

Uncle Otto cleared his throat. 'In spite of what I just said about clerks and labourers, Clive isn't an ordinary husband and yours isn't an ordinary marriage. You knew he was an artist when you married him.'

'Of course, I did,' said Julie.

'Don't you like living in Camden?'

'It isn't the house I object to, it's Clive not being here to share it with me.'

Avoiding Julie's eye, Otto said, 'Clive isn't lacking in – ah – passion, is he? I mean, he doesn't neglect you – ah – upstairs?'

'Lord, no!' Julie said. 'On the contrary.' She stubbed out the unwanted cigarette in a tin ashtray. 'I thought you were going to give me a lecture about marrying in haste and repenting at leisure.'

'That's more your father's line than mine,' said Otto. 'But Stan will come around in his own good time.'

'And Anna?'

'Anna has concerns enough of her own.'

'What sort of concerns?'

'Haven't you heard? Verity Millar's very sick indeed.'

'What does that have to do with Anna?'

'Verity has asked us to call at Holland Park tomorrow

evening. Between you and me,' Otto said, 'I've a sneaking suspicion Anna may not be averse to meeting up with Howard Buskin again. In any event, we can hardly refuse the request of a dying woman, can we?'

'Is Verity Millar really dying?'

'So it would seem,' said Otto just as the door flew open and Clive, all hale and hearty, burst in to pump Otto's hand, plant a kiss on Julie's cheek and call out to Maisie to bring on the beef.

Anna had never seen anyone die before. She had no clue how to deal with the situation or what was expected of her. The enormous first-floor bedroom was lit by a single lamp that isolated the frail figure in the bed. On a tray on a bedside table were three china bowls, three silver spoons, a water glass and a pile of small towels, like baby napkins. Uncle Otto, looking very sombre, stood on the far side of the bed while Howard strode about the room, railing against modern medicine and Sir Robert Templar-Agnew in particular.

'Thereby proving,' Howard went on, 'that a bloody knighthood confers neither tact nor wisdom on a man but only the authority to strike the fear of God into anyone foolish enough to be impressed by a frock-coat and a title. Syphilis,' he barked. 'Syphilis, my backside! Half an hour in the London Chest – which is where we should have gone in the first place – gave the lie to that calumny. Did Templar-Agnew think my mother was a street walker? Did he think she has no pedigree just because she doesn't speak with a plum in her mouth? Did he think the thirty guineas I put in his hand was tainted? Didn't stop him pocketing it, I can tell you. Thirty bloody guineas to give us both fits when all it took was an examination by a chap in shirtsleeves with a stethoscope to come up with the answer.'

'Which was?' Otto said.

'Inflammation and a bit of swelling round the heart. What can you expect at her age? Little bit of inflammation isn't going to kill her. Be back on her feet in no time. Won't you, Mama?'

'Treatment?' said Otto.

'Pills and rest. Lots of rest. No worries, Mama. Right?'

Anna noticed that her uncle was sucking his moustache, a habit he'd supposedly broken years ago. He took a half step forward and stooped over Verity whose eyes remained closed.

'I don't think she can hear you, Howard,' Otto said.

'Oh, yes, I can,' said Verity.

The studio wasn't as large as the Trafalgar but at least it had a gas fire, a gas ring and a small cold water sink.

'Not much to it, is there?' Julie said. 'Where's the red divan?'

'I left it in Chelsea.'

'Where do you pose your models now?'

'I'm not using life models – well, not in studio poses. Look.' He steered her to the drawing board. 'I'm well ahead with my preliminary designs. The Midland asked for six but I'll trot out ten or a dozen roughs and let the board members choose the ones they like best.'

'Can I do anything to help?' Julie said.

'Like what?'

'Cleaning.'

'Wouldn't dream of it,' Clive said. 'You're my wife not my skivvy. Any cleaning that has to be done, I'll do myself. Now, would you like to see what I've been up to while I've been neglecting you?'

'Indeed, I would,' said Julie.

He cleared space on the end of the work table and put down on it a large cardboard box covered with a dustsheet. He tugged off the dustsheet to reveal several rolls of heavy paper tied with ribbon.

'Fortunately,' Clive said, 'the printers are expert lithographers so I won't have to shepherd them through the entire process.' He fished out a roll, untied the ribbon and carefully unfurled it. 'What do you think, darling?'

The figure of a wrestler in a leotard filled the frame, a huge man backed by stylised white walls. The picture bore no resemblance to anything Julie had seen before but the effect was undeniably powerful.

'How do you do that?' she asked.

'Do what?' Clive said, smirking a little.

'Give the figure such depth.'

'The walls are exaggeratedly concave which throws the figure out towards the viewer. I gather you approve.'

'I do. I do,' said Julie. 'Show me another.'

He plucked a second roll from the box. It showed two athletes in profile, heads dipped. There was no ground, only a blue wash against which the runners stood out as if, like messengers of the gods, they were racing through the sky.

'Speed,' Clive said. 'Speed and power, that's what railway companies want and what I intend to give them. My only concern is that my designs might be a little *too* progressive for the bowler hat brigade.' He brought another picture from the box, a diver caught in mid-air, torso gracefully elongated against a band of brilliant yellow. 'However, I have a friend – a brand-new friend – who's promised me a favourable mention in the *Standard*. I doubt if the Midland's bowler hats will ignore the recommendation of a respected art critic who also happens to be on the British Olympic Council.'

'Who is this new friend?'

'Cook, Theodore Cook.' He fished a folder from under the drawing board, threw it open and brought out an ink and chalk drawing of a handsome man with a pert moustache and eyeglasses perched on his nose. 'That's the chap. It's really only a quick sketch but he seems to like it. I'll have it mounted and framed before I hand it over.' He stirred the drawings in the folder, fished out another. 'Do you know who this is?' Ink and chalk on grey paper; a ridiculously good-looking young man with a lock of jet-black hair hanging across his brow stared out at Julie.

'Telfer Scully,' Clive told her. 'Oxford's most promising athlete since Desborough. His father's a stockholder in the White Star shipping line.'

'What does that have to do with you?'

Clive rubbed forefinger and thumb together. 'Money,' he said. 'Money goes with power and influence. And I want some of it, darling, don't you?'

'I certainly wouldn't say no,' said Julie.

Otto was not averse to enjoying a good cigar and a glass of French brandy but he would have enjoyed them more if he'd had his dinner first. He'd counted on a brief visit, a few minutes with the invalid, another four or five offering condolences to the not quite bereaved son then off, with

Anna, to Wilton's for a bite of supper. It had given him quite a turn, however, to see his former lover so close to death's door and he'd been relieved when Howard had carried him off for a snifter and a smoke in the drawing room downstairs, leaving Anna to attend the patient.

'Ah!' He gestured with his glass. 'Finished at last.'

'Beg pardon?' Howard followed the line of Otto's gaze. 'Oh, that! Yes, pride of place above the mantle, as you can see. The old devil made not a bad fist of it in the end. Took him bloody long enough. If it hadn't been for the arrival of a pretty little nursemaid to care for the new infant, and Edgar's interest in bedding her, I suspect it would never have been finished at all.'

They stood side by side looking up at Banbury's portrait of the widow Millar who, robed in a flowing gown and crowned with an ostrich feather, bore no more than a passing resemblance to the feeble figure in the bed upstairs.

'Who did the framing?' Otto asked.

'Briggs. It's all right, isn't it?'

'Not bad. Serves its purpose.'

'And the painting?'

'The painting,' Otto said, 'is just what you'd expect from Banbury.'

Howard sucked on his cigar, blew smoke and nodded. 'For a time there,' he said, 'I thought it might be all I'd have to remember her by.'

'I doubt if your mother is quite out of the woods yet.'

'I'm only too well aware of it,' said Howard. 'I've been assured by the fellows at the London Chest that the inflammation in her lungs will disperse but that the congestion around her heart might never heal.' He inhaled another mouthful of cigar smoke. 'Something like this does give one pause.' He crossed to a sofa and seated himself on the arm. 'My mother is much taken with your niece and – and, well, I am too.'

Otto placed his empty glass, like a votive offering, beneath Verity's portrait.

'Howard,' he said, 'just what are you trying to tell me?'

Howard held the cigar at arm's length, the glass close to his chest. He might, Otto thought, have been posing, not for a Banbury but a cartoon in *Punch*.

'I've decided to marry your niece,' he blurted out. 'Honestly, Otto, do you think I stand a chance?'

'Why don't you ask her?' said Otto.

Propped against a bank of pillows with one of the baby napkins tucked under her chin, Verity allowed Anna to place the silver spoon against her lips and, sticking out her tongue, lapped at the contents as daintily as a cat laps milk.

'Cold consommé,' she said. 'Cook's idea of nourishment, I suppose.'

'Will I send down for something more substantial?' Anna offered.

'No,' said Verity. 'Thank you. I don't have much appetite.'

Anna dipped the spoon in the bowl and steered it to Verity's mouth.

'Enough,' Verity said. 'I've had enough for now.' She extracted a scrawny hand from under the sheet and tugged the towel from her throat. 'Take this away, my dear. It makes me feel like a dribbling old fool.'

Anna dropped the towel into a wicker basket by the bedside table and returned to the bedside.

'Did Howard tell you I was dying?' Verity said.

'He did rather give my uncle that impression.'

'He's right,' said Verity, 'I am dying – but not this week, or this year. It isn't syphilis or anything like it, thank heaven. I do, however, have a weakness of the heart which, in due course, will do me in.' She rested for a moment, fingers spread across her breast. 'I'm so glad Otto came. And I'm glad you came with him.'

'It's the least I could do after all your kindness.'

'Oh, you think that's kindness, do you?' Verity rested again. 'It's nothing of the sort. Pure selfishness, I assure you. From the minute I realised Howard liked you I've been setting snares. Now look at me. See where plotting has got me.' She put her hand to her chest once more. 'Otto will look after me, won't he?'

'Of course, he will,' said Anna.

'And you'll look after Howard?'

'Well,' Anna said cautiously, 'that remains to be seen.'

14

However disparaging Clive might be in private about the 'bowler hats' who controlled the advertising budget for the Midland Railway, when it came to sitting round a table with them he was courtesy itself and had nothing but respect for their professionalism. Being neither fools nor philistines they did not recoil in horror from his bold designs and, after some discussion, chose six from the ten on offer. No doubt his cause had been helped by Theodore Cook's article on the poster as art that had appeared in the *Standard* and the fact that Cook had praised him as a young artist who knew how to extract the best from modernism without resorting to painting purple horses or women with green hair.

Clive was feeling very pleased with himself when he opened the door of his studio that chilly March morning. He lit the gas fire, arranged his inks and stencils and, without dallying, applied himself to the tricky business of lettering.

Soon he was so caught up in balancing word with image that he became oblivious to the racket from the street and the thumps and bumps upstairs where Manfred seemed to be throwing lumps of clay at the walls.

Clive barely heard the first knock and, with a little *tut* of annoyance, chose to ignore the second. He was sure it would be Manfred down to scrounge tobacco or, more likely, Charlie Moore up to chat about the *Standard* article and wheedle an invitation to meet Theodore Cook. He shifted the stencil a quarter-inch and fixed the outline on the tracing paper. When the knocking sounded again he threw down his pen and shouted, '*What?*'

'It's me,' said a voice from the landing. 'Anna.'

He jumped to the door and pulled it open.

'My God!' he said. 'What the devil are you doing here?'

'That isn't much of a welcome,' she said.

'I'm sorry. Do come in.'

She stepped over the threshold and looked around.

'How did you find me?' Clive said.

'Uncle Otto let it slip.'

'Does Julie know you're here?'

'No,' Anna said, 'and I'd prefer to keep it that way.'

Being alone with his sister-in-law made him nervous for some reason.

He said, 'Julie and I have no secrets.'

'As it should be,' Anna said. 'But just this once – oblige me. I shan't keep you long. I can see you're busy.' She glanced at the board. 'Tracing?'

'Applying captions.'

Clive brought the stool from behind the drawing board and all but shoved it under her. Anna smoothed her skirts and folded her hands primly in her lap.

After a moment, she said, 'Howard has asked me to marry him.'

'Good for old Howard.'

'I haven't given him my answer yet. Clive, I need your advice.'

'Really?' said Clive. 'What sort of advice?'

'I take it you've heard about Verity's illness.'

'Of course,' said Clive. 'How serious is it?'

'Serious,' said Anna, 'but not quite as bad as we'd feared. That's the nub of my problem. Is Howard offering to marry me just to please his mother, or does he really love me?'

'Howard claims to be wedded to his art, you know,' Clive said.

'Howard's nothing but a frightened little boy who hides behind an easel.'

'There's a lot more to him than that, Anna.'

'What? Please, tell me what?' She reached into her pocket, brought out a handkerchief and dabbed her eyes. 'I'm so confused.'

Clive knelt by the stool and took her hand.

'Now, now, Anna, don't upset yourself.'

'Oh, Clive,' she said softly. 'Oh, Clive. Why can't it be you?'

He was on his feet at once. 'Now, Anna,' he said. 'I don't mind giving you advice but I am married to your sister. I've no intention of cheating on her, especially with you.'

'I think,' Anna said, 'you've misjudged me.'

'That I have,' Clive said. 'Now I really do have a great deal of work to do. I'd be obliged if you'd let me get on with it.'

'What shall I tell Howard?'

He put a hand on her shoulder and turned her towards the door.

'Tell him you'll marry him,' Clive said, 'then wait.'

'Wait?' she said over her shoulder. 'Wait for what?'

'For Howard to change his mind.'

★

The house reeked of mutton which meant that supper would be another of Julie's greasy stews. He was hungry enough to do it justice, though, for he had eaten nothing all day save a few stale crackers.

It had taken him the best part of an hour after Anna's departure to focus on the job. Infatuation is all it was, all it could be. Anna was just a silly little girl, full of repressed desire, longing for what she couldn't possibly have.

Julie's head appeared above the level of the stairs, face flushed by the heat of the kitchen. 'Maisie thought she heard you. You're early.'

'I'm bang on time,' Clive said. 'And as hungry as a hunter.'

She came up into the hall, put an arm about his waist and kissed him.

'You look tired.'

'I spent all damned day lettering.'

'No interruptions?'

'What?' he said; then, 'No, darling, no interruptions,' and, satisfied that she believed him, followed her downstairs.

15

They chose the ring together in a jewellery shop in the Burlington Arcade. It appeared modest enough on the cloth but once on Anna's finger the diamond and sapphire cluster looked suitably ostentatious. Howard promised there would be other gifts to mark their engagement and suggested, diplomatically, that perhaps she might care to purchase him a silver cigarette case, engraved, so that he might keep her, as it were, close to his heart.

When the ring, duly fitted and paid for, was tucked into his pocket, he took her to lunch at Jules, after which they walked to St James's Park. There, by the edge of the ornamental lake, observed only by waterfowl and a curious nursemaid or two, Howard put the ring on her finger and kissed her. It was, Anna supposed, a nod towards romance on Howard's part but she'd have felt better about it if the breeze that strode across the water had been less chill, the afternoon light less bleak and if Howard had kissed her lips and not her cheek.

'Now,' Howard said, as Anna fitted her glove carefully over the unfamiliar lump on her finger, 'now we can tell everyone.'

'Meaning,' Anna said, 'your mother.'

'Mama, of course,' Howard said. 'First and foremost, Mama. I was also thinking of your sister. She'll be your maid of honour, I assume?'

'Matron,' said Anna off-handedly. 'But not for some time yet, Howard. Remember, we agreed on a long engagement, a year at least. I'm just not ready yet for all that marriage entails.'

'I understand, my dear.'

'Where are we going now?'

'Home, I thought.'

'Home?'

'To Holland Park. I can't wait to tell Mama our news.'

'Hold on,' said Stanley Martindale. 'Are you telling me you had the impertinence to present my daughter with an engagement ring without asking my permission? Did you know about this, Otto?'

'Not an inkling,' said Otto smoothly.

'In my day you'd be horsewhipped for your temerity, young man. What if I refuse Anna permission to marry you?'

'What's wrong with you, Papa? I thought you'd be pleased.'

Anna pressed her nose into her uncle's chest and pretended to weep. A little piece of her, a sliver of ice, despised Otto for being taken in but at the same time she was gratified by her ability to deceive.

Chastened, Stanley said, 'I am. You just caught me on the wrong foot.' He seated himself on a straight-backed chair. 'I didn't mean to offend you, Anna, or you, Mr Buskin – Howard.'

'How did Verity take it?' Otto asked.

'As you'd expect, she was delighted,' Howard answered.

'At least someone's pleased for us,' said Anna. 'Would you like to see my engagement ring, Papa?'

'Why, of course I would,' said Stanley.

He left the support of the chair, took his daughter's outstretched hand and peered at the ring. 'Good Lord!' he said. 'That trinket must have cost a pretty penny. I'm afraid I won't be able to match your extravagance, Howard, when it comes to paying for the wedding.'

'The wedding won't be for some time, Papa,' said Anna. 'Howard and I have agreed that a long engagement will be best for both of us.'

'Why?' said Otto.

Anna slipped an arm into the crook of Howard's elbow. 'We want time to get to know each other, don't we, darling? We want to have fun before we set up house.'

'This house,' Otto said, 'will it be in London?'

'Too soon to say,' said Anna. 'I suppose we might settle abroad.'

'Verity won't like that,' Otto said. 'She'll want you nearby, especially after the children arrive.'

'The children?' said Howard. 'What children?'

'Your children, silly,' said Anna. 'Our children.'

'Oh, God, yes,' said Howard.

She had sent the nurse downstairs and with the invalid tray balanced on her midriff nibbled a slice of toast dripping with rhubarb jam. She'd never been all that partial to rhubarb jam but something in her constitution craved it now and she had taken to consuming it at every opportunity. Perhaps, she thought, the stimulating effect of the bitter tincture that the nurse forced down her throat four times a day had something to do with it.

The nurse was po-faced and wore a grey uniform that seemed to be nothing but pockets; pockets for thermometers, watches, peppermint sweets, eye-droppers with red rubber bulbs on the end and curious little spoons for measuring this and that from the battery of medicines that the physician in the London Chest had prescribed and the butler, Percy, collected from the big new pharmacy at the Marble Arch end of Oxford Street.

Of course, she'd been thrilled to waken from an afternoon nap to find Howard and Anna standing shyly beside her bed waving an engagement ring in her face. It was only after the couple had gone off to break the news to Anna's father that it dawned on her that Howard had finally given her what she wanted.

Sitting up in bed, she'd let out a whoop of joy and had promised herself that as soon as she was well again she'd toast the happy couple not in rhubarb jam but pink champagne and with Emily or, perhaps, Anna in attendance would head for Harrods to inspect, albeit prematurely, the latest lines in baby wear.

'I'm not sure you should be sketching me in this sorry state, Clive,' she said.

'Why not? It's the next best thing to a death mask.'

'You can be cruel sometimes.'

'Part of my charm, Verity, all part of my charm.'

Clive had appeared out of the blue in the dead part of the afternoon. He was seated now at the foot of her bed, a sketch pad balanced on the rail, his head going up and down, up and down, like a dabbling duck.

'Didn't you know I was ill?' Verity asked.

'Not until Otto Goldstein came to dinner last week,' Clive answered. 'I'm none too pleased with Howard for keeping me in the dark. It's a relief to find you on the road to recovery. You are on the road to recovery, aren't you?'

'I think it's safe to say I am.' She sipped lukewarm tea and wiped her lips with a napkin. 'I'll be up and about soon, thank the Lord. There's much to be done before the wedding.'

'Have they set a date yet?' said Clive.

'They're talking, rather vaguely, about next year. A year? I mean, what's wrong with them? I wish Howard would take a leaf out of your book and sweep the dear girl to the altar before she changes her mind.'

'Howard isn't like me. He doesn't rush into things.'

'Are you happy, Clive?'

'Yes, Verity, I am.'

'And Julie?' said Verity. 'Is she – I mean – is she – babies?'

'No,' Clive said. 'Not just yet. Shall I take the tray?'

'If you please.'

Not for the first time, Verity wished that her son could be more like his friend, not just tall and handsome but courteous too. Clive placed the tray on the floor and returned to his chair. He leaned his forearms on the bed rail and studied her with uncharacteristic gravity.

'I'll let you into a little secret, Verity,' he said. 'I rather thought you wanted to keep Howard to yourself.'

'I know,' said Verity. 'Edgar told me. I may have frightened off one or two naïve young things but I've always wanted Howard to take a wife and raise a family. All that "wedded to his art" is just nonsense. Well, the bloom will be off the peach soon enough.' She adjusted the pillow behind her back. 'After he's married and fathered a few babies he'll have a lot more to concern him than producing perfect works of art. She'll see to that.'

'I thought you liked her?'

'Oh, I do,' said Verity. 'Anna Martindale is exactly the right sort of wife for Howard. He doesn't need a pretty pair of ankles or a pert little bustle to inspire him. What he needs is a woman of strong character to draw him out.'

Before she could say more, a clock in the hallway chimed, the bedroom door was flung open and the nurse appeared in the doorway.

'Oh!' Verity groaned. 'Time for my medicine.'

Clive gathered up his sketch book and pencils and got to his feet.

'High time I left. I do hope I haven't tired you.'

'On the contrary. Howard will be sorry he missed you,' Verity said. 'Before you go, however, let's see what you've made of me.'

'I don't think that's a good idea.'

'Humour a poor sick old woman, there's a good boy.'

Clive flipped open the sketch pad and, with a shrug, handed it to her.

She held it out at arm's length, squinted, then brayed with laughter. Clive had drawn her with cap askew, neck stretched, head tipped back and mouth wide open greedily devouring a piece of toast.

'Cavendish out of Goya,' Clive said. 'Not bad, eh?'

'You really don't like me, do you?'

'No,' Clive said, 'I really don't like you.'

'May I keep it?'

'If you wish,' Clive said and swiftly took his leave.

'She may have money,' Julie said, 'but she will never have class.' Clive's elbow chafed her bare arm. 'Do you think it's snobbish of me to state the obvious?'

'Verity Millar may be a parvenu,' Clive said, 'but she came by her money honestly – relatively honestly – and that's more than one can say for half the toffs I deal with. Anyway, I'm too tired to argue. Go to sleep.'

Rubbing his shin with the ball of her foot, Julie said, 'I can't imagine my sister and Howard Buskin in bed together.'

'Is that what's bothering you?' Clive said.

'Don't tell me it hasn't crossed your mind?'

'What hasn't crossed my mind?' Clive said.

They'd been in bed for twenty minutes. He'd done his duty by her but in a manner she could only describe as mechanical.

'Howard and Anna making love,' she said. 'That's really what marriage is all about, isn't it? Having sex? I can no more imagine going to bed with Howard Buskin than I can imagine going to bed with a pig.'

'It's just as well you married me then,' said Clive.

'Oh, you're all pigs really,' Julie said. 'Universal suffrage isn't just about voting rights. It's really about free love and having lots of sex.'

'Now you're just babbling. Have you been at the sherry, or what?'

'Gin,' she said. 'Good old mother's ruin. I'll have to give it up soon.'

She waited for the penny to drop but he was clearly

thinking of other things. Ten seconds went by before he sat upright. 'Give what up?'

'Gin.'

'Why will you have to give up gin?' he asked suspiciously.

'It isn't good for expectant mothers.'

'Julie, are you . . .'

'Harbouring a little secret?' Julie said. 'Yes, dearest, I do believe I am.'

16

The gymnasium was only a few streets from the Queen's Club in West Kensington but if you didn't know what you were looking for you'd have passed it without a second glance. It didn't seem like the sort of place where a man might go to hone his physique and the bevelled glass doors with huge brass handles had the discreet appearance of a government office with no plate to hint at what went on inside.

The little foyer was manned by several potted plants and a porter in a smart uniform who, poised on the balls of his feet, gruffly enquired as to the nature of Clive's business. Fixing a pair of glasses to what was left of his nose, he scanned Mr Cook's letter of introduction then, with a nod and a jab of the thumb, directed Clive to a flight of stairs that climbed steeply into the gloom.

Knockabout football, obligatory outings with the school cricket team and a bit of swimming in pond, pool and river had been the limit of Clive's sporting activity but as he climbed the stairs the heady aroma of sweat and disinfectant quickened his pulses and when he stepped into the huge first-floor room the sight that met his eyes occasioned the sort of pleasure usually reserved for squaring up to an altarpiece by Bellini or Rubens.

Dust motes swirled in slanting light. In solitary corners young men in singlets skipped rope or twirled Indian clubs. Trainers spurred their charges to greater efforts on bars, rings and vaulting horse. Clive fished his sketch book from his satchel and, kneeling on the floor, immediately began to draw.

'I see you're already hard at it, Mr Cavendish?'

Clive scrambled to his feet. The man, in his fifties, was dapper, fresh-faced and youthful-looking. He beamed, winked and held out his hand.

'Scully, Max Scully,' he said. 'What do you make of our hideout?'

'Most impressive,' Clive said.

'Cook introduced you, I suppose.'

'He did.'

'Rather decent of him,' Max Scully said, 'given that he doesn't approve of what goes on here. Theo hasn't quite grasped that international meets are no longer gentlemanly contests but combat, pure and simple. We've the Americans to thank for that.' He paused to watch Telfer, his son, thud down on a wooden springboard and sail over a vaulting horse. 'The days of the Christchurch Beagles scampering over the pasture in hobnails are long gone. If we wish to succeed in track and field we must follow the lead of our American cousins and adopt a scientific approach.'

'What sort of approach is that, sir?'

'Body control,' Max Scully told him. 'Where better to learn it than an indoor gymnasium rather than a muddy field? As an artist, you must surely appreciate the combination of style and strength required to make the human body function at its highest capability.'

'Like high divers and gymnasts?'

Max Scully clapped a hand to his shoulder. 'Exactly.'

'Your son's a jumper, is he not?'

'He is,' Max Scully said fondly. 'He can jump high and he can jump long but he'll be matching himself against the best the Yankees have to offer. It's no longer a question of muscle power but, rather, of timing, poise and balance.' Max Scully paused. 'I'm sorry, Mr Cavendish, I'm rattling on. Would you care to dine with Telfer and me after we're done here?'

Clive thought of Julie retching into a bowl and the little creature, his son, the foetus, barely ten weeks old, bobbing about within her like a tadpole in a jar. He really ought to go home, hold Julie's hand, share with her, as best he could, the burdens of pregnancy.

Sensing his hesitation, Max Scully said, 'I've a little piece of business to put your way, Mr Cavendish, if you're interested?'

'What sort of business, sir?' said Clive.

Julie had been three when her mother had died. She had no concrete memory of the event. Tucked in some byway of her brain, though, was a shadowy recollection of bearded men in black frock-coats gathered in the hall, men who had replaced her mama with an infant to whom Papa, Uncle Otto and Nanny Cairns had introduced her, as if trading Mama for a baby was their idea of fair exchange.

She had survived encounters with doctors ever since by simply making the best of it. Some were kindly, some stern, some, like whiskery Dr Gloag, a little too keen to examine her intimate parts. Her stoicism had evaporated, however, when on being ushered into Dr Maben's consulting room she'd been confronted by a table with straps and padded leather holders and, shivering in her shift, had been forced to lie down and open her legs.

She'd stared at the ceiling cornices, cleaner than those in Faversham Garden, while the doctor's fingers probed her flesh and, transported back to the hall in Ledbetter Street all those years ago, she'd experienced an irrational dread that Clive would exchange her for a baby, and that soon she would be dead.

'Try to eat something,' Maisie said.

'I'm not hungry.'

'You're eatin' for two now, remember,' Maisie insisted.

Maisie had a kind heart and was sincerely concerned about her welfare which, Julie thought, was more than could be said for Clive. All Clive seemed to want was to put his thing into her with never a thought for her wishes. It was, she knew, a woman's lot to suffer but surely she had a right to expect some sign that the promises he'd made at the altar had not been entirely forgotten.

'Maisie, where is he? Do you know?'

'Gone to a club, I fink.'

'A club? What? A drinking club?'

'A club where fellers train.' Loyalties divided, Maisie hesitated before adding, 'He's gone lookin' for Mr Scully.'

'Mr Scully, the gorilla?'

Maisie chuckled. 'He ain't no gorilla. I saw his picture in *Health and Strength*. He's lovely.'

'Why is Mr Cavendish so interested in Telfer Scully?'

'He's a toff, Mrs Cavendish.' Maisie said. 'It's the armatures, see. You gotter be a toff to be an armature.'

'Amateurs,' said Julie. 'Wealthy amateurs, you mean?'

Maisie nodded. 'The other kind ain't got no cash for paintings, 'ave they? There's them what paint dancers an' them what paint 'osses but you want a picture of a toff holdin' up a silver cup, Mr Cavendish is gonner be your man. He's doin' it for you, Mrs Cavendish. He's doin' it for you an' the little 'un.'

'Is that true, Maisie?'

'Plain as the nose on your face.'

Julie folded her hands across her stomach and contemplated the skinny little girl who seemed to know so much more about life than she did.

'Maisie,' she said, after a pause, 'what do we have in the pot?'

'Minced beef with onions. You hungry after all, Mrs C?'

'Actually, Maisie, I am.'

At Papa's insistence, Howard had been dragged from Holland Park to break bread chez Martindale. Verity had also been invited but she was still too weak to venture out. She'd sent an effusive note to Papa by way of apology and another, apparently no less gushing, to Uncle Otto who, on reading it, had turned a funny shade of pink and had hastily stuffed it into his trouser pocket.

Irish lace and wax candles graced the dining table and Mrs Sims had dug out the very best china. Anna had wheedled Papa into paying for a new evening gown in soft *soie-de-chine* and had had her hair professionally arranged. She judged it money well spent, for Howard had been knocked sideways when he'd entered the drawing room and had kissed her as if he really meant it.

Dinner progressed from soup through fish to a perfectly cooked saddle of lamb. Anna had just begun to relax when the doorbell chimed and, a moment later, Julie's voice echoed in the hall.

Papa threw down his napkin and leapt to his feet. 'What the devil . . .'

'Now, now, Stanley,' said Otto, rising too, 'keep your hair on.'

'What's *she* doing here?' Papa hissed. 'Otto, did you invite her?'

'I'm as surprised as you are, Stan.'

The maid appeared in the doorway.

'Mr and Mrs Cavendish, sir. Shall I ask them to wait in the drawing room?'

'No, damn it, you'd better show them in,' Stanley barked.

Julie entered first, Clive close behind.

Anna's first thought was that Verity Millar had passed on and Clive had been despatched to break the news to Howard. But Julie was smiling, Clive too. In fact, they looked so blissfully happy that she suffered a stab of envy and, dropping her fork, cried out in a shrill voice, 'Can't you see we're having dinner?'

'I'm sorry,' Julie said. 'I had no idea you had a – a guest.'

'It's only Howard,' Uncle Otto said. 'Come along, sit down and join us. There's plenty for all.' He turned. 'Stanley?'

As if he were speaking to two street urchins, Papa asked, 'Are you hungry?'

'No, Mr Martindale,' Clive answered. 'We're pregnant.'

The cab was an old-fashioned 'growler' with four wheels and a cart horse in the shafts. It clipped along at a fair rate, though, and Howard, with Julie's permission, lowered the upper half of the window to let in a breath of fresh night air. He would, of course, be paying the fare. He had no objection to that, for a detour via Camden was just what he needed to clear his head of the fumes of all the alcohol he'd consumed after Martindale's dull little dinner party had turned into a celebration.

Light from passing streetlamps illuminated Julie's features like images in a magic lantern show. She looked so peaceful cradled in her husband's arms that Howard was tempted to believe that marriage might be no bad thing after all.

Then Julie said, 'He offered you money, I suppose.'

'He did,' Clive said. 'Wasn't that the intention?'

'Part of it,' Julie said. 'I knew Papa would come off his high horse as soon as he learned I was pregnant. You didn't accept, did you?'

Clive stroked a lock of her hair. 'No, I did not. Haven't I told you often enough that our fortunes are on the rise. Don't you believe me?'

'Not entirely, no.'

Howard cleared his throat to remind them that they were not alone.

Clive said, 'Julie thinks I'm tarred with the same brush as Edgar Banbury. What can I do to convince her otherwise?'

'I have no idea.'

'Where is Banbury, by the way? Have you heard anything from him?'

'Absolutely nothing,' Howard said. 'He's still in Florence, far as I know.'

'With his wife *and* his sweetheart?' said Julie. 'We'll have to find *you* a pretty nursemaid, Clive, to keep you amused when baby arrives.'

'The last thing I need,' Clive said, 'is another woman in my life. It's complicated enough as it is.'

Julie sat up. 'What about you, Howard?'

'What about me?'

'Is that what Anna is to you – a complication?'

'Careful, Howard,' Clive said. 'My wife will have you on toast no matter what answer you give.'

'No need for me to have Howard on toast,' Julie said. 'Anna will do an excellent job of that when the time comes. Have you had her yet?'

'Pardon me?' said Howard.

'Come now,' Julie said. 'We're all grown-ups here. Well, Howard, *have* you tested the waters – or is my little sister still playing hard to get?' She laughed. 'Have you even kissed her?'

'Yes, I've kissed her,' Howard said.

'How daring of you,' Julie said. 'What else?'

'None of your business,' Howard said.

'Pure as the driven snow,' Julie said. 'I knew it.'

'Chastity before marriage is not a crime, even in this day and age,' Howard said. 'Some people have moral standards, Julie. I happen to be one of them.'

'Oh, dear,' Julie said. 'I think I've just been told off.'

'You did rather ask for it, dearest,' said Clive.

'I notice you aren't rushing to defend me.'

'Not when you're too tipsy to know what you're saying.'

'Am I tipsy? Yes, I suppose I am.' She yawned, settled back against Clive's chest and pulled his arm around her as if it were a blanket. 'Nighty-night, Howard,' she murmured. 'Dear stuffy old Howard, night-night,' and to all intents and purposes fell asleep.

17

Easter fell in mid-April just a few days before the opening event of the London Olympics took place at Queen's Club. The first round of racquet singles was hardly likely to stir the blood of the average working chap and even bookmakers expressed little interest in the outcome. Clive was too busy to trot out for the modest ceremony at which Lord Desborough made one of his patriotic speeches that only *The Times* bothered to report in full.

It had been a frantic few weeks for Clive. He had delivered his poster designs and had spent a full day with the printers in Holborn explaining his colour requirements. The Midland board were delighted with the results of his labours and, with a fat cheque nestling in his pocket, he'd treated his good lady to dinner at Paddington's Rialto Restaurant and presented her with a necklace that may not have matched Anna's engagement ring in monetary value but was worth a king's ransom – so Clive said – in sentiment.

To spread a little more butter on Julie's paws he took her, and Maisie, to view the Great Stadium at Shepherd's Bush which, together with the pavilions of the Franco-British Exhibition, was rapidly nearing completion. That same evening he sprang for seats at the Gaiety Theatre for Julie and himself and the following morning, duty done, went back to work.

In Holland Park things were rather less hectic.

Verity had recovered sufficiently to take up the reins and, appetite restored, insisted on large luncheons, full-scale afternoon teas and five-course dinners. Howard, meanwhile, skulked in the studio upstairs and, idle for once, frittered away the time between meals brooding on what Anna might expect of him once they were man and wife.

'Foxhailes,' he said, as if the idea had just occurred to him. 'We could jog down to Foxhailes for a week or two. Better yet, we could stay for the summer.'

'That,' said Verity, biting into a teacake, 'would not be sensible.'

'What wouldn't be sensible?' said Howard.

'Leaving Anna for so long.'

'We'll take her with us.'

'Without a chaperone?' said Verity.

'You'd be our chaperone.'

'Mothers cannot chaperone their sons.'

'Says who?'

'Polite society. Don't you want your children to be brought up properly?'

'For heaven's sake, Mama, you might at least see me married before you start yammering on about children. In any case, I see nothing wrong in taking Anna to Devon with us. We're engaged, after all.'

'It wouldn't look right.' Verity tackled another teacake. 'Besides, I don't think Anna's all that keen on the country – and her father wouldn't approve.'

'You can talk her into it if anyone can,' Howard said. 'And

if Daddy Martindale feels it's not "the done thing" then invite Otto along.'

'Otto?' Verity raised an eyebrow. 'Well, now, there's a good idea.'

'Impossible.' Otto scowled at Verity's letter. 'Absolutely impossible. I can't go dropping everything just to satisfy her whims. The cheek of the woman.' He squinted over the breakfast table at his niece. 'Did you put her up to it?'

'I've no idea what you're talking about,' Anna said.

'Verity wants me to accompany you to Devon next week.'

'Why can't I go on my own?'

'Tell her, Stanley,' said Otto.

'I see no reason why she shouldn't go if she wishes it,' said Stanley. 'After all, this is the twentieth century and she is engaged to the fellow. But if you ask me, Otto, it isn't Anna's company Mrs Millar wants, but yours. Now she has Howard settled – or almost so – she's probably looking to her own future. You could do worse than the widow Millar, you know.'

'Whatever there was between Verity and me is long gone,' Otto said.

'Not according to Verity,' Anna put in. 'She still thinks you're a catch.'

'Ah!' Stanley was beginning to enjoy himself. 'Spring on Dartmoor: the voice of the turtle dove is heard in the land and the stealthy sound of sap rising in every young man's – ah – heart.'

'I am not, repeat not, a young man, Stanley.'

'But the sap still rises, does it not?'

'This conversation is becoming obscene,' said Otto. 'In

any case, I can't take time off. Someone has to keep our employees bowed to the lathe.'

'I think,' said Stanley, 'I can still remember how to do that.'

'The point's moot, anyway,' Otto said. 'I'm sure Anna doesn't want to go.'

'Oh, but I do,' said Anna.

On a dull April evening Clive slipped into the house with a parcel under his arm. He hid the contents in the basement until Maisie, adept with needle and thread, had shifted the waist buttons and lifted the trouser cuffs an inch or so. The following night, just before supper, Clive appeared in the kitchen and, with a kick of the heel and a little pirouette, said, 'What do you think of your hubby now?'

'How much did it cost?' was Julie's first response.

'Four guineas, off the peg, as advertised in *Tailor & Cutter*. Sort of thing only a young man with flair can get away with, apparently.'

'I have to admit,' said Julie grudgingly, 'you do look rather dashing.' She picked a fleck of lint from his lapel. 'Dare I ask what it's in aid of?'

'The London Athletic Club are hosting a dinner for British Olympic officials. I have' – he bowed – 'been included on the guest list.'

'Why?'

'Theo Cook has ordained me – unofficially, of course – as a BOC artist and, like it or not, I'll have to pass muster as a gentleman.'

'I fink,' said Maisie, 'you look bumper, Mr Cavendish.'

'Why, thank you, Maisie,' Clive said, with another bow.

'I assume this dinner is exclusively male?' said Julie.

'Of course.'

'When?'

'Wednesday.' Clive paused. 'There's another on Saturday, though.'

'Really?' said Julie. 'Where?'

'The Savoy.'

'Oh, swanky, like,' said Maisie.

'Indeed.' Clive shot his cuffs. 'Now, young lady, tell me, what's for supper?'

'Cavvie-har, sir,' said Maisie. 'You want it wiff or wiffout the cabbage?'

Great skirts of cloud trailed across the moor and veiled the tottering chimneys of Foxhailes as the trap the widow Millar had despatched to the railway halt turned into the gate. Rain dripped from the hood and in spite of her proofed overcoat and the canvas across her knees Anna was damp and miserable.

When Uncle Otto said, 'Well, here we are at last,' she answered with something between a grunt and a whimper, for she was well aware that he'd made the trip only to please her and that she had no right to complain.

Howard was lurking in the stable doorway looking, Anna thought, more like a French peasant than heir to this dismal pile. He had obviously being working, though what he could possibly find to paint in such weather Anna couldn't imagine.

When the trap drew up at the porch Verity rushed out, embraced them and led them quickly indoors. Twenty minutes later Anna was sipping tea before a blazing fire in the spacious wood-panelled room that Verity referred to as the library, though it contained not a single book.

Making himself at home, Otto had changed into a quilted smoking jacket and red leather slippers and, with hair slicked down and moustache curled up, needed only a fez and a hookah to complete his impersonation of a minor eastern potentate.

'By gum, Verity,' he said. 'You look better than the last time we met. It gave me quite a turn to see you knocking on death's door.'

'No cloud without a silver lining, my dear. My imminent departure brought Howard to his senses. All I have to do now is convince him – and you, Anna – that long engagements are out of fashion.'

Howard had exchanged his smock for a lounge suit but there were paint stains on his hands and his fingernails weren't clean. He helped himself to tea and a slice of cherry cake that he held, without a plate, on the flat of one hand. He stuffed cake into his mouth and spoke through the crumbs.

'I've more to do than fuss with wedding preparations.'

'He means he's painting again,' Verity put in.

'Happily, I am,' said Howard. 'Something about this old place inspires me.'

'Don't I inspire you?' Anna said. 'Why don't you paint me, Howard?'

Howard slid the remnant of cake into his mouth and chewed thoughtfully.

'Yes,' he said at length, 'why not?'

*

Immediately after breakfast Howard led her to the stable building. On the easel was a small unfinished study of an ancient wall patched with moss and lichen, the detail so far confined to a jagged zigzag of colour that split the canvas like a gash.

'Well,' Howard said, 'do you still want me to paint you?'

'Not covered in moss and lichen.'

'I think you'd look better in taffeta or silk.'

'Or,' Anna said, 'in nothing at all, perhaps?'

'Why do you insist on teasing me, Anna?'

'That's what girls do, Howard.'

'Not all girls.'

'No, not all girls,' Anna said. 'I thought you might care to see your future wife in her natural state.'

'Nudity isn't a natural state.'

'What an odd thing for an artist to say.'

'I don't know you well enough to paint you *au naturel*,' Howard said. 'I'm not a fast worker, like Cavendish.'

'How long will it take to get to know me? A week, a month? How long to – how does Edgar Banbury put it? – to capture my essence?'

'I won't flatter you, Anna,' Howard said. 'As a painter I'm ruthless. Tell you what, we'll have a rake about in your trunk, pick something suitable for you to wear and then choose a room where we won't be disturbed.'

'I thought you weren't a fast worker?' Anna said.

'There's a first time for everything, I suppose,' said Howard.

The Savoy dinner was less rowdy than the Wednesday night affair, the speeches longer and more formal. Not entirely by chance, as it transpired, Clive found himself seated next to a lanky American, Edward Norris, whose connection to the Olympic committee was even more tenuous than Clive's. He was, he said modestly, a pole-vaulter who'd come a cropper at the trials in Albany and, bowing to the inevitable, had shipped over to London not only to offer his support to his fellow countrymen but also to scout the English art market.

'Have you seen Picasso's latest work?' The American's enthusiasm was palpable. 'Matisse? Braque? Derain? Wow!'

'My friend Banbury keeps me abreast of what's happening on the Continent,' Clive said defensively.

'Banbury? Edgar Banbury? You know him?'

'I know him very well,' Clive said. 'He's in Florence right now.'

'He certainly is,' Teddy Norris said. 'I split a bottle with him just last week.'

'Did you, indeed? How is he?'

Teddy Norris hesitated, then, leaning over the parfait dishes, said, 'In love.'

Clive laughed. 'That doesn't surprise me. The nursemaid, I assume.'

'Yep, poor girl spends more time nursing Edgar than she does his kid.'

'Is he painting?'

'He says he is.'

'Did he show you anything?'

'Couple of watercolours. I didn't care for them enough to make an offer.'

'Oh!' Clive said. 'You're a dealer, are you?'

'More of a collector, I guess,' Teddy Norris said.

'An expensive hobby,' Clive said.

'Not really,' said Teddy Norris. 'I'm only interested in the old masters of the future, if you see what I mean. You can pick them up for dimes right now but in ten or twenty years they'll be fetching thousands of dollars in the auction rooms.'

'And,' Clive said cautiously, 'who in England might fall into that category?'

Teddy Norris crossed one long leg over the other. 'Okay, I may as well come clean. I asked Mr Cook to seat us together. I guess you've realised that?'

'It had crossed my mind,' said Clive.

'Banbury told me to look you up but I didn't figure you'd be bumping elbows with the sporting crowd.'

'And I didn't "figure" I'd run into an American collector at a BOC dinner,' Clive said. 'I'm sorry I don't have much to show you at present.'

Teddy Norris sat forward. 'I'd love to see some of your work sometime, Mr Cavendish, but right now I'm trying to track down Howard Buskin. Banbury said you'd know where to find him.'

'What do you want with Howard?'

'Banbury tells me he's the best young painter in England.'

'That,' Clive said, 'is a matter of opinion.'

'*Do* you know where I might find him?'

'Yes.' Clive nodded. 'He's in Dartmoor.'

'What, in prison?'

'Unfortunately not,' said Clive.

18

Howard had picked out a satin dress with a fan collar for her to wear and had spent the best part of half an hour posing her on a chair in the library. He tugged her hither and thither like a rag doll and when everything was arranged to his satisfaction peered at her over the top of the drawing board as if she were an object on the distant horizon and not a beautiful young woman seated six feet away.

Using a fine pencil he carefully defined the planes of her face. His approach was meticulous, the outcome exact, though the finished drawing would give no hint of painstaking labour.

They paused for tea and, later, for dinner. Twice in the interim, when Anna's muscles rebelled, Howard allowed her to walk about the room and stretch her limbs while he sat motionless at the board and waited patiently for her to return. Finally he put the board down and let her see what he'd done.

'There,' he said and, to Anna's surprise, kissed her behind the ear.

'What are you doing, Howard?'

'Rewarding myself for a job well done.'

'It's not very big, is it?'

'It doesn't have to be,' he said. 'Don't you like it?'

'Oh, yes,' she said dutifully. 'I do.'

'He's in love, you know,' Otto said.

'If he wasn't before he certainly is now,' Verity agreed. 'Perhaps now he'll open up and begin exhibiting.'

'I wouldn't count on it,' said Otto.

They lay side by side on Verity's bed. In nightgown and bed-jacket, Verity was beneath the covers; Otto, still dressed, on top of them.

Otto passed her the brandy glass. She sipped from it and said, 'I take it you're aware that Howard's going to spin out this portrait of Anna as long as possible. You're liable to be here for months.'

'Can't be done,' said Otto. 'I must be back in harness on Monday. Stanley's fine with ledgers but lost when it comes to glue and varnish.'

'If you were to marry me,' said Verity, 'you wouldn't have to work at all.'

'I've no fancy for being a kept man.'

'We could travel the world together, see all the sights.'

'What would Howard do without you?'

'Anna will look after him.'

'And who will look after Anna?' Otto said.

'Anna, I think, can look after herself.'

'You know you'll be required to provide Howard with his father's name to put on the marriage certificate?' Otto said.

'I don't know his name,' Verity said. 'I was tiddly at the time. Besides, I doubt if Howard would be thrilled to learn that he's the son of a son of the soil.'

'Oh, God, Verity, surely Howard's daddy wasn't a farmer?'

'Not even that,' said Verity with a sigh. 'What an impulsive fool I was in those days. I just wanted to be loved, I suppose.'

'Flat on your back in a barn?'

'You're a fine one to talk, Otto Goldstein. Do you recall the first time we—'

'Only too well,' Otto put in. 'But I didn't leave you holding a baby.'

'More's the pity,' said Verity. 'You'd have made a very good father.'

'But not, I suspect, a very good husband.'

'I think I might have forgiven you an occasional fling.' She handed him the brandy glass and stretched an arm straight up in the air. The sleeve of her bed-jacket slithered down to her elbow. 'Look at that,' she said. 'Nothing but scrag. Do you recall how plump and juicy I used to be?'

'You were never plump, dearest,' said Otto. 'You were perfectly proportioned – and stop fishing for compliments. None of us is getting any younger and the years do take their toll.'

Verity shook down her sleeve. 'It's so unfair. Here we are, much of an age, and I'm a skinny old lizard and you're still bounding about like a young buck.'

'If only that were true,' said Otto.

'How many sweethearts do you have right now?'

'Nary a one,' said Otto.

'What about the redhead – what was her name?'

'Ariadne? Gone.'

'I can't believe she turned you down,' said Verity.

'In fact I never quite got around to proposing.'

'Then it's your own fault you lost her,' Verity said. 'In any relationship it's vital for a woman to know where she stands.'

'Does that hold true for men too?'

'You know where you stand with me, Otto.'

'I was thinking of Howard, actually,' Otto said.

Verity laid an arm across his chest. 'I'd like to think my son and your niece are, at this moment, sharing a bed. You wouldn't disapprove, would you?'

'Probably not,' said Otto. 'There's a fat chance of it happening, though. Howard's far too strait-laced to jump the gun.'

'And Anna?'

He hesitated, frowning. 'Hard to tell.'

'She's a woman, Otto,' Verity said. 'Believe, me, she'll throw caution to the winds now she's found the right man.'

'Do you think Howard's the right man?'

'I just wish I could be sure,' said Verity.

'Well, we're both agreed he loves her.'

'Yes, dear, but does he want her? That,' Verity said, 'is the rub,' and, pursing her lips, allowed him to kiss her goodnight.

Fickle though her moods were, Anna was pleased to be the sole focus of Howard's attention and, in the silence of the library, undisturbed, had begun to feel a degree of affinity with her intended.

'What are you doing?' she asked.

'Making ready,' Howard answered.

The library table had been moved back and a portable easel erected in its place. The table was covered with newspaper upon which tubes and brushes were randomly scattered. In this respect Howard was slapdash, unlike Clive who, so Julie had told her, was scrupulous in his preparations. Only when the brush was charged did the balance between the artists shift, for Clive was swift in his execution and Howard slow and limping.

The pencil drawing was pinned to a leg of the easel as Howard transferred her likeness from paper to canvas with a charcoal pencil. She had put on the satin dress and spent some time before the mirror arranging her hair. She was, therefore, annoyed when Howard paid her no attention, as if the image he'd created meant more to him than the reality.

'Would you like me to leave?' she said.

He didn't look up. 'No. Why?'

'You seem to be otherwise occupied.'

'Well, I won't really need you for at least an hour. Go, if you wish.'

She wandered to the window and looked out across the lawn.

It had stopped raining but broken cloud tumbled above the trees and the little patches of blue sky seemed very far away. She wondered if she should go for a walk and if Uncle Otto would care to accompany her or if, as seemed likely, he'd already settled down with Verity by the drawing room fire to browse through yesterday's newspapers.

She was on the point of leaving the window when she caught sight of a gig turning in at the gate. Pressing her nose to the glass, she watched the conveyance advance towards the house.

'Oh, my goodness!' she said.

Howard looked up. 'What?' he said. 'What is it?'

'It's Clive,' she said. 'Clive and a stranger,' and rushed out of the library to greet the unexpected guests.

★

'You must excuse the informality, Mr Norris. We had no idea anyone would be dropping in,' Verity said. 'Why didn't you let me know, Clive?'

'We took it into our heads at the last minute, caught a late train to Exeter and put up there for the night. There's no need to fuss, Verity,' Clive said. 'We're not staying over.'

'Then why are you here?' said Howard.

'To see what you have to offer,' Clive said.

'Offer?'

'Paintings.' Mr Norris smiled. 'Edgar Banbury tells me—'

'Bloody Banbury,' Howard said. 'I might have known he'd be behind it. Well, I'm not running a market stall, Mr Norris. I don't have anything to "offer".'

'Calm down, Howard,' Clive said. 'Mr Norris is a serious collector.'

'I don't care what he is,' said Howard, red-faced. 'And, if I may say so, Cavendish, you've a diabolical liberty turning up unannounced.'

'Howard's painting my portrait,' Anna put in.

'Is he now?' Clive said. 'Well, there's a turn-up for the book.'

'Would you like to see a drawing he did of me?' Anna said.

'I'd love to see it,' Teddy Norris said.

'So, indeed, would I,' said Clive.

It was impossible not to be charmed by Teddy Norris's impeccable manners and distinctive Yankee drawl. He had, he said, two sisters and a much younger brother and, when not travelling, lived with his parents in 'a place' on Fifth Avenue, New York. He was too modest to be drawn on just how large or how grand 'the place' might be and ducked Verity's questions about his father's profession by wagging his hand and shrugging: 'A little of this, a little of that. Steel, mostly. Some railway stock, I think.'

He displayed no trace of the brash self-confidence that was Clive's trademark and seemed impervious to the insults that Howard threw at him over the coffee cups. He continued to heap praise on the drawing that Anna had put into his hands even after Howard had retrieved it and, as if it had no more value than a doodle, tossed on to the window seat.

Anna sat quietly on the sofa, cup and saucer balanced on her knee.

How peculiar, she thought, to have the only three men she'd ever cared about, Papa excepted, assembled in a room in a ramshackle house on the edge of Dartmoor: Otto, Clive, Howard – and a stranger towards whom she was already beginning to feel an unsettling attraction.

Uncle Otto brought over the coffee pot.

'Anna?' he said. 'What's wrong?'

'Nothing,' she said. 'I think I need a breath of air, that's all.'

'Poor child,' said Verity. 'Howard's been too hard on her.'

'Have you, Howard?' Clive said. 'Have you been too hard on her?'

'She didn't complain,' said Howard.

Mr Norris said, 'Now it's stopped raining, perhaps Miss Martindale would care to show me the grounds,' and when she nodded, took away her saucer and cup and gallantly offered his arm.

★

'Stop it, Howard. Stop it this very minute. You're behaving like a child. Rushing off into the library and locking the door. Refusing to turn up for dinner. Are you trying to drive her away? Stop fiddling with your dressing gown and listen to me.'

'Am I not entitled to any privacy, Mother, even in my bedroom?'

'I'll leave when I've said my piece, not before.'

'All right, say your piece and get it over with.'

'Anna,' Verity began, 'is a lovely girl.'

'She had no right to show him my drawings.'

'One drawing,' Verity corrected. 'He thought it was marvellous.'

'I don't care what he thought. I don't like anyone showing my work to strangers.' Howard tightened the cord of his dressing gown with such force that it seemed as if he might cut himself in half. 'What say you'n'me step out for a breath of air, Mizz Martindale? – making up to my fiancée right under my nose, as if she were the bloody queen of Egypt.'

'He was merely being courteous. There was no impropriety.'

'Impropriety? Dear God, Norris could have stripped her naked and painted her blue and she wouldn't have raised a finger to stop him. As for Cavendish, he's only smarming around in the hope that the American might buy some of his stuff,' Howard said. 'By the by, if you think we've seen the last of Norris, think again. He may present himself as a connoisseur but when it comes down to it, I'll wager he's a dealer just like all the rest and only interested in profit.'

'He'd have bought that drawing of Anna if you'd given him half a chance.'

'I'm not selling my soul to please Anna Martindale.'

'All the same,' Verity said, 'I think you'd better apologise.'

'Now why would I do that?'

'You don't want to lose her, do you, dear?'

'Oh, I won't lose her, Mama, have no fear. Now, I'd be awfully grateful if you'd push off and let me get some sleep,' Howard said and, none too gently, steered his mother towards the door.

When they were very young Julie and she had spent many hours dressing up. Seated on a quilted stool before the dressing table in the gloomy bedroom in Foxhailes, Anna amused herself by playing the childish game again. She propped the electrical lamp on the dressing table and, bathed in a pool of light, furled her nightgown up to her waist, improvised a wimple from a pillowslip and preened and pouted at her reflection as if she were not only beautiful but irresistible and might bring any man, even charming Teddy Norris, to his knees.

'What the devil do you think you're doing?' said a voice behind her.

She snatched the pillowslip from her hair, pushed down her nightgown and spun round to find Howard watching from the doorway. He was bare-legged and barefoot, a silk dressing gown cinched tightly around his middle.

'How long have you been spying on me?' Anna asked.

'Long enough,' Howard answered. 'You really should lock your door.'

'What do you want?'

'You know damned well what I want.'

'I've no idea what you're talking about, Howard.'

'You've been leading me on for months.' Coming up behind her he clumsily cupped her breast. 'You're very sure of yourself, aren't you, Anna?'

'Howard, you're hurting me.'

'You're not teasing some stranger now,' he said. 'You don't have to impress me with how desirable you are.'

Anna squirmed a little. 'Howard, this isn't right.'

'Show me.' He stepped back. 'Take off your nightgown and show me.'

For a moment she was inclined to refuse but she feared he might do her harm if she resisted. Obediently, she let her nightgown slither to the floor. She stood stock still, the stool pressing into the back of her thighs, and let him study her. She almost expected him to fashion a frame from his fingers and enclose her within it, a vertical oblong of impersonal flesh.

'Well?' she said at length and, when he didn't answer, said again, 'Well?'

Piqued by his lack of response she leaned into him and attempted to kiss him.

He jerked his head away, caught her by the arm, swung her across the room and threw her on to the bed. He pushed her knees apart, loosened the cord of his dressing gown and let it fall open. When he positioned himself between her legs she braced herself for pain. But there was no pain, only an abrupt splash of sticky warmth on the flesh of her inner thigh.

Howard pulled away, as shocked, she thought, as she was.

Then, spinning round, he stumbled out into the corridor and slammed the door behind him, leaving her bewildered and unsatisfied to ponder on just what she'd done wrong.

She appeared at breakfast ready for the road. She had packed her bags and put them in the hall beside Uncle Otto's luggage. When Verity, rather upset, said, 'Oh, Anna, are you leaving us too?' she answered coolly, 'I'm afraid I must get back to London sooner than expected.'

'Why, my dear, why?'

'I'm anxious about my sister, Julie. She isn't well.'

'Really?' said Otto, then, waving a fork to cover his gaffe, added, 'Yes, of course, none too well.'

'Howard *will* be disappointed,' Verity said. 'Does he know you're leaving?'

'Yes,' said Anna. 'He knows.'

'He might at least show up for breakfast. I'll send Emily to fetch him.'

'No need,' said Anna. 'I'll find him,' and headed for the library.

The easel had vanished, all the tubes and brushes too. Even the sheets of newspaper that had protected the polished table had been removed. The chair on which she'd posed had been kicked into a corner. There was nothing in the room to suggest that Howard Buskin had ever plied his trade there, nothing but a sheet of drawing paper torn into a hundred pieces and scattered across the carpet.

Ten minutes later Anna was seated in the pony-trap with the luggage stowed behind her, Mr Moss at the reins and Uncle Otto by her side.

Verity stood in the porch with a shawl over her shoulders,

waving and blowing kisses. Anna guessed that Howard was already high up on the moor, an easel on his back, a satchel bouncing at his hip.

'May I ask,' said Uncle Otto, 'what made you change your mind?'

'Boredom,' Anna said curtly. 'Sheer boredom,' then, holding out her hand, added, 'Oh, look, it's beginning to rain.'

19

It hadn't occurred to Julie that she might be an asset in her husband's assault on the ladder of success. Her father was 'trade', after all, and no amount of money would change his standing in society. On the other hand, Clive was the son of a provincial lawyer which gave him an advantage over the Martindales. More to the point, he was that oddest of odd fellows – an artist; a slippery item in the eyes of the gentry. If he had something the toffs thought they wanted, however, he would be tolerated and if he played his cards right and kept his nose clean might even be accepted by those and such as those, which, in Clive's book, meant anyone with influence and a private income.

'Max Scully, for instance,' Julie said.

'He fits the bill perfectly.'

'And this American chap?'

'Norris, yes,' said Clive. 'He's still hell-bent on buying up Buskins. I think my little trip to Devon will pay dividends, though. Our dear Howard was even more obnoxious than usual. He's too polite to say so but Norris wasn't impressed. He was, however' – Clive gave her a squeeze – 'somewhat enamoured of your sister.'

'Did she flirt with him?'

'Not too obviously,' Clive said.

Now that the nausea had dwindled Julie felt well, very well. Any small niggles in the downstairs department were simply comforting reminders that she was advancing towards motherhood.

'I'm hosting a supper party next week,' Clive informed her.

Julie sat up in bed. 'Not here? Surely not here?'

'God, no! Rules.'

'Rules? Can we afford it?'

'If we go easy on the champers we can bring it in at around three and sixpence a head.'

'We?' said Julie with a hint of sarcasm. 'Are you actually inviting *me*?'

'Hmm,' said Clive. 'Mixed doubles. Are you in, or out?'

'Of course, I'm in. I'm not so far gone that I can't fit into an evening dress. Who else will be there?'

'Max Scully and his wife, Teddy Norris and' – he paused – 'your sister.'

'I thought Anna was in Devon.'

'She came home with Otto at the weekend. I dropped by the gallery this afternoon to see how the land lies. I gather there was a bit of a contretemps after Norris and I departed. Howard said things he shouldn't have said and Anna, very wisely, left him to cool off.'

'Good for Anna.'

'Good for us,' Clive said.

'Oh?' Julie angled to face him. 'Why is it good for us?'

'The idea of a supper party wasn't entirely my idea.'

'Whose was it?'

'Matter of fact, the hint came from Teddy Norris.'

'Then why isn't he paying for it?'

'He's a bachelor, all alone in London. He can't go inviting young women to supper without a good excuse.'

'Young women meaning my sister, of course,' Julie said. 'What are you up to, Cavendish? What underhand game are you playing?'

'Nothing underhand about it,' Clive assured her. 'That said, I do have a faint suspicion that Teddy Norris's interest in Anna may be no more than a means of getting to Howard.'

'What if you're wrong?' Julie said.

Clive shrugged. 'Then it could be a match made in heaven.'

Teddy Norris might be a hand-reared sophisticate weaned at a table in Delmonico's but even he was impressed by Rules and the fact – made up by Clive – that Sir Joshua Reynolds had once dined there. He was much at ease in the select company, talked knowledgeably about art and sport and even listened attentively when Max Scully's wife, Maude, held forth.

In spite of her husband's wealth Maude was no snob. She claimed to come from humble origins, though, Julie thought, you never quite knew what 'humble' meant these days. She had informed opinions on everything and a store of anecdotes with which to back them up. When she learned that Julie was expecting she embarked on a hilarious account of how Telfer, her first-born, had plopped into the world on a liner in mid-Atlantic shortly after it had been rammed by the steamship *Britannic* in a thick, white fog.

'What was the name of the ship you were on?' Clive asked.

'The *Celtic*,' Maude Scully answered. 'No joke at the time. Seven dead. We were fortunate to reach New York in one piece.'

'Being a stockholder in the White Star Line isn't all fun and games, you see,' Max Scully said. 'How do you travel, Mr Norris?'

'I came over on the *Lusitania*.'

'Really?' Anna put in. 'Is she as luxurious as everyone says she is?'

'Very comfortable,' Teddy Norris answered. 'And very fast.'

'Blue Riband, of course,' said Clive.

'Hah!' Max Scully threw up a hand. 'Hang on three years or so then we'll see who has the Blue Riband for the quickest Atlantic crossing. We've designs on the drawing board for three Olympic-class super-liners. The first keel will go down before the end of the year. When she's launched she'll knock the Cunarders into a cocked hat for size, speed and opulence.'

'Where's she being built?' Teddy Norris asked.

'Harland and Wolff, Belfast,' Max answered.

'I've never been on a boat,' said Anna.

'Yes, you have,' Julie reminded her. 'We went to Greenwich on the steamer.'

'That doesn't count,' said Anna. 'I mean, I've never been to sea.'

'Persuade your husband to bring you to New York,' Teddy Norris said. 'It's a very exciting city. Well worth a visit.'

'My husband?' said Anna.

'Mr Buskin.'

'Howard isn't my husband.'

'Not yet,' said Julie.

'No,' said Anna, looking Teddy Norris straight in the eye, 'not yet.'

How Norris occupied his days when he wasn't taking tea with Julie and Anna was a mystery. America's track and field athletes weren't due to arrive in England for several weeks and Clive couldn't imagine the elegant Mr Norris consorting with the handful of Irish-Americans, mainly boxers, whose 'managers' had already installed them in boarding houses in London's less salubrious suburbs.

'From what Teddy tells us he just trails round the galleries,' Julie said. 'Every gallery you can name, public and private. If you're so concerned about where Teddy goes and who he's dealing with why don't you ask him?'

'I don't want him to think I'm pushy.'

'But you are, darling, you're very pushy. That lovely evening at Rules was rather a give-away, don't you think? Added to the fact that you're willing to let your wife take tea with a young, handsome, unattached male. Some people might think that's carrying hospitality a step too far.'

'Norris isn't averse to taking you to tea, is he? I mean, we know he's interested in Anna.'

'What makes you think he's not interested in me?' Julie said.

'Because you're pregnant.'

'Glowing,' Julie told him. 'Teddy says I'm glowing.'

'Does he, indeed?' said Clive.

Scraps of this odd conversation floated in Clive's head as he trickled chrome yellow into a pool of raw umber to duplicate the colour of the floor of the gym and give it depth. He was unaware of the men behind him until a familiar voice said, 'Well, if it isn't my old friend, Cavendish.'

Teddy Norris was clad in a cotton singlet and cream-coloured flannels. His hair was damp and he smelled faintly of chlorine. Behind him, Telfer Scully bounced on the balls of his feet as if to express his delight at meeting Clive again.

'Been swimming, Teddy?' Clive asked.

'That we have. I miss my regular exercise when I'm away from home.'

'You really should have made the American team, Teddy.'

'I guess it was a blow not to make it through the Albany trials, a salutary lesson in humility, you might say. Anyhow, I've lots of other fish to fry.' He glanced, without comment, at the watercolour pinned to Clive's drawing board. 'How is your good lady wife?'

'Glowing,' Clive said. 'You had tea with her last Thursday, I believe.'

'Sure did. I appreciate having two charming young ladies to squire me around. Sorry you can't join us.'

Clive waved the brush. 'Busy, as you can see. Very busy.'

'More posters?' Teddy Norris asked.

'No,' Clive answered. 'Not more posters.'

'Dad's buying a portrait from Clive,' Telfer Scully put in, 'as soon as the Games are over. Meanwhile' – he wrapped an arm round Teddy's waist – 'perhaps we should snatch our opportunity on the vaulting horse while it's free.'

'I must warn you,' Teddy said, 'I'm no great shakes on a springboard.'

'Oh, I'll be there,' Telfer Scully assured him, 'to catch you if you fall.'

★

'I'm glad you've stopped sulking,' Julie said. 'I did rather miss you, you know.'

'I wasn't sulking,' Anna said. 'I was otherwise occupied.'

'Doing what?'

'All sort of things.'

'With Howard?'

'Sometimes.'

'Well, at least we're back on speaking terms,' Julie said. 'I'll be glad of your support when baby comes. Will you like being an aunt, do you think?'

'I suppose I will,' said Anna. 'I don't have much choice, do I?'

She had her back to the river, her eye on the French doors that led from the rear of the Old Bridge Hotel into the sunlit garden where a number of ladies and gentlemen were nibbling sandwiches and sipping tea at wrought-iron tables. She had no idea why they were meeting Teddy so far out of town. There were no galleries worth the name on the Putney shore and it wasn't as if they had anything to hide.

'Shall we order?' Julie asked.

'It's only gone the quarter,' Anna said. 'He's probably been delayed.'

The breeze was warm, the sun high, the scene so gay and colourful that it might have been painted by Renoir.

'Is Howard still in Devon?' Julie asked.

'I really don't know.'

'Doesn't he write to you?'

'No.'

'You're not committed to him, you know,' Julie said. 'Engagements are made to be broken. Correct me if I'm wrong, but I have the distinct impression you don't like Howard Buskin very much.'

'He's all right, I suppose.'

'Hardly a ringing endorsement for the man you intend to marry,' Julie said.

'Were you sure Clive was the man for you from the beginning?'

Julie wagged an admonishing forefinger. 'Now, now, you know perfectly well Clive and I were compatible, shall we say, before we took the plunge.'

'Do you think I should take the plunge?' said Anna.

'It depends what plunge you mean,' Julie said. 'It also rather depends on the nature of your feelings for Mr Buskin. Do you see yourself as his muse, Anna, or his mistress? What you don't want to do is become his serf. There are too many meek wives in the community as it is, women so besotted by their husbands' extraordinary "gifts" that they put up with every insult, every betrayal out of a sense of – well, I don't know what. Perhaps they enjoy being martyrs for art's sake. Perhaps they've been told so often that they're inferior to the men who marry them that they actually begin to believe it.'

'This isn't you, is it?'

'Good Lord, no!' said Julie. 'I put up with that sordid house in Camden because I know Clive loves me. If he ever betrays me then I'm off, bag and baggage. No compromises, no negotiations, no second chances. If Clive's intent on flying to the moon he must take me with him. Me, and nobody else.'

'I'm not sure I feel that way about Howard.'

'Ah!' said Julie. 'But does Howard feel that way about you?'

Before Anna could answer Teddy Norris appeared in the doorway. He was dressed in a seersucker shirt open at the neck, a striped blazer and cream-coloured flannels with broad turn-ups. His hat, tipped back, was a straw boater. He looked, Anna thought, like a cross between a fairground huckster and an Oxford don.

Seeing her, he took off the boater and held it against his chest as if he were about to break into song. From the corner of her eye she noticed ladies at nearby tables ogling him, though whether in admiration or disapproval was a matter for conjecture. He kissed Julie's hand but, to Anna's annoyance, greeted her with nothing more intimate than a smile.

'Now,' he said, 'what shall it be? Tea and trimmings all round?'

'Please,' said Julie. 'I'm famished.'

Anna watched him summon a waiter, a young boy with sticking-out ears and a shock of ginger hair who was not impressed by seersucker shirts or American accents. He took the order glumly and disappeared through the French doors.

'I wonder if we'll ever see him again,' said Teddy, 'or our teas.'

'It's that sort of place,' said Julie. 'Very English.'

'Couldn't we have found somewhere a little more convenient?' Anna said.

She was annoyed with herself for being annoyed with him. He was too good, too amiable, too engaged with everything around him: the garden, the river, the skiffs and sculls that flitted like dragonflies across the shimmering surface of the water, even the little puffs of cloud that gave the blue sky its depth. He seemed, Anna thought, to be occupied with every single thing – except her.

She said, 'You did rather keep us waiting, you know.'

'For which you have my apology,' he said. 'Julie, I ran into your husband at the gymnasium. He was painting.'

'And what,' said Anna, 'were you doing in a gymnasium, Mr Norris?'

'Taking exercise,' he answered, then, without so much as a pause, added, 'I've had a letter from Mr Buskin. I take it you're behind it?'

'Behind what?' Anna asked.

'He wants to sell me a painting,' Teddy Norris said.

20

Clive wasn't prone to fits of temper and Maisie and she were both taken aback when he reared from his chair and, casting around frantically, picked up the second-best teapot and hurled it across the kitchen to smash into pieces in the sink.

'God damn the man to hell,' he shouted, then, deflated, sat down again and immediately apologised for his outburst.

'I'm sorry,' he said. 'It's just so bloody demoralising.'

'It's only a painting, Clive,' Julie said, while Maisie picked shards of china from the sink. 'It doesn't mean Teddy won't buy something from you as well.'

Clive slumped over the table. 'Norris said nothing to me when we met this morning. He must have received Howard's letter by then. No doubt he was sniggering at my pathetic efforts to interest him in my work.'

'Teddy isn't the sniggering sort,' said Julie.

Clive raised his head and glowered. Julie moved the dish of cauliflower and cheese out of his reach. Maisie took herself out of the line of fire.

'What did Anna have to say about it?' Clive asked.

'She was flabbergasted,' Julie answered.

'As well she might be,' said Clive. 'He's doing it for her, you know.'

'Really?' Julie said. 'I'm not sure I follow you.'

'Howard, the recluse; Howard, the misanthrope, too wrapped up in himself to care what anyone thinks, now, suddenly, pops out of hiding and offers work to an American fellow he barely knows. Why? I ask myself. The answer's obvious. It's a gesture of apology. He wants Anna back.'

'I don't think it's going to make much difference,' Julie said. 'Teddy's far too clever to be taken in by your – by our little ruse. Once he has his Buskin, or a whole cartload of Buskins, he'll shake Anna off and that's the last any of us will see of him. Console yourself, darling; perhaps Teddy won't like Howard's work.'

'No,' Clive said. 'I wouldn't want that to happen.'

'Why ever not?' said Julie.

'Because it'll wreck Howard's confidence completely. It's one thing keeping Howard out of the way while I court the Yankee but I've too much regard for my profession to . . .' He paused, sighing. 'Banbury's right. Howard is an original. I might sneer and do him down but that's only because I know I can't compete.'

'You're just as talented as he is,' Julie assured him.

'Unfortunately, I'm not – and never will be,' Clive said. 'When will this great unveiling take place?'

'Tomorrow, I believe.'

'Where?'

'Holland Park.'

'Will you be there?'

'No,' Julie said.

'Why not?'

'Because, darling, I haven't been invited.'

'Has Anna?'

'Now what do you think?' Julie said. 'Of course, she has.'

'I wonder if I should drop by,' Clive said. 'Keep an eye on things.'

'I wouldn't if I were you,' Julie said. 'Teddy knows what he's doing.'

'That's what I'm afraid of,' said Clive.

Some Fifth Avenue boulevardiers complained that gored skirts, tailored jackets and shirtwaist blouses made women look masculine but Teddy liked the latest fashions that took the froufrou out of sex appeal.

Anna Martindale was certainly no Gibson girl, no S-shaped, giraffe-necked creation with a bouffant hairstyle, a hand-span waist and a protruding bottom. Heaven knows, Anna's bottom was cute enough without a bustle skirt to show it off. She'd looked particularly attractive in the simple evening gown she'd worn to dinner at Rules and it had been all he could do to keep his mind on the jugged hare and not poke his nose into her cleavage.

On that first day in chilly Devon he'd been almost as impressed by her intelligence as her looks. In fact, if her fiancé hadn't been hovering over her, and Cavendish smarming all over *him*, he might have made a pitch there and then. But young Miss Martindale had depths he couldn't fathom, not least of which was her engagement to the half-mad Buskin whose hatred of everyone and everything might be the source from which great art sprang but was hardly a sterling attribute in a husband-to-be. Now his partner in the gallery in the shadow of the Park Avenue viaduct in New York was badgering him with letters urging him to hasten back to Paris to buy more stock. He'd no intention of quitting London before he'd acquired at least one painting by the intractable Howard Buskin, however, and, if luck was running his way, got to know the luscious Miss Martindale a whole lot better than might seem right and proper.

Anna arrived at Verity's house only minutes before Teddy. Howard barely had time to greet her, as if nothing nasty had taken place in the depths of Devon, before Percy was summoned to the front door once more and she heard Teddy's voice in the hall and felt her heart rise in her throat like mercury in a thermometer.

They met in the big sunny drawing room where Howard had propped three cloth-draped canvases on chairs in the window bay. To his credit, Teddy managed to ignore the shrouded paintings. He shook Anna's hand and looked into her eyes with such warmth that she felt her cheeks redden. She might even have blurted out something unwise if Verity hadn't dragged Teddy off to admire the Banbury portrait that hung over the mantelpiece.

Anna drifted to the table where coffee and cake were laid out. She filled a cup from the silver pot and carried saucer and cup to the chairs in the window bay. Three chairs: three shrouded canvases. She reached out to lift a corner of a cloth and peep at the painting beneath.

'No,' said Howard. 'Don't spoil the surprise.'

'The only surprise,' Anna said quietly, 'is that you're doing this at all.'

'You didn't have to come, you know,' said Howard.

'Why did you invite me if you didn't want me here?'

'But I do want you here,' said Howard. 'After all, you still wear my ring.'

'That's true,' Anna admitted. 'Would you like it back?'

He shook his head and looked so dejected that she almost felt sorry for him. He said, 'Whatever you decide to do, Anna, the ring is yours to keep. I don't intend to lose you over a simple misunderstanding.'

'Oh, is that what it was?' said Anna. 'I prefer not to discuss it right now.'

She was conscious of Teddy gliding across the drawing room. He put a hand on her arm and, in a voice as soft as caramel, said, 'I'm not the only one who's curious about what you're hiding under there, Mr Buskin. Shall we get on with it?'

Howard took up position behind the chairs. He reached over a chair and tugged the cloth from the painting. Folding the cloth across his arm, he leaned back as if to distance himself from the bleak landscape that his action had revealed.

Teddy cupped a hand to his chin and studied the canvas. He held his thoughtful pose; a forefinger twitched, tapping his nose. At length, he sucked in breath and, looking up, gave Howard a nod. Howard unveiled a second canvas. The still life was smaller than the landscape; fruit and wine bottles arranged round a reddish-brown pitcher, linked in sensuous harmony by a scarf of patterned silk.

'Oh,' said Verity brightly. 'I've seen that one before.'

For all her father's lectures and her lessons with Mr Rodale, Anna still could not fathom what special quality Teddy Norris found in Howard's paintings.

'Are they both for sale?' Teddy asked.

'I'll sell one, if you're interested – but only one.'

'May I make you an offer?'

'You haven't seen them all yet.' Howard swirled the cloth

like a matador's cape and threw it into a corner. 'First, I'd like to know what you intend to do with it? Keep it, or sell it?'

'Display it,' Teddy said, 'in my father's house on Fifth Avenue.'

'Who's the collector, you or your papa?'

'Dad buys for investment,' Teddy said. 'I buy for love.'

'Love,' Howard said, with a little snort. 'Ah, yes, love.'

'You'll be in good company, Mr Buskin,' Teddy said, 'if you don't mind rubbing shoulders with Seurat, Sisley and Bonnard.'

'I don't particularly care who I rub shoulders with,' Howard said. 'Twenty guineas for a single canvas. That's my price. Twenty guineas whichever picture you choose. Framing and shipping are your problem.'

'I am prepared to pay more, you know.'

Howard stripped the covering from the final painting.

'How much for a portrait, then?'

Anna stared at her image on the canvas, her pitiless twin. It was as if Howard had reached into her, tugged out shreds of her character of which she was unaware and rendered them with tiny flicks and flecks of the brush that made her seem vividly, insolently alive.

'Well now!' Teddy Norris exclaimed. 'Now that is something special.'

'A pretty girl in a satin dress,' Howard said smugly, 'is hardly anything to get excited about. Ten for a penny on every postcard stall in London.'

'When did you finish it?' Anna heard herself say. 'You tore up the drawing.'

'Not before I'd transferred it to the canvas, Anna. What

a waste it would have been otherwise.' He propped the painting on the chair again. 'In art as in life nothing is ever thrown away. Am I not right, Mr Norris?' He didn't allow Teddy time to answer. 'Now, would any kind person care to offer me twenty guineas for one of my magnificent paintings? You, sir? Then take your pick. Just one, though, just one.'

Howard was selling her likeness for twenty guineas, practically giving it to Teddy Norris to carry home to New York. She clung tightly to Verity's arm while waiting for Teddy to announce his choice.

'I'll take the landscape, Howard,' he said.

21

The grand opening of the Franco-British Exhibition, presided over by the Prince of Wales, had been marred by drizzling rain. It had rained on and off for days thereafter but now, at long last, the sun shone from a clear sky, the pavilions glistened like alabaster and the waters of the artificial lagoon were almost blue.

Julie settled into the canvas seat of the little pleasure boat and sighed contentedly. 'It's just like being in Venice.'

'Not quite,' said Uncle Otto from the seat behind her. 'It doesn't smell.'

'I didn't know you'd been to Venice,' said Anna.

'Once, long ago, with your mama,' Otto said. 'And it smelled.'

'You're not feeling sick, dear, are you?' Papa asked solicitously.

'Not in the slightest,' Julie answered. 'But you're not getting me up in that Flip Flap machine for all the tea in China. The Scenic Railway was bad enough.'

'In your condition I'm not sure you should even be on a boat,' said Howard.

'I survived the tube journey, didn't I? And that mêlée at the gate? Like lemmings. Kindly stop fussing, all of you, and let me enjoy the view.'

'It is rather splendid, isn't it?' said Papa. 'I confess I'm glad I came.'

'Too much to take in, really,' said Anna. 'We'll have to come again.'

'We'll bring Mama next time,' Howard said. 'We can hire a chair for her.'

'She won't take kindly to that,' said Otto. 'However, there's plenty to do that won't knock the stuffing out of her. Let me know when you're coming and I'll tag along to make sure she doesn't overdo it.'

They had met by arrangement under the soaring arches of the Wood Green entrance. Even Howard had been impressed by the grandeur of the 'Franco'. His grumbles that the exhibition was just an overblown exercise in international relations had tailed off when he'd discovered that paintings by Corot and Courbet were on display in the Fine Art Palace, a fact that gave the whole enterprise validity in his eyes and raised it above the level of a fun fair.

Sunshine had brought out the crowds. There was a cosmopolitan air to the promenades. The queue on the steps of the Court of Honour, where they had boarded the pleasure boat, was livelier than might be expected from a gathering of staid Londoners. Music helped, of course; as the boat chugged between the ivory palaces the strains of various orchestras floated, zephyr-like, from the colonnades.

'Oh,' said Anna. 'What building is that?'

'Palace of Women's Work, I believe,' Howard told her.

'I'm surprised they finished it in time,' Anna said.

Papa fell into the trap. 'Why is that, my dear?'

'Well, you know what they say: women's work is never done.'

Otto tweaked the ribbon on his niece's hat. 'You're not taking this educational experience seriously enough, young lady.'

'Am I meant to?'

'Take it any way you like,' said Julie. 'I think it's intended to be all things to all men. Spirit of Empire. *Entente Cordiale*, and all that. Aren't you glad you closed the shop for the day, Papa?'

'Indeed, I am. Just sorry Clive couldn't be with us.'

'Oh, he's here,' said Julie. 'We're meeting him at the café by the Elite Gardens at four o'clock. He came up early this morning to sketch the elephants.'

'Elephants?' said Anna.

'In the Ceylon village.'

'God!' said Howard. 'Does the man never stop?'

'Can't afford to,' said Julie. 'When the Games begin in earnest in July I doubt if we'll see him at all.'

'Bloody Games!' Howard said. 'Now that *is* a waste of public money.'

'Howard, please,' Anna said. 'Do stop complaining.'

'What? Yes, of course, my dear. My apologies,' Howard said. 'I'm just not very sporting, that's all. Can't understand what all the bloody—'

'Howard!' Anna said sharply.

'Right. Sorry.'

Howard was walking on eggshells these days. He had no means of knowing that Anna's 'forgiveness' of his outrageous behaviour at Foxhailes had more to do with Teddy Norris's rejection than his, Howard's, contrition. Anna couldn't forget her disappointment when Teddy had chosen the sullen landscape over her gorgeous portrait. Whatever his other faults

Howard had painted a beautiful picture and for that deserved clemency. She reached over and patted his hand.

Then Julie said, 'Is that who I think it is?'

Anna looked up. Crossing the Venetian bridge he was tall enough to stand out from the throng, tall and easy of manner, strolling, it seemed, in a dreamy little world of his own – except that he wasn't alone.

'Norris,' Howard said, sitting forward. 'My God, what's he doing here?'

'More to the point,' said Julie, 'what's he doing with my husband?'

'Five thousand people in this park and you just happened to bump into Teddy,' Anna said. 'Well, I for one don't believe you.'

'You must admit, darling, it is stretching coincidence,' said Julie.

'Believe what you like,' Clive said. 'I'd no idea Norris was visiting the Franco today. Besides, I didn't bump into them; they bumped into me.'

'They?' said Anna.

'He's here with Telfer Scully. They're making a day of it.'

'I didn't see Scully on the bridge,' said Anna.

'Possibly because he'd sprinted off in search of a gentleman's lavatory.'

'Oh!' said Anna. 'I'm sorry.'

Howard said, 'I thought you were painting elephants.'

'I was. Gathered quite a little crowd, too. Should have put round the hat, made a few bob,' Clive said. 'Don't give me that superior look, Howard. You did all right out of Norris, so I've heard. Surprised you haven't had a mob of dealers hammering on your door now you're open to offers.' He hoisted up his sketch book and showed it round. 'Elephants,' he said. 'See.'

'Are they mating?' said Julie.

'No, they're dancing,' said Clive.

'I've never painted an elephant,' said Howard.

'Well, now's your chance,' said Clive. 'Turn left at Australia and—'

'Teddy isn't really a collector, is he?' Anna interrupted.

'I've never been quite sure where collecting ends and dealing begins,' Clive said. 'If Norris claims he's a collector why not believe him?'

'Did he say anything about me?' Anna asked.

'Not about you, no. He didn't even tell me what sort of painting he'd purchased from Howard, though I got the impression he was pleased with it.'

'If you didn't talk about me and you didn't talk about Howard's painting,' said Anna, 'what did you talk about?'

'The high jump,' Clive said. 'We talked about the high jump and the broad jump and whether Hefferon or Hayes will win the marathon. And to save you craning your neck, sweetheart, Messrs Norris and Scully will not be joining us for *cafés crèmes*. They've more important things on their minds than oil paintings or pretty girls. In fact, they've headed over to the stadium. By the way, where are Otto and your old man?'

'Gone on ahead to secure a table,' Julie said.

'Shall we toddle after them?' said Howard.

'Yes,' Julie said. 'I think perhaps we should.'

'Are you all right, darling?' Clive asked.

'Never better,' Julie answered and snaring her husband by the strap of his satchel, dragged him off towards the café before her sister could throw another tantrum and spoil a lovely afternoon.

Maisie unwrapped two ham sandwiches from newspaper and put them on a plate. She put the plate on one side of the painting table, together with a knife, a pot of English mustard and a mug of tea.

'I like them elephants,' she said. 'You gonner paint them proper?'

'Some day,' said Clive, 'but not right now.'

'Yer, I can see how you've got your 'ands full with the big feller.'

Clive wiped his fingers on a rag, picked up a sandwich and bit into it.

'What do you think of it, Maisie? An honest opinion, please.'

The girl cocked her head and gave the canvas her full attention.

'It's comin' on,' she said. 'Bit dark, though, ain't it?'

'You're right,' Clive said. 'I can't seem to get the dusty feel of the gym without losing contrast. I don't want the figures to be too bold.'

'Is that Mr Scully in mid-air?'

'It's a composite – you know what that means, Maisie?'

'Like no one an' everyone.'

Hands on hips, she continued to appraise his morning's work.

Clive dabbed a corner of the sandwich into the mustard pot and chewed the hot mouthful thoughtfully. He'd developed considerable affection for the blithe little servant and had too much respect for her to consider asking her to take off her clothes. He hadn't lost his appetite for sex but his 'brush' – if that was the word – with his sister-in-law had alerted him to the danger of regarding every pretty girl as an opportunity to test his manhood. He was far too engaged with all his various projects to risk complicating his life and, unlike his mentor, Edgar Banbury, had no need to go looking for 'inspiration'.

'Is Mrs Cavendish all right?' he asked.

'Right as rain,' said Maisie.

'Is she lying down?'

'She was peeling spuds when I left.'

Clive washed down the first sandwich with tea and tackled the second.

'Would you like a bite, Maisie?'

'No fanks. Going 'ome in a minute to make lunch for Mrs C.'

Maisie returned to the gouache and ink sketches he'd brought back from the Franco and tacked to the studio wall. She moved down the line with the patient sideways step he associated with inveterate gallery-goers. He was pleased to have an appreciative audience, even if she was only a serving girl.

'Them elephants,' Maisie said, 'are they – I mean, are they doin' it?'

Clive laughed. 'No, Maisie, they're dancing.'

'Can't be comfortable, like, if you're a elephant.'

'I don't suppose it is. But elephants are easy to train, so they say.'

'Like Barnardo girls,' said Maisie and, with a wink and a wave, left him to get on with his work.

★

Neither Otto nor Verity could be sure when the embers of their long ago romance sparked into life again. Perhaps it came about on an evening in early June when Otto, trotting out of Ledbetter Street for a breath of air before supper, found himself arrested by the sight of a pretty little flower-seller plying her trade by the railings of St Martin-in-the-Fields.

On impulse he purchased a posy of violets and loitered on the kerb while inconsiderate strangers bumped into him and taxicabs and omnibuses growled past. Then it dawned on him that he was thinking of his oldest friend – who might not be around much longer. And if it wasn't quite an epiphany, Otto said later, it came dashed close.

'For me,' Verity said. 'You bought violets for me?'

'Actually,' said Otto rather ruefully, 'yes.'

She held the posy to her nose and sniffed, sniffed again and then, to Otto's astonishment, shed tears.

'Dear God, Verity,' he said. 'It's only flowers.'

'I know, I know. But *you* bought them for *me*.'

He took her into his arms and hugged her.

There was more substance than he'd expected and her bones didn't creak. The velvet evening gown slid against his fingers and her hair against his cheek was soft enough to tickle. There was nothing seedy about two old friends sharing a moment of – well, Otto thought, let's call it affection.

Fishing in her sleeve for a handkerchief, Verity blew her nose.

'I'm sorry,' she said. 'I don't know what came over me. You're just being Otto, aren't you?'

'Probably,' he said. 'Who else would I be?'

Evening sunlight in the white-painted room brought out

the colours of the carpet, the fireplace and the Banbury portrait. It added colour to Verity too, made her seem somehow young again as if, Otto thought, the best of it had not been lost and he, like Verity, hadn't quite reached the dreaded watershed after all.

'Are you coming down this summer?' Verity said.

'Down?'

'To Devon, to your cottage?'

'I hadn't thought of it,' Otto said. 'I haven't been there in ages.'

'Stay with me in Foxhailes, just you and me.'

'That,' said Otto, stroking his moustache, 'is a highly improper suggestion. We'd be the talk of the town.'

'The "town" has more to interest it than two old fogies doddering about in darkest Devon,' Verity said.

Otto nodded. 'Unfortunately, I think you may be right. Howard, however, would be outraged. I'm not sure I can face up to a blast of his moral indignation.'

'Howard's moral indignation can be rather tiresome,' Verity admitted. 'I've every hope he'll mellow with age or, if not with age, with marriage.'

'By the way,' Otto said, 'where *are* the children?'

'Howard's upstairs in the studio but I've no idea where Anna is. I thought she was at home with you.'

'No, she went sailing out soon after tea.'

'Perhaps she's visiting her sister.'

'Yes,' Otto said. 'That's probably it.'

22

The steak was inches thick and smothered in fried onions. In any other circumstances the smell alone would have put her off but there was something so novel in sitting in a wooden booth in a pub in the East End cheek by jowl with a soft-spoken American, that she picked up the worn horn-handled knife and cut into the meat with relish. When Teddy offered her a helping of fried potatoes she nodded enthusiastically and murmured 'Hmm,' like a child welcoming a fruit jelly or a dish of ice cream.

Teddy had bundled her into a cab without a word of explanation. His silence and her acquiescence were all part of the adventure. She had no idea why he'd brought her out here or quite where she was. She'd caught a glimpse of Tower Bridge from the cab window before docks, quays and colossal warehouses had closed around her and only familiar hoardings plastered to high brick walls indicated that she was still in London and not some foreign port.

The eating house was low-beamed and reeked of beer and tobacco smoke. The raucous sounds of men in drink emerged from an inner room, backed by a tinny piano hammering out a music-hall tune.

'How is your steak?' Teddy asked.

'Good.'

'Not too bloody?'

She shook her head and reached for her glass. The beer slipped so smoothly down her throat that she downed half the contents of the glass in a swallow. She watched Teddy cut his steak into neat cubes. He ate with his fork held in his right hand, his left tucked below the level of the table as if, she thought, wickedly, he might be touching himself.

She wasn't the only woman in the eating house. Two frowsy ladies of a certain age were tucking into meat pies at a nearby table. In a booth in a corner three giggling girls were being courted by a couple of rough-looking young men in cotton ducks and pea jackets.

'Is it always this crowded, Teddy?'

'No idea,' he said. 'It's the first time I've been here. I guess it's busier than usual because of the fight.'

Anna helped herself to a fried potato. 'What sort of fight?'

'Boxing – in the ring in the yard out back.'

'Oh, you've brought me to a boxing match, have you?' Anna said. 'Is this how you entertain young ladies in New York?'

'Have you never been to a prize fight?'

'Of course not.'

'I figure you might enjoy it,' Teddy said. 'I'll take you home if you wish.'

Anna put down her knife and fork. 'Tell me this, my dear Mr Norris, do people make wagers on this boxing match?'

'Sure they do.'

'And who's our money on?'

'Malone,' Teddy told her. 'Mikey Malone.'

'Irish?'

'Irish-American.'

'He can't lose then, can he?'

'He'd better not,' said Teddy.

Howard said little over dinner. It wasn't until they'd repaired to the drawing room that he revealed what was on his mind. Percy drew the curtains and a maid set out coffee things. Emily brought Verity three white pills and a glass of water and watched her mistress knock them back, after which Howard excused himself and followed the servants from the room.

'What's he up to?' Verity hissed as soon as the door closed.

'He's your son, not mine,' Otto answered. 'Is he coming back?'

'I rather hope he doesn't,' Verity said.

'I rather hope so too,' said Otto, adding, 'Unless, of course, he's gone to fetch me one of his good cigars.'

'Devil!' Verity chuckled. 'You probably mean it.'

'Oh, I do. I do.'

It wasn't a cigar Howard had gone to fetch but his portrait of Anna Martindale. He carried the canvas casually into the drawing room, swung it on to a chair and left it there while he poured coffee and lit a cigarette.

'Hah!' Otto said, not disparagingly. 'My niece in all her glory. I assume this is one of the pictures you showed Norris?'

'One that he turned down,' Howard said.

'Is it for sale?'

'No.'

'Why not?' said Verity.

'It's a gift of sorts,' Howard said. 'How would you frame it, Otto?'

'Are you asking for an estimate?'

'No, just your expert advice.'

'In that case, I'd go for something modern with, say, a simple bevel edge. Briggs will do a good job for you,' Otto said. 'When will you give it to her?'

'I'm not giving it to her,' Howard said. 'I'm putting it up for the Academy, though I greatly doubt if they'll accept either it or me.'

Otto said, 'And if they don't, what then?'

'I thought the Carfax in Ryder Street.'

'You'll be lost among the avant-garde,' said Otto.

'Don't you think it's good enough?'

'Oh, yes, I think it's good enough. Too good for the Carfax,' Otto said. 'You know damned well how good it is, Howard. If you really want to please Anna and show her how much you care why don't you just give it to her?'

'Because,' said Howard, blowing smoke again, 'I want to see her hung.'

It was late now and the light had all but gone. Clive was on the point of packing up and heading home when a motorcar drew up outside the studio and a Cockney voice called out, 'Hoy, Mr Cavendish, you hup there?'

Clive opened the window and looked out. The chauffeur was clad in a strange greenish-blue uniform and sported a hat like an Admiral of the Fleet.

'You Mr Cavendish?'

'I am,' said Clive.

'What floor, like, sir?'

'One up, left.'

The chauffeur nodded, leaned into the passenger window

and conveyed the information to his employer, Max Scully, who climbed from the motorcar, waved cheerily to Clive and a few minutes later stepped over the threshold into the studio.

He tipped back his hat and looked round.

'So this is the art manufactory, is it?'

'I'd hardly put it like that,' Clive said.

'Got light?' Max Scully said.

'What? Oh, yes, light,' Clive said.

He clicked the wall switch that lit the electrical bulb that dangled on a cord from the ceiling then crossed the studio and turned on the lamp attached to the drawing board. 'Is that better?'

'Marginally,' Max Scully said. 'I should have come earlier.'

'I usually only open my studio to invited guests, you know.'

Max looked at him suspiciously then, seeing the joke, laughed.

'Getting a bit above yourself, aren't you, Cavendish?' he said. 'Be asking for a pavilion at the Franco next.' He rolled the easel into position beneath the bulb. 'This it?'

'If you mean what I think you mean,' Clive said, 'yes, that's it.'

'I heard you were haunting the gym. Telfer told me. Rather thought you might be setting up an oil.'

'It isn't finished.'

'I can see that,' Max Scully said. 'How long?'

'Three weeks, possibly four. I've promised sketches of the Franco to *John Bull* magazine and daren't make them wait,' Clive said. 'Frankly, I need the cash.'

'Well, you aren't exactly sleeping rolled up in a carpet on your studio floor,' Max Scully said, 'but work is work, I suppose.' He turned from the easel to the drawing board and glanced at the pen and ink sketch that was pinned to it. 'How many drawings are the *Bull* paying you for?'

'Four tailpieces.'

Max had barely stopped moving since he'd stepped through the door. He took himself to the rear wall, where the elephant drawings were tacked, planted his hands on his thighs, stooped forward and peered at them.

'My God,' he said, 'are they . . .'

'No,' Clive said, 'they're dancing.'

Clive had more savvy than to rush his backer. His first thought was that Scully had come to formalise a commission for a portrait of Telfer but instinct told him there was more to the visit than that.

'You don't hang about twiddling your thumbs, Cavendish, do you?'

'I work quickly. I have to.'

'Some patrons might see that as a disadvantage,' Max Scully said.

'They might,' Clive said cautiously, 'if I had any patrons.'

'This one' – Max jerked his thumb – '*Athletes in Training*, are you sending it to Maule's for the summer show?'

'Not,' Clive said, 'necessarily.'

'Will you sell it to me?'

'Did our American friend, Norris, put you up to this?'

'Norris? Hell, no. Don't tell me he's after it too?'

Clive shook his head. 'No, it's for sale all right. Fifty pounds and it's all yours, Max – if you really want it, that is?'

Max Scully didn't hesitate. He stuck out his hand to seal the bargain.

'Fair price,' he said. 'When it's finished have it suitably

framed – my expense – and delivered to the London Athletic Club in Piccadilly. It's my gift to the club, though it'll be put up in Telfer's name.'

'Don't you want to see it finished first?'

'No, lad, I trust you to do an honest job.' Another handshake. 'By the way, I'm requesting grandstand seats for you and your family at the Olympic track and field events. I'll make it four, shall I?'

'Please,' Clive said.

'Tickets and my personal cheque by the week's end: all right?'

'Yes, of course. Fine, yes, fine,' Clive said. 'Max, are you sure about the painting? I mean, you didn't take much time to—'

'You're not the only one who works quickly,' Max Scully said. 'Besides, I know a winner when I see one.'

'I'm flattered, Max. Truly, I'm flattered – and very grateful.'

They moved to the door. Clive reached out and opened it.

Max adjusted his hat and put on his gloves. He looked up at Clive, frowning a little. 'Do you ever paint boats?'

'Boats?'

'Ships. Ocean liners.'

'I haven't done so, so far,' Clive said. 'Why do you ask?'

'Just curious,' Max Scully said, then, with a little click of the tongue, wished Clive goodnight and rattled off downstairs.

Anna had attended several Hyde Park rallies for the women's cause and had joined the great press of people who turned out to see the King drive in state to the opening of parliament. She had never been part of a crowd like the one that packed the stable yard behind the East End tavern, however, nor had she rubbed shoulders with such a motley assortment of men, from West End toffs to Irish horse-copers, dockers, sailors, butchers, bakers and costermongers and, she suspected, quite a few who made their living in ways too shady to contemplate.

The gates to the yard were guarded by men armed with sticks whose purpose, Anna guessed, was not to keep the mob in but to keep the coppers out. In addition, several small boys were perched precariously on the rooftops of the upper gallery to act as scouts, for the match, however well managed, would surely not be conducted according to Queensberry rules.

The heat, the smell and the din, far from causing Anna dismay, induced a visceral excitement. With Teddy close behind, she wormed through the crowd until she reached the ring. Four ropes attached to padded bollards formed a measured square, empty save for stools and wooden buckets set out in opposite corners.

She found Teddy's hand and looked up questioningly.

'It's no bare-knuckle brawl, if that's what you're thinking,' Teddy told her. 'The only reason the match is being held here and not in a licensed hall is because Michael Malone is being paid to fight.'

'What's so shameful about being paid?' Anna said. 'Boxing isn't illegal.'

'It is if you're a member of an Olympic team and, theo-retically, an amateur.'

A diminutive man in a bowler hat leaned across and said affably, 'You'd do well to keep that pretty lip o' yours buttoned when you gets 'ome, sweetheart. Wouldn't want to cause no trouble for big Mikey, would we now?'

'I wouldn't dream of it,' Anna heard herself say. 'I know the score.'

'That,' the bowler hat said, 'I doubts,' then, squinting up at Teddy, 'Who's yer money on, Yankee?'

'Malone, of course,' Teddy answered.

'Fancy another fin?'

'Too rich for my blood,' Teddy said.

'How about the lady? Looks to me like she's good for a five. How about it, sweetheart? Quick, afore the gloves go on.'

A voice in Anna's ear rasped, 'Don't trust 'im none. He'll 'ave the drawers off you, give the beggar 'alf a chance. Ain't that right, Sydney?'

'Not your drawers, Fran, since you don't wear none,' said the bowler hat.

The woman, Fran, wore a flowered cotton dress that clung to her frame like rust. Her hat was decorated with an assortment of faded ribbons and broken feathers sewn not to the crown but the brim so that when she leaned towards Anna the feathers bobbed aggressively.

'Put a 'arf crown in me 'and, love,' she said, 'an' I'll give yer three to two on Malone going darn before the eighth.'

'Clear off, you cow,' Sydney told her. 'You're queerin' me pitch.'

'You're queer enough already, Sydney,' Fran said. 'An' you ain't no patriot neither or you'd 'ave yer tin on Tommy Rogers. He'll spiflicate that Irish nobody.'

'Rogers, Rogers? He's got no more clout than a wet

'erring,' Sydney said, then ducked, or tried to, as Fran caught him by the scruff of the neck and led him off, still squabbling, into the crowd.

'I take it, Mr Norris,' Anna said, 'you've laid your wager with someone a little more reliable?'

'My bet's with Telfer Scully. Even money on Malone.'

'Why isn't Telfer here?'

'It's more than Telfer's reputation's worth to be seen in this sort of crowd.'

'But your reputation doesn't matter?'

'Not to the Olympic committee, thank God.'

'Are you a gambler, Teddy?'

'Yeah, I am.' He paused. 'But I prefer to back sure things.'

'Is Howard a sure thing?'

'I think he is.'

It was on the tip of Anna's tongue to ask if she were a sure thing too, but she thought better of it. 'The other fighter, Rogers, is he also an amateur?'

'Nope, he's a professional scrapper from up north – Liverpool, I think. Malone's keen to cut him down to size and collect a few bucks in the process. Malone's manager sets up the money fights. This, I believe, is big Mikey's third back street bout since he landed in England. If he wins a gold medal in July he'll go home to Pittsburgh famous – but fame won't feed his wife and kiddies.'

'I had no idea sport could be so corrupt.'

'It's a dirty business all right,' Teddy said. 'Does that bother you?'

'Not one little bit,' said Anna.

★

To Anna's regret the fight didn't last long. In the fifth of fifteen slated rounds the Irish-American's superior strength took its toll and the Liverpool scrapper, backed against the ropes, received a series of brutal blows that sent not just sweat but blood flicking into the crowd. Thirty seconds later Tommy Rogers's trainer threw in the sponge and led his dazed and bleeding charge away.

America's best hope for an Olympic gold medal leapt up and down and shook both fists skywards. The crowd, or most of it, jeered and drifted back into the tavern to settle scores and drown its xenophobic sorrows at the bar.

The sheer aggression of the fighters had held Anna spellbound.

Glossy with sweat, dainty leather boots dancing, they embraced like lovers, then, breaking away, threw more thudding punches whose force she'd felt like an echo on her flesh. She blew out her cheeks and gasped for breath, taken by unfamiliar sensations that, like a winded boxer, caused her to drop her guard.

Teddy took her by the hand. 'This way.'

Skirting the ring, they reached the gates and slipped out into a back street.

The sky above the buildings wasn't dark enough to show stars but the gas lamps down by the thoroughfare already glowed like fireflies in the gathering dusk. Four or five top hats and two or three posh young women were hurrying off to find a cab stand, badgered by a gang of urchins, male and female, begging for pennies.

Anna rested against the wall, a hand to her breast.

'Give me a moment, please,' she said.

'Are you unwell?'

'No. I'm – I don't know what I am. How much did you win?'

'Fifty,' Teddy said.

'Shillings?'

'Pounds.'

'You don't do things by half, do you?' Anna said.

'No,' he said. 'It does tend to be all or nothing.'

She put up no resistance when he kissed her.

He might have done more if, at that moment, the urchin pack hadn't rushed upon them. Teddy hurled a handful of coins into the gutter to keep the little devils occupied while he and Anna ran to find a taxicab.

In the back of the cab he kissed her once more.

It didn't seem to matter that her lips tasted of onions. He kissed her tenderly and passionately, which, Anna thought, as she opened her mouth to his tongue, was a whole lot more than Howard had ever done.

The lions were roaring in the Zoological Gardens as if the heat of the summer afternoon stirred memories of the African plains. The sound, faint but unmistakable, stood in contrast to the decorous cooing of the pigeons on the gravel walk who, with enquiring little nods, seemed to be begging more for attention than crumbs. 'I don't know why you bother,' Anna said. 'They never seem to know when they've had enough.'

'If you didn't know where your next meal was coming from,' Julie said, 'perhaps you'd be the same.' She crumbled up the empty paper bag and pushed it into the wire basket that hung from the back of the bench. 'Now, my dear, what's all this about? I don't believe for a moment you've dragged me all the way to Regent's Park just to watch me feed pigeons. Out with it.'

'If anyone asks, will you say I was with you last night? You owe me a favour, Julie. You know you do.'

'In other words it's my turn to provide you with an excuse for not turning up for supper at home. Where were you?'

'You wouldn't believe me if I told you.'

'Try me,' Julie said.

'I went to a boxing match in a public house in the East End.'

'Of course,' Julie said. 'Now, where were you really?'

'Teddy Norris took me.'

'Did he? To a boxing match? In the East End? Now why would he do that?'

'He thought I might enjoy it.'

'And did you?'

'Very much.'

Julie wrinkled her nose. 'Can't think why.'

'It was exciting, very exciting.'

Mockingly, Julie said, 'Oh, my goodness! What will you get up to next?'

'Will you cover for me?'

'What choice do I have? How did Teddy Norris get in touch?'

'By letter. We met at the gate of St James's Park opposite the Waterloo steps. I thought he would take me to dinner somewhere – well, discreet.'

'You certainly weren't going to bump into anyone we know in a pub in the East End,' Julie said. 'Will you see him again?'

'He wants me to.'

'Perhaps he'll take you bathing in the Serpentine next time.'

'Julie, this is not a joke.'

'No, I can see that.'

'Do you think it's wicked of me to deceive poor Howard?'

'Howard isn't poor,' Julie said, 'and he isn't your husband.'

'I do have his ring, however. That's a promise of sorts.'

'I've told you before: you're not Howard Buskin's wife. You're at perfect liberty to change your mind about marrying him.'

'Verity and Papa, they expect it of me.'

Julie threw up her hands. 'It's got nothing to do with them. Look, if you want to have an affair with Teddy Norris then have one.'

'I wasn't actually thinking of an affair.'

'What were you thinking when you tripped down the Waterloo steps with your heart beating like a drum?' Julie said.

'He's not married.'

'Who's not married?'

'Teddy.'

'Oh, God!' Julie sighed. 'Don't tell me you think he'll spirit you off to his castle on Fifth Avenue and make an honest woman out of you? Now you are being naïve. However, I'll let you into a secret: if I weren't happily married and more than somewhat pregnant I wouldn't hesitate to have an affair with Teddy Norris. Don't look so shocked. You'll be none the worse of the experience, believe me.'

'Won't Howard realise I'm not – not pure?'

'Only if you marry him.'

For a long moment Anna stared out across the park, saying nothing, then she got to her feet and offered Julie her hand. 'You're right,' she said. 'You're absolutely right. You *will* cover for me, won't you?'

'Of course, I will,' said Julie.

23

The plaster buildings of the Franco exhibition were drab in the drizzle and what was reputed to be the finest sports stadium in the world looked decidedly less than glamorous in the dismal English weather. The little canvas tent that Clive had brought to protect his sketch book proved too awkward to use and he packed it away together with the rest of his equipment just before the clouds lifted and, around three in the afternoon, the rain miraculously ceased and, half an hour prior to the arrival of the King and Queen, the sun poked out and the scene in the vast arena changed dramatically.

The cinder running track displayed all sorts of interesting shades of russet and the banked cycle track took on a velvety sheen. The contrast between the dove-grey water of the swimming bath and the vivid green of the wet grass was startling and when the diving tower was cranked, dripping, from the depths of the pond the first of the afternoon cheers went up, not only from the sparse crowds in the east stand but also from the privileged seats in the royal boxes and the flanking area, open to the skies, where pressmen, judges and sundry lesser lights, Clive's party among them, were stationed

The British championships, held in the stadium in June,

had provided Clive with a rich harvest of sketches. Squeezed between morning stints in his studio and late night shindigs at various London hotels, he had somehow managed to fill six fat notebooks and, on one dazzling evening, had dashed off a half-decent gouache from a viewpoint high up in the stadium roof.

The Scully purchase, *Athletes in Training*, had been duly framed and delivered to the Piccadilly address and hung on a panel in the foyer where even the least attentive member could hardly fail to notice it.

'I say, are you the chap who – ?'

'Yes,' modestly. 'Yes, I am.'

'Damn fine daub. Damn fine.'

Clive was confident that by the year's end he would no longer require parental subsidy and might soon be in a position to quit Faversham Garden for Hampstead and a life better suited to a successful artist with a burgeoning family.

Right now, the burgeoning family was hidden beneath a three-quarter-length cape that, given the filthy weather, was not out of place in the next-to-royal boxes. Julie had needed no persuasion to accompany her husband to the opening ceremony of the IV Olympiad, for while she might not care a fig for sport she couldn't possibly resist the allure of a royal occasion.

In watery sunshine the centre of the west stand looked wonderfully gay. It was railed with posts and white cords and smothered in marguerites and crimson ramblers. The armchairs upon which King Edward and his wife, Alexandra, would plant their regal posteriors were still empty but behind the armchairs the Princes of Greece and Sweden, their wives and children and a collection of other noble figures, including Princess Louise, occupied a double row of gilt cane chairs.

They, like everyone else, were expectantly awaiting the drums and pipes of the band of the Scots Guards that would signal Their Majesties' arrival in Wood Lane. Meanwhile there was no shortage of diversion.

The competitors' dressing rooms were situated directly beneath the west stand and a babble of voices, in umpteen languages, rose from below. Every now and then officials in frock-coats or athletes in shorts and braided jerseys would pop out to take in the scene and at one point a squad of bicyclists from the mother country wheeled out their tandems to test the traction of the track and, barked at by an officer of the IOC, promptly wheeled them in again.

Julie was lady enough to contain her excitement but young Maisie bobbed up and down like a jack-in-the-box.

It had been Clive's idea to bring the girl along. He'd said, not without a hint of sarcasm, that it was quite permissible for a woman in Julie's condition to have a lady-in-waiting in attendance, though just what use Maisie would be if her mistress went into early labour was anybody's guess.

In frock-coat and topper, Papa was almost indistinguishable from the dukes in the royal box. He'd been so eager to take up Clive's offer of a 'free ticket' that Otto had agreed to mind the shop for the afternoon and allow the King of England and Stanley Martindale, monarch and monarchist, to breathe the same damp air and applaud the British contestants together.

A skirl of bagpipe music floated over the stands.

'What's that?' Maisie cried. 'Are they 'ere at last?'

'It certainly looks like it,' said Clive.

The director of the ceremony, a certain Mr Mitchell, who, much to the annoyance of the major in charge, had been busily organising the band of the Grenadier Guards, suddenly sprinted for the tunnel, then, swerving, headed instead for the flagpole to make sure the bluejackets who would hoist the royal standard knew which ropes to pull.

On the far side of the stadium the crowd, such as it was, had its first sight of the royal party. The citizens rose in a ragged wave of hats and caps and released an uncertain cheer that was mercifully swallowed up by the playing of the National Anthem. The three rousing cheers that followed the Anthem were more enthusiastic, though Julie thought that His Majesty appeared slightly less than elated at his reception. He remained on his feet while a queue of top-hatted gentlemen formed on the steps and along the walkway to shake his hand.

'Who're they?' Maisie whispered, as if afraid that the King might hear her.

'That's Lord Desborough,' Clive said. 'He's introducing members of the International Committee and the *Comité d'Honneur.*'

'He looks bored, does our Edward,' Julie said.

'Probably is,' Clive said. 'It was touch and go whether he'd turn up at all.'

'That,' Papa Martindale said, 'is treason. Is it true?'

'So the rumours have it,' Clive said.

'I thought the King was a keen sportsman,' Julie said.

'He is, but he really prefers shooting,' said Clive.

'Perhaps 'e could shoot some Americans,' said Maisie, 'then Britain might win a few more medals. Is that Telfer Scully down there?'

Trooping into the stadium from left and right the competitors were taking up positions beyond the swimming pond, ready to advance, nation by nation, in one long line as soon as the King had done his stuff with committee men and saw fit to declare the Games open.

The sight of two thousand young men and a handful of women in the pink of condition was impressive enough to smother Julie's cynicism. Banners and flags, green, white and red; the blue cross of Sweden, the crescent of the Turks, the French *tricouleur*, the shield of Italy, a troupe of Danish girl gymnasts in short white skirts, Dutch in blue serge, Germans in black and red, Americans in mufti with badges in their caps, and the Australians, a magnificent few in shorts and green jerseys, all came marching proudly on to the field. The British contingent, headed by Oxford and Cambridge 'blues' in tailored jackets, filed on to the grass, young Telfer Scully, shoulders back and chest out, among them.

'What a pity Anna isn't here to see all this,' Papa Martindale said.

Julie stiffened. 'Oh, but she is here,' she heard herself say.

'What?' Papa said. 'Surely Howard didn't bring her?'

'No, she's with Mr Norris, Clive's American friend.'

'What's she doing with him?' said Papa.

'He had a seat to spare,' Clive put in, 'with his Harvard cronies.'

Papa scanned the crowd. 'I wonder if Anna's spotted us?'

'Somehow I doubt it,' Julie said and, to her relief, heard the crowd fall silent as King Edward stepped up to make his little speech about peace and unity among nations, and give the Games the go-ahead.

★

He had been patient and considerate the first time he'd made love to her and had taken her virginity almost, it seemed, as an afterthought. He'd drawn the curtains in the hotel room, high over Chamberlain Square, and had allowed her to take her time undressing while he'd cooled his heels in the bathroom.

Anna had felt very odd putting on a nightgown in mid-afternoon. She'd been grateful for the curtains that kept daylight out, grateful too that Teddy hadn't switched on the marble lamp on the bedside table.

When she'd called to him he'd emerged from the bathroom clad only in a dressing gown that he'd shed just before he slipped into bed. He'd lain for half a minute, his feet tickling her feet, then he'd kissed her and told her how beautiful she was and how privileged he felt to be sharing a bed with her. Then he'd stroked her stomach lightly for a while before slipping a hand between her thighs to find her moist and ready. Patient and considerate he might be, but it hadn't taken Anna long to realise that however much of a gentleman Teddy Norris might appear, when it came to making love he didn't lack experience.

Once she had shaken off her inhibitions, the afternoons they spent together in the big hotel bed brought nothing but pleasure. It was all she could do not to cry out when he thrust into her, his face buried in her hair, while she, without a shred of dignity, locked her legs about his hips and bucked beneath him.

Teddy was as ardent as ever that afternoon but as soon as it was over he gave her a little tap on the behind and told her to bathe and dress quickly, for they were due to meet the Harvard gang who had travelled up that morning from digs in Brighton to take part in the athletes' parade.

'Why are they staying in Brighton?' Anna asked.

'To keep them from the fleshpots of London.' Teddy pulled on his trousers. 'Booze and women don't add up to gold medals, and the Irish-Americans – well, you've seen one of them in action.'

'Aren't you afraid of ruining *your* health?' she said.

He grinned. 'I'm not much of a drinker – and I'm not in training.'

'I'd hate to see you if you were,' Anna said. 'Do "the Harvard gang" know you have a girl in London?'

'I don't have a girl in London.' He paused to kiss her. 'I have a woman, a beautiful, beautiful woman.'

'Don't play the fool, Teddy. You know what I mean.'

'Yes, they know I have a sweetheart and they're kinda anxious to meet you.'

'To give me the – what is it? – the once-over?'

She was still a little soggy after lovemaking and did not like to be rushed. She adjusted her nightgown, rolled from the bed and began picking up her clothes from the carpet where, in her haste, she'd tossed them.

'The question is – will I match up?' she said.

Fiddling with his collar stud, Teddy shot her a glance. 'Match up?'

'To your other girls?'

'My legions of other girls? Of course, you will. You'll top them all.'

'How many girls have you had, Teddy?'

'Hey, that's not the sort of question a fellow should answer.'

'Too many to count?'

He came across the room and took her in his arms.

'You're my girl. My only girl and the fellers will just love you.'

'Is their approval important to you, Teddy?'

'Nope, not really.'

'Just a little, or rather a lot, which is it?'

'Just a little,' he admitted. 'Can't blame me for that, can you?'

'I don't blame you for anything,' Anna said and, hugging her clothes to her chest, headed for the bathroom to dress.

The procession of athletes had been marred not only by the fact that some competitors had dared to parade in mufti but more particularly by the refusal of the American contingent to dip the Stars and Stripes before the King, an arrogant gesture that would lead to much bad blood between the two nations in the course of the next few weeks.

It was an unfortunate start to the London Olympiad and no one was unduly surprised when the King and his guests nipped off, without much pomp, at around half past five. The ground by then was less than half full. Only the heats of the 1,500 metres foot race held much interest. The Olympic record was smashed not once but twice by American runners and such fast times promised a thrilling final tomorrow evening. The heats in the swimming pond and on the cycle track were far from gripping, however, and with skies darkening and Julie grumbling about a sore backside, Mr Cavendish's party headed for the Wood Lane exit shortly before six.

It was not by chance that Teddy Norris and his friends were hanging about the gate chatting to Miss Martindale.

When Clive's party emerged from the gate Anna and Teddy broke away from the Harvard boys to greet them. If Stanley was surprised to find himself shaking the hand of a tall, elegantly dressed and very courteous young man, instead of some waddling middle-aged colonial, he hid it well.

After exchanging a few comments on the afternoon's events, which Teddy and Anna had rehearsed, he accepted receipt of his daughter and thanked Teddy for taking good care of her.

'Care to join us for supper, Mr Norris?' Papa Martindale asked.

'Kind of you, sir,' Teddy answered, 'but, as you see, my friends are waiting to carry me off to show them the sights.'

'Another time, perhaps,' said Papa.

'Sure, another time,' said Teddy.

24

The London Olympics had been brought to a close without the presence of the King who, it seemed, was still sulking over slights, real and imagined. Some minor competitions would drag on in various parts of the country but as far as Clive was concerned there was nothing now to excite his imagination. All that remained was to pick up on the promises of commissions that had come his way and buckle down to an autumn of hard work in the studio.

In spite of poor weather and a great deal of squabbling between Britain and the USA, the Games had been a great success. Clive had watched Telfer Scully fail to qualify in both broad and high jump. He'd also been present on a baking-hot afternoon when the little Italian confectioner, Dorando Pietri, had staggered into the arena ahead of Johnny Hayes, an almost unknown American, and, with quite a bit of help from British officials, had made it across the finishing line of the marathon before collapsing; yet another instance, so the Yankees claimed, of blatant anti-Americanism and one for which the unfortunate Theodore Cook had been obliged to issue an official apology.

One visit to the Games had been enough for Julie but Otto and Stanley had enjoyed Clive's hospitality on several occasions. Maisie had been in the vast and vociferous crowd when her hero, Jock Halswelle, had survived a bumping, boring, all-in scrap with the Americans in a contentious semi-final of the 400 metres – later declared void – and had hurled some very salty insults at the Yankees while Clive, rather half-heartedly, had tried to shut her up.

Clive was nursing a whisky and soda at the bar in the London Athletic Club and waiting for Max Scully to join him, when he caught the first whisper of the scandal that would come to haunt the Martindales. Somewhere off to his left a voice said, 'I guess Teddy might hang on to her if she had a little more class.'

Clive pricked up his ears.

'Think what his old man would say if Teddy turned up with some English floozie on his arm. You know what old Norris thinks of the English.'

'Florence won't much like it either. Fiery Flo will have Teddy's nuts if he ditches her for some piece of baggage he's picked up on his travels.'

The voices were pitched low but the accents were unmistakably American.

Clive discreetly observed the speakers in the mirror behind the bar.

They were dressed for the opera and, in spite of their tanned complexions, looked at ease in formal wear. Whether or not they were Harvard alumni Clive had no way of knowing. They were obviously taking advantage of the temporary membership the London Athletic offered to select foreign visitors. They certainly looked at home propping up the bar and, oblivious to Clive's flapping ears, continued to converse.

'Who is this female, anyhow?'

'Anna somebody.'

'I assume she doesn't have royal connections?'

'No, but she is a peach, a real peach – and she's got it bad for Teddy.'

'Already had a taste of the legendary appendage, you reckon?'

'Be surprised if she hasn't. This kid would tempt a eunuch.'

'Is Teddy sailing home with us?'

A shrug: 'Couldn't say.'

Clive was tempted to corner the pair but with Max due at any moment, he had no wish to make a scene. He watched the couple pay the bill and head off towards the foyer, then, shakily, downed the remains of his whisky and soda.

Max Scully clapped a hand to his shoulder.

'You look like you could use another of those,' he said.

'I really and truly could,' said Clive.

She'd steeled herself to speak out, had even rehearsed the speech as she'd lain in bed that morning, but somehow it didn't come out as she'd intended.

'Frankly, Teddy,' she said, 'it isn't good enough.'

'I thought you enjoyed it.'

'I don't mean that – I mean, well, us.'

Teddy opened the curtains. Rain drummed on the window glass, a hard rain that flooded the guttering high up on the hotel roof and sent noisy little cascades down the face of the building.

'What's wrong with us?' Teddy said.

'You'll be going home soon, won't you?'

'I will have to go home eventually.'

'Take me with you,' Anna said.

He guided her to the bed, seated her on the edge of the mattress and, sitting too, put an arm about her. 'I can't just steal you away from your family.'

'You've done this sort of thing before, haven't you? Perhaps you even have a wife waiting for you in New York.'

'Hell, no,' he said, 'I'm not that much of a cad. I love you, Anna. I love you just as much as you love me. As soon as I've gotten my old man used to the idea, I'll come back for you.'

'Who do you take me for, Teddy? Madam Butterfly?'

'I don't know what you're talking about.'

'Puccini: the opera. One fine day and all that.'

'I don't want to let you go,' Teddy Norris said. 'But, really, I do have a lot of things to clear up before I can take on a wife.'

Anna rose from the bed. 'I'm not the fool you take me for, Teddy. I know what I am to you or, rather, what I've been to you. You're going to make all sorts of promises you've no intention of keeping just to stop me creating a fuss. Well, you're not the only one with responsibilities.'

He nodded. 'Howard?'

'Yes, Howard.'

'You're not in love with Howard.' He paused. 'Are you?'

'I'm engaged to him, in case you hadn't noticed.'

He said, 'Have you spoken to Howard about us?'

'I haven't spoken to anyone about us except, as you know, my sister. In any case, what would you have me say to Howard? Would you have me tell him we've been . . .' She couldn't bring herself to say the word, as if the word were more awful than the act it described. 'You know what I mean,' she concluded lamely.

'Let's go talk to Howard,' Teddy said.

'Howard's in Devon, painting.'

'All right,' Teddy said. 'Let's go talk to your papa.'

'And say what?'

'That we're in love and hope to marry,' Teddy said. 'Come on, we'll go see him right now. What are you afraid of? I thought you said you loved me.'

'I did. I do. I need just a little more time to get used to the idea.'

'See,' he said, 'you don't know whether you really love me, or if you just enjoy having sex with me.'

She walked to the window and looked out at the clouds spinning across the sky. She could just discern the face of Big Ben far off through a gap in the rooftops. A torrent of water from the gutters splashed suddenly against the pane. Teddy came up behind her and put an arm around her waist.

'You see, darling,' he said, 'I'm not the only one who needs time to make things right. Promise you'll wait for me. That's all I ask.'

'Yes, I'll wait for you,' Anna said, 'but not for ever.'

'I wouldn't expect you to.' He kissed her lightly on the lips. 'Now that's settled, darling, shall we go?'

'Go?' said Anna. 'Go where?'

'In search of lunch,' Teddy said, smiling.

Clive was well aware that both he and his dear, foolish, pregnant wife had been complicit in Anna's downfall. The loss of Anna's virtue was far from the only thing on his mind, however. Max Scully had made him an offer that would take him away from home for at least part of the year.

'Belfast?' Julie said. 'Are you suggesting we live in Belfast?'

'Of course not,' Clive said. 'I wouldn't dream of living in Belfast.'

'Isn't that what Scully expects of you?'

'Max only expects me to deliver eight or ten paintings, recording stage by stage the building of White Star's Olympic-class ocean liners which, he tells me, will be the largest ships in the world. How I go about it is my business.'

'Why has he chosen you?'

'He likes my work. He thinks I'll capture the scale and grandeur of the ships. However, it does mean I'll have to spend time away from home. The liners are being built by Harland and Wolff in their Belfast yard. Didn't you hear Max bragging about them during dinner at Rules?'

'If I did,' said Julie, 'I've forgotten. How many ships?'

'Three. The first keel will be laid in December.'

'So you're leaving me with a new baby in the middle of winter to trot off to Ireland? Ireland of all places. My God!'

'Perhaps Anna will come over to keep you company.'

'Anna has her own life to lead.'

'Yes,' Clive said. 'She does, doesn't she?'

'How much will these paintings fetch?'

'Thousands,' Clive said. 'Industrial landscapes are boardroom treasures.'

'You said much the same thing about sporting pictures.'

'True,' Clive admitted, 'but I'm not stuck in a rut, like Howard. I can turn my hand to anything. The White Star Company is owned by Pierpoint Morgan and managed by Bruce Ismay. The board has more millionaires on it than you can shake a stick at. Once I get a foot in that door there'll be no looking back. Besides, we all have to move on.'

'Are you moving on from *me*?'

'No, Julie, I'm not some wealthy American with an eye to the main chance.'

'He told you, didn't he?'

'If you mean Teddy Norris, I haven't seen him for weeks.'

'Who told you? Was it Anna?'

'So it is true,' Clive said. 'She has been having an affair with Norris and you've been covering up for her.'

'She did it for me – for us – didn't she?'

'That was quite different. I married you.'

'What makes you suppose Teddy Norris won't marry Anna?'

'All right, no need to fly off the handle. I'm only repeating what I've heard.'

'Do you mean to say people are gossiping about my sister?'

'It's all over London,' Clive said. 'Norris is famous for his conquests.'

'Oh, God!' said Julie. 'What if it gets back to Papa?'

'What if it gets back to Howard?'

'You've certainly changed your tune,' Julie said. 'You were all for throwing Anna at Teddy Norris when it suited you. You're as much to blame as I am.'

'I don't think anyone's to blame,' Clive said. 'Anna's not the sweet little girl you like to pretend she is. She's just as predatory as he is.'

To his surprise, Julie nodded. 'It's true. All she lacks is experience.'

'Now, on the other matter . . .'

'What other matter?'

'Scully's offer.'

'Didn't you give him an answer on the spot?' said Julie.

'I wanted to consult you first.'

'Tell me again,' she said, 'how much will these paintings earn us?'

'Thousands,' said Clive, 'but the earning thereof will take me away from home quite a bit.'

'I think I can put up with that – especially if we're living in Hampstead.'

'Let's not get ahead of ourselves, dearest,' Clive said.

'Why not?' said Julie. 'You do it all the time.'

The desk clerk, an elderly chap with a dapper moustache and sleeked-down hair, had seen it all before. He sighed, reached behind him, whipped the letter from the pigeonhole and, elbows on the counter, whispered, 'Miss Martindale, is it?'

Anna looked up. 'Yes.'

'This is for you, I believe. From the American gentleman.'

'Thank you,' Anna said. 'When did Mr Norris check out?'

'Last evening before dinner.'

'Ah!' Anna said, as if that explained everything. 'I assume he took his luggage with him?'

The clerk hesitated before he answered. 'Everything, miss. I'm sorry.'

She went out into the square. Leaning on the railings, she opened the letter.

'*My Dearest, Darling,*' it began, and rambled on over three pages of hotel stationery, three pages of flowery prose which boiled down to: *It was fun while it lasted and I'll never forget you. Bye-bye*. No mention of 'paving the way'. No promise that he would return for her one fine day. No apology. No forwarding address.

She folded the letter and returned it to the envelope.

She pinched the envelope between fingers and thumbs and tore it into small pieces which she dumped in the nearest litter basket before she set off for home.

She was halfway down Regent Street before she burst into tears.

PART THREE

Troubled Waters
1910

25

At last little Maisie Fellowes had a man of her own. The fact that he was only two feet and eight inches in height and weighed less than thirty pounds was neither here nor there; from the moment she'd taken him into her arms she was his to command.

Fortunately Master Walter Cavendish was just as enchanted by his nursemaid as she was by him. He would stretch out his tiny fists, explore the landscape of her face and chuckle as if he couldn't quite believe his luck. He was a good-natured baby, not given to tantrums or noisy demands for attention, perhaps – as his father pointed out – because he'd never known its lack. Come October, however, Master Walter would no longer have things all his own way. The bump in Mummy's tummy would turn into a sister or brother and his brief time as the only star in the Cavendish firmament would be over once and for all.

Maisie wasn't Julie's idea of an ideal nursemaid. She'd envisaged someone more akin to Nanny Cairns who had been as tall as Nelson's column and had worn a starched apron that offered no comfort. No starched apron for Maisie Fellowes, then, no awful green serge uniform. At Clive's insistence Maisie was allowed to be just Maisie and when she bowled out into the park with Walter in the perambulator no one, least of all the other nursemaids, could be quite sure of her status – which was just how Maisie liked it.

Babies, Clive said, thrived on routine and Maisie had been raised on routine. She took pleasure in bathing, changing and, in due course, weaning the little mite and, unlike Julie, seemed to know by instinct what was best for her precious charge.

It wasn't until young Walter found his voice that the flaw in the 'Maisie arrangement' showed itself.

'Cockney,' Julie said. 'My God, he's speaking Cockney.'

'I don't know how you can tell,' said Clive. 'It sounds like nothing on earth to me. Anyhow, Maisie doesn't speak proper Bow Bells.'

'Don't you start,' said Julie. 'It'll be rhyming slang next.'

'Nuffink wrong wiff a bit uv the old "apples and pears".' Clive knelt on the carpet and addressed the question to his son. 'Is there, me lad?'

'Ain't nuffink wrong wiff it at all, Pa.' Walter appeared to answer in a high-pitched voice that caused his mother's mouth to pop open.

'Wha – what did he just say?'

'Awright, Ma, keep yer bleedin' 'air on,' Clive squeaked while Walter rolled about chuckling at Dad's little joke.

'You – you thing,' Julie said and, quite gently, lobbed a cushion at her husband's head, a cushion that almost before it struck the floor had become a bone over which big dog and little pup wrestled for possession.

'Clive,' Julie said, 'do you *have* to leave tomorrow?'

'I'm afraid so, darling.'

'How long will you be gone?'

'A week should do it.'

'A week,' said Julie. 'A whole week.'

'Be back before you know it,' said Clive and, holding the cushion to his stomach, let his son butt against it like a little ram.

The proximity of the moor offered no more comfort in summer than it did in winter. Anna had spent the morning in the library reading Mr Maugham's slum novel, *Liza of Lambeth*, and the early part of the afternoon in the garden dozing in the shade of the awning that Howard had had the servants erect to keep his little wifey cool.

Whether in London or Devon, keeping his little wifey cool had become something of an obsession with Howard, one to which Clive Cavendish and Edgar Banbury – 'Passing through, my boy, just passing through' – attributed the changes in his technique. Gone were the taut draughtsmanship and meticulous brushwork that had distinguished the canvases of his bachelor years; he painted now in great thick slabs of contrasting colour and his gigantic Dartmoor landscapes, though still devoid of figures, had all the gaudiness of Eastern bazaars.

The radical new style might endear him to French Fauves but it was far too beastly for English taste. In fact, only blackmail by golden boy Clive Cavendish had persuaded Maule's to take Howard on and hang his latest work side by side with the handful of the early self-portraits that Howard had consented to release.

One by one the smaller pictures had been sold but the lurid canvases Howard had produced in the past year were stacked in Maule's storeroom safe from moth, mouse and mould, where, Howard cheerfully predicted, they would probably remain for the rest of the bloody century.

It wasn't only his approach to painting that had altered. Howard, too, had changed. In London he was still sufficiently civilised to wear suits but in Devon, where he spent most of his time, he reverted to what Verity euphemistically called 'rusticity'. He purchased a stout two-wheeled cart and a shaggy, bad-tempered pony and with a haunch of beef or a rack of lamb wrapped in brown paper and a flagon of rough cider in his satchel would ride off into the blue every morning, easel and canvas rattling in the back of the cart.

Where he went and who, if anyone, he met remained a mystery, though Anna liked to imagine him chasing across the moor, like a character from a Brontë novel, in search of an unsuspecting country lass upon whom to expend his passion.

He certainly wasn't expending his passion, not one drop of it, on her.

On honeymoon in Paris he'd made one futile attempt at penetration, an attempt that had sprinkled her parts with more of the sticky stuff but failed to reach inside her. She'd done her best to wheedle him back to bed but he'd spent the night crouched on a chair by the hotel window and next morning had packed up and whisked her back to England.

Howard might give an appearance of rough-hewn masculinity but she, Anna, knew better. No matter how imaginatively she strove to rouse his interest his response was always the same and when, in the early months of bed-sharing, she'd inadvertently draped an arm about him he'd struck out at her with the flat of his hand as if he were swatting away an insect.

After half a year of tense, bruising, sexless nights Anna had suggested they sleep in separate rooms, an arrangement that astonished poor Verity.

'Why wouldn't you want to sleep with your husband?'

'Because,' Anna answered, 'he snores.'

'Clarence snored,' Verity said, 'and it didn't bother me.'

'Well, it bothers me,' Anna told her. 'There's no scarcity of empty rooms. I'd be obliged if you'd arrange for me to have one of my own.'

'What does Howard have to say to it?'

'Ask him.'

'If that's what she wants,' Howard said, 'so be it.'

Next time Otto came to visit, Verity buried her head in his chest and, sobbing, told him what had happened. Ever tactful, Otto assured her that snoring was the reef upon which many a marriage had foundered and that sleeping apart did not exclude intimacy and, indeed, might make things more exciting.

'She should be suckling a baby by now,' Verity said. 'You don't think there's something wrong with her, do you?'

'With Anna? I doubt it.'

'Perhaps we should we call in a doctor?'

'It's far too early for that,' Otto said. 'You don't want to scare the girl, or, worse, burden her with guilt.'

Otto had sold his little cottage in Brampton and given up the life of a fancy-free bachelor. He spent weekends and holidays 'relaxing' in Foxhailes where, nothing loath, he sometimes shared a bed with Verity.

It would have suited Anna better if her uncle had married

her mother-in-law, for then she might have been able to persuade Howard to decamp from his mama's house and set up in a place of their own. She even feigned envy of Julie's new home in West Heath Road, a lovely little detached villa with eighteenth-century staircases and twentieth-century plumbing, though, deep down, she didn't much care where she lived, since any house with Howard in it would never really be home.

At night, alone in bed, she fizzed and fumed at the trap in which she'd put herself. The information that came her way via Clive only fed her bitterness: Teddy Norris's Viaduct Gallery written up in *Art Today*; Teddy Norris's father nominated to the board of the Metropolitan; Teddy Norris elected to this council or that committee. Never a word, however, about Teddy Norris betting on back-yard boxing matches or Teddy Norris deflowering English girls in shady hotel rooms.

Bored and listless, Anna drifted through each day, waiting for night when she was free to remember how Teddy had made love to her and to tease herself with sad, solitary simulations of desire.

In the sunlit garden, in the shade of the awning, she lay like a corpse, eyes closed, only the cooing of wood pigeons and, distantly, the chuckling of grouse to remind her that she was still alive.

Otto and Verity had ridden into Exeter on the motor bus; a long day trip.

Howard had gone off to convene with nature in the lofty wilderness where he would gnaw on his rack of lamb, slosh down cider and, for all she knew, bathe nude in the pools of Bishop's Brook.

In ten minutes or half an hour – she'd lost track of time – a maid would trot down from the house and ask if she wished to partake of tea. She would stir herself, shake her head, force a smile and thank the girl, then sink into lassitude again and like an old, old woman give herself over to reverie.

She couldn't be sure which variation in the familiar drone of the moor's edge caused her to open her eyes. He was still too far away to cast a shadow.

He approached with an easy, loping stride that made him seem weightless.

She didn't flinch, didn't blink in case he vanished again.

He ducked his head under the scalloped edge of the awning.

'Anna,' he said. 'Darling.'

'Go away, Teddy,' she said. 'Please, please, go away.'

It didn't take long for Belfast to cast its spell on Clive. The energy of the city on the Lagan was addictive. The pubs were noisy, the streets crowded, the chat dominated by arguments about Home Rule. Men who seemed incapable of standing up without a wall to support them could quote you verbatim Carson's last Westminster speech in defence of Unionism and others, snarling, would invoke the sainted name of Parnell as if the great man were still alive and might come riding over the Queen's Bridge at any moment at the head of a Republican army.

On his first visit Clive had found rooms in a hotel, the Cromarty, not far from the Northern Railway station. His bedroom window looked out over timber ponds, engineering works, docks and shipyards, a vast panorama that had had him reaching instantly for his sketch book as if the sprawling industrial landscape might slip its moorings and be gone before morning.

The Cromarty was owned by a Scotsman who, together with his sons and grandsons, was a member of the Orange Order. Clive was grilled on the nature of his allegiances from time to time and, as an Englishman, treated with some suspicion. Relations had warmed considerably when he'd presented the family with a head and shoulders chalk drawing – framed by Martindale of the Strand, no less – of the oldest granddaughter who thereafter had wafted in and out of his room and gave him the sort of eye that might have tempted him to stray if he hadn't been resolutely married to Julie.

It wasn't the winsome dark-eyed granddaughter that lured him back to the banks of the Lagan, though, but the challenge of rendering in paint the White Star's great iron monsters, shrouded in scaffolding, rising, frame by frame, from the slipways. He had no interest in the technical aspects of marine construction. He drew and painted the rigid geometric shapes as freely as if they were beanstalks. He made endless rapid oil sketches of men perched on airy beams, clustered, coven-like, over braziers and dwarfed by gargantuan bits of machinery. He toted the sketches home by steamer and railway train to the studio in his house in Hampstead, where, working with new-found confidence, he put all the pieces together.

'It don't look like no boat to me.' Maisie juggled Walter from one arm to the other. 'Does it look like a boat to you, sweetheart?'

Walter was more interested in getting his hands on those

lovely fat tubes of paint that his daddy had temptingly laid out on the table and only Maisie's restraining arms prevented him sliding to the floor and wreaking havoc.

'Much as I value your opinion, Maisie, I hope you're not going to linger.' Clive reached out a forefinger and dabbed a tiny smudge of cobalt on to his son's cheek. 'Well, Big Chief Cavendish, are you behaving yourself?'

'Ow!' Walter answered obligingly, and began to struggle again.

'I'd better get 'im out of 'ere,' Maisie said. 'By the by, you're wanted downstairs. You've got visitors.'

'Visitors?' Clive groused. 'Who the devil's calling at this early hour?'

'Mr an' Mrs Buskin,' Maisie said. 'An' another chap.'

'Another chap? Didn't he give a name?'

'Nope,' Maisie said. 'But judgin' by the way 'e talks he's a Yankee.'

The drudgery of sustaining a sexless marriage had hardened Anna's heart. She wouldn't have cared if Howard had ridden his stupid little cart into the Foxhailes yard that golden afternoon a week ago and caught her with her skirts up and her drawers down. The stable was a wonderfully incongruous place in which to commit her first act of adultery, with Howard's easel looking on, his gaudy paintings, some still wet, ranged round, a mess of rags, brushes and twisted tubes of paint bouncing on the table top while dear, darling, ardent Teddy thrust into her.

'How long will you be in London?' Clive asked.

'A couple of weeks, three at most,' Teddy answered.

'A flying visit,' said Clive. 'And its purpose?'

'I've been in France,' Teddy said evasively. 'Paris, mainly.'

'Where, I believe,' Howard put in, 'every oyster-seller in the city has bought himself a set-square to turn out Cubist masterpieces. You'll pay a pretty penny for anything decent now, Norris. No more twenty pound bargains, I fear.'

Anna had hoped to slip back to London alone but Howard had insisted on accompanying her. A few days later, at Teddy's invitation, the three had met for lunch in the opulent dining room of the Strand Palace, a stone's throw from Ledbetter Street. Howard had amused himself by needling his host throughout the meal and now, in Julie's drawing room, he was at it again.

'Did you visit Matisse?' Clive asked. 'I hear he has a grand new house at Issy and the Bernheims have contracted to take everything he produces. Is it true?'

'He's not quite as well off as the peons choose to believe,' Teddy said, 'but, yes, it seems Henri is coming into his own at last.'

'Much like you, Clive, eh?' said Howard. 'Big house, big reputation. Not sure I'd want to squander my talent painting nothing but boats, though.'

'No worse than painting Dartmoor landscapes day after day,' said Anna.

Howard conceded the point with an unapologetic nod.

Since the visitors hadn't shown much interest in admiring her son, Julie had instructed Maisie to take Walter away. It was, Anna supposed, too close to noon to offer coffee and not close enough to one o'clock to coax cook into dishing up an impromptu lunch for five.

'Norris wants to see what you've been up to,' Howard said. 'Your boats.'

'Ships,' Julie corrected him. 'Ships, Howard.'

Julie and Anna were seated on a chintz-covered settee but the men, all three, remained on their feet. Clive was clad in a plaid shirt and baggy corduroys while Howard, in suit and waistcoat, looked more like a stockbroker than a painter. Only Teddy, in a linen suit, embodied the essence of summer. He appeared so cool and unruffled that just looking at him made Anna shiver.

'Come now, Clive,' Howard went on, 'you're not going to pull a Buskin on us' – he laughed at his little joke, though no one else did – 'and pretend you're too bashful to show us what you have on the stocks. On the stocks?' He laughed again. 'Good one, eh?'

'All right.' Clive sighed. 'If you insist. The studio's this way.'

'Anna,' Howard said, 'are you coming?'

'Later, perhaps,' Anna answered. 'Later,' and, with some relief, watched the men trail out of the drawing room.

The little creature that snuggled in Julie's womb had become restless of late. She or he gave her gyp when she remained in one position for too long. She'd survived one pregnancy, though, and was sure she'd survive another. Nothing came as much of a surprise this time and a bit of nudging and lurching from Cavendish minor indicated an active baby, so the doctor said. She did rather resent the rude noises that emanated from her body, however, especially the fact that wind would break, upwards and downwards, without a moment's notice; an unladylike phenomenon that caused the servants to wrinkle their noses and look pained.

Only Maisie was forward enough comment and, covering

Walter's ears, would say, 'Naughty Mummy. Naughty Mummy,' and laugh in a manner to which Julie couldn't possibly object.

As soon as the men left, she hoisted herself to her feet and, hands on hips, took a little toddle about the drawing room.

Anna watched, frowning.

'Are you in pain?'

'No,' Julie said, 'just stretching.'

'You're very large.'

Julie looked down at the dumpling-sack she carried before her.

'So I should be,' she said. 'I'm due in seven weeks.'

'Will Clive be here? I mean, in London.'

'I certainly hope so.'

'And if he's not?'

'We'll just have to manage without him.'

Julie lowered herself into an armchair and spread her knees to support the weight of her stomach. 'Now,' she said, 'tell me – what's going on? What's Teddy doing here? Have you started up again?'

Anna let out a little wry *huh*. 'Of course, we have.'

'He broke your heart once and he'll do it again.'

'I'm having sex with him and, if you must know, enjoying every minute of it. When he sails off into the blue once more – and he will: oh, yes, I know he will – I'll thank him kindly and wave a fond farewell.'

Julie shook her head. 'You're being used, Anna, horribly used.'

'Not by Howard, I'm not.'

'Explain yourself.'

'What is there to explain? All that stuff about deceiving

Howard on our wedding night – absolutely, totally unnecessary,' Anna said. 'Howard has never made love to me.'

'What?' said Julie sceptically 'Not even once?'

'Not once,' said Anna.

'Have you talked it over? Has he told you why?'

'He can't, that's all.'

'Can't?' A little eruption of gas rose into Julie's throat. She covered her mouth with her fist. 'I find it hard to believe that when you're in bed together you can't interest Howard in – well, you know what I mean.'

'We're never in bed together. We have separate rooms. Two years, virtually two years of marriage and I'm still technically a virgin.'

'Hardly,' said Julie. 'You weren't a virgin when you married him. What does Howard make of your friendship with Teddy Norris?'

'I think he's pleased to have another man do to me what he can't do himself.'

'That,' said Julie, 'is utter nonsense. I can't say I blame you for being glad to see Teddy again but to suggest that Howard's colluding in your affair is a step too far even for you, Anna.'

'Really?' Anna said. 'In that case why does Howard let me go out for hours on end without so much as a raised eyebrow or a question as to where I've been? He keeps Verity from badgering me too. Makes excuses on my behalf. Howard knows what's going on. In fact, I'm sure he's encouraging me.'

'Is Howard that perverse?'

'Oh, he's perverse all right, take my word on it,' Anna said.

'Does he beat you?'

'He doesn't hurt me, if that's what you mean.'

'Anna, does he beat you?'

Her sister sighed. 'Sometimes I almost wish he would.'

'Oh, this is bad, very bad,' said Julie. 'Have you spoken to anyone about it?'

'Like who?'

'Uncle Otto, for instance.'

'I'm not spiteful enough to talk to anyone about Howard's weakness, no matter how much I despise him for it. Swear to me on the life of your child that you won't say a word to anyone, Julie.'

'You have my promise,' Julie said, though there was something comical in the notion of a beautiful woman marrying a man to whom intercourse was anathema. Seated in her elegant drawing room, heavy with child, she felt proud that her husband was not only talented but normal. 'You could sue Howard for divorce, I suppose,' she went on. 'Or – what's that other thing? – an annulment.'

'Can you imagine the sort of dirty laundry that would be washed in court if I went to law,' said Anna. 'No, I'm happy enough to take what I can from Teddy and give Howard what he wants.'

'And what *does* Howard want?'

'He wants to please his mama by giving her a grandchild,' Anna said.

'Don't tell me you're pregnant?'

'No, but at the rate Teddy's going it may not be long before I am.'

Julie covered her stomach with her forearms and blew out a breath. 'Surely Howard will realise that the baby isn't his.'

'He'll know, and I'll know – but no one else will.'

'He'll wind up hating it, you know.'

'Which,' Anna said, 'will make a nice change from hating me.'

'This is wrong, all wrong.'

'Is it? I really don't see why,' Anna said. 'Actually, I'm satisfying the needs of two men simultaneously. Rather clever of me, don't you think?'

'No,' said Julie. 'I think it's very dangerous.'

'What a prude you are,' said Anna, rising. 'Now, dearest, since you haven't offered to feed us, I do believe I'll trot up to the studio, find my menfolk and persuade one or other of them to take me out to lunch.'

'Or both,' said Julie bleakly.

'Yes,' Anna said, 'or both.'

Puffing on a cigar, Howard dithered by the corkboard upon which Clive had arranged his sketches in a sequence that added cohesion to the final composition. He had deliberately kept his brushwork loose to suggest an organic element in the shapes of the great half-built ships caged in their gantries and to avoid the static, over-detailed approach that leached life from so many maritime paintings. Max had already earmarked the painting for presentation to Lord Pirrie, one of several influential gentlemen with whom Max hoped to curry favour, so, Clive told himself, it didn't really matter what Howard, or Norris, thought of it.

'How many of these damned things have you knocked off?' Howard asked.

'Five,' Clive answered.

'All sold?' said Teddy Norris.

'I have a patron,' Clive said. 'I paint for him exclusively.'

'I hope,' Teddy Norris said, 'he pays you well.'

'He does,' said Clive. 'Very well.'

'Are you free to market your sketches?'

'Yes,' Clive said, 'but I've no intention of doing so.'

'Why not?'

'They don't do justice to the subject.'

Teddy stretched out a hand and held it an inch from the canvas as if to test the picture's worth by its temperature. 'Interesting work, Cavendish. I'd very much like to buy one for my collection.'

'Your gallery, you mean?' said Howard.

'Yeah, my gallery,' Teddy said. 'You'd sell well in America, Clive. The new realism is much in vogue.'

'The *new* realism,' said Howard. 'Whatever happened to the old realism?'

'Come over some time,' Teddy went on, unperturbed. 'Stay a while. Bring the family. Why don't you come, too, Howard? Ship over twenty canvases apiece and let me mount a show for you. It's a small gallery but we do have some forward-thinking clients who like to spend money.'

'Not interested,' said Howard.

'And you, Clive?' Teddy said.

'Do you really like my pictures?'

'I like this picture.' Teddy returned to the canvas, 'It's the White Star's new Royal Mail steamer we've heard so much about, is it not?'

'The *Olympic*,' Clive said. 'She's due for launch in October.'

'And this vessel in the background?'

'Works' number 401,' Clive said. 'She'll be put in the water next May.'

'Haven't they settled on a name for her yet?' Howard asked.

'Oh, yes,' Clive answered. 'They're calling her *Titanic*.'

26

Clive lay on his back, arms raised above his head as if he were stretching or, Julie thought, surrendering to the fact that she took up so much of the bed he was unable to sleep comfortably on his side.

'Showing in New York wouldn't be such a bad idea, would it?' he said. 'We could go over for a few weeks, see the sights.'

'Go when?'

'Not right now, of course. I've too much to do in Belfast. Max has been very generous and I wouldn't dream of letting him down.' He paused, awaiting a response. When she said nothing, he went on, 'In a couple of years, after the liners are fitted out and in service and my work's finished – by that time Jemima . . .'

'Jemima?'

'Or Jeremiah, as the case may be.'

She dug an elbow into his ribs. 'Be serious.'

He snuggled against her, placed a hand gently on her breast and nuzzled her cheek. 'In a couple of years she – or he – will be old enough to travel. Crossing the Atlantic on a super-liner will be an unforgettable experience, something Walter will remember for the rest of his life.'

'And when we get there?'

'Norris will look after us.'

'Do you trust Teddy Norris?' Julie said.

'Yes, of course, I do. I mean, he may go on rather about his friendship with French artists – I don't believe for a moment Matisse regards him as a "buddy" – but he does know his art from his elbow, and he is rich.'

'So you'd trust a man who's having an affair with my sister?'

Clive sat up. 'I thought that was all over.'

'Well, it isn't,' Julie said. 'I gather Teddy more or less stepped off the boat straight into Anna's arms. No point in being indignant, Clive. If I recall you were quite keen on throwing Teddy and Anna together.'

'That was before she became Howard's wife.'

'Yes, it is different now, isn't it?' Julie sighed. 'I thought Teddy would return to New York and Anna would never see him again.'

'At least he didn't leaving her nursing a baby.'

'One thing's for sure,' Julie said, 'she won't be bearing a child to Howard.'

'You've lost me completely,' said Clive.

'Howard can't.'

'Can't what?'

'Perform. Function. Can't, or won't, have intercourse.'

'I don't believe a word of it.' Clive hesitated. 'Mark you, Banbury did say something I found rather odd. Edgar wasn't flush with details but I got the impression it involved a girl in Paris.'

'A prostitute?' said Julie.

'Probably.'

'You've seen Howard undressed. Is he – I mean, normal down there?'

'He has everything a man should have, though he is rather small.'

'How small?'

'Very small.'

'Microscopic?'

'Julie!'

'I'm only trying to determine if Anna's telling fibs.'

'She's not telling fibs about doing it with Norris, is she?'

'No,' said Julie. 'She's far too self-satisfied to be lying abut that. She has a plan, you see, an insane notion that Teddy will impregnate her and Howard will be forced to acknowledge the child or risk having his "condition" exposed.'

'I'd no idea Anna was so vindictive.'

'You know what they say about a woman scorned,' Julie said. 'It must be ten times worse when the man who does the scorning is your husband.'

'It occurs to me that if Norris takes Anna back to New York Howard might actually be relieved.'

'Somehow I don't think that's going to happen,' Julie said.

'Which leaves us with the question of what're we going to do about it?'

'You could tell Howard.'

'Oh, no, not me. I don't want my head bashed, thank you all the same.'

'Or you could threaten Teddy.'

'Threaten him with what? I don't know him that well.'

'What *do* you know about him, Clive?'

'Only what I've read and what Theo Cook tells me. Norris's father is the nineteenth-richest man in America, apparently. He made his pile in iron and steel, in cahoots with Andrew Carnegie, but he is a genuine art collector. Teddy's a partner in a gallery in New York that his old man helps finance.'

'I wonder why Teddy doesn't have a wife.'

'He's promised to one of the Gunderson girls, so Theo says. That's the same Gunderson family who owns half of Manhattan. Of course, it may be one of those arranged things, to bring two wealthy families together,' Clive said. 'But if you think Teddy Norris is desperately in love with your sister and that true love will find a way, think again. There's no romance there, Julie. Teddy Norris is sowing his wild oats while he can and Anna is revelling in what she hasn't been getting at home. I assume she is – revelling, I mean?'

'I'm afraid she is,' Julie said. 'I'm in no position to deny my sister her share of happiness. I'm just afraid she might push Howard too far.'

'Perhaps Howard wants her to have a child.'

'By another man? That's disgusting.' Julie eased on to her side and propped an elbow on her husband's chest. 'Anyway, I'm glad it's not your problem, darling.'

'The question remains,' said Clive 'what *are* we going to do about it?'

'Nothing. Let it run its course, I say.'

'And if a kiddie does come out of it?'

'Knowing Anna, she might even get away with it.'

Clive snorted. 'Unless she calls him Teddy, of course.'

It galled Stanley that quantity rather than quality was required by photographers and print shops these days and that Martindale's had become more of a factory than a supplier of hand-wrought frames. Otto's latest money-spinner involved selling boxes of polished wooden strips, complete with an edging tool, screws, mounts and, in the deluxe version, a sheet of glass that could be cut to size. His hunch that knocking up your own frames would appeal to lower-class customers, where every man fancied himself a craftsman, had proved right and Martindale's framing kits were fairly flying off the shelves.

Now that his daughters were married and Otto spending much of his time hobnobbing with the widow Millar, Stan was often at a loose end. He turned up regularly for Sunday lunch at Julie's new house in Hampstead and was easily persuaded to stay for dinner, particularly if Clive was detained in Ireland. Walter was the magnet, of course, for Stanley and his grandson got on famously. Casting aside his natural reserve, Grandpa Martindale was more than willing to go down on all fours and let the boy ride him round the lawn or, on damp afternoons, play noisy games of hide and seek indoors.

It was a different story in Anna's house which, strictly speaking, wasn't Anna's house at all. The Holland Park mansion was Verity Millar's property and Otto's 'territory' and it made Stan uncomfortable to watch his brother-in-law fawn over the widow Millar. Otto's vow not to become a 'kept man' didn't prevent him enjoying Verity's hospitality, it seemed. He returned the compliment by purchasing good seats at London's most talked-about shows, taking her to supper and sleeping with her now and then. In London and in Devon, he provided the widow with an arm to cling to, a shoulder to lean on and an ear to bend, for which items of support Verity was exceedingly grateful.

It was probably just as well that Stanley wasn't dining chez Millar that Sunday evening, for, after a morning visit to church and an afternoon wriggling under her Yankee lover in his room in the bustling Strand Palace Hotel, Anna had invited Teddy to dine in Holland Park.

'I hope I'm not intruding?' Teddy said while Percy relieved him of his hat. 'We met by chance in the park and Anna took pity on a poor lonely stranger.'

'You're not intruding in the slightest,' said Verity. 'We're very pleased to see you again, Mr Norris. Aren't we, Otto?'

Otto nodded guardedly. 'We are. Of course, we are.'

'And where,' Anna chirruped, 'is my loving husband?'

'Upstairs,' said Otto.

'Painting, I suppose,' said Anna. 'Painting, always painting.'

'Shall I send someone to fetch him?' Verity said.

'No, he'll come down in his own good time,' said Anna. Taking Teddy's arm, she moved into the drawing room which, with a late summer sun low in the sky, held the lingering light in mirrors and polished surfaces. She threw herself down on the long settee, tossed her hat and gloves on to the cushion, and lay back. 'I could do with a stiff gin and tonic,' she said. 'Teddy?'

'Whisky, if you please, with a splash.'

Verity rang the bell to summon Percy then asked, 'What were you doing in the park, my dear?'

'Soliciting congenial company,' said Anna.

'What park would that be?' Otto said.

'The old Jekyll and Hyde,' said Anna.

'I don't think I've heard it called that before,' said Verity.

'Well, you have now – Mother.'

Verity's credulity had its limits. She exchanged an anxious

glance with Otto who, sensing trouble, rang the servants'
bell again and when Percy appeared made a show of
dispensing drinks. There was still no sign of Howard who
must surely have heard the commotion in the hall and who,
Otto assumed, was deliberately steering clear. He watched
his niece hold the glass to her lips and twinkle – yes, twinkle
– at Teddy Norris.

'We took tea,' the American said, as if that excused
everything.

'Loads of tea,' said Anna. 'And cake, very creamy cake.
Yum.'

'Anna,' Otto said, 'are you changing for dinner?'

'You do look a little grubby, my dear,' said Verity. 'And it
is Sunday.'

Anna tossed back the gin, handed the empty glass to Otto,
then, snatching up her hat and gloves, leapt to her feet.
'Sunday,' she said. 'Of course, it is. I shall bathe in asses'
milk, dress in raiment fine and return like the angel I am
– anon.' Then, trailing her hand down Teddy's sleeve in
passing, she vanished into the hall.

Howard was affable at first. Over dinner Teddy and he
discussed the market in America and the prevailing opinion
of east coast conservatives that art was intended to preserve
tradition, not tear it down. Teddy confessed that his father
inclined to that view but, being a man of taste as well as
sound business sense, didn't dismiss modernism lightly.

'In fact,' he said, 'Dad purchased your Dartmoor
landscape.'

'What did he pay for it?' Howard asked.

'Two hundred dollars.'

'Didn't you give him a discount?' said Otto.

'Certainly not,' said Teddy. 'And I didn't go foisting it on him either. He saw it on the wall of our gallery and insisted on having it for himself.'

'Are you hoping to buy more of my son's paintings?' Verity asked.

'I have already,' Teddy answered. 'Four canvases from Maule's.'

'You said nothing to me,' Anna said. 'Howard, did you know of this?'

'News to me too,' Howard said.

'I've only just clinched the sale,' Teddy said. 'No doubt Sam Maule will be in touch with you early in the week.' He glanced at Anna, brows raised. 'Did I do something wrong?'

'Of course you didn't,' said Verity. 'It's high time Howard's work was given the prominence it deserves.'

'What, out of interest, did you buy?' Howard said.

'One little self-portrait.' Teddy demonstrated size with his long fingers. 'Sam Maule calls it "early work", though I can't imagine why.'

'And the others?'

'All landscapes, big landscapes from the storeroom. I had to twist Sam's arm to show me the stuff in back.'

'He doesn't care for them,' Howard said. 'No one cares for them. You'll never sell them in New York, you know.'

'If you won't let me mount a show for you,' Teddy told him, 'I'll just have to do it my way. Gamble, in other words.' He put down his spoon. 'Sooner or later the world will catch on to what you're doing, Howard. You're just too far ahead of your time, that's all.'

'Hah!' said Howard, pleased. He ran a hand over his hair

then attacked the summer fruit crumble in his dish. He wiped cream from his chin with his napkin, sat back and lit a cigarette.

'What's this about a show?' said Verity.

'It's nothing, Mother. He isn't after me. He's after Clive.'

'On the contrary,' Teddy said. 'It's you I want.'

Howard blew smoke. 'Not my wife?'

'Beg pardon?' Teddy said.

'I mean,' Howard said, 'not my picture of my wife?'

'I thought we were talking about a show in New York,' Otto put in.

'We're not,' Howard said. 'We're talking about my portrait of Anna. Would you like it, Teddy?'

'Sure, I would,' Teddy said.

'Well, you can't have it. It's mine now. It hangs above my bed – like an icon.'

'That's a queer way of putting it, Howard,' Otto said.

'You know me, Uncle: queer as they come.'

'So,' Teddy said, 'it's no longer for sale?'

'Not at any price,' said Howard. 'Sorry.'

'Well, at least we know where we stand,' Teddy said.

'I hope we do,' said Howard. 'I really hope we do.'

It had been an exhausting day one way or another. She was almost asleep when Howard threw open the door and switched on the overhead light. She sat up, blinking. He didn't approach the bed but skirted it, prowling in a half circle. He was still buttoned up in the evening suit that didn't quite fit. He'd been drinking, of course, but there was nothing unusual in that.

After the tense little exchange across the dinner table

Howard had gone back to being genial and, without obvious irony, had thanked Teddy for having faith in him. They'd talked of Derain, Vlaminck and Epstein's monstrous sculptures and the influence of the primitive, talked and talked until Otto had fallen asleep on the drawing room couch, head resting on Verity's shoulder. When Verity, mouth open, had fallen asleep too Anna had separated her lover and her husband and had shooed Teddy out into the night.

For a moment in the hall she'd been tempted to kiss him. She might have done so too if Otto hadn't been stumbling about trying to find his overcoat, for, weekend over, Otto was sharing a cab with Teddy and heading home to Ledbetter Street. She wondered what they'd talk about as the cab clipped through the quiet streets, if they'd talk about her and if so what they would say.

Head deep in the pillow, she was just drifting off to sleep when the door flew open and Howard snapped on the light.

'Do you want him?'

'Beg pardon?'

'Do you want him – Norris, I mean?'

'I do wish you'd stand still, Howard. You're making me dizzy.'

'Just answer me, Anna. It's a fair question.'

'I don't know what you mean by "want him".'

'Do you want him inside you, between your legs?'

She leaned against the bed-head, nightgown slipping from one shoulder.

'What makes you think Teddy wants me?'

'Of course he wants you. Every man wants you.'

'Every man except you, Howard.'

'Is it so important to you to have sex?'

263

'Yes,' she said.

'Isn't it enough to be loved?'

'Loved?' she said. 'Loved? How can you possibly claim to love me when you can't bear to touch me? What's wrong with me, Howard? Am I so repulsive you can barely bring yourself to look at me?' She cupped her breasts and offered them to him, nipples erect. 'See. You can't even look at me now, can you?'

'Stop it, Anna. You're behaving like a whore.'

'Really? What would you know about whores?'

He placed his hands on the rail at the foot of the bed and forced himself to look at her. 'How long will he remain in London?'

'I don't know,' Anna said. 'Another week – two at most.'

'I don't want you to lie with him, but if you do . . .'

'What?' she said.

'Don't leave me, Anna. That's all I ask.'

She threw back the covers.

'Come to bed, Howard. Come to bed with me right here and now.'

He levered his chin upward as if his head were balanced on a rusty spring. His neck seemed to bulge out of his collar and his face was red.

In anger, she thought, he's going to take me in anger.

But when he spoke his tone was even, almost matter-of-fact.

'I can't,' he said. 'Anna, I can't. I'm sorry.'

'I'm sorry too, Howard,' she said, then, pulling up the bedclothes and turning on her side, told him to switch off the light.

27

Howard left for Foxhailes early next afternoon. He insisted that his mother go with him. Verity wasn't happy at leaving Anna to fend for herself but, as Howard pointed out, if his wife couldn't struggle by with five servants to tend to her needs then how would she ever manage a household of her own.

There was, Verity conceded, a degree of logic in Howard's argument. She was too timid to raise the question of Teddy Norris who, even she could see, was paying far too much attention to her daughter-in-law. She penned a hasty letter to Otto and then, with Emily and cook in tow, set off for the railway station. They were halfway to Exeter before it dawned on her that Anna had offered no excuse for staying behind in Holland Park – and Howard had demanded none.

'He just caved in and let you stay, did he?' Teddy asked.

'It was his suggestion,' Anna said. 'Naturally, I bowed to his wishes.'

'Is he looking for grounds for divorce, maybe?'

'Whatever else,' Anna said, 'not that.'

'I can't believe Howard's happy at being cuckolded, though I have heard of fellows – even met a couple – who

265

like nothing better than watching their wives make love with another man.'

They were dining in a Sicilian restaurant frequented by exiled Italians who loved good food cooked in the traditional style. Anna suspected that Teddy had brought her here to remind her of that evening in the East End when she'd gorged on beer and steak and been roused by the sight of half-naked men fighting. The Sicilian eating house was much more respectable, of course, but it still had a faintly exotic air as if odd things might be going on in the rooms upstairs.

She said, 'Would you like to see me with another man?'

'If you were my wife I'd kill any man who even looked at you.'

'Really?' Anna said. 'Shoot him dead with your six gun?'

'I mean it.'

'I believe you do,' Anna said. 'But what would I do if you were locked up in the clink for thirty years – or if they hanged you?'

'You'd have the satisfaction of knowing I'd died for love.'

'Now I know you're not being serious,' Anna said. 'No one dies for love.'

'Or the lack of it?' Teddy asked.

'That,' Anna said, 'is a different story. Miss Gunderson's story, perhaps? Come now, darling, don't look so surprised. You're not some hermit living in a log cabin in the mountains. You're practically public property. Your name and Miss Gunderson's are never out of the society columns. You even made it – hand in hand, as it were – into *Art Today*. I'm not jealous, not even a little bit. I have a life here in London and you have a life over there in New York. Tell me about Miss Gunderson. Is she as lovely as the newspapers make out?'

'She is quite gorgeous when she's posing for photographs.'

'And when she's not posing for photographs?'

'They don't call her Fiery Flo for nothing.'

'Are you and she engaged?'

'There's what you might call "an understanding", but it has nothing to do with me. My old man and Halcome Gunderson got together and stitched up a marriage contract when I was still at school and Florence still in pantaloons.'

'Have you slept with her?'

'No,' Teddy answered: Anna knew he was lying.

'Why isn't she pressing you for a ring, Teddy?'

'Florence is having too good a time to want to settle down. She has me, she thinks, on a string. If and when she's had enough of the high life – or the high life has had enough of her – she'll reel me in.'

'Won't you put up a fight?'

He paused. 'I don't know.'

'You don't know?' said Anna incredulously. 'You can't expect me to believe you haven't thought about marriage?'

'It's there, always there – lurking.'

'Lurking? My God, Teddy! Don't tell me you're afraid of marriage?'

'There!' he said. 'My secret's out.'

'If I didn't have a husband would you try to reel me in?'

'You're not a fish, Anna.'

'And there are plenty more like me in the sea, *n'est-ce pas*?'

'No, you're unique.'

'You liar.'

'No lie. You are unique. I've never met anyone like you and, though I rove the whole world over, like they say, I probably never will.'

'Yet you'll climb aboard the *Lusitania* and just sail away.'

'Yep.'

'Why? Because I'm Howard Buskin's wife?'

'Yep.'

'Stop being so damned laconic.'

'Howard dotes on you, you know.'

'As if that mattered to me.'

'It matters to me, Anna, which is why I'm taking responsibility.'

'For what, Teddy? Tell me – for what?'

'For asking you to drink up while I settle the bill.'

'Are we going back to the hotel?' she asked.

'No,' he answered. 'We're popping round the corner to the Royal Opera House. Curtain up in fifteen minutes.'

'Oh, yes! It's Puccini tonight, isn't it?' said Anna.

'Of course, it is,' Teddy said and, to the amusement of the Italians at a nearby table, leaned over the chequered cloth and kissed her.

Entertaining Master Cavendish was an exhausting business. When he put his mind to it he could wear his grandfather out in half an hour and his mother in fifteen minutes. Even Maisie had now and then to prop herself on the arm of a chair or collapse against the door of the nursery just to catch her breath. Only Clive seemed able to keep up with the little dervish, to trade blow for blow and come out on top.

The first sign that Walter's surrender was imminent was

a cat-like curling up on the sofa or, more often than not, on the carpet, and a cross-eyed stare filled with surprise that his energy wasn't boundless after all. Then he would put his thumb in his mouth and, forefinger pressed against the base of his nose, hum quietly, suck noisily, and fall asleep.

Grandfather Cavendish, a staunch traditionalist, had told Julie off for allowing the boy to nap whenever he felt like it. But Grandfather Cavendish's case for the virtues of a strict upbringing was lost in protests from Grandmother Cavendish, not to mention Uncle Walter, who were swift to point out that little Walter was happy, lively and inquisitive and that Julie must therefore be doing something right.

On afternoons when work didn't demand his attention, Clive would spend an hour in the drawing room with his son in his lap while Maisie tidied up the nursery or lay on her bed and read the latest Nat Gould novel, and Julie, heavy and hot in the sultry weather, sprawled in an armchair and did nothing more strenuous than watch her son, and sometimes her husband, nap.

On that particular afternoon, though, Clive was wide-awake.

'White Star will launch the *Olympic* in October,' he said quietly. 'Like it or lump it, dearest, I'll have to be in Belfast for a week or ten days. She really is a beautiful vessel. I'll be sorry to see her go.'

'You'll still have the other ones, won't you?'

'The *Titanic* next.' Clive nodded. 'Bigger and better. The wrights at Harland and Wolff are frightfully proud of their luxury liners. Can't say I blame them.'

'Will you sail with her when she's fitted out?'

'The *Olympic*? I doubt it. I don't want to leave you and the children. Let's hang on until *Titanic* makes her maiden voyage and we'll all go out together.'

'It won't come cheap.'

'Nothing worthwhile ever does,' Clive said. 'Must say, I like the idea of a two-man show in a New York gallery. I'm just cocky enough to think I'd come out of it rather better than old Howard – or, more accurately, the new Howard.'

'Of course you would, darling,' Julie said. 'You have the vulgar touch that Howard has always lacked, the enviable vulgar touch.'

'Is that meant to be a compliment?'

'Take it how you will,' said Julie. 'May I ask you something?'

'Ask away.'

'Just how much *are* we worth?'

Clive had been reared in a tradition of financial reticence. If Walter hadn't been snuggled on his lap he might have locked his hands behind his back, rocked on the balls of his feet and told her it was none of her business.

As it was, he hesitated before he answering. 'I earned over a thousand pounds last year. Nothing I've done so far is going to hang in the New Art Club or the Royal Academy. On the other hand, my paintings are on show in the Olympic Rooms, the London Athletic, the Teddington Club, and now, thanks to Max, in the boardrooms of half a dozen shipping magnates. With a little effort, I can probably fill my diary with commissions – but I don't want to paint fusty old gentlemen in striped waistcoats no matter how profitable.'

'What do you want to do, Clive?'

'I want to see America. I want to paint America.'

'All of it?' said Julie teasingly.

'I want to paint the skyscrapers of Manhattan, Boston's mansions, Washington's marble monuments, the stockyards in Chicago, and all the mountains, lakes and rivers I can reach.'

'How long does a crossing take?' Julie asked.

'A week at sea in the lap of luxury,' said Clive eagerly. 'Will you think about it, sweetheart?'

'I'll think about it,' Julie promised as little Walter stirred in his father's arms and, groping blindly, found his mouth with his thumb once more.

Verity was waiting in the porch when the trap arrived. It was already almost dark. Moths and other insects swarmed about the electrical lantern. Verity looked haggard in the wan overhead light and was in no mood for small talk.

'Where is she, Otto? Where's Anna?' she snapped. 'Why isn't she with you? Didn't you get my letter?'

Otto put an arm about her and kissed her brow.

'I did my best,' he said. 'She refused to leave London.'

'She's with him, isn't she? She's with Teddy Norris.'

'I really have no idea,' Otto said. 'Shall we go inside?'

'Tell me the truth, Otto.'

'I don't know who she's with, if she's with anyone at all. You know what she's like, Verity. She just doesn't care for the country.'

He had always known that sooner or later he would become the scapegoat for his niece's waywardness but he was fond of Verity and chose his words with care. 'Calm yourself, dearest. All this fretting does your heart no good. Anna told me to tell you she'll be down next week sometime.'

'You saw her? You spoke with her?'

'Yes,' Otto said. 'She dropped in at the shop.'

'Did she stay, stay for supper?'

'Yes,' he lied effortlessly. 'I put her in a cab about half past ten.'

'Thank God,' Verity said. 'I really thought she might be running off with this Norris chap. How did she seem, Otto?'

'Much as usual,' Otto answered. 'I think she's just going through a phase.'

'A phase? Married women don't have phases.'

'Do let's go inside,' said Otto, 'before these damned gnats eat me alive.'

'Howard's in the drawing room. I don't want to worry him.'

'Is he worried?' Otto said.

'He pretends not to be.'

'Would you like me to have a word with him?'

'No, the less said the better.'

Otto put a finger to his lips. 'Mum's the word then.'

They went inside. The house had held the heat of the day and the atmosphere was stifling. Howard, dressed for dinner, was seated on the stairs.

'No Anna?' he asked.

'No Anna,' Otto answered.

'Well, thank God for that,' said Howard.

She had considered inviting Teddy to make love in her bed or, even more perversely, in Howard's bed. Neither prudence nor guilt had stayed her, only an unacknowledged reluctance to hurt her husband more than she had done already.

She returned home to Holland Park each evening, alone.

Teddy had wound up his business in London to spend his last few days with her. It was all she would have of him, all, she believed, he would have of her: five precious days to lunch by the river, stroll in the parks, visit the theatre, dine late and make love. When he'd gone she would do penance by travelling down to Foxhailes for what was left of the summer. It might be months or years before Teddy returned, though she didn't doubt that he would.

She rose early that morning, the last morning, and took an age to dress.

She promised herself she wouldn't weep, wouldn't cling and, when the train pulled out of the railway station, wouldn't even wave. She would maintain an immaculate image, adult, cultured and totally in control, a slender figure in Prussian blue with a lavish, wide-brimmed 'Merry Widow' hat to hide the wistful smile that she felt sure would say it all.

Teddy's purchases, Howard's paintings among them, had been packed and shipped early in the week. His trunks had gone ahead to Southampton. All he carried that mid-morning was a slim leather valise. The linen jacket had been replaced by a single-breasted reefer with button cuffs and a prominent ticket pocket, the boater by a wide-awake. He looked, she thought, like a dockside artisan pretending to be a gentleman, though no labourer could ever duplicate the ease of manner that came with confidence and cash.

'How are you, Anna?'

'I'm well.'

'I love you.'

'I know you do.'

'Won't you say it?'

'Say what, Teddy?'

'That you love me.'

The carriages ran off in a great brown curve. She couldn't see the engine, only a plume of white smoke billowing up to the arched glass roof. In her nostrils was the earthy odour that pervaded every railway terminal and in her ears the urgent sound of whistles and slamming doors. It hadn't dawned on her until that moment that he might be saying goodbye for ever, might be going home to New York to marry Florence Gunderson and that their lovemaking had all been a sham.

She began to cry. 'I do,' she said. 'I do. You know I do.'

He took her in his arms and held her tightly.

'I will come back for you, you know,' he said, 'just as soon as I can.'

Her hat was twisted out of shape and the feathers came between them. She tugged at the pins and took the hat off and let him kiss her, kiss her, kiss her until her lips felt bruised. Then he released her, spun abruptly on his heel, picked up the valise and was gone.

She watched him recede into the distance, weaving between passengers, well-wishers and half-open doors. He did not look back, but just before she lost him he thrust up an arm and punched the air, not, she thought, in triumph but despair.

She lingered until the train pulled out but did not see him again.

She crossed the concourse to the ladies cloakroom, washed her face, tidied her hair and pinned on her hat. She was empty now, too hollow to cry. She purchased a cup of tea from a railway bar and drank it piping hot before she caught a cab back to Holland Park.

By half past three she was on a train from Paddington to Exeter and at nine o'clock that evening sat down to dine with Verity and Howard in Foxhailes House, a little pale but otherwise composed.

Five days later, in the middle of a warm afternoon, a niggling cramp roused her from a soft sweet dream and, an hour later, her monthly bleeding began.

PART FOUR

The Voyage Out
1912

28

The first letter arrived only a few weeks after Teddy returned to New York. It was typewritten on cream laid paper, bore a die-stamped likeness of the Viaduct Gallery on the upper left-hand corner and was signed by Harold K. Gaines, Teddy's partner and business manager. The letter was addressed to Howard at Holland Park and, rather formally, informed him that the proprietors of the Viaduct Gallery would be pleased to consider mounting a show of his work in the spring of 1912, if he was open to discussing terms.

Howard didn't mention the letter to anyone. It would probably have lain unanswered in a drawer in his dressing table if, in February 1911, Harold K. Gaines hadn't written again. The tone this time was a deal less formal and boiled down to 'What the hell are you playing at, Buskin?' The letter carried a little postscript written in blue ink across the bottom of the typewritten page: 'At least have the decency to let us know your thoughts on the matter, Howard,' and signed simply, 'Teddy'.

Howard dumped the second letter in a drawer too, but he couldn't stop thinking about it. Shut away in his London studio that wild, wet spring, he felt as if he were painting towards an end at last and not just passing the time.

'Percy?' Verity said. 'Why on earth would you want to paint Percy?'

'Look at his features,' Howard said. 'Supercilious deference engraved in every line. You can't tell whether Percy hates or respects us. He's so wonderfully enigmatic, don't you think?'

'He's only a butler,' Anna said, 'not the blessed Mona Lisa.'

'Good face, I agree,' said Otto. 'But why, may I ask, are you suddenly so eager to paint from the life?'

'I've always painted from the life.'

'I mean,' said Otto tactfully, 'from a model.'

'Yes,' Verity said, 'and why Percy? He can't afford to buy paintings.'

'Not the point, Mama,' said Howard. 'There's something worth exploring in old Perce, don't you think? What lies behind that basilisk stare, for instance?'

'He's probably plotting how to get Emily's drawers off,' said Anna. 'Why don't you paint Emily? I'm sure she'd be delighted to pose for you.'

'I don't do women,' said Howard.

'You did me, didn't you?' said Anna. 'In paint, I mean.'

'You don't count,' said Howard.

'That's nice to know,' said Anna. 'Have you given up still lifes?'

'I'm tired of painting objects,' Howard said. 'And I've done all I can with landscapes. I feel a need for change, a change of direction, something different. Something challenging.'

'People?' said Anna. 'Surely you don't mean people?'

'Well, yes,' Howard said. 'I suppose I do mean people.'

'I'd love to have a portrait of Otto to hang in the drawing room, a companion piece to my Banbury,' Verity said.

'And risk invidious comparisons?' said Anna. 'That isn't your style, is it, Howard? After all, you're *so* original, *such* an individualist that no one can possibly compete with you.' She tossed aside the novel she'd been reading and stretched her arms above her head. 'This sudden change of direction wouldn't have anything to do with Clive, would it? He's been invited to show in New York. Didn't he tell you?'

'No,' said Howard, after a pause. 'No, he didn't tell me.'

'He was rather under the impression you'd been invited too.'

Another pause: 'What – I mean, what's Cavendish sending?'

'Portraits,' Anna said, adding, 'People, Howard. Real people.'

'I thought he was still painting boats for Scully's cronies?'

'Oh, he is,' said Anna. 'He's putting the finishing touches to a huge canvas right now. Really quite awe-inspiring. The critic in the *Standard* calls him the next—'

'What the critic in the *Standard* calls him is no concern of mine,' Howard interrupted. 'They're all tarred with the same brush, that lot. Is Clive really sending pictures to Norris for a show in New York?'

'Oh, yes. His portrait of Telfer Scully will be the centre-piece, I think,' Anna said. 'But lots of other portraits, sportsmen mainly, will be there too, plus some Belfast paintings. Teddy says the show will be a curtain raiser for an enormous exhibition of modern art the American Association of Painters is setting up in a couple of years' time when all sorts of international artists will be represented: Monet, Seurat, Cézanne, Sickert . . .'

'Sickert! Ye Gods!' Howard exclaimed. 'That charlatan.'

'Teddy says the Viaduct show will help pave the way.'

'Teddy says? Teddy says?' Howard said. 'How do you know what Teddy says and who, if I might enquire, is he saying it to?'

'Clive,' Anna replied promptly. 'He writes regularly to Clive.'

'Did you know nothing of this, Howard?' Otto put in.

'Nothing – well, not much.'

'Perhaps Mr Norris thought you wouldn't be interested,' said Verity.

'Or that your stuff isn't good enough,' said Anna.

'Well, I am interested,' Howard blurted out. 'And, damn it, I've more to offer than the bloody picture postcards Cavendish passes off as art.'

'Pity you haven't been invited,' said Anna. 'I would so love to see New York.'

'And Norris, I suppose?' Howard said.

'Oh, yes,' said Anna brightly, 'and Teddy too, of course.'

Soon after Howard indicated his willingness to talk terms, letters from Gaines came thick and fast. What Howard did not know was that the communications Clive received from the Viaduct Gallery contained intimate letters from Teddy to Anna, letters Clive passed on, unopened, to his sister-in-law.

Anna saw little of her husband in the course of the summer. Howard spent most of his time in Devon painting a series of pictures to ship to the Viaduct. He followed a full-length portrait of Percy with a head and shoulders of Mr Moss, the Foxhailes steward, together with oil studies of the pot boy at the Storr Inn, the blacksmith at Brampton and, trailing in the wake of Van Gogh, a grizzled local postman complete with cap and uniform. Real people, Howard called them, without frill or flounce to lure him into turning 'chocolate box'.

Life in Hampstead was just a little too real for Julie. In the autumn of 1910, while Clive was in Belfast for the launch of the *Olympic*, she'd given birth to a little girl, Frances Marian, who'd popped into the world so suddenly that the midwife arrived just in the nick of time to cut the cord.

Little Fran was far too young to understand what her father was blathering about when he leaned over her crib and sang her to sleep with versions of 'Camptown Races', or 'My Old Kentucky Home', spiced with an occasional sea shanty. By the time she reached fifteen months, however, she was old enough to grab the wooden model of RMS *Titanic* that her brother had been given for Christmas and gnaw on it for all she was worth.

The White Star Line had tentatively announced a departure date for the *Titanic*'s maiden voyage but an unfortunate collision between an armoured cruiser, HMS *Hawke*, and RMS *Olympic* in Southampton Water shot a hole in the company's plans. *Titanic*'s fitting out was put on temporary hold while the *Olympic* returned to Belfast for repairs. The cost to the company of this little mishap, Max gloomily reported, would run to a quarter of a million pounds and declared that come hell or high water an April date for *Titanic*'s westward crossing would be met even if the crew had to row the damned boat across the Atlantic.

Shortly before Christmas Otto and the widow Millar slipped off to a registry office in West Kensington where, with Stanley and Emily as witnesses and no others present, they quietly tied the knot – mainly, Otto sheepishly explained, because a spring honeymoon aboard the most luxurious ocean liner in the world was too good an opportunity to miss.

Predictably, Howard was devastated by his mother's furtive marriage to a Jew, so devastated, in fact, that he took to the bottle and spent most of Christmas week blotto in the billiard room in Foxhailes. Julie and Anna were more magnanimous. They wished the happy couple well, while Stanley resigned himself to a lonely year or two in Ledbetter Street and an early retirement.

As soon as *Titanic*'s departure date was confirmed Buskins and Goldsteins reserved suites in New York's Park Avenue Hotel where Max Scully and his missus would also be staying. The Cavendishes settled for a double room at four dollars a day in the Hotel Woodward which lay at the entrance to the Great White Way, whatever that might be.

The private viewing of 'Two English Artists' was slated for the evening of Saturday, April 20th, four days after the *Titanic*'s arrival in New York. Twenty-two works by Clive and eighteen by Howard would be on display. Wine and canapés would be served and selected members of the press invited to an informal 'Meet the Artists' supper at Delmonico's, hosted by no less a personage than Charles Edward Norris, Teddy's father, who, it seemed, knew a thing or two about whipping up publicity. Whether Charles Edward Norris knew a thing or two about Teddy's plans for the future remained moot. It was one question Teddy never got around to answering no matter how often Anna put it to him.

He was more forthcoming about his tenuous engagement to Fiery Flo Gunderson, which was well and truly off.

Flo, or possibly her father, had grown weary of waiting for young Norris to abandon his harebrained pursuit of tomorrow's great masters and, having no patience with 'Art' in the first place, replaced the vacillating ne'er-do-well with a middle-aged Wall Street stockbroker, who accompanied Miss Gunderson to the altar with half of New York's social elite looking on.

And the way, Teddy wrote, was clear.

Clear for what? Anna wondered, as she lay in bed surrounded by Teddy's letters, reading and rereading them as if his flowery declarations of love required interpretation. She kept the sheaf of letters locked in a cash box in the home safe which, at her suggestion, Howard had bought to house her jewellery. The safe was tucked into a corner of her shoe closet where no one could trip over it. The safe had a key lock, not a combination, and she hid that key, together with the little key to the cash box, in a box on the top shelf of her wardrobe where she was sure they wouldn't be found.

The problem was what to do with the letters now she was leaving for good. She couldn't bring herself to burn them. They were, after all, precious reminders of what it was to be truly loved. Finally, with time running out, she tied them with ribbon, stuck them in a toilet bag and buried them a corner of her Vuitton case only minutes before the carrier arrived to take away the luggage. Then at eight next morning she met the Cavendish clan on the boat train to Southampton and, at a little after the hour of noon, left England behind for ever.

29

'What's wrong with the child?' Howard said crossly. 'Is he cutting teeth, or what?'

'He's three years old, Howard,' Anna informed him. 'The hustle-bustle has upset him, that's all.'

'Well, thank God we're not next door to Clive's brats if they're going to snivel all way to New York. Did Scully pay for Cavendish's ticket, by the way?'

'Clive wouldn't hear of it.'

'He must be doing well if he can fork out for a stateroom. Did they have to bring that common creature with them, though?'

'Creature? Oh, you mean Maisie?'

'Is that her name? Emily doesn't think much of her.'

'Emily doesn't think much of anyone,' Anna reminded him. 'Maisie's been brought along to look after the children.'

'I thought that was Julie's job.'

'Howard . . .'

Anna's reprimand was drowned by a blast from the whistle of one of the tugs that hugged the harbour wall. Turning, she scanned the throng for her sister. She could see nothing of Julie in the forest of feather hats and toppers but caught sight of Clive with little Walter perched on his shoulders.

'See,' she said. 'He's stopped crying now.'

'Has he?' said Howard, without interest, and went to join the queue at the gangway.

'All a bit much for you, Chief?' Clive gave his son's knee a squeeze. 'All a bit much for me, too, if you must know. She really is daunting when you see her up close.'

Reassured, Walter sniffed up his tears and whispered in his father's ear, 'You painted her.'

'I did,' Clive said. 'But I haven't seen her since she was fitted out.'

'Wiff funnels?'

'Yes, with funnels. How many funnels, Walter?'

Arms clasped about his father's neck, Walter stared upward. Viewed from eighty feet below the level of the decks the funnels reared into the sky at an angle so acute it seemed as if they might topple over.

'Free,' Walter declared, nodding.

'Four,' Clive said. 'Three for smoke and one for ventilation. Are you feeling better now?'

'Hmm,' Walter said, still trying to count funnels.

'I'm going to put you down,' Clive said. 'I want you to hang on to my hand when we climb up the gangway and do exactly what the sailors tell you to do. First, though, we must find your mother and sister.'

'And Maisie,' Walter reminded him.

'Oh, yes,' said Clive. 'We mustn't forget Maisie.'

Maisie hoisted the carpet bag stuffed with essential baby supplies into the crook of her elbow and tucked the beige wool blanket round Fran's bottom.

Mrs C had been none too pleased at having baby wrapped in a blanket. She'd said, rather sniffily, it reminded her of a shawl and did she, meaning Maisie, think they were travelling steerage. The blanket, Maisie had explained, was to keep Fran secure and had insisted on taking it along which, as it turned out, had been a wise thing to do. No tears from Fran then, not so much as a whimper when the passengers from the early train jostled to be first to the quay and nothing but big round eyes when the boat loomed up in front of them.

Julie plucked at Maisie's sleeve. 'Where's the luggage? Have you seen the luggage? I'd really like to be sure . . .'

'It'll be in our cabin by now, Mrs C,' Maisie told her.

'Oh, do they take it there for us?' Julie scuttled to keep up. 'I thought we had to collect it or – or something like that.'

'For what Mr Clive paid for them tickets,' Maisie said, 'I'm surprised they don't 'ave somebody carry *us* to our cabins.'

'Where's my husband? Can you see Mr Cavendish?'

'He's waiting by the gangway with Master Walter.'

'And my uncle, can you see him?'

'Mrs Goldstein and 'im – he – 'ave gone on board already, I fink.'

The doors in the side of the ship looked very small, Maisie thought, and the folk who lined the rails high overhead quite tiny. How easy it would be to get lost inside this huge tin bucket or, worse, lose the children. She experienced a moment of panic at the prospect of one of her precious charges vanishing from sight and, looking up, had a horrid vision of Fran squeezing through a porthole or Walter toppling over a rail.

Pulling herself together, she hoisted Fran and the carpet bag higher in her arms and, with Mrs C treading on her heels, headed for Mr Clive whose enthusiasm was never less than reassuring.

'All well, Maisie?'

'All well,' said Maisie.

'Right,' Mr Clive said. 'Now we're all together why don't we line up, women and children first, and let them pipe us aboard.' Then, herding his clan to the gangway, he followed them on to the steamship.

'Why, Howard,' Anna said, as soon as the stewardess had left, 'how thoughtful.'

'Thoughtful?' he said. 'I don't know what you mean?'

'Two beds.' Anna bounced a little on the coverlet. 'It really is most considerate of you to arrange it so we don't have to sleep together.'

Howard was busy sniffing the wall panels.

'Cedar,' he said, half to himself. 'Might be sandalwood.' He ran a hand over the panelling. 'Smooth as bloody silk. No expense spared, eh?' He turned. 'What's all this about beds? Aren't you satisfied?'

'Perfectly,' Anna said. 'Did you pick this room from the brochure?'

'God, no,' said Howard. 'Mama – possibly Otto – made all the arrangements. They're just next door. We share a bathroom. It's through – ah – that door, I think. Do you want to make use of it?'

'Not at present,' Anna said. 'I think I might begin unpacking.'

'Stewardess will do that for you.'

'I prefer to do it myself.'

'Just as you wish,' said Howard. 'Dutch, that's it.'

'Dutch? What about Dutch?'

'The décor,' Howard said. 'It's rather like stepping into a painting by Vermeer, don't you think?'

Anna looked around and shrugged. 'A little, I suppose.'

She was less impressed by the ship than she should have been. Wrapped in a cocoon of anticipation, all she could think of was that Teddy would soon be with her.

Howard said, 'Are you coming?'

'Coming?' she said. 'Where?'

'On deck,' Howard said. 'To wave goodbye to England.'

'What? Are we leaving?'

'Any minute,' Howard said. 'You can't possibly miss seeing her cast off.'

'Yes,' Anna said. 'I can. When's lunch?'

'Lunch? I've no idea. As soon as we clear the harbour probably. Come along, my dear. Everyone will be up top, you know.'

'No,' said Anna, 'not everyone.'

Julie had read an article on 'Motherhood' that claimed that children under five respond only to that which affects their immediate welfare and that all else is simply an assembly of irrelevant sights and sounds. What nonsense, she thought, as she watched her son's exhilaration swell and heard questions tumble out of him so fast that Clive barely had time to answer them.

Walter sported a little sailor's cap that Papa had bought him and clutched a Union Jack that Otto had magically produced; a little paper flag on a stick that cracked and snapped when you waved it. He had both elbows on the rail, head thrust forward as if he were drinking in everything and committing it to memory with the same effortless concentration as Clive dashed off his thumbnail sketches. Even little Frances, not yet out of baby clothes, wriggled in Maisie's arms as if she too couldn't get enough of the raucous activity which she clearly found fascinating.

From her vantage point high on the boat deck Julie observed hawsers being loosed and tugs take charge. She felt the first vibration of *Titanic*'s engines beneath her feet as the ship eased away from the quay. Following the stately movement of the ship, the crowd flowed along the quay, waving, blowing kisses, cheering and weeping.

Leaning on the rail, Maisie on one side, Clive on the other, Julie watched sheds and cranes slide quietly by and in a voice as piercing as a policeman's whistle, heard Walter cry, 'We're moving, we're moving. Daddy, we're moving,' and saw him flap his little flag to bid everyone farewell.

Howard laid a hand on her shoulder. 'Quite a sight, isn't it?'

'It certainly is,' Julie agreed.

'She doesn't know what she's missing.'

'Where is Anna? Isn't she with you?'

'Sulking in the cabin.' He waved a hand indiscriminately at the well-wishers. 'I've no idea what's wrong with the woman. I thought she fancied this trip.'

'I'm sure she does,' Julie said. 'She's probably tired.'

'Tired?' Howard said, still waving. 'Tired of me, perhaps. Well, I hope she isn't going to spoil it for everyone else. How's your child – the boy – Walter? He seems to be in fine fettle now.'

'He is, thank you.'

Julie had little or no affinity with her brother-in-law. She'd been relieved when the friendship between Clive and he had lapsed and Howard had stopped visiting. He was, she realised, making an effort to be affable now but his friendliness seemed insincere.

'I say, I don't much like the look of that.'

'Of what?' Julie said.

The liner nosed into the river channel. Bow wash slapped on pilings. Up ahead, moored along a section of the dock, were two other ocean-going liners, their decks crowded with passengers.

'Hoh-ho!' Howard exclaimed. 'We're running into trouble here, I fear.'

Clive fenced his son with his forearms. Maisie, Fran in her arms, stepped hastily back as *Titanic* came abreast of the smaller of the berthed steamers. Howard's hands closed on Julie's waist. The mooring ropes that secured the smaller ship snapped and, arcing high in the air, lashed into the crowd of spectators on the dock. The back end of the little ship – her name, *New York*, plainly visible on her stern – swung out into *Titanic*'s freeway and a collision seemed inevitable.

'Hold tight everyone,' Clive said calmly.

A great turmoil of water surged from one of *Titanic*'s propellers and generated enough wash to hold *New York* at bay. With only a few feet to spare, the smaller ship slipped stern first along the side of the great new liner and, almost gracefully, swung out in front of her as the *Titanic* shuddered to a stop.

Belching smoke, the tugs moved nimbly to manoeuvre

the *New York* back to her berth and allow the White Star's queen of the seas to get under way again.

Passengers on the *New York* leapt and yelled in nervous excitement but, Julie noticed, there were no such displays of emotion on the deck around her, only a disquieting contempt for the smaller vessel as if, she thought, *Titanic* was not only indestructible but charmed.

'It's the suction that does it. Acts like a magnet.'

'I thought it was the wash.'

'Happened with the *Hawke*, you'll recall. Same thing.'

'Thank God it didn't dent our plating.'

'Proves just how big she is, how powerful.'

'Cumbersome, don't you think? Hard to handle.'

'She stopped quickly enough when required.'

'That's true. Captain Smith knows what he's doing.'

'Should do. God knows, he's been at it long enough.'

Julie listened to the chat around her and hung on to Howard who, whatever his failings, had been shrewd enough to spot danger in advance.

'Well,' he said, 'that was quite a little show, wasn't it?'

'Crash,' Walter piped up, beaming. 'We crashed.'

'Almost, but not quite, Chief,' his father told him. 'Not a bad omen, I hope.'

'Surely you don't believe in omens?' Howard said.

'Of course I don't,' said Clive.

'I, for one,' Howard said, 'could use a drink. Where's the bar, I wonder?'

'I think it's that way,' Clive told him. 'You'll find a steward in the lounge.'

Howard strode off along the deck without a backward glance.

'Boats, more boats, Mummy,' Walter said. 'I want to see more boats.'

'And so you shall, darling,' Julie said. 'But first we'll have to find a place to wash your hands and put some food in your tummy. How long before we reach Cherbourg, Clive?'

'We should be there by six,' said Clive.

The Channel crossing was unusually smooth, much to the relief of stewards and stewardesses who were almost as unfamiliar with the layout of the ship as the passengers. An hour into the crossing Walter finally ran out of steam. After an *al fresco* lunch, with ice cream, at a side table in the first-class restaurant he fell asleep sprawled on a couch in the downstairs reception area from which embarrassing position Maisie redeemed him while Julie finished feeding sieved rice pudding to the baby and, that done, followed Maisie to the stateroom where, between them, they put the children down, side by side, to nap.

Lax Clive might be in his approach to child rearing but he was still subject to the rules that governed proper social behaviour. When Julie reminded him that children – decent, respectable children – were meant to be seen only occasionally and heard not at all he promised to let Maisie do what Maisie was paid to do, namely keep the children fed, watered and out of mischief while he and his wife, together, sampled the many pleasures that *Titanic* had to offer.

Otto and Verity were doing whatever a honeymoon couple slightly past their prime might be expected to do – snoozing on steamer chairs behind the glazed screens of the port-side promenade deck, most likely – and Howard was prowling the length and breadth of the ship with the same loping stride as he prowled the heathery slopes of Dartmoor, when the Normandy coast, beautiful and serene in placid evening light, hove into view.

Only Maisie, Walter and little Fran bothered to hop from port to starboard to watch the clutter of Cherbourg's sheds and warehouses appear through the gathering dusk and the *Titanic* drop anchor between the breakwaters. The tender, the *Nomadic* – a name Walter couldn't get his tongue around – pulled out from harbour to load and offload passengers, including, so rumour had it, Colonel Astor and his blushing bride of eighteen for whom he'd divorced his wife.

Maisie had never seen a scandal in the flesh before, let alone one as rich as Colonel Astor. She joined several hundred inquisitive souls at the rails to watch the *Nomadic* snuggle up to *Titanic*. A door in the hull opened. A gangway was rolled out. Ropes were tied, stewards assembled and passengers, mainly Americans, scrambled on board, while the few who had used the liner as a cross-Channel ferry, prepared to disembark. It was by then almost dark and difficult to make out who was who in the influx of transatlantic passengers.

'There he is,' a voice cried and a half-hearted cheer went up, punctuated by jeering from third-class louts who had found their way up from the well deck and clearly didn't know their place.

'Who?' said Walter, and Fran, not to be outdone, uttered a series of owl-like hoots that Maisie, under other circumstances, might have applauded.

If it was Colonel Astor and his pretty little wife, Maisie

had no more than a fleeting glimpse of them before they stepped over the coaming, followed by a rangy young man who, without so much as a valet to carry his bag, clambered up the gangway with his hat tugged down to hide his face.

30

It was after eight o'clock before *Titanic* weighed anchor and left Cherbourg behind. By then little Frances Marian was too tired to eat and with a feeding bottle filled with sweet malted milk to soothe her – although Julie did not approve of feeding bottles – she fell asleep as soon as Maisie put her to bed.

In a pale mauve satin-silk evening dress that had cost Clive eight pounds of his hard-earned, Julie popped into the cabin to bid her children goodnight and give Maisie last-minute instructions. Maisie already knew how to summon a stewardess or, by simply opening the door, attract the attention of the section steward who stood duty at each end of the corridor. She had even chosen her supper from the dinner menu and had asked for it to be delivered at nine by which time, surely, Walter too would be asleep.

'Shame, Maisie, that you can't join us for dinner.' Clive leaned nonchalantly in the doorway that connected the rooms. 'We'll try to find a half-hour or so for you to take the grand tour tomorrow.'

'This is grand enough for me, Mr Clive,' said Maisie. 'I'll be 'aving myself a fine old feed in peace an' quiet – which is better than muckin' in with the other servants in that dismal dining room downstairs.'

'Did you order the oysters?' Clive asked.

Maisie grinned. ''Course I did.'

'Good for you,' Clive said and, picking up Walter by the nightshirt, gave his son a gentle shake. 'You, lad, behave yourself. Into bed and off to sleep – and don't dare waken your sister.'

Walter nodded. 'Where you going, Daddy?'

'We're having dinner with Aunt Anna and Uncle Howard.'

'Will Uncle Otto be there?'

'I expect he will.'

'Uncle Otto gave me a flag. Where's my flag?'

'Right 'ere.' Maisie had thought of everything. 'In the water glass beside your bed, all ready for the morning.'

'You'll be here in the morning, Mummy, won't you?'

'Of course I will. Just next door.'

'And Daddy?'

'All of us.' Clive ruffled his son's hair, kissed his daughter's brow, then, on impulse, kissed Julie too, a gesture that seemed to reassure his son that all was well.

Maude Scully told her that the dining saloon was not only the most palatial but also the largest room afloat and for sheer luxury set *Titanic* a notch above her sister ship, *Olympic*, and, need it be said, far above anything Cunard had to offer.

Leaded windows looked out from Jacobean alcoves. The smell of new leather and brocade wasn't quite hidden by the aroma of cooking and the ladies' fragrant perfumes. A Babel of voices in several different tongues all but drowned out the strains of a waltz played by the musicians in the reception room. The dining saloon was so long it was difficult to pick out the captain and identify the gentlemen and ladies who shared his table. Maude and Max were not among them, though, for having money to burn or being a stockholder in the White Star Line didn't guarantee you a place at the captain's table.

Anna had spent most of the afternoon unpacking and laying out her evening clothes. She'd chosen a beautiful dress of pink chiffon decorated with satin bows and crystal beads that displayed just a little more of her figure than Howard considered decent. When he'd returned from his wanderings he'd gone straight into the bathroom to shave. Anna had been tempted to throw on a stole and hurry on deck to watch the passengers embark from the Cherbourg tender. But she had contented herself by slipping into the corridor and peeping through a baize-covered door at an alleyway crowded with stewards, valets, maids and servants all trying to find the way to their various rooms.

She had been back in place, seated on the bed in the stateroom, before the bugle sounded the call to dinner, followed a few minutes later by a reminder from the deck steward that the sitting, though late, was about to begin.

Otto said, 'I see they've relaxed the rules for this evening. Fellow over there in country tweeds. Probably just arrived. Surprised they didn't insist on sticking the new arrivals in the *à la carte*.'

'At twelve and sixpence extra per head,' said Verity, 'that would hardly be fair, my dear. I wonder where Mr Astor and his little trollop are dining.'

'You're a fine one to talk, Mother,' Howard said.

'That isn't him at the captain's table, by any chance?' Julie said.

'No, that's Andrews. Very decent chap,' Clive told her. 'He's the marine architect who designed *Titanic*.'

'Do you know him?' Verity asked.

'We met once or twice,' Clive answered modestly.

'And, I suppose,' Howard said, 'he bought one of your paintings?'

'Matter of fact, Howard, he didn't.'

'Just think,' Howard said, 'if you'd screwed him for a couple of quid you could have signed for the wine tonight.'

'I'm signing for the wine tonight,' said Otto.

'Paid for with Mama's money, of course,' said Howard.

'That's quite enough, Howard,' said Anna mildly. 'If you're so concerned about who's paying, why don't you sign the bill yourself?'

'Please,' said Verity. 'No more squabbling. After Mr Norris sells your paintings we'll all be rich, won't we, Clive?'

'Absolutely,' Clive agreed.

'Is Teddy meeting us at the dock in New York?' Julie said.

'Oh, he'll be there for sure,' said Howard. 'Won't he, Anna?'

'How would I know a thing like that?' Anna said.

'I thought perhaps he'd written to you,' said Howard.

'He wrote to me,' Clive put in. 'And, yes, he'll be at the dock.'

'Hugs and kisses all round, no doubt,' Howard said, then, with a little bow in Anna's direction, 'What's it to be, my dear? Squab or duckling?'

'I think I'll have the chop,' Anna said. 'Yes, Howard, the chop.'

★

The band stopped playing at a quarter past nine which, henceforth, would be a signal for diners to decamp to the smoking room or the lounge or even go to bed. Running late this evening, the serving of dinner dragged on, however. Mr Goldstein's party were still short of dessert – a treat Verity would not forgo – when, with a spirited little flourish, the music ceased and, as if to compensate, the hubbub in the saloon grew louder.

A dark-skinned gentleman in a very white shirt and very tight evening suit was caught laughing too loudly while his companion, a beautiful, willowy woman in a sheer silk evening gown, tried not to appear embarrassed. Four whiskered gentlemen, clearly of the old school, were digging into rum cakes and lemon meringues and, between mouthfuls, exchanging comments about the dark-skinned man that Anna felt sure were not complimentary.

In an alcove on the port side, Max and Maude Scully were entertaining a brace of distinguished-looking men. One had bristling white hair and a dapper moustache. The other, a tall, broad-shouldered chap with, Anna thought, a military bearing, nodded to her and Maude gave her a wave and mouthed something the sense of which Anna could not make out.

By half past nine the racket in the saloon had become a drone through which the tinkling of the piano in the reception room was barely audible. When the sound of the piano ceased, Anna put down her napkin, allowed a steward to draw out her chair and got to her feet.

'If you'll excuse me . . .' she said, and let it go at that.

'You can't be sick,' Howard said. 'It's as flat as a pancake out there.'

'No,' she said. 'I'm not sick. I just need to . . .'

'Howard,' Verity said, 'let the poor girl go. Do you know where it is?'

'Yes.' Anna stepped away from the table

'Don't you want pudding?' Otto asked.

'No, I'll meet you in the reception room,' Anna said, adding, 'shortly.'

Then she headed for the elevators and the forward cabins where, God and White Star willing, Teddy was waiting to greet her with something more filling than dessert.

He had spent three days in the brand-new Normandy Casino in Deauville and had lost only seven thousand francs which, given the stakes at the baccarat table, was almost as good as winning. He had hired a motorcar and driver to take him to Cherbourg and had slept all the way in the back seat. He had also taken the precaution of eating an early dinner in a café close to the harbour and had been on the dock in time to watch *Titanic* steam over the horizon and, growing ever larger, tower over the vessels that clustered between the breakwaters.

It was a fine evening, calm as you like, the air so clear that every sound seemed as sharp as a pistol shot. He was a seasoned transatlantic traveller and had sailed on the biggest and best of the Cunarders but the great looming bulk of the White Star's pride and joy raised in him an unexpected feeling of awe. He peered up at the faces that lined the steamer's rails and half expected to see her there, waving and blowing kisses if she were his sister or his wife and there was nothing secretive in their meeting and no stealthy plan to follow.

Colonel Astor, his child-wife and an entourage of servants were passengers on the tender too. The colonel eyed him up and down but Teddy looked away as if he didn't even know who Astor was. There were others in the crowd who might also recognise him so, with hat pulled down, he'd hurried up the gangway on the heels of Astor's gang while the curious craned over the rails and, for some reason, jeered. Ten minutes later he was safe in his single-berth cabin with ample time to shave and bathe and, tipping the steward to leave him alone, unpack a change of clothing from his trunk.

He sat tensely on the side of the bed, smoked a cigarette and felt the motion of the ship around him, silky smooth, as she headed through the darkness for Queenstown on Ireland's southern tip.

At some time after nine o'clock, a little later than arranged, Anna knocked on the stateroom door.

And Teddy jumped to let her in.

'Well,' Howard said, through a cloud of smoke, 'you took your time. Are you sure you're not ill?'

'Quite positive,' Anna said. 'Is that brandy?'

'It is,' Otto said. 'Would you care for a snifter?'

'Indeed, I would, thank you.' She seated herself carefully on a chair at the table while Otto flagged down a steward.

'You look a little flushed, my dear,' Verity said.

'Where's Julie?' Anna said.

'Clive and she have gone for a stroll,' said Otto, adding, 'to look at the stars.'

'I hope you're not coming down with something.' Howard was concerned enough not to blow smoke in Anna's direction. 'How inconvenient that would be.'

'A turn on deck would do *you* no harm, Howard,' Verity said.

'Unlike some,' Howard said, 'I've already been on top.'

'I mean,' said Verity, 'with your wife.'

Teddy had taken her instantly, upright against the door, had taken her as if he'd been waiting there not for minutes or hours but weeks and months. When he'd thrust up into her, she'd let out a cry that had brought a steward hurrying to the cabin door. She would never forget that moment, poised and breathless, Teddy inside her, her skirts furled around her waist, her cheek pressed against the door as if she were eaves-dropping, her belly clenching and unclenching as she came.

'Everything all right, sir?'

The drawl, the easy drawl, unshakeable: 'Everything's fine, thank you.'

He'd felt huge within her, swelling within her. He'd put a hand around her throat and a finger into her mouth, a forefinger tasting of tobacco. She'd sucked on it until the steward went away and, tugging at her hips, Teddy had driven into her once more.

'No,' Anna said. 'I think I'll have an early night.'

'What about you, Otto?' Howard said. 'Fancy a hand of cards?'

'With that bunch of sharpers in the smoking room? I think not.'

'They look decent enough to me,' Howard said. 'I'm not ready for bed yet so I think I might join them for an hour or so.'

'What time do they put out the lights?' Verity asked.

'About eleven,' said Otto. 'In the smoking room – midnight.'

The steward arrived with drinks. Anna took the brandy

from the tray and, with a little 'thank you' tilt of the glass in Otto's direction, drank half the contents while Howard, his eyes clouded, studied her closely.

She said, 'Where is the smoking room, anyway?'

'Two decks up, aft,' Howard answered.

'You seem to know your way about, dear,' Verity said. 'It's such a big ship, I find it rather confusing.'

'You find everything rather confusing, Mother,' Howard said.

'Why don't you go and play cards, Howard,' said Otto snappishly.

'Do you know, I think I probably will.'

He made to rise then sat down again as Julie and Clive appeared.

'You'll never guess who *we* just bumped into,' Julie said excitedly. 'Teddy. Teddy Norris. He boarded at Cherbourg, apparently.'

'Well, why isn't he with you?' said Howard.

'He wanted to surprise us at breakfast,' Clive said.

'Teddy,' Anna got out. 'Oh, my goodness!'

'Did you know about this, Clive?' Howard said.

'About what, old man?'

'That Norris would be joining us on the voyage.'

'Of course not,' Clive said. 'I gather he meant it to be a surprise.'

'When – I mean, where did you bump into him, Julie?' Anna asked.

'On the stairs,' Julie answered. 'He was searching for the smoking room.'

'Really?' Howard said. 'To keep out of sight until breakfast, I suppose.'

'Actually,' Clive said, 'he said he was going to play cards.'

'Oh, good,' said Howard, rising again. 'Nothing like a friendly face to make sure the game is straight. I think I'll go and look for him. Do you think he'd mind?'

'I don't think he'd mind at all,' said Anna and, hiding her disappointment, signalled to a steward to bring her another brandy.

31

Of all the devices invented by man few held as much appeal for a small boy as a revolving door. It was all Maisie and Clive could do to keep the little imp from racing off downstairs to hurl himself at the heavy oak and glass and go spinning round and round, much to the annoyance of the gentlemen within who regarded the smoking room, with its veined marble mantelpiece, coal-burning fire and deep leather armchairs, as an exclusively male preserve.

No matter how hard Maisie tried to interest Master Cavendish in seagulls and views of the sea or in sitting nicely with his sister – who wasn't sitting nicely at all – on a wicker chair in the Verandah café, the little chap had but one thing in mind, one aim and object, which was to shuttle round and round in the smoking room door. A trip to the gymnasium, a ride on the 'bucking horse', and the promise of a visit to see the swimming pool did nothing to allay his obsession with the merry-go-round upstairs. Even when Clive took him firmly in hand and threatened a spanking, all he could talk about was the door, the door, the big door that moved with you inside it.

Smoking was discouraged in the starboard section of the café which meant it was quiet enough for mothers and nannies to let their charges scamper between the tables and generally keep the stewards, balancing trays of scalding-hot coffee, on their toes. Older children, even those trained to be demure, soon forgot their manners and, stimulated by sunshine and a light sea breeze, pitched in by organising games of tag and hide-and-seek in which little Fran did her unsteady best to join and from which Julie and Anna, between sips of coffee and snippets of conversation, were frequently obliged to rescue her.

'Of course, I didn't know he was joining us for the crossing,' Anna lied.

'But you are pleased to see him,' said Julie.

'I am,' said Anna, 'or, at least, I would be if I knew where he was.'

'You saw him at breakfast.'

'We all saw him at breakfast.' Anna paused. 'It isn't quite the same.'

'What was he doing in Europe?'

'Buying pictures, I suppose.'

'Come along,' Julie said. 'I know he's been writing to you. Clive told me. Admit it: you knew Teddy was boarding at Cherbourg. Is that why you disappeared from the dinner table last evening? Was it a joyous reunion?'

'Very joyous indeed,' said Anna.

'Oh, you didn't?'

'Actually,' said Anna, 'we did.'

'You,' said Julie, grimacing, 'are beyond redemption.'

'Unfortunately, Teddy has more or less ignored me ever since.'

'He's probably being tactful.' Julie darted forward to scoop her daughter from the deck, dust her off and set her back on her feet again. She returned to the table but, perched on the edge of her chair, remained alert. 'Did you go to his cabin later last night?'

'How could I? He was playing cards with Howard – Howard of all people – until midnight. I was asleep when Howard came stumbling into the room and woke me, not, I might add, intentionally.'

Last night Julie had strolled on the promenade deck hand in hand with her husband, the sea calm, the stars bright, and, later, had made love in the stateroom's brand-new bed, snug and secure in Clive's arms. She was a little aggrieved at Anna, not for cheating on Howard, who probably deserved it, but for her selfish disregard of the trouble her affair would cause.

Fran was tottering round in circles, giggling, while a small boy, not much older than her, pursued her. The small boy's mother seemed quite unconcerned at the possibility of a collision and Julie remained poised to rush to the rescue if Fran took a tumble.

'Have you written to Papa?' she asked.

'What? No.'

'Perhaps you should.'

'Are you writing?'

'If I can snatch a spare moment before we reach Queenstown.'

'Give him my fondest and tell him I'll write from New York.'

'I'm sure,' Julie said, 'you'll have plenty to tell him by that time.'

'Meaning what?'

'All about your adventures at sea, so to speak.'

'Julie . . .' Anna began, then, 'Look, she's fallen again.'

Julie sighed, rose and lifted her weeping daughter into her arms. She glared down at the small boy as if the accident were his fault, carried Fran to the table, seated her on her knee and wiped away the tears with a handkerchief.

Fran sniffed, pouted, squeezed out a last little sob, then, ever the opportunist, reached for the wafer biscuit that nestled in Julie's saucer.

'If you give her that now,' said Anna, 'she won't eat her lunch.'

'Better this than uproar,' Julie said.

Snapping the wafer in half, she presented a piece to Frances Marian who, with a remarkably deft touch, removed it from Mummy's fingers and, holding it in both fists, nibbled on it like a squirrel with a nut.

'Julie,' Anna said, 'I'm not coming back.'

'Why, where are you going?'

'I'm not coming back from New York.'

'You mean you're leaving him, leaving Howard?'

'Yes.'

'Have you told him?'

'Not yet.'

'I assume,' Julie said, 'Teddy has promised to take you on.'

'Take me on? Oh, yes, we've been planning it for months.'

'When *do* you intend to tell Howard?'

'Not before the Viaduct show. I'll let him have his moment of glory.'

'That's very decent of you.'

'Disapprove all you like, Julie. It's my life, not yours,' Anna said. 'Teddy will put me up in an apartment until he can straighten things out with his father. I'll sue Howard for divorce and, when that's settled, we'll be married.'

'All cut and dried, I see. What happens to Howard in the meantime?'

'He can travel home with Verity and Otto. They'll take care of him. Howard doesn't need me. He'll be happier on his own.'

'He may not need you, Anna, but he's stubborn enough not to let you go without a fight.'

'Howard doesn't have the guts for a fight.'

'He may surprise you.'

'I doubt it,' Anna said. 'He had his chance and . . .'

Walter appeared through a door in the trelliswork. Trying, without success, to maintain a semblance of dignity, Clive scooted after him.

'Where's Maisie?' Julie asked.

'Using the facilities,' Clive answered. 'She'll be here in a minute.'

'Good.' Julie got to her feet. 'I must, really must write to Father.'

'Better hurry,' Clive said. 'We'll be in Queenstown in an hour or so.'

'Will you keep an eye on them, darling, please?'

'Do I have a choice?'

'Not really.'

Julie lowered Frances to the deck and, brushing crumbs from her dress, headed for the door that she hoped might lead her to the writing room.

Clive sank thankfully into the chair his wife had vacated.

'Where is he?' Anna said.

'Howard?'

'Do not be obtuse, Clive. I'm not in the mood for games.'

'He's touring the decks,' Clive said. 'I hadn't realised our friend Mr Norris was quite so well connected. He seems to know half the folk on board. Last I saw of him he was chatting with Max and two other gentlemen. In fact, he asked me to invite you to join them.'

'Where?'

'Go through that door, cross to the port side and you'll find them.'

Anna detached herself from her nephew who, for some unfathomable reason, insisted on clinging to her skirts.

'And Howard?' she said. 'Have you seen Howard?'

'He's with them,' Clive said. 'Just one big happy family, eh?' and gave a sardonic little waggle of the fingertips to send her on her way.

The coast of Ireland was in sight. Soon they would pick up the lighthouse at Roche's Point. Soon after that the anchors would go down and a boatload of Irish emigrants all, or most of them, third-class, would clatter aboard and head down into the bowels of the ship which, Howard thought, was the best place for them.

He propped an elbow on the rail and watched the doorway through which his wife would appear, if, that is, Cavendish had found her. He was bored and angry, bored not with cruising which, to his surprise, he rather enjoyed, but with the company in which he found himself and angry that Norris had turned up to steal his thunder.

He'd been trying to sneak off to the lounge when Norris and Max Scully had nabbed him to introduce him to two strangers, one of whom he knew by reputation.

He had seen many reproductions of Francis Millet's so-called 'classical' paintings and had no liking for the old buffer's polished studies of young girls in togas lounging on marble benches, or his huge murals of American Indians cavorting on the dusty plains.

What did it matter that Millet had once been a surgeon in the Civil War, a writer, a journalist, a translator of unreadable tomes, had served as a trustee for umpteen American art institutions and had just retired from the exalted post of secretary to the American Academy in Rome? He was an old-school Academic which, in Howard's view, made him an enemy of progress. He was even less impressed by Millet's somewhat younger travelling companion, a big barrel-chested fellow, who, Howard gathered, was some sort of military panjandrum and on intimate terms with both Roosevelt and Taft.

'War,' Max was saying, 'is a long way off.'

'Not so far off as you might imagine,' Major Butt put in.

'Whatever problems we may have in Europe our diplomats will fix them,' Max said. 'We've centuries of experience in this sort of thing. We're quite capable of sorting out our differences without resorting to warfare. I hear you met with the Pope, Major Butt?'

The major answered, 'I did.'

'Does His Holiness believe we should be beating our ploughshares into swords?' Teddy asked.

'It was a private visit,' the major replied. 'I carried personal greetings to the pontiff from President Taft.'

Howard had been stuck away for so long in one studio or another that he'd lost contact with what was going on in the world. He knew, vaguely, about the troubles in Ireland, the clamour for Home Rule, that women were making a fearful fuss to obtain the vote, that there had been rioting in Liverpool and Manchester, even in London, though quite what the rioters wanted – better wages, like as not – he hadn't bothered to find out. He'd heard Mama and Otto discussing disruption in Europe but had assumed they were talking about railway timetables or crazy foreign anarchists blowing up pillar boxes.

Splashing paint on canvas might give him a modicum of status in the enclosed world of dealers and collectors but meant little or nothing to men who dined with presidents and had the ear of the Pope. What was even more mortifying was the realisation that Teddy Norris was no languid dilettante but a member of an elite fraternity that not only understood what was going in the world but had the power to change it. And what did he, Howard Buskin, the bastard son of an artist's model, have that might make them sit up and take notice?

Anna appeared in the doorway, framed by the ivy leaves that trailed from the trelliswork and, Howard thought, had never looked more beautiful.

He stretched out a hand and summoned her to him.

'Gentlemen,' he said proudly. 'My wife.'

The choice was simple, stay on deck to observe the transfer of mail and passengers from the Queenstown tender or pop down to the dining room for a sitting of lunch. Otto, Verity and Howard chose lunch but, to keep little Walter happy, Clive, Julie and Maisie found a corner from which to watch the tender off load its human cargo. Anna had gone with them but, spying Teddy alone on the upper deck, had slipped along the alleyway and climbed upstairs to join him.

The whole of County Cork, it seemed, was laid out before her, the fretted coastline dwindling away into a faint haze peppered with chapels and white-painted houses perched on the edge of green pastures or knitted to sandy shores. It was too gentle a scene to appeal to either Howard or Clive, though, when last seen, Clive had balanced his notebook on top of his son's head, and was dashing off thumbnail sketches of the rough-and-tumble passengers who were trooping up the ramp from the tender.

'You're acquainted with far too many people on this ship, Teddy,' Anna said. 'How on earth are we ever going to be together with so many eyes upon you?'

'Patience, darling,' Teddy told her. 'Once we're out on the Atlantic things will settle down and we'll have more opportunities to be alone.'

'If you're not playing cards with my husband, that is.'

Though the port side was almost deserted, he didn't dare kiss her. She turned her back to the rail and looked up at the funnels rearing over them, at gulls swooping out of a cloudless sky and all the bits and pieces of rigging that, from this angle, seemed to be holding the ship together.

Teddy sighed. 'Part of my purpose in crossing with you is to introduce you to friends and acquaintances who might be useful to us in New York.'

'Useful? What does that mean?'

'Like it or not,' Teddy said, 'I'm the son of a famous father. If you're to be my wife some day you'll have to be accepted, not just by my family but in the circles we move in.'

'Those two gentlemen . . .'

'Are close friends of Father's. It's important they approve of you. You charmed them, you know – I was sure you would – and that will get back to Dad. Butt and Millet are small beer compared to, say, Lucy Duff Gordon, Issy Straus or Ben Guggenheim – though Guggenheim has his mistress with him and might not be too interested in anyone else.'

'His mistress?'

'Some French chanteuse. Quite well known, I believe.'

'I'm not sure I want to be paraded like a prize heifer.'

'A heifer you ain't, darling,' Teddy said, smiling. 'A prize you certainly are.'

'What sort of prize, Teddy?' Anna said. 'I'm not just the English equivalent of Mr Guggenheim's French chanteuse, am I? Once Howard sails off without me I'm at your mercy.'

'I thought you liked being at my mercy.'

'I do. I'm just worried that something will happen to ruin our plans.'

'Nothing will happen,' Teddy assured her. 'We'll have a relaxing voyage, a successful show then, in due course, I'll take Howard aside and tell him the truth.'

'No,' Anna said. 'When the time comes, I'll tell Howard myself. I'm not that much of a coward.'

'What if he turns on you?'

'He won't,' Anna said.

'How can you be sure?'

'Because he loves me,' Anna said and then, for no logical reason she could think of, suddenly began to cry.

Teddy Norris wasn't the only one who had friends in high places. No children on the bridge was an order not even

Mr Andrews cared to challenge but as *Titanic*'s designer he had, otherwise, free run of the ship. He was only too pleased to take Clive and his son to inspect that wonder of modern science, the Marconi room, where wireless messages were received and transmitted, and also the boiler and engine rooms which were, of course, off limits to all but the most favoured.

If Walter was frightened by the sight of dozens of sweating stokers feeding the fiery furnaces he had too much Cavendish in him to let it show. He clung to his father's hand as they peered down into the pit from the top of a metal ladder and when they entered the engine room where turbines hummed and pumps and pistons hissed and thrashed, he clapped his hands to his ears and, looking up at his daddy and then at Mr Andrews, grinned a huge grin and showed no fear at all.

'We're picking up speed, I see,' Otto said. 'Must be young Walter helping out the stokers.'

'Many a true word, Mr Goldstein,' said Maisie who, temporarily relieved of the burden of childcare, was tucking into a large slice of sponge cake. 'He'd love to get 'is 'ands on a coal shovel.'

Seated in a wicker chair in the starboard side of the café with Frances Marian settled comfortably in his lap, Otto Goldstein had seldom felt so at peace with the world. All it would take to make it perfect would be the taste of a good cigar but for that lack he was amply compensated by the purring of his niece's daughter who toyed dreamily with one end of his moustache and, Maisie predicted, would soon sail off to the Land of Nod.

The first-class passengers who had joined the ship at Queenstown were doing justice to afternoon tea and the café was packed to overflowing. Several Americans had already set up camp at two tables and seemed intent on spending the rest of the afternoon, if not the voyage, there. In days of yore Otto would probably have paid court to the pretty ladies at the surrounding tables but marriage to Verity had stifled his desire to flirt.

'She's not ill, is she?' Julie said. 'Verity, I mean.'

'Lord, no,' Otto said. 'She's in the best of spirits and having the time of her life but neither she, nor I, are quite as young as we used to be and a lie-down before dinner is almost a necessity.'

'Shouldn't you be lying down with her?' Julie said.

Maisie coughed into her napkin.

'I mean,' Julie corrected, 'shouldn't you be resting too?'

'I am resting,' Otto said. 'What could be more restful than sitting here with this little mite snoring on my lap?'

'She doesn't snore, Mr Goldstein,' said Maisie. 'She 'ums.'

'Yes,' Otto said. 'Her mother used to 'um too.'

'I did nothing of the sort,' said Julie. 'You're confusing me with Anna.'

'Never,' Otto said. 'Is Anna still sulking, by the way?'

'Who knows?' said Julie. 'I can't keep up with her moods these days.'

'I thought she'd perked up when Norris arrived.'

'Oh, she did,' said Julie. 'He's introducing her to all sorts of interesting people – well, interesting if you like influential Americans.'

'Is that what he's doing now?' said Otto.

'I don't know what he's doing now,' said Julie. 'All I do

know is that Anna and Howard will not be joining us for dinner. Teddy has other plans.'

'What sort of plans?' said Otto.

'He's showing Howard off to potential clients.'

'How does Clive feel about that?' said Otto.

'I don't think Clive cares very much.' Julie paused. 'He's rather written Howard off to tell you the truth.'

'Written him off as a painter?' said Otto, surprised.

'As a rival,' Julie said. 'Clive no longer feels a need to compete.'

Otto was silent for several seconds. At length, he said, 'Does Howard have another sort of rival?'

'I wouldn't know about that,' said Julie. 'All I do know is that Clive has me and seems perfectly happy with the arrangement.'

'And you, my dear,' said Otto, 'are you happy with the arrangement?'

'Oh, I can put up with it, I suppose,' said Julie.

'Put up with it?' said Otto.

'For another forty or fifty years,' said Julie.

'And after that, Mrs C?' said Maisie.

'After that,' Julie said, smiling, 'we'll see.'

32

Howard said, 'Has she been taking her pills regularly, Emily?'

'Yes, sir,' Emily answered. 'Regular as the clock.'

'Are you sure?'

'Quite sure, Mr Buskin. I put them out for her myself.'

'She looks exhausted.'

'Been a lot for her to put up with,' said Emily.

'That's true,' Howard conceded. 'She has Mr Goldstein to thank for that.'

The stateroom was smaller than the bedroom in Holland Park and made Emily seemed taller than she actually was. Short in the leg and narrow in the waist, she carried before her a ponderous bust that seemed about to pop the buttons or tear the laces of whatever garment she wore. Her hair was wiry and unnaturally black which Howard put down to one of the chemical dyes that had lately come on the market, for Emily was on the cusp of forty and should be showing at least a trace of grey in the upper storey.

Verity opened her eyes. 'I've Mr Goldstein to thank for a lot of things.'

'Oh,' Howard said, 'I'm sorry, Mama, did we waken you?'

'I wasn't asleep, though I am supposed to be resting. I would, therefore, be obliged if you'd stop hovering, Howard, wringing your hands and fretting over the state of my health.' She turned her head on the pillow and rolled her eyes upwards to take in her maid. 'And you, Emily, had better give over complaining. If it wasn't for Mr Goldstein you wouldn't be here at all.'

'I know he doesn't like me, ma'am.'

'He liked you well enough to insist on having you along.'

'I've been your lady's maid for fifteen years, Mrs Millar. I trust I've always give good service, but if you want rid of me . . .'

'No one wants to get rid of you, Emily,' Howard said.

'Then why am I eating with the servants? Mrs Cavendish's maid don't eat with the other maids and valets.'

'Mrs Cavendish's maid has children to look after,' Verity said. 'I had rather hoped you might give her a hand with them, in fact.'

'I'm not no nanny, Mrs Millar.'

'Goldstein,' Verity reminded her. 'I'm Mrs Goldstein now.'

'Well, Mrs Goldstein, I'm not trained to look after children. I've got enough to do looking after . . .'

'Yes?' said Verity, sitting up. 'Go on.'

'Your wardrobe,' said Emily, then, sucking in a breath, blurted out, '*She* don't have to eat with that lot in a crowded hole downstairs. *She* don't have a cabin you couldn't swing a cat in. *And* she's only young.'

'My God!' said Verity. 'You're jealous of Maisie Fellowes.'

'I'm not jealous of anybody. I just feel I'm not being given my due.'

'You're travelling to America, Emily, on the finest ship ever built and have a cabin to yourself. What more do you want?' Howard said with more patience than the woman deserved. 'As for Maisie Fellowes, she has two small children to feed, which is why she sits upstairs at breakfast and lunch and – by a special arrangement that costs Mr Cavendish extra – has her dinner served in the cabin. Do you think Maisie is living on champagne and caviar? If that's what's bothering you, I'll see to it that you have a bottle and plate in your cabin every evening, but what I will not do – do you hear me, Emily? – I will not make a place for a maid at our table in the dining saloon upstairs.'

'They don't like me downstairs, those others.'

'That's hardly surprising,' Verity said. 'They can smell a snob a mile off.'

'I have made my grievance known,' Emily said stiffly. 'I'll say no more about it, Mrs Goldstein.'

'I should hope not,' said Verity. 'Now, if you've nothing else to do here – which you haven't – I suggest you put on your coat and take a walk to calm yourself.'

'Take a walk where?' said Emily.

'Anywhere,' said Howard. 'You're on a first-class family ticket so only the private promenade decks are closed to you. My mother won't need you until an hour before dinner. I'll sit with her for a while.'

'Mrs Mill— Goldstein?'

'Go, Emily, just go,' Verity said, lying back, 'and give me peace.'

Anna was in no doubt that Teddy had had many girls in his time – his expertise as a lover attested to that – but it seemed he had never learned how to offer comfort when only comfort was required. She had no idea what had come over her up on the boat deck, why tears had flowed or why

Teddy had hustled her off to the nearest ladies lavatory as if emptying her bladder would make everything all right again.

At least he hadn't abandoned her. When she emerged from the ladies room he was waiting in the corridor, leaning against a pillar and smoking a cigarette.

'I'm sorry, Anna,' he said. 'I realise now I made a mistake.'

'What?' she said. 'Inviting me to New York?'

'God, no! Joining you on this hothouse of a ship.'

'It isn't that. It's . . .' But she didn't know what it was or how to explain it.

'To hell with it,' he said. 'I know what you need. Come on.'

Money changed hands, a bribe to the steward to ensure they wouldn't be disturbed. Then Teddy ushered her into his cabin, stretched her out on the bed and, without undressing, made love to her. Only moments after release, however, she experienced a vague sense of disappointment that he'd misinterpreted her need of him. All she could think of was the expression on the steward's face when money changed hands, a wordless transaction between men of the world, and the swift sly glance the steward had thrown at her, as if he were sizing her up and putting her down as just another trollop.

'Are we moving?' she said. 'The ship, I mean.'

'Yep, the anchors are up and we're on our way. Next stop New York.'

'We should go,' Anna said. 'I should go.'

'Will Howard be looking for you?'

'I don't know. Probably.'

'What would he say if he found us like this?'

'I don't know that either.'

'Nothing to be gained from taking risks.' Teddy rolled away and stood up.

'Are you going to play cards again?'

'I thought I might rustle up a partner for a game of racquet ball. Howard doesn't play racquet ball, I guess.'

'Howard doesn't even know what racquet ball is.'

He reached out a hand, hoisted her from the bed and kissed her.

'Better now, darling?' he said.

'Yes,' Anna said. 'All better.'

One of the valets, a middle-aged chap with an Italian name, had tried to strike up a conversation last night over dinner and, ignoring her frosty response, had made sheep's eyes at her again over breakfast this morning. She'd read about foreigners and their evil ways and how they wouldn't take no for an answer. Well, Emily thought, he'd better take 'no' for my answer or I'll have Mr Buskin report to him to the purser.

Still smarting at Mr Buskin's refusal to rescue her from the servants' dining room, she strode along the deck and up stairs, following her nose towards the bow. She was surprised how steady everything was, how nothing slid or tipped or rattled the way Mr Percy had said it would; it was clear that Mr Percy knew nothing about boats. The sea, though, the sea that everyone raved about was definitely a disappointment. It just lay there doing nothing, and when you stood still and stared at it for a while even the waves, such as they were, all looked the same.

The ship *was* very grand, though. The lounges and

reception rooms reminded her of visits to the Ritz with Mrs Millar – Goldstein – but were so spanking new you could still smell the paint and varnish. Then, through an open doorway, in a long room packed with people drinking coffee she caught sight of Mr Goldstein, Mrs Cavendish and Maisie – Maisie sitting there like Lady Muck, stuffing her face with cake while someone else took care of the kiddies who were supposed to be her responsibility. Emily retreated to an enclosed deck, where toffs were lolling in steamer chairs, and continued in the direction of the bow.

She pushed through a baize-covered door with a little window in it and found herself at one end of an empty passageway flanked by cabin doors.

She was on the point of withdrawing when one door opened and a man stuck his head out. Emily stepped back, the corridor door closing in front of her.

On the tips of her toes, she peeped through the oval window and saw Mr Norris, Mr Buskin's American friend, emerge from the cabin arm in arm with a young woman, a young woman she instantly recognised.

'Well, well, well,' Emily murmured, and prudently made herself scarce.

'When all is said and done, existence itself is a gamble,' Mr Reibling said. 'Do we not all gamble with our lives when we cast our bread upon the waters?'

'That's a gloomy thought.' Maude Scully pulled a face. 'I was under the impression we were talking about Mr Buskin's paintings.'

'Which, God knows, are gloomy enough,' Max put in. 'Not my intention to give offence, old chap,' he added, reaching over the table to pat Howard's arm, 'but you must admit your early Dartmoor landscapes aren't exactly jolly.'

'They've improved in that respect,' said Howard who, Anna thought, was taking it all in good part so far. 'I change my palette to match my circumstances.'

'Marriage certainly changed your palette,' Maude declared. 'Colours, I've never seen such colours. I was dazzled to near blindness at your last exhibition.'

'Oh,' said Miss Vazana, 'you have exhibited before, Mr Buskin?'

'Once or twice,' said Howard. 'Here and there.'

'But not in our country?' Miss Vazana said.

'Which country would that be?' Howard asked.

'America, of course,' the woman answered.

Anna expected Howard to come out with a cutting remark but he merely nodded. He really was on his best behaviour tonight, which was all the more surprising given that he didn't much care for Jews.

Maude had told her that Mr Reibling and Miss Vazana were not a couple; no hanky-panky there. Miss Vazana was Mr Reibling's sister-in-law and it had fallen to the old boy to escort her back across the Atlantic after a visit to Paris where he'd been lecturing on Old Testament theology at the Sorbonne and Miss Vazana had toured the fashion houses to top up her wardrobe for a hot summer in St Louis where, Maude had said, she was famous for her Friday evening salons. It was just as well she was famous for something other than her beauty, Maude had added, for, setting prejudice aside, Miriam Vazana was too tall to be fashionable and too old now – sixty if she was a day – to wear the latest French styles with anything approaching aplomb.

Howard said, 'No, Miss Vazana, I haven't exhibited in your country.'

'It is all a matter of acceptance.' Mr Reibling had apparently failed to notice that he was talking to himself. 'Only the breath of the Almighty gives us the assurance of a correct outcome. Take Zerubbabel, for instance, who put his faith in the stellar cults of Mesopotamia and not Divine Providence. He, if you recall . . .'

'Are you returning to St Louis directly, Miss Vazana?' Teddy asked.

'No, I'm staying in New York with Tula, my sister, for a week or so.'

'In that case why not come along to the Viaduct Gallery tomorrow week and judge Mr Buskin's work for yourself,' said Teddy.

'Your father, he will be there?'

'He certainly will,' said Teddy.

'Careful, Miriam; you might be expected to buy a painting,' Maude said.

'Oh, you are *selling* paintings,' said Miss Vazana. 'For charity, I suppose?'

'Howard,' Anna said quickly, 'be good enough to pass me the horseradish.'

'By all means, my dear.' Howard ferried the sauceboat down the table with a honeyed smile. 'Anything else I can get for you?'

'No, thank you,' Anna said. 'I have everything I need now.'

Mr Reibling released a bark of laughter that startled everyone into silence. His eyeglasses dropped from his nose and hung, swinging gently, on a silver chain. 'I am forced to conclude,' he said, 'that nobody is interested in Providence, or poor old Zerubbabel. Teddy, I will buy a painting. You see, I do listen while I talk. What sort of painting can I buy and what will it cost me?'

'Belshazzar's Feast for ten dollars,' Howard said. 'How's that?'

'My husband's teasing, Mr Reibling,' Anna said. 'He doesn't do religious subjects.'

'Anyway, you wouldn't get anything of Howard's for much less than three hundred,' Max said. 'Genius doesn't come cheap, Reuben.'

'Genius?' Miriam Vazana's eyebrows vanished into her hairpiece. 'You are saying this man is a genius?'

'Of course, he is,' Max went on. 'The world just doesn't know it yet. My advice: get in on the ground floor.'

'Your sister's husband, is he not a painter too?' Mr Reibling asked.

'He is,' said Anna, 'but I don't think Clive would call himself a genius.'

'So he comes cheaper,' Miriam Vazana said.

'He comes bigger, certainly,' said Howard. 'Buy a Cavendish and you'll get more canvas for your money, Miss Vazana. Covers a lot of wall, does Clive.'

'Who then is the better man?' said Reuben Reibling.

'The better man or the better investment?' said Max. 'Well, old chap, that's pretty much in the lap of the gods.'

'I will buy one of each and cross my fingers,' Mr Reibling said.

'Banking on Divine Providence while hedging your bets,' said Maude. 'Is that what the Talmud teaches?'

'The Talmud—' Mr Reibling began, but Teddy cut him short.

'Speaking of bets,' he said, 'is anyone up for a wager on our running speed?'

'I am,' said Howard promptly. 'Science not theology, Mr Reibling, is my forte. How is the distance measured, Norris?'

'Noon to noon in nautical miles.'

'And when's it posted?'

'Shortly before one every day on the board in the A Deck hall.'

'I believe the purser runs a sweepstake,' Max said.

'I don't much hold with sweeps,' Teddy said. 'I prefer to back my judgement eyeball to eyeball – and for a lot more than a shilling.'

'I'll have a piece of that, if I may,' Max said.

'Sorry, Max. You're far too familiar with White Star steamers. I expect you even know how fast this leviathan can shove along when she's given her head,' Teddy said. 'I've no intention of loading the dice in your favour.'

'Not when you've already hooked your fish, Teddy,' Maude Scully said. 'Be careful, Howard; this is a man not to be trusted.'

'I'm well aware of that.' Howard dug into the pocket of his dress suit, brought out a little silver case and extracted from it two visiting cards. 'Write down your mileage, Norris, and I'll do the same. Max can hold the cards. Closest to the number sent down from the bridge on Saturday wins.'

'Saturday?' Teddy said. 'What's wrong with tomorrow?'

'I prefer to wager on a full day's running.'

'Very well,' Teddy said. 'Fifty all right with you?'

'Make it a hundred,' Howard said. 'Pounds.'

★

The ship's band was playing in a corner of the lounge. By half past nine, it had run through a medley of songs from popular musical shows and a couple of ragtime tunes that had Julie tapping her toes. Otto had strolled over to the band leader ostensibly to enquire if dancing was permitted which, it seemed, it was not, not in the first-class lounge at any rate, though Palm Court was there for anyone who desperately wanted to cut a rug. What went on downstairs was anyone's guess, of course, and there were, the band leader said, a few spots on deck where the romantically inclined could catch enough of the music to take a little twirl.

'Well,' said Otto, taking his seat by Verity's side, 'I tried.'

A moment later the band struck up with 'Beautiful Dreamer' and Verity, who had downed a brandy or two by that time, threw up her arms in delight.

'Otto, you devil,' she cried. 'You requested it, didn't you?'

'Hmm,' said Otto smugly.

'They were playing that very song the night Otto and I first met,' Verity explained.

'I'm surprised the band still has the music for anything that old,' Clive said.

'Cheek!' Verity dug him in the ribs. 'You will be old too one day.'

'All too soon,' said Otto. 'What song will you remember: Wabash Blues?'

'Never heard of it,' said Clive. 'Besides, Julie and I are not going to grow old, are we, sweetheart? We're going to go on sailing, sailing for ever just as we are now.'

Verity sought her husband's hand.

'"Beautiful dreamer, out on the sea,"' she crooned,

'"mermaids are chanting the wild lorelie." Oh, dear, I can't remember the rest.'

'"Over the streamlet vapours are borne,"' Otto prompted.

'"Waiting to fade at the bright coming morn,"' said Anna.

'You see, you knew it all the time,' said Verity.

'Otto used to sing it in the bath,' said Julie.

'While thinking of me, dearest?' said Verity.

'Of no one else,' said Otto.

'Howard never sings in the bath,' said Verity. 'He isn't very musical.'

'Or has nothing to sing about,' Anna said.

'Then you must give him something to sing about,' Verity said.

'What, for instance?' Anna said. 'Aces and spades and clubs are trump.'

'Playing cards again, is he?' said Clive. 'What a waste of a lovely evening.'

'Howard doesn't think so,' Anna said.

'Nor does Teddy, by the look of it,' said Julie. 'What is it tonight?'

'Bridge, I believe,' said Anna. 'Teddy needs a partner to match stakes with Mr Millet and Major Butt who are, Teddy says, a very accomplished pair. Howard was only too willing to oblige. Now, if you'll excuse me. I think I'm going off to bed.'

'I hope we're not boring you, my dear?' Verity said.

'No,' said Anna. 'I'm just tired.'

She was neither bored nor tired, of course. She was angry with Howard for stealing her lover or – the thought rose in her mind like a noxious vapour – at her lover for stealing her husband. Who, she wondered, was competing with whom and what was the prize? If she was the prize why were they both avoiding her? When she saw Verity flirting with Uncle Otto and Julie and Clive so much in love they could hardly bear to be apart she was at a loss to understand why she was lying in bed alone in a cabin on a ship in the middle of the ocean on a voyage tailor-made for romance. She was still wide-awake, when, just after midnight, Howard stumbled in.

'Ah, you're up?' He crossed to the bathroom. 'Waiting to kiss me goodnight, are you – or to tell me what a naughty boy I've been?'

Through the half-open door, she heard him make water.

He was, she guessed, at least half seas over.

He emerged from the bathroom and began to undress.

'I take it you lost,' Anna said.

'Fact, no.' Fumbling with buttons, he chuckled into his chest. 'When you partner Teddy Norris – no, you don't lose. Took them for quite a few bob, if you must know.' He stripped off his waistcoat, shirt and under-vest and rubbed a hand over his hairy chest. 'Dear old Major Buttocks was none too pleased.' He lowered his trousers, kicking them over his shoes. 'I'd rather take money from Norris, though. I'll have his cods on toast when the numbers come through on Saturday. He won't like that.'

Anna was pressed into a corner of the bed, a pillow beneath her back. She watched him hop on one foot to detach the trouser leg from his shoe heel. He hopped, thumping, for half a minute before he collapsed on the side of his bed.

'You could give me a hand, you know,' he said.

'Why should I?' Anna said. 'You're the one who's drunk.'

'Not drunk, dearest, just merry.' He separated trousers from shoes, then, head lowered, fell to his knees and crabbed across the space between the beds. 'You don't grudge me a little innocent merriment, now do you?'

When he rested his head against her knees and squinted up at her she realised he wasn't nearly as drunk as she'd supposed him to be.

He said, 'Bet you a century you wish he was here.'

'You're talking nonsense, Howard.'

'Am I?' he said. 'If Norris was here right now you wouldn't be so shy. Aren't you going to give me a goodnight kiss?'

'No.'

'Or a goodnight anything else?' Before she could answer he slapped his thighs and got to his feet. He turned his back, stripped off his under-shorts and looked down. 'Alas, too many whiskies, Anna,' he said. 'The little feller seems to be already asleep.'

A moment later she heard the whisper of sheets and the sigh of the mattress as he climbed into bed. She was sure there was more to come, a parting shot before he closed his eyes.

He cleared his throat and said, 'You shouldn't be fooled by Teddy Norris. All that charm is just a front. Underneath, he's reckless beyond belief.'

'Make it a hundred,' Anna said.

'Beg pardon?'

'Make it a hundred, your very words.'

'Well, yes,' Howard said. 'Point taken,' and at least had the decency to laugh.

33

Quite a little crowd gathered in the A Deck hall shortly after noon on Saturday to await the posting of the daily progress report on the board on the starboard side of the stairs. Couches and armchairs were occupied mainly by ladies and elderly gentlemen who were, on the surface, too proud to 'have a flutter' on anything as vulgar as a sweepstake but who had somehow managed to register a number in the name of a maid or a valet and who, with the peerless indifference of the well-to-do, kept just as beady an eye on the staircase as everyone else.

Friday's posting had recorded 386 miles but that figure had included the stop at Queenstown and neither Howard nor Teddy had been fooled into using it as a yard-stick for twenty-four hours of uninterrupted running.

In a heavy mantelet that appeared to have been cut from an Afghan rug and sporting a hairpiece more suited to the law courts than the lounge, Miriam Vazana lounged in an armchair and brazenly smoked a cigarette in an ivory holder so long that Mr Reibling claimed it would reach New York a half-hour before she did. Her sweepstake number reposed in Mr Reibling's vest pocket and she had about her an air of absolute confidence, for, she said, she'd had a word with an officer who had been kind enough to give her a lesson in maritime arithmetic and the conversion of knots into miles. Mr Reibling, on the other hand, had put his faith in Divine Providence – and had no confidence at all in the outcome.

Four young sprats and two giggling girls formed a wedge in front of the board and were giving up their places to no one, while dedicated gamblers, to whom wagering a shilling on mere guesswork was anathema, loitered in the space behind the elevators sipping pre-lunch whiskies and casually puffing cigars.

Howard too was puffing a cigar but a good deal less casually than his confrères round the corner. He swayed nervously from foot to foot as if, Teddy said, he hadn't found his sea legs yet. With a hand on Clive's shoulder, Max viewed the excitement with an amused smile. He had seen it all before many times and neither he nor prudent Mr Cavendish had attempted to predict the speed of *Titanic*'s majestic progress across the face of the deep.

'Here he comes,' someone called out.

All eyes turned towards the staircase. Tripping down it with the dainty step common to all uniformed personnel, the Third Officer, hat under his arm, danced into the hall and, with a bow here and there to the ladies, crossed to the board and pinned a tiny strip of paper to the chart.

The four sprats crowded forward. One of them shouted, 'Five. One. Nine.'

'Five hundred and nineteen miles,' the Third Officer announced. 'Anyone close to that figure?'

'Me, me,' a gentleman called out. 'Five hundred and twelve.'

'I have the same,' a female voice piped up. 'Five, twelve.'

'Call at the purser's office at four o'clock,' the officer said. 'If there are no other claims then the prize will be divided between you, less a percentage for a seaman's charity. May I remind you that, tomorrow being Sunday, there will be no sweepstake, although the running figure will be posted as usual.'

Clive said, 'She's making fair speed, Max.'

'About twenty knots, I reckon,' Max said. 'She still has untapped boiler capacity so she won't really open up until we turn the corner.'

'The corner?' Clive said.

'Swing towards the coast of Nova Scotia. We're on the Southern Route so we shouldn't encounter too much field ice at this time of year.'

'Field ice?' Clive said.

'In any event, ice won't stop this beast,' Max said. 'I doubt if Bruce Ismay will let her slow down. Mark you, he's not supposed to be here officially as president of White Star, so I doubt if Captain Smith will pay much attention to anything Ismay might have to say about running speed and course setting.'

'Field ice,' said Clive again. 'I say, Max, any chance of spotting an iceberg? My little lad would be thrilled to catch a glimpse of one of those.'

'The weather's exceptionally clear so you never know your luck,' said Max.

Howard and Teddy had consulted the little strip of paper on the chart together to ensure there was no possibility of error.

As they approached, Teddy was smiling; Howard was not.

'The cards, please, Mr Scully,' Teddy said.

Max took his wallet from his pocket and drew out the visiting cards. He glanced at one then the other before he handed them to Teddy.

'Five hundred and ten, Howard,' Teddy said. 'Damned good guess.'

'But not good enough, uh?' said Howard.

Teddy exposed a card in the palm of each hand.

'Five, sixteen,' he said. 'See.'

'By gum, Yankee, you've won the sweep,' said Max. 'Congratulations.'

'I didn't enter the sweep,' said Teddy. 'I have, however, beaten Howard.'

'What do I owe you?' Howard asked.

'A hundred pounds was the sum agreed,' Teddy answered.

Howard picked a fleck of tobacco leaf from the tip of his tongue.

'Double or quits?' he said.

Otto had booked two steamer chairs on an enclosed section of the deck and made sure that Verity was warmly tucked up under a travelling rug before he took off on his post-prandial constitutional. In spite of his cheerful assurances to the children he was worried about his wife's health. Verity claimed she had never felt better but, sea air and good food notwithstanding, she was not quite herself. After he'd made love to her in bed at night she would wrap her legs and arms around him as if she feared some deep-sea monster might reach into the cabin and snatch her away.

It was odd, Otto thought, as he started along the prom-enade deck, how swiftly one became accustomed to the routine of life aboard ship; a life so orderly it was hard to believe he'd only been four days at sea.

Fine weather helped, of course; cloudless skies, a passive sea, ships passing on the horizon as smoothly as swans gliding across a lake. Even so, he couldn't shake off a nagging feeling that all was not as it should be and a fear that if New York lived up to its hectic reputation three weeks touring the city might do Verity more harm than good.

'Mr Goldstein, a word, sir.'

'Oh, I thought you were still at lunch, Emily.'

'Lunch!' the woman said. 'Some lunch!'

'Well, there's a chair vacant beside Mrs Goldstein if you wish to use it.'

'No,' Emily said. 'I need a word with you, private like.'

It dawned on him that the meeting had not been by chance. Sighing, he said, 'Look, if this is about the dining arrangements—'

'No,' she said, 'it's worse than that.'

'Worse?' said Otto. 'Is it Verity – Mrs Goldstein, I mean – is there something she hasn't told me? Something I should know?'

Emily pressed herself against his stomach and, looking him dead in the eye, said, 'It's Mrs Buskin, sir, Mr Buskin's wife.'

'Yes,' said Otto impatiently, 'I do know who Mrs Buskin is.'

'She's – she's misbehaving, sir.'

'Misbehaving? What, giving you a hard time?'

'With another.'

'Another what?'

'Man, sir, another man what isn't Mr Buskin.'

With some difficulty Otto maintained his composure.

He felt awkward enough with the stout little woman pressed up against him in a position that might suggest familiarity or even be construed as intimacy. He'd had his suspicions about Anna ever since Norris had sneaked on board at Cherbourg. Only Norris's apparent lack of interest in his niece – his preference for her husband's company – had partially allayed his concern.

He stroked his moustache for half a second then said sternly, 'I think you'd better be careful, Emily. It doesn't do for a lady's maid to make accusations against her employer.'

'She ain't – she isn't my employer. You are.'

'Well, I suppose that's true,' Otto conceded.

'I didn't want to go to Mr Buskin, not right off.'

'That would be a foolish move on your part,' Otto said. 'All right, I suppose you'd better tell me what you think you heard.'

'Saw.' Emily nodded grimly. 'I saw her come out of Mr Norris's cabin. No mistake, Mr Goldstein. It was her all right.'

'When did this – this thing occur?'

'Thursday afternoon, when Mr Howard was busy with Mrs Goldstein.'

'What, may I ask, were you doing prowling about the first-class cabins in the forward part of the ship? Were you spying on Mrs Buskin?'

'No, Mr Goldstein, no. Went for a walk and got lost.'

'What exactly did you see?'

'Mr Norris came out of the cabin first,' Emily said. 'He looked about careful then brought Mrs Buskin out by the hand.'

'Did Mr Norris and Mrs Buskin do anything else?'

'Like what?'

'Embrace,' Otto said. 'Kiss.'

'No, sir, nothing like that.'

'Then,' said Otto, 'you saw nothing.'

'Oh, but I did. I saw—'

Otto put a hand on her shoulder. 'Nothing. Do you hear me? Did it not even cross your mind that Mr Norris might simply be showing Mrs Buskin his cabin? Now, where is Mrs Buskin?'

'Don't know, sir.'

'Mr Buskin?'

'I think he's playing cards.'

'Mr Norris is Mr Buskin's friend,' said Otto. 'In addition to which, he's Mr Buskin's picture dealer, so, honestly, Emily, do you think it's likely he'd misbehave with Mr Buskin's wife?'

'No, Mr Goldstein, I don't think it's likely.'

'There you are then,' said Otto, far too breezily. 'Mystery solved.'

She cocked her head and frowned.

She was still suspicious but surely, Otto thought, horse sense and self-interest would prevail. He said, 'Trot along and see if Mrs Goldstein needs anything and, if she doesn't, make yourself comfortable on the steamer chair until I get back.'

'Are you going to have words with Mrs Buskin, sir?'

'I most certainly am not,' said Otto. 'Now, cut along before you try my patience too far. And remember – you saw nothing.'

'No, sir, nothing,' said Emily.

*

It really was an exceptionally beautiful room, Julie thought. Everything was brand new, of course, but even after it weathered, as no doubt it would, the oak panelling would mellow and the light through the ornamental windows would still reflect the shimmer of the sea in mirrors and marble surrounds.

Clive had promised that on their twenty-fifth wedding anniversary they would sail across the Atlantic on this same ship and, without Walter and Frances to distract them, make love all the way from Southampton to New York, which struck Julie as a very pleasant prospect, if a shade impractical.

She lay on the bed digesting the crab salad she'd consumed at lunch, with Fran, fast asleep, lying on her stomach. She amused herself by breathing deeply and watching her daughter, all unaware, rise and fall like one of the 'living' waxworks in Tussaud's; my sleeping beauty, she thought, and lightly brushed Fran's curls with her fingertips. She loved being alone with her daughter, not that she didn't love Walter but it was already evident that he was a man's man and very much his father's son.

Maisie had taken him up to the gymnasium to get his mind off revolving doors. Between the hours of one and three o'clock small boys and girls, closely supervised by a trainer, were allowed to ride the electric horse or one of the stationary bicycles or even pretend to lift weights. Walter hoisting an empty barbell above his head, grunting and groaning like the mighty Sandow, was certainly a sight to behold, Clive said, and had recorded his son's efforts in a series of lightning cartoons that everyone, Walter excepted, found highly amusing.

The ship made scarcely a sound save a steady rhythmic pulsation and a faint silken hiss as the bow cleaved the waters of the Atlantic. There were bells and bugles, of course, and random voices in the passageway but at that hour of the afternoon it was all so peaceful that Julie's eyelids drooped. She had almost joined her daughter in Nod when someone knocked on the door.

'Who is it?'

'Me,' Otto answered. 'Are you decent?'

'Yes.'

The door opened and Otto stepped into the cabin.

She could tell by Otto's expression that the peace of the afternoon was about to be shattered. She eased Fran from her stomach and settled her, still asleep, on the bed by her side.

Without preamble, Otto said, 'Is Anna having an affair with Teddy Norris?'

'Who told you that?' Julie said.

'She hasn't been exactly discreet about it. Is it true?'

'Yes,' Julie said. 'It's more than a casual fling, though. She's not coming back to England with us. As soon as the Viaduct show is up and running she intends to tell Howard that their marriage is over and ask for a divorce.'

Otto groped for one of the room's upright chairs. He leaned forward, elbows on knees and, out of consideration for the sleeping child, spoke softly. 'What a complicated legal process that'll be.'

'Is that all you have to say about it?'

'Stanley will be broken-hearted.'

'What about Howard?' Julie said.

'Howard will be more than broken-hearted,' Otto said. 'He'll be furious.'

'Anna and Teddy have been planning it for months, apparently.'

'Letters, I suppose. How did—'

'Clive was the post box,' Julie said.

'Clive? Hah! The ultimate victory.'

'What do you mean?'

'If you can't rob a man of his talent at least you can rob him of his wife.'

'Clive isn't like that,' Julie snapped. 'If you think Clive knew Anna was bent on leaving Howard and encouraged her to do so then you don't know my husband very well.'

'Hell!' said Otto, very softly. 'Hell and damnation!'

'You're thinking of Verity, aren't you?'

'Of course, I am. Good God, the shock could kill her.'

'At least she'll have her precious son all to herself again.'

'She doesn't need Howard now she has me.'

'She wants grandchildren,' Julie said. 'If Anna deserts Howard you can bet your last sixpence Howard will never marry again. Besides . . .'

Otto glanced up. 'What?'

'I gather it wasn't much of a marriage.'

'That isn't for you to say,' Otto said. 'Have you tried to talk Anna out of it?'

'If Anna believes Teddy Norris is the man for her what right have I to tell her she's wrong?' Julie said. 'I've no intention of saying a word to Anna or Teddy in case it queers things for Clive. This New York show is important to my husband. I don't want anything or anyone to spoil it, least of all my selfish sister.'

'Now you're the one who's being selfish,' Otto said.

'With good reason,' Julie said. 'I've a husband, whom I

love and two small children to look out for. I won't tolerate anything that threatens their future. To be frank, Otto, I've never liked Howard, never trusted him. It might be no bad thing for Anna to be rid of him once and for all.'

'Trade him for a rich American, you mean.'

'The size of Teddy Norris's fortune isn't a factor. In any case, Howard isn't exactly poor.' She paused, frowning. 'Don't tell me you've persuaded Verity to leave everything to you?'

'Julie, Julie.' Otto shook his head. 'I hope you know me better than that. In fact, I insisted that Verity revise her will before we left London. Everything goes to Howard and Anna, except for one or two small personal things.'

'Like what?'

'Banbury's portrait for one.' Otto shivered. 'God, but this is a morbid topic. Neither Verity nor I are tottering on the brink, Julie. We've plenty of years left. To nail your misgivings once and for all, I've no intention of giving up my partnership with your father. I may live with Verity and be responsible for looking after her but in all other respects I'm still my own man.'

'Of course, you are,' Julie said. 'I'm sorry.'

'I'll let you into a secret,' Otto said. 'I was always of the opinion that you might be the one to go to the bad.'

'Shaking off a useless husband is hardly going to the bad,' Julie said. 'But I count myself lucky I found the right man to marry. Now, before we start saying things we might regret, Uncle, what are you going to do?'

'About Anna?' Otto hesitated. 'I don't know. I mean, what can I do? If I challenge Norris and demand explanations there's bound to be a scene. I'm not sure I want to spoil this wonderful trip for everyone else.'

'Then wait,' Julie said. 'Please, for Clive's sake and my sake, wait.'

'For how long?'

'At least until we reach New York.'

'Yes,' Otto said, rising. 'Who knows? Perhaps Anna will change her mind.'

'She might,' Julie said, as Fran opened her eyes and yawned. 'But I doubt it.'

'I doubt it too,' said Otto.

'But you will wait, won't you?'

'Yes,' said Otto. 'For your sake – and Verity's – I will.'

34

Anna saw no irony in following Divine Service in the first-class dining room at half past ten o'clock on Sunday morning with an act of adultery in Teddy's cabin at half past three in the afternoon. Although she considered herself a good Christian, raised in the habit of worship, she had no difficulty in packing her conscience away, like the White Star's prayer books, as soon as the service was over.

Uncle Otto had volunteered to look after Frances and, with Maude and Max Scully's help, kept the toddler amused by fashioning rabbit's ears out of napkins in the Verandah café while Walter experienced his first brush with 'religion' which, with Dad singing lustily on one side and Maisie on the other, he thoroughly enjoyed.

White Star policy-makers did not encourage integration between the classes even on Sunday. Second- and third-class passengers assembled below decks to pay homage to God and, in the case of Roman Catholics, receive mass from the hands of an Irish priest. For an hour or so, the ship hummed with devotional melodies after which members of all classes headed off in search of a snifter before lunch.

With no sweepstake, the crowd around the chart board was thin. Only those interested in matters maritime and a few incorrigible gamblers – Howard and Clive among them – even bothered to glance at the slip of paper the officer brought down from the bridge.

Howard groaned. 'How much do I owe you now, Norris?'

'Couple of hundred, I guess.'

'Same again on tonight's run.'

'Are you sure, Howard?'

'What's wrong? Can't you stand the pace?'

'Sure, I can,' Teddy Norris said. 'Double or quits, it is.'

By three o'clock Howard was asleep in his cabin.

Late nights and an excess of whisky had taken their toll and he lay on his back, flat out, snoring loudly. By a quarter past three Anna was flat on her back on the bed in Teddy's cabin and by half past was almost convinced that Teddy not only loved her but would make good on all his promises.

She snuggled, naked, against him.

'I should never have doubted you, darling,' she said.

'Have I given you reason to doubt me?'

'Actually, you have – a little.'

'Why – because I spend time with Howard?'

'That – and other things.'

'It's not that I don't want to be with you every hour of every day – I do, I definitely do – it's just that Howard has to be appeased.'

Anna sat up. 'Appeased? That's a peculiar word for it.'

'I guess I mean kept sweet. He's too impulsive for his own good.'

'That's more or less what he said about you.'

Teddy stroked her shoulder with the tip of a finger. 'So you and Howard talk about me, do you?'

'It would be odd if we didn't,' Anna said. 'If you must

know, he thinks you're a fine upstanding fellow and a credit to your profession.'

'A fine upstanding fellow I'm not,' Teddy said, 'but I do like to think I'm a credit to my profession.'

'What precisely is your profession? I've never been too clear on that point.'

'I'm a dealer in modern art.'

'Is it profitable?'

'Can be. Will be.'

'When we're married will you take me with you?'

'Take you where?' Teddy asked.

'France, Italy – on all your travels.'

'Sure, I will,' he said, a shade too quickly for Anna's liking.

'You won't just dump me, Teddy, will you?'

'Dump you?'

'Leave me alone in New York while you go off jaunting for weeks on end.'

'Heck, no, I'm not going to dump you.'

'You will have to dump Howard, you know.'

'Don't remind me,' Teddy said. 'I hate giving up on a great artist.'

'Is he a great artist?'

Teddy frowned. 'Don't you know just how good Howard is?'

She sensed she'd disappointed him and sought, belatedly, to rectify her mistake. 'He's certainly very dedicated. Perhaps I'm too close to him to fully appreciate his – his qualities.'

Teddy pulled away, slid from the bed and reached for his trousers.

Anna said, 'I'm giving up things too, darling. I'm giving up my family, my friends, my – my country to be with you.'

'There's still time for you to change your mind,' Teddy said.

'Do you want me to change my mind?'

'I've gone to too much trouble to fetch you to New York to have you change your mind now.' He paused, listening. 'I reckon you'd better get dressed. There's someone lurking in the passage.'

'The steward . . .'

'No – right outside my door.'

They dressed swiftly, silently.

When Teddy opened the door, Anna hid behind it.

She heard him say, 'Emily, what the devil are you doing here?'

'It's Mrs Buskin, sir. Mr Buskin sent me to find her.'

'What makes you think she might be with me?'

'If she is,' Emily answered tactfully, 'tell her she'd better come at once.'

Anna took a deep breath and showed herself.

'Why, Emily?' she said. 'What's wrong?'

'Don't know, Mrs Buskin. All I know is, he wants you back.'

The instant she stepped into the stateroom and found Howard kneeling on the floor surrounded by Teddy's letters Anna knew that the game was up. She had personally unpacked the Vuitton but had carelessly left the toilet bag inside and, with the case yawning at her feet and the toilet bag flung into a corner there was no possibility of denying that the letters belonged to her, even if they hadn't been full of intimate promises addressed to her by name.

For a moment she felt sick at the hurt she was causing,

then, with Emily still bobbing about in the corridor, she closed the door and tossed her hat on the bed.

'How did you find them?'

'Hunting for a nail file.' Howard showed his hand, thumb cocked. 'I wasn't prying, Anna. Honestly.'

Pages, a great shoal of them, were scattered across the carpet and several little balls of crumpled paper tossed against the cabin wall hinted at anger.

He seemed calm enough now, though, icily calm.

He sat back on his heels. 'Were you with him just now?'

'Yes.'

'I mean, were you doing sex with him?'

'Yes.'

'Was it satisfactory?'

'Yes. Very.'

He adjusted his position, easing his legs out in front of him. He looked almost endearing in that pose, like a bear in a zoo pit, Anna thought, a letter resting in his lap like a sugar bun. 'At the risk of sounding banal,' he said, 'may I ask how long this thing between you and Norris has been going on?'

'If you hadn't spent so much time—'

'I'm not after excuses, Anna, just answers.'

She seated herself on an upright chair, her silks sticking to her thighs. She pressed her knees together and folded her arms.

'How long?' he said.

'Almost four years.'

'Then you were with him before we were married?'

'Yes.'

'Did you think you were pregnant when you married me?'

'No,' Anna said. 'Perhaps if Teddy hadn't come back to London . . .'

'Did you send for him?'

'No.'

'Did you send for him to give you what I couldn't?'

'No, Howard.'

'But you didn't turn him down.'

'No, I didn't turn him down. You didn't want me: Teddy did.'

He spoke with a sardonic edge that she found hurtful. 'Well, if you want to live with him in New York, which seems to be the plan, I'm not going to stop you.'

'Are you writing me off, Howard? Aren't you even going to ask me to stay?'

He plucked the letter from his lap and discarded it as if it had neither value nor meaning. He elbowed himself to his feet, tugged down the wings of his waistcoat and ran a hand over his hair. 'What's the point?' he said. 'Norris can have you. What he can't have is my paintings. I'll burn them before I'll let Norris have them.'

'The show, the Viaduct show is all set up.'

'Too bad!'

'Clive will be very upset.'

'Clive can reap all the glory. By the by, Clive hasn't had you too, has he?'

'That's a filthy thing to say.'

'Yes, I suppose it is,' Howard conceded. 'He's far too enthralled by his skinny little wife to be interested in you.' He stirred the pages on the carpet with the toe of his shoe. 'I'm afraid you're going to have to clear up this mess by yourself. Probably not wise to ring for a stewardess, not if we want to keep "our little problem" to ourselves for a while. I don't want to spoil the voyage for Mama. Time enough for confrontations after we land.'

'Aren't you going to talk to Teddy?'

'Of course, I am. I'm going to break bread, crack jokes and play cards with him as if all was as it should be. And you, my sweetheart, are going to say nothing. You're an expert in duplicity, after all. And if you feel the urge to slip off for a bit of horizontal exercise I shan't stop you.'

'What am I going to tell Teddy?'

'Tell him I sent for you because Mama wasn't well. Tell him I couldn't find my bloody cufflinks. You'll think of something. Just don't tell him I know what's going on. We'll settle the matter like gentlemen after we reach New York. Now, clear up this litter and dress for dinner, please. I want you to be at your best tonight.'

'Where are you going, Howard?'

'Right now? Off to the bar for a drink.'

She was doing her best to avoid him which, she realised, was a strange way to behave towards a man with whom she hoped to spend the rest of her life. She had crafted a lie but hadn't polished it and she was sure that Teddy would see through it at once. He trapped her on the landing of the grand staircase. The elevator had been crowded as usual and he had no difficulty in separating her from Howard as the elegant crowd moved on.

'What did Howard want with you?' Teddy asked.

'Phooh!' she answered. 'He had a blazing row with the steward about towels and needed me to back him up. A storm in a teacup, in other words.'

'Did the woman, Emily, say anything out of turn?'

'No,' Anna said. 'She knows she'll lose her position if she does.'

'Maybe I should give her a few dollars just in case.'

'No bad idea,' said Anna.

She addressed him nonchalantly, smiling, then, with Teddy behind her, went downstairs to join her husband. She was just about to enter the saloon when Teddy said, 'I won't be joining you for dinner tonight. The captain's laid on something special in the *a la carte* and Major Butt has finagled me an invitation. I should be through socialising by ten, Howard, if you're game for a hand or two.'

'I'm always game for a hand or two,' said Howard, then led Anna into the dining room to join the rest of the family.

Concerts were taking place all over the ship. In the second-class dining saloon there was a communal hymn-sing and, deeper below decks, the third-class passengers were raising the roof with marching songs and sentimental Irish ballads.

The music in the first-class reception rooms was rather too sedate and Julie, for one, was glad when the lights were dimmed to indicate an end to the Sunday evening's entertainment. She hadn't been alone in sharing Anna's embarrassment at the number of whiskies Howard poured over his throat or his insistence on ordering unwanted brandy for everyone. Only Verity was taken in by her son's bonhomie and laughed at his brittle remarks and, in spite of Otto's disapproval, matched him glass for glass.

It came as a relief when Teddy appeared on the stairs and signalled to Howard that his presence was required in the smoking room. Soon after, the band put away its instruments and people streamed out of the reception rooms to settle in one of the lounges or take a last stroll on deck before turning in.

Maude and Max Scully paused to say goodnight and, as soon as they'd gone, Otto got to his feet and offered Verity his hand. 'No nightcap for you, my dear,' he said. 'I think you've had quite enough for one evening.'

'Do you see how mean he is,' said Verity. 'Denying his poor old wife a little something warm. Are *you* going to warm me instead, Otto?'

Otto raised an eyebrow. 'Now, now, Verity, enough of that. We don't want to embarrass the children, do we?'

'The children? Oh, if only I were young again, Mr Goldstein, you wouldn't have a leg to stand on.' She chuckled, then, with a hand to her breast, said, 'I think you may be right, my dear. I am just a little out of puff.'

'Time for bed then,' Otto said firmly. 'Say goodnight to everyone.'

'Goodnight everyone.'

Leaning on her husband, she swayed unsteadily across the room and picked her way upstairs. The last Julie ever saw of her was a glimpse on the gallery as she waved, rather grandly, to all and sundry before Otto whisked her away.

There was no moon but a million stars glittered brilliantly in the arching sky. The Cavendishes had hoped to be alone on the boat deck but the rails were dotted with couples braving the chill. The temperature had dropped close to freezing. Using the cold as an excuse, Clive wrapped his arms round Julie and waltzed her across the breadth of the ship from port to starboard until they bumped into Miriam

Vazana clad in a heavy coat with a massive fur collar and a hat like a Mexican bandit's.

Mr Reibling had added a white silk scarf to his evening attire but was so enraptured by the starry night sky that he didn't seem to feel the cold. He was in the process of treating his long-suffering sister-in-law to a discourse on the stellar cults of ancient Egypt and their connection to the constellation of Orion but politely broke off to greet the young couple.

'Beautiful night,' he said.

'But cold,' said Julie. 'I don't believe we've met.'

'You are Mrs Buskin's sister, are you not?' Miriam Vazana stuck out a gloved hand. 'And this must be the painter who is not a genius.'

'I beg your pardon?' Clive said.

'A little joke,' Miss Vazana said. 'Do not take offence, young man.'

She proceeded to introduce herself and her brother-in-law who was on the point of launching into another astrological lecture when Miriam tugged his sleeve. 'Come now, Reuben, the Cavendishes have no wish to listen to old goats bleating. They are company enough for each other. Tomorrow, Mr Cavendish, tomorrow you will tell me all about your paintings and suggest to me which one I should buy.'

'Two,' Mr Reibling said. 'We will take two.'

Clive laughed. 'I might just hold you to that, sir, though I suspect promises made on a chilly night in mid-Atlantic aren't binding.'

'He will tell you,' Miss Vazana said, 'it is written in the stars – but you must not believe him. Tomorrow we will find Maude and Max and have coffee and talk more. Yes?'

'I look forward to it,' Clive said.

Cigarette-holder wagging, Miriam Vazana inclined towards Julie and, in a stage whisper, remarked, 'Handsome. He is so handsome,' then, with a chuckle, dragged her brother-in-law off towards the stairs.

'Who the devil are they?' Clive said, as soon the pair had gone.

'Teddy had them at his table with Howard, Anna and the Scullys.'

'Where were we?'

'Feeding the five thousand,' said Julie. 'Early supper, remember?'

'She's obviously a woman of taste,' Clive said.

'Just because she said you were handsome doesn't mean she's going to buy one of your paintings,' Julie said. 'Besides, it's dark up here.'

'Not that dark,' Clive said. He kissed her. 'Not dark enough.'

'Dear me! I hope you're not suggesting somefink improper, sir.'

'Would I do such a thing? Even if I am considered 'andsome by some, I wouldn't go pressing me attentions on an innocent young flower like yourself.'

'I might not be as innocent as you think I am.'

'Really! And me a married man too. Have you no shame?'

'None,' Julie said.

It was on her mind to tell him about Anna's decision to leave Howard. She hated keeping secrets from her husband but when the truth did come out she was sure Clive would forgive her.

'Shall we go down now?' Clive asked.

'You mean, to bed?'

'Of course I mean to bed. Where else are we going to go at this hour?'

'Yes,' Julie said. 'Let's go to bed. It's too cold to stay out.'

He guided her towards the stairs, then, pausing, stared out at the sea.

'Max tells me we might spot an iceberg tomorrow, if we're lucky.'

'Oh, Walter will love that,' Julie said.

'I wouldn't mind seeing one myself,' said Clive.

And then, arm in arm, they went below.

35

Seated in a tub chair before the electrical heater in her stateroom, Anna was trying to coax a little warmth into her feet when an unusual sound disturbed her, a sound like the scratching squeal of chalk scraping the surface of an old blackboard. It was accompanied by a slight jarring that interrupted the familiar rhythm of the engines. If Howard had been with her she might have asked him what had caused it but she was too wrapped up in her own predicament to be curious. It certainly didn't occur to her that the ship that was carrying her towards her destiny might have any part in shaping that destiny.

She was still dressed in her evening gown, a blanket draped over her shoulders. She flexed her toes inside her stockings and sank into introspection once more. 'There's still time for you to change your mind,' Teddy had told her but now that Howard had learned the truth changing her mind was no longer an option.

It was only when voices were raised in the passageway that Anna realised the ship was no longer moving forward.

She sat up, head cocked, and, curiosity tweaked at last,

slipped on her shoes, shed the blanket and opened the stateroom door.

The steward had just delivered a glass of warm milk to Otto's cabin when the engines went into reverse and, soon after, stopped.

There was no great shaking or shuddering but the skin on the surface of the milk trembled a little as Otto lifted the glass to Verity's lips. He peered into the glass, frowning, for half a second, then, still frowning, held it and the three little sugar-coated pills out to his wife and urged her to take them.

He had managed to get her dress off and her corset. She was seated on the side of the bed in what was described in steamy novels as déshabille. In a younger woman, Otto thought, guiltily, the effect would have been arousing but Verity was young no more – and no more was he. He ignored the enquiring voices rising and falling in the passageway, held the glass in one hand, lifted Verity's hand with the other and tipped the pills into her palm.

'Take them, dearest,' he urged. 'They'll make you feel better.'

Her gaiety had evaporated almost as soon as she'd entered the stateroom. She'd gone into the bathroom merry and had emerged, minutes later, a sickly wreck, a transformation Otto had put down to alcohol. He'd ordered warm milk from the steward and, to save Verity's blushes, had dismissed Emily for the night.

The words dropping singly, like coins from a slot, Verity said, 'Too. Much. Brandy. Otto. Silly. Me.'

He put the glass on the bed-stand and, gripping her wrist firmly, lifted her hand to her mouth and watched her lick up the pills.

She coughed. He pressed a forefinger to her lips to keep the pills in and, reaching behind him, picked up the glass once more.

'Are you going to vomit?' he asked.

She shook her head.

'Then' – he offered the glass again – 'do try to drink some of this.'

Her eyes shifted focus, slanting towards the glass.

'Milk? I'm not. A Baby.'

'You are,' Otto said. 'You are my baby, Mrs Goldstein.'

Otto flattened his hand between her shoulder blades and held her steady while she sipped from the glass. He wiped milk from her upper lip with his finger and watched her throat contract as she swallowed. Then the door from the passageway opened and Anna, fully dressed, stuck her head into the room.

'Otto,' she said, 'what's happening?'

'Drop too much to drink, that's all.'

'I mean,' Anna said, 'why have we stopped?'

'I've no idea,' Otto said. 'What does the steward say?'

'He thinks we may have dropped a propeller. What does that mean?'

'No idea,' said Otto again. 'I'm no sailor.'

'Do we have to stop to pick up the propeller, is that it?'

'I doubt it,' Otto said. 'Whatever it is, the worst that can happen is we'll be delayed in reaching New York.'

Anna advanced into the room. Verity seemed unaware of her presence. She sagged against her husband and appeared to be asleep.

'Otto, I don't think she's very well,' Anna said.

'Howard shouldn't have poured all that brandy into her.'

Otto rubbed his wife's back with his hand. 'She'll be fine come morning. Won't you, my honey?'

'It's freezing in here,' said Anna. 'Couldn't you at least put on the heater?'

'Better yet,' said Otto, 'you could help me get her into bed.'

'Where's her nightgown?'

'Never mind the nightgown,' Otto said. 'She's slept in petticoats often enough. Now, be good enough to turn down the bedclothes.'

'I think we should send for a doctor,' Anna said.

Otto said, 'No, no. Verity won't thank us for causing a fuss. She'll be as right as rain in the morning, though she might have a bit of headache.'

The voices in the passageway had dwindled into silence. For two or three seconds there was no sound save Verity's laboured breathing.

'All right,' Anna said. 'Lift her up, please.'

Otto drew his wife into a sitting position.

She opened her eyes. 'Otto?' she said. 'Otto, is that you?'

'It certainly is, dear,' Otto said.

'What's. Happening?'

'Anna's here. We're putting you to bed. Please, lie down.'

Anna tucked the bedclothes around Verity's neck. Her hair on the pillow was as brittle as straw but her features seemed oddly youthful.

'You see,' Otto said. 'She's better now. I'll lie beside her for a while.'

'Otto . . .' Anna began.

'You're going to fetch Howard, aren't you?' Otto said.

'Yes,' Anna told him. 'I am.'

★

Archie Butt and Frank Millet were playing bridge with another couple. Howard and Teddy, left to their own devices, were experimenting with the new American game of gin rummy at a small table in a nook of the smoking room when the collision occurred. At a quarter to twelve, the smoking room was still crowded. Teddy could see Major Butt over Howard's shoulder. At first Major Butt, like most men present, appeared unconcerned but when the engines stopped he placed his cards face down on the table and left the room.

Teddy said, 'Can't be the weather.'

'What can't be the weather?' said Howard.

'The weather can't be the reason we've stopped.'

'Oh, we've stopped, have we?' Howard looked round. 'Whatever it is, I expect it'll be fixed shortly.'

'I don't like it,' Teddy said.

'Don't like what? The game? You're winning, aren't you?'

'The silence: I don't like the silence. Perhaps we should quit.'

Howard gathered the cards, squared and boxed the deck and, without looking up, said, 'Is she waiting for you?'

'Beg pardon?'

'Is my wife waiting for you?'

'What the heck are you talking about, Howard?'

'Anna thinks you're going to marry her.' He dealt the cards deftly. 'You're not, are you?'

'I don't know what you've heard, but—'

'Of course,' Howard went on, 'she may have given up on you. She has very little patience when it comes to getting her own way. If you feel the need to pop along to your cabin just in case, I won't stop you.'

'By God, you're a rum 'un, Howard.'

'I'm just trying to be civilised.'

'You mean, if I want her I can have her.'

'I didn't say that,' Howard told him. 'Besides, you've had her already.'

'How long have you known?'

'That you intend to take her from me? Not long.'

'I asked her to say nothing until after the show opened.'

'Ah, yes, the show.' Howard arranged his cards. 'We'll have to have a little chat about the show, Teddy. I'm not sure I want to be part of it.'

'You're not pulling out, are you? You can't pull out now.'

'Oh, come now,' Howard said. 'It's only a little gallery show. It's not going to cause a sensation or change the course of history. In fact, boiled down, it's really of no consequence to anyone.'

'It is to me,' Teddy said. '*Are* you pulling out?'

'You'll still have Clive.'

'I don't want Clive. I want you.'

'My paintings *and* my wife? What a greedy fellow you are.'

'I thought painting meant everything to you.'

'Not quite,' Howard said. 'No, not quite everything.'

Major Butt strode into the room, the door flapping behind him. He seemed surprised to find himself the centre of attention but, spreading his hands, made the announcement in a loud voice. 'Ice. We've struck into ice. Nothing to worry about,' he declared then, pulling out his chair, sat down and picked up his cards again.

'You see,' Howard said, 'nothing to worry about.'

Ten seconds after the first grating impact Maisie was out of bed and on her feet. She put on the small light over the dressing table.

Shivering a little, she crossed to the cots where the children slept and checked that they hadn't been disturbed. Walter, a sound sleeper, was curled up under the eiderdown, only his hair and the tip of his nose visible. Fran lay on her back, mouth open, snoring lightly. Maisie paused, then, very gently, turned the little girl on to her side. She felt the motion of the ship alter and, a minute or so later, cease. She reached for her dressing gown and slippers, put them on and went out into the passageway. She looked left and right, saw no one and, with barely a second's hesitation, hurried to the door of Mr Clive's cabin and knocked upon it.

After a lengthy pause, Clive opened the door an inch and peered out.

'What is it, Maisie? Is it the children?'

'Ship's stopped. We 'it somefink. Didn't you feel it?'

'Can't say I did,' Clive told her. 'Are you sure?'

'Certain,' Maisie said. 'Listen: no engines.'

'Hmm, you're right,' Clive said. 'We may have run into field ice and are having to lie up for a bit. The children . . .'

'Fine, they're fine,' Maisie assured him. 'Both fast asleep.'

'All right,' Clive said. 'If it'll make you feel any better, I'll put on some clothes and go for a wander.'

'What is it?' came a voice from the cabin.

'Nothing, darling. Maisie thinks we've hit something.'

'Oh, Maisie!' Julie exclaimed. 'What's wrong with the girl?'

'Want me to come wiff you, Mr C?' Maisie asked.

'No, stay with the children. I'll let you know if anything's wrong.'

Then he went back inside and closed the door.

★

'Stupid girl.' Julie pulled the sheet up to cover her breasts. 'I don't know what comes over her sometimes. She was probably dreaming.'

'She's right about one thing.' Clive tugged on his trousers. 'The engines have stopped.'

'It can't be anything serious,' Julie said. 'You watched this ship being built. She's supposed to be unsinkable, isn't she?'

'Of course, she is,' said Clive. 'She rides on watertight compartments and has a double bottom. You could cut her in half and the two halves would still float.'

'Then why not come back to bed?' Julie said.

Clive stooped to tie his shoe laces. 'I'm up now. May as well take a snoop around and put Maisie's mind at rest.'

'Sometimes I think you care more for that girl's feelings than you do mine.'

'Rubbish!' He slipped on his tweed overcoat, kissed Julie on the brow. 'Keep your boiler stoked. I'll be back in a tick. Meantime, perhaps you should put on your dressing gown.'

'Really? Why?'

'Just in case,' said Clive.

Those who were bored with cards or lounging idly in the club-like haze of tobacco smoke left the room singly and in pairs. They were careful to show no haste and exchanged jocular remarks in passing with the more resolute of their friends as they made their exit. The stewards were a little more agitated but Howard put that down to the fact that they'd had a long day of it and were anxious to have the room cleared so they could go to bed.

He was in no hurry to go anywhere, no hurry at all. He had Teddy Norris against the ropes and revelled in the American's discomfort.

He drew a card from the pack, stroked his chin, and made his discard.

Teddy opened his mouth, closed it, opened it again. The questions would not take shape. Perhaps, Howard thought, he's afraid that my answers will saddle him permanently with my dear, sweet, vacuous little wifey, who might fit nicely between Mr Norris's thighs but would not fit nicely into the drawing rooms of the very rich.

Smiling, he watched Norris fumble his cards.

'Knocking, are you knocking?'

'What?' Norris said. 'No, not yet.'

The drift towards the doors continued but Butt and Millet remained where they were, calm as you like. They might be Americans, Howard thought, but they had the unruffled air of *noblesse oblige* that he'd never been able to emulate – which, he supposed, was one of the disadvantages of being Hoxton born and Hoxton bred.

'I assume,' Howard said, 'Anna will sue for divorce.'

'That – yeah, that's the plan.'

'The best laid plans gang aft askew, of course.'

'You'll fight it, won't you?'

'No,' Howard said. 'I see no point in delaying the inevitable. No doubt your family will marshal an army of legal experts to cut through the red tape. Even so, it might be some time before she's free of me. What grounds, I wonder, will Anna put forward to ensure I emerge as the villain of the piece?' He glanced up enquiringly. 'Cruelty, perhaps? Ah, yes, Buskin the monster, the brute, the devil incarnate.

Just look at his horrid paintings if you want proof of his nastiness. Poor woman, married to a man like that. Eh?'

'Howard, listen . . .'

'Then again Anna might claim the marriage was never consummated,' Howard went on. 'And it would be her word against mine and involve a great deal of scandalous conjecture in the newspapers on both sides of the Atlantic – which, come to think of it, might do my reputation as an artist no harm. What's that called, by the way? Is that annulment?'

'I know what you're up to,' Teddy said. 'You think I don't want Anna enough to ride out a scandal. Well, you're wrong, Howard. Dead damned wrong. Can't you get it into your thick head that I love her?'

'Do you suppose I don't?' said Howard. 'Are we playing cards or aren't we?'

'We're not.' Teddy tossed down his hand. 'I've better things to do than sit here and listen to you slander the woman I . . .'

A steward appeared at Howard's elbow and the sentence was never finished.

'There's a lady in the vestibule looking for you, Mr Buskin,' the steward told him. 'Says she's your wife.'

Howard closed his eyes and sighed. 'Ah, sweet mystery of life – what now?'

Then, without apology, he got up and left.

36

A small crowd had gathered in the foyer on A Deck but Clive had no difficulty in locating Max who, with a long black overcoat flung over his pyjamas and a bowler hat on his head cut an even more ridiculous figure than most of the half-dressed passengers who had climbed out of bed in search of explanations. There was no sign of Mr Reibling but Miriam Vazana, dressed as Clive had last seen her, was hanging on to Max's arm, a cigarette, minus holder, adhering to her lip.

'I don't own the blessed boat, Miriam,' Max was saying. 'I hold stock in the company, that's all. I can't go charging up to the bridge to find out what's wrong. In any event, we won't know much until the powers that be finish their tour of inspection. They're down below right now assessing the damage.'

'Maude, where is she?' Miriam Vazana asked.

'In bed, where you should be,' Max answered irritably.

'Waiting to drown in my sleep?'

'No one is going to drown,' Max told her. 'Modern steam-ships don't sink; that's the long and short of it. Ask *him*, if you don't believe me.'

'A painter?' Miriam said. 'What would a painter know about steamships?'

'Not much, Miss Vazana,' Clive said, 'which is why I'm willing to take Max's word that everything's as it should be.'

'If everything's as it should be,' Miriam Vazana said, 'why are we meeting here in the middle of the night?'

'Oh, very well, Miriam,' Max said. 'I'll go and see what I can find out. Clive, will you join me?'

'You are abandoning me to my fate?' said Miriam Vazana.

'Come with us, by all means,' Max said.

'No, it is too cold outside.'

Clive trailed Max through the main lobby and up on to the boat deck. The air was bitter. He flipped up the collar of his coat to protect his ears.

In pyjamas and a thin overcoat, Max gasped and stamped. 'Look,' he said, 'I haven't been exactly truthful with Miriam. I don't want to ruffle feathers unnecessarily but the situation may be more serious than anyone's letting on. We struck against an iceberg on the starboard side. She's holed below the waterline, apparently, and shipping water.'

'The watertight compartments, what about them?'

'I don't know,' Max said. 'But I've an odd feeling this floating fortress may be not be impregnable after all. I can hardly believe it myself and I may be completely wrong but – well, if I had children to look out for, Clive, I'd be taking precautions.'

'Precautions?' Clive said. 'What sort of precautions?'

'Wrap them up warmly – your wife too – and get them on deck.'

'Which deck?' Clive said. 'We've had no instructions, no boat drill.'

'I know,' Max said. 'Heads will roll when we reach New York.'

'You mean' – Clive paused – 'if we reach New York.'

'We're on one of the busiest shipping routes in the world,' Max said. 'There are bound to be vessels nearby, but . . .'

'Max, you're scaring me,' Clive said.

'Have you counted the lifeboats?'

'Sixteen and four collapsibles in accordance with the Board of Trade regulations.'

'Regulations that are sadly out of date,' Max said. 'If *Titanic* does go down – and I'm not saying she will – she'll take half the passengers with her. There just aren't enough boats for everyone, Clive, not nearly enough.'

Clive sucked in a breath. 'First come, first served, you mean?'

Max said, 'Naturally, women and children will have priority. No one's ready for this, though. No one's going to believe it's possible.'

'What's the launch procedure; do you know?'

'No,' Max said. 'I've a horrid feeling the crew may not know either. For all the crossings Maude and I have made – some very rough – I've never had to do more than strap on a life preserver. Lifeboats – I don't know much about lifeboats.'

'More than I do,' Clive said. 'Have a stab at it, Max.'

'If they do it by the numbers one of those would be my guess.' He nodded at the shrouded boats that hung passively from davits on the starboard side. 'Fetch your family up, Clive, and if I'm wrong I'll offer my apologies at breakfast.'

'What are you going to do?'

'Rouse Maude.'

★

Maisie had made her bed and had laid out upon it three life preservers, though they weren't the preservers she'd found on top of the wardrobe which weren't a good fit for a three-year-old and a toddler.

She'd rung the bell for the cabin steward but Mr McIntosh hadn't answered. After a few minutes, she'd gone out into the passageway just as a man in steward's uniform – not McIntosh – had come skipping down it, rapping on cabin doors and calling out to everyone to put on their life preservers. The man might have brushed past her if Maisie hadn't pinned him with a forearm and demanded to be told if there were special life preservers for young children. A brief – very brief – altercation had ensued before the substitute steward had capitulated and leading Maisie by the arm had taken her to a cubby at the corridor's end where, kicking open a cupboard, had told her to help herself.

Two little preservers and one of adult size lay like kippered herring on the eiderdown together with two piles of warm clothing, each topped with a small pair of shoes. Fran's 'special' blanket, though in need of a scrub, was there too and resting upon it was Walter's paper flag.

Seated on a chair, skirts hitched up, Maisie was trying to squeeze her boots over two pairs of stockings when Clive found her. There was quite a bit of activity in the passage now as doors opened and closed and voices were raised in enquiry. Mr McIntosh, it seemed, had returned to his duties and his soothing Scottish burr stood in contrast to the shrill demands of his clients.

Clive closed the door and leaned his shoulders against it. 'You've been busy, Maisie,' he said. 'I see we're almost ready. Mr Scully thinks we should get ourselves up to the boat deck just to be on the safe side. Will you wake and dress the children while I attend to Mrs Cavendish?'

'I will,' said Maisie. 'Never thought this would 'appen, though.'

'No one did,' Clive said. 'Mark you, nothing drastic has happened yet and it probably won't. Tomorrow we may well look like fools for galloping up to the lifeboats but I'd rather be safe than sorry.'

'Lifeboats,' said Maisie. 'Gawd Almighty! Are we all going together, Mr C?'

'What?'

'Up to the deck,' said Maisie. 'What you fink I meant?'

'Yes, Maisie,' Clive said. 'All together.'

'And you'll be leading the way?'

'I will,' Clive said. 'Of course, I will.'

If there hadn't been such a commotion in the passageway Julie might have remained in bed. She was irked by the interruption to her lovemaking and, for a little while after Clive left, blamed Maisie for it.

Instinct rather than common sense eventually told her that something was wrong and when the steward came thumping past calling for everyone to put on lifebelts, she wasted no time in leaping out of bed and getting dressed. She was fumbling with the ties of the life preserver when Clive returned and, without saying a word at first, fitted the clumsy garment around her and did up the tapes.

'Splendid,' he said. 'You look simply splendid.'

'Stop it, Clive,' she said. 'You're not talking to Walter now.'

He seated himself on the rumpled bed and pulled her on to his knee.

'We – the ship, I mean – we struck an iceberg a glancing blow. There is damage but no one seems certain how bad it is. This' – he tapped the cork capsule that covered her chest – 'is nothing but a precaution. If the worst comes to the very worst – and I'm sure it won't – it's better if we're upstairs near to the lifeboats.' He drew her closer, an arm about her middle, holding her the way he held Fran when she was fractious. 'If we do have to abandon ship . . .'

'Abandon ship?' Julie wriggled. 'What are you talking about?'

'There won't be enough places in the lifeboats for everyone.'

'The children . . .'

'Maisie's taking care of the children. Now, listen, Julie, listen: we're all going up to the boat deck together. There's not much happening right now so if we're fast off the mark we'll be first in line if – and I say again, *if* – the lifeboats do have to be launched.'

'What about Anna?'

He ignored her question. 'I'll take Walter. Maisie will have Fran. I want you to carry three extra blankets – pull them off the beds, if you have to – and stick close to me. While I'm fetching the children I suggest you gather your trinkets, wrap them in a scarf and put them in your pocket.'

'My trinkets?'

'Your jewellery. Wrap the pieces in—'

'Yes, yes,' Julie said impatiently.

'And gloves, don't forget your gloves.'

'Clive, it's freezing upstairs. The children . . .'

'Listen,' he said again, 'please listen. If the captain does decide there's a threat to the ship he'll order the women and children into the boats. That doesn't mean to say the ship's sinking. The boat crews will be instructed to hang around at a safe distance. If the ship's still afloat by daylight and the damage repairable you'll all be brought on board again.'

'We,' Julie said. 'You do mean we, don't you?'

'The men will probably be expected to stay on board for a bit.'

'I'm not setting foot in a lifeboat without you.'

'Yes,' Clive said. 'You are.'

He tipped her from his knee and, standing too, took both her hands in his.

For the first time she realised just what sort of man she'd married, that the time had come to match up to him.

'If it comes to it,' he said, 'you, Maisie and the children will go without a fuss. No fuss, Julie. Do you hear me? No tears and no fuss.'

'And you,' she heard herself say, 'what about you?'

'I won't be far behind,' said Clive.

It had been quiet for some time, uncannily quiet. Otto had not undressed. He had removed his shoes and had propped himself in a sitting position on the bed by Verity's side. She seemed more settled now but no matter how vigorously she protested tomorrow he would keep her in bed and make a point of summoning a doctor to cast an eye over her. He had no awareness of immediate danger. His thoughts leapt ahead to what might happen in New York and how Verity would react to Anna's news that she was leaving Howard.

Crippled marriages were common and adultery almost obligatory among so-called artists like Edgar Banbury but it galled him to think that Anna's marriage to Howard had been a sham from the start. He questioned if there was more to her affair with Norris than sexual gratification and feared that she might live to regret her impetuosity. How he would break the news to Stanley was also a worry but he would cross that bridge when he came to it.

There were voices in the passageway, the thud of feet on the stretch of decking overhead. Glancing at Verity to make sure she was asleep, Otto slipped stealthily from the bed and put on his shoes. He was on the point of opening the door when Howard burst in, Emily at his heels.

Howard hurled himself at the bed. Otto only just caught him in time.

'Mama.' Howard struggled in Otto's embrace. 'Mama, what's wrong?'

Otto said, 'Pull yourself together, Howard. She's asleep.'

Emily cried, 'I ha'n't got a lifebelt. Where do I find my lifebelt?'

Otto said, 'Kindly stop yelling, Emily. You've no need of a lifebelt.'

Howard said, 'She's not dead, is she?'

'Of course she's not dead,' Otto said. 'She's drunk, if you must know. If you hadn't poured all that brandy into her . . .'

Emily clutched Otto's arm. 'We hit a rock. I heard we hit a rock.'

Howard told her, 'We ran into ice, that's why we've stopped.'

Emily said, 'Then why is everybody going upstairs?'

'Howard.' Otto gave his son-in-law a shake. 'Where's Anna?'

'We've got to get Mrs Millar upstairs,' Emily said. 'I'll help her dress.'

'You'll do no such thing, Emily,' Otto said. 'Mrs Goldstein's staying right where she is.'

'At least let me speak to her, Otto,' Howard said, and Otto released him.

Howard leaned over the bed and peered intently into his mother's face.

'Mama, it's me. It's Howard.' He looked up. 'She's not answering.'

'Because she's asleep,' said Otto with a little less conviction than before. 'She's had her pills and they always make her sleepy.'

'Listen,' Emily said.

'I don't hear anything,' Otto said.

'That's them telling everybody to put on lifebelts.'

'I still don't hear—'

'There,' said Emily. 'All passengers on deck with lifebelts on.'

'We can't leave Mama here,' Howard said.

'No one's leaving her here,' said Otto. 'I'll stay with her.'

'But what if we're sinking?' Emily said.

'Damn it, we're not sinking,' Otto said crossly. 'This is the *Titanic*. A little scrap of ice isn't going to send her to the bottom. If you're so concerned, Emily, why don't you put on your life preserver and go upstairs. Mrs Goldstein's down for the night and there's nothing to keep you here.' He turned to Howard. 'And you – let me ask you again: where's Anna?'

'With her lover, I expect,' Howard said. 'In bed with Teddy Norris.'

'Oh!' Otto said lamely, then again, 'Oh!'

'Doing it, I expect,' said Howard. 'Doing sex.'

'If you don't need me, Mr Goldstein . . .' Emily stammered and before Otto could answer darted from the room.

'You see, even Emily knows what's going on,' Howard said. 'Everyone knows – except me. Well, Otto, I'm not the fool you take me for.'

He dipped into his pocket, brought out his case, drew a cigar from the slot and, without ceremony, lit it. He rolled the cigar between finger and thumb and, calmer now, inhaled a mouthful of smoke.

Otto, saying nothing, perched himself on the end of the bed.

'What does Mama have to say about it?' Howard asked.

'Mama – Verity – doesn't know.'

'So, you've managed to keep it from her. How thoughtful,' Howard said. 'I take it you've heard that Anna's leaving me as soon as we reach New York. No.' He held the cigar out like a pointer. 'I stand corrected; not as soon as we reach New York. As soon as Norris has his grand opening and been fêted for discovering – shall we say "discovering"? – two brilliant young painters in England. Well, who am I to grudge him that?'

'Has Anna told you what she intends to do?'

'In no uncertain terms.'

'Have you tried to talk her out of it?'

'Why would I?'

'I thought you loved her.'

Howard licked the end of the cigar. He rocked on his heels, almost but not quite swaggering. 'I decided not to go along with their plan after all,' he said. 'Had it out with Norris, man to man. He knows how the land lies.'

'And how,' Otto said, 'does the land lie?'

'I thought you were the great wise owl who knows everything.'

'No, Howard,' Otto told him. 'You've always been a mystery to me.'

Howard snorted. 'My epitaph, eh? No one knows how the bastard did it? Well, my friend, I'll let you into a little secret: the bastard doesn't know how he does it either – or why he does it – or, frankly, how to stop doing it.'

'Are we talking about painting – or Anna?'

'Take your pick. It's all one to me now.'

'What do you mean by that? What have you done, Howard?'

'Me?' Howard said. 'Nothing – as yet. Let's just say our little Anna will come with strings attached.'

'Strings? What strings? What the devil are you talking about?'

Howard took a long pull on the cigar and buried it in the ashtray on the bed-stand. 'Enough!' he said. 'You will stay with her, won't you?'

'If you mean Verity, of course I will.'

'What a chivalrous fellow you are, Otto – for a Jew, I mean,' Howard said. 'By the way, I think my mother may have passed away,' then, turning on his heel, left the cabin without another word.

For all his alacrity Clive had not been fast enough. There were already people on the top deck when he led his troop upstairs into the cold night air. Fortunately there was no breath of wind. Even the breeze caused by the forward motion of the ship had died away now the engines had stopped and the vessel rode peacefully on a glassy sea. Nothing much seemed to be happening. There was evidence of uncertainty but no panic among the passengers. Some were warmly clad but others had simply slung coats or dressing gowns over their nightclothes and a few were even barefoot, as if they expected to be back in bed in no time, the irksome so-called emergency written off as a false alarm.

Julie felt like a fool wrapped up like a Christmas package and clutching an armful of blankets. Maisie was carrying Fran, Fran swaddled in so many clothes that almost nothing of her was visible. She had grizzled a little when Maisie had dressed her but, snug inside a cocoon of blankets, had soon fallen asleep again and appeared oblivious to what was going on around her – which, Julie thought, wasn't much at all. Walter, on the other hand, was wide-awake. He clung to his father like a monkey, twisting and turning to take it all in and waving the paper flag that Maisie – typical Maisie – had stuck into his fist to keep him occupied.

'What sort of nonsense is this, Max?' Julie came up to a group of men gathered by the rail. 'Is it the White Star's idea of a joke to hold a boat drill in the middle of the night?'

'It's not a drill,' Max Scully told her. 'It's a safety measure.'

Walter leaned his chin on Clive's shoulder and peered down at her. He had on his little sailor's cap. It had tipped over one eye and he looked, Julie thought, quite piratical.

She adjusted the blankets over her arm and reach up to sort out her one-eyed son who wriggled coyly away.

'There doesn't seem to be any hurry about telling us what's going on,' Julie said. 'Do they want us all to . . .'

Her question was drowned by a monstrous roar of steam belching from a pipe high up on one of the funnels. Fran wakened with a start and wailed. Walter clapped his hands over his ears and buried his face in the folds of Clive's scarf.

'Blowing the boilers,' Max shouted at the top of his voice. 'That's all.'

'I've had enough,' Julie yelled. 'I'm going below. Maisie, bring the children.'

Maisie had wandered off a little way along the deck, rocking Fran in her arms to soothe her. Separating herself from Clive, Julie took a few steps after Maisie – then stopped stock still.

Crewmen were crawling all over the lifeboats, peeling away canvas coverings, checking oars, unloading masts and other paraphernalia. Sailors on deck were coiling the ropes that ran through the pulleys.

For whatever reason, on whoever's orders, the lifeboats were being made ready for launching. Clive had been right after all.

'Maisie,' Julie shouted at the pitch of her voice, 'come here and stand close to me. I think we may be leaving soon.'

If Anna had known what was about to happen she might have taken more pleasure in lovemaking. There was no sense of urgency, though, no illicit thrill now that Howard had learned the truth and, according to Teddy, cared not a toot what they got up to provided they were discreet. And what could be more discreet than stealing away to have sex standing up in a first-class forward cabin at half past midnight with all, or most, of your clothes on?

The door handle jerked behind her, smothered by the bulky roll of skirts and petticoats that cushioned her bottom.

'For Chrissake!' Teddy hissed, then, raising his voice, called out, 'What is it? What do you want?'

'Clearing the cabins, sir. Gotter lock them, sir.'

'Lock them? What the hell for?'

'In case of theft, sir. Can't be too careful. You need help with your lifebelt?'

'No, I do not need help with my lifebelt,' Teddy said.

Anna could feel his anger through his member, a bizarre sensation that did nothing to increase her ardour. He jerked back and slipped out of her, still erect. He pushed her to one side and addressed the door as if the door itself was responsible for the interruption.

'Thought you'd heard, sir,' the steward said. 'Everyone required on deck.'

'On whose orders?'

'Captain's orders, sir.'

Anna tugged up her underclothes and smoothed down her skirts. Teddy tucked himself away and buttoned his trousers while still arguing with the inside of the door. 'Supposing I refuse to go up on deck,' he said, 'what's the old feller going to do about it? Clap me in irons?'

Five seconds of respectful silence, then: 'I got my instructions, sir. You do as you like. Not my fault if you get left.'

'Left?' Teddy yanked open the door. 'Wait.'

The steward was a man of middle age who, in spite of his willingness to take bribes, had the obsequious habit of holding his fists loosely in front his chest. He had a moon face, Anna recalled, and hair so sparse that not all the careful combing in the world could disguise the fact that he was almost bald.

Teddy said, 'Are you telling me we're abandoning ship – this ship?'

The steward stepped aside as an elderly gentleman and his wife, both sporting fur-lined capes and carrying life preservers, sailed past and floated aloofly towards the door at the end of the passage.

'*This* ship?' Teddy repeated. 'Do you expect me to believe *this* ship . . . ?'

'Best get the lady up top, Mr Norris, is my advice,' the steward said. 'Don't know proper what's going on but they're making the lifeboats ready and they'll want the women loaded first.'

'Lifeboats? What the hell . . .' Teddy began, then, with a little gasp, said, 'We struck ice, didn't we? I mean, Jesus, we actually ran into it?'

'I believe that to be the case, sir,' the steward said. 'Would you like me to escort the lady to the stairs?'

'No,' Teddy said. 'That won't be necessary. We're leaving together.'

Teddy came inside.

Anna said, 'Why are they manning the lifeboats?'

'In case we go down, I suppose,' Teddy said. 'It's probably just panic on the captain's part. Damned inconvenient, though.'

'Inconvenient is putting it mildly,' Anna said.

'Other ships will be standing by in no time,' Teddy said. 'Look, darling, can you find a lifebelt and make your own way up top?'

'I expect I can,' Anna said. 'Why? Where will you be?'

'Looking for Howard,' said Teddy, and left.

37

The rocket rose in a long arcing curve and burst in a shower of stars high up in the heavens. Faces turned upwards, brightly illuminated, at the sound of the hissing roar and the sight of the white light that dispelled all doubt that the ship was in distress. Funnels and rigging were outlined like props in a grand opera before sliding away into darkness again as the fiery globules cooled and fell into the sea.

Another rocket followed and a third. Walter, mouth open, followed each trajectory eagerly, throwing himself back with such force it was all Clive could do to support him. He glimpsed Maisie from the corner of his eye, Maisie cowering a little, shoulder raised to protect Frances Marian as if the rockets were weapons that might rain down fire.

The boats had been manned by crew members. Seamen were standing by the pulley ropes ready to lower away. Several boats had already been dropped, the space where they had been now open to the sky.

Clive looked round for Max but there was no sign of the man, or Maude. Shouting to make himself heard above the infernal screaming of the steam pipe, he strode across the deck and guided Julie and Maisie to the nearest boat. There was no panic, none at all, but places had not been assigned and the women were reluctant to leave their men. Clive wasted no time. He detached his son from his back and handed him, squirming in protest, to Julie.

'Walter,' he said sharply. 'Walter, you're going for a boat ride and Mummy needs you to look after her. Chief, Chief, do you hear me?'

Walter stopped squirming and settled his weight into his mother's arms. Paper flag clutched in one fist, the sailor's cap tipped over one eye, his attention had been caught by the lifeboat and he appeared to lose interest in his father.

As soon as the crewmen had helped his family safely into the lifeboat, Clive stepped back into the crowd of husbands, brothers and sons and became, as it were, anonymous, for he knew, somehow, that he would never see Julie again.

'Mother?' Howard said. 'God, no! Mother's a goner, I'm afraid. Even if this bloody tub doesn't go down, she'll never make it through the night. Poor old Otto, trying to pretend he's doing a noble thing by staying with her while she breathes her last, telling himself she's tipsy when anyone with half an eye can see her heart's packed in.' He swirled whisky in his glass but didn't drink. 'I suppose you think I should be with her, holding her hand and telling her how much I love her – well, I don't. I never did. Besides, the bird has flown – chirp, chirp – the soul has fled. If Otto's hoping for a few last words of farewell he will, I fear, be disappointed.'

Anna said, 'Stop it, Howard. Please stop it.'

'I wonder,' he said, 'if they'll bury her at sea.' He sipped from the glass and offered it to Anna, who shook her head. 'Cheated at the last,' he went on. 'My God, she couldn't even wait for me to go first. I ask you, what kind of a mother's that? And now this farce.' He waved the glass without spilling a drop. 'Perfect! Just perfect! Who'll give a flying fig if the finest young painter in England goes down with *this* ship? My grand gesture, my curtain call, my revenge blown away by a bloody iceberg. Where is he? Where's Norris?'

'Looking for you, I think,' said Anna.

'Looking for me when he should be looking after you. Touch of the old irony there, don't you think? On the other hand, Teddy may – I say may – be charging about up top looking after himself.'

They were seated on the staircase, hunched against the base of the plinth from which the gilded figure of a cupid looked out into the deserted reception room. All but a few first-class passengers had surrendered to the realisation that the ship was slowly sinking and that their precious lives were at risk. There had been a mad dash at some time just after one o'clock when the noise of rushing water had become audible and by peering down the stairwell you could see the flooded landing five decks below, the sea-green water transparent in the lights.

It had crossed Howard's mind that it might be no bad way to go, slithering over the balustrade and dropping straight down through the ship's vertical planes, deck by deck, layer by layer, until that lovely opalescent swirl sucked you in and gobbled you up. He was, however, just cynical enough to assume he would hit something en route and instead of dying a nice clean death would hang there, broken, bleeding and in awful pain, until someone fished him out in the morning.

'Well,' he said, 'since Teddy hasn't come galloping to the rescue it must be just about time for you to take your leave.'

'I'm not leaving without you, Howard.'

'Touching, very touching. I'm tempted to ask why.'

'Because you're a stubborn pig and martyrdom doesn't become you.'

'Who do you take me for – St Jerome? No, Anna, martyrdom isn't my style. I'm not sacrificing myself for your sake. Hell, no, there are many causes more worthy than that.' He grunted wryly. 'It's just occurred to me that some lucky beggar is going to earn a fortune painting pictures of *Titanic*'s final hours. Clive!' He laughed. 'Old Clive! Of course! Just the ticket for our mutual friend. Keep him in clover for years to come. Is your sister safe away?'

'Yes – and the children.'

'Good,' Howard said. 'That's good. Why didn't you go with them?'

'I told you, I'm not leaving without you.'

'Guilt, is it guilt?' he said. 'Or are you punishing me for you know what?'

'Both,' Anna told him.

Howard fashioned a little O with his lips and looked up at the iron and glass dome that crowned the staircase. 'What a hoot it will be,' he said, 'if she doesn't go down after all. What a bunch of mugs we're going look come morning if she's still afloat.' He finished off the whisky and, with a sweep of the arm, propelled the empty glass across the floor like a curling stone. He clasped the plinth with both hands and hoisted himself up. 'Is it my imagination or are we sliding slowly southward?'

'It isn't your imagination,' Anna said.

'Last chance, my dear. It's now or never, I reckon. Please, go.'

She looked up at him, not smiling. 'I told you, Howard, I'm not—'

'Damn it, Anna!' he said. 'Why do you always have to do things the hard way?' Then, flexing his knees like a wrestler, he lifted her into his arms, threw her over his shoulder and headed upstairs at the double.

The band near the port side entrance had stopped playing ragtime and had broken into something a tad more appropriate; not a hymn but a waltz, cheerful enough, but not – not jittery, Teddy thought. It was colder than he'd anticipated. He wished he'd grabbed a coat from his wardrobe before he set out on his – his what? – his rescue mission, his senseless drive to make restitution before it was too late? When he first came up top several men were still playing cards in the smoking room, Butt and Millet among them, and Astor and his wife were sitting astride the horses in the gym chatting as casually as if nothing was amiss. He had arrived upstairs with laudable intentions but they'd soon dribbled away and he'd wound up helping Scully dig out his wife and get her, complaining loudly, on to the promenade deck.

More than half the lifeboats had gone; he could see them floating below or, shading his eyes, lying off to port in a cluster just on the limit of the light spill. He had no doubt now that the ship wouldn't survive.

Max was shouting at his wife and his wife was shouting back at him.

Maude loomed large with a life preserver strapped over

her furs and a feather boa wrapped around her neck. Her hat, all feathery too, was clasped to the back of her head, her hair sticking out as if she'd been electrified. She was very concerned about Miriam and seemed unwilling to accept Max's assurances that Miriam had already gone off.

When Max gave him the nod Teddy grasped Maude by the left arm and, with Max firmly attached to the right, hustled her round to the port side near the bridge, a long way from the after cabins where Howard might be hiding and the staircase where he'd last caught a glimpse of Anna.

There had been a delay, apparently, a bottleneck; confusion.

A group of first-class passengers, shuttled back and forth between the boat deck and the promenade, had been hanging around waiting to be told what to do for almost an hour. The Second Officer had finally taken charge. A window on the enclosed deck had been prised open and the great and the good were being herded across a ladder of steamer chairs into a lifeboat that hung several feet away from the hull. Astors and Ryersons, Carters, Wideners and Thayers, the very cream of the crop, were gathered there. Teddy felt better at once. No pipsqueak White Star officer would dare refuse a man like John Jacob Astor the right to a place in a lifeboat. Come one, Teddy thought, come all. Shuffling up behind Maude Scully, he made ready to take his turn.

They were handing down Astor's pregnant young wife. Leaning from one of the windows Astor asked if he could go with her.

Teddy moved again, shifting closer to Astor. Then, to his dismay, he heard the Second Officer say, 'No, sir. No men until all the women are loaded.'

'What is the number of this boat?' Astor asked.

'Four, sir,' the officer answered and, standing his ground, shot out an arm to bar the way of any man who dared defy the law of the sea. Astor smiled a bleak little smile that augured ill for the Second Officer when – or if – they reached port.

Then Astor stepped meekly aside.

'Maude,' Max Scully said, 'you're a woman, last I heard.'

'I am not going without you, don't you even think it.'

'Well, I'm blowed if you're staying here,' Max said.

With another nod to Teddy, he grabbed his wife's arm and between them they bullied her into the window space. A crewman caught her, dragged her across the ladder of steamer chairs and the last Teddy saw of her was a pair of stout legs in lisle stockings and an enormous rump cloaked in fur vanishing over the sill. Max let out a whistle of relief instantly followed by a savage little sob. He fell back against the wall of the promenade deck and covered his face with his hand.

No hope here, Teddy thought. Swinging away from the window, he separated himself from the impotent elite and headed for the stairs to the boat deck.

She was furious with him, absolutely furious at being treated like a wilful child. She kicked his belly, kneed his chest and beat her fists against his back while he lugged her up the staircase as if she weighed no more than a bag of sugar. She thought he would set her down as soon as he reached the promenade deck but he did not. He continued to carry her slung across his shoulder, like booty. Ignoring her indignant protests, he headed for the crowd by the open window, yelling as he bumped along, 'I have a woman here. I have my wife here. Hold up on that lifeboat. Hold up.'

It was all a jumble then, a kaleidoscope of arms, hands and faces.

Lights danced overhead, lights reflected in the glass of the windows and then the night, that dark space, like a hole, taut vertical ropes running down it like icicles from an eave – and Teddy peering anxiously into her face while she dangled, helpless, over Howard's shoulder.

She stretched out her hands to Teddy and heard him shout, 'No, Howard, no,' as Howard swung her round and, like a coalman tipping out a sack, propped her bottom on the rail and released her.

She sat there, balanced in the edge of nothingness, while two crewmen and a uniformed officer fought to haul her back in.

Howard spread his arms and, with a dip of the head, brought his mouth to hers and brushed her lips with his.

'Goodbye, my peach. Goodbye,' he whispered.

And gave her an almighty shove.

Self-sacrifice had never been high on Otto's agenda. He had always considered himself to be, at root, quite selfish. True, he'd rescued his sister from Vienna and, after a fashion, had looked after his nieces' interests, and Stanley's, but somehow he'd managed to avoid giving his heart to anyone until, that is, his past had caught up with him, that far-off time when he'd been full of the rich red stuff of life. Verity had been part of his rambunctious youth. He had agreed to marry her only to redeem a little of that happy time, to have someone to share it with as the lights dimmed and the orchestra struck up the final waltz of the evening, that wistful melody to which everyone must dance in the end.

If he'd been sure that Verity had gone from him and not all his pleading could bring her back, then, and only then, he might have left her in the bed and ordered the steward to lock the cabin door. But the steward, disgruntled, had gone now and there were no voices in the passageway, only the creaking and groaning of the ship; a curiously old-fashioned sound as if the *Titanic* was no twentieth-century masterpiece of riveted iron but a wooden-walled hulk settling softly into the silt of the Mersey or the Tyne.

He put on a sweater and, in a moment of uncertainty, hauled the life preserver from the rack and tied it on. The steward, of course, had no notion what was really happening and, even if he had been inclined to do so, would surely have been hard pressed to find a doctor now that lifeboats had been launched.

For a fleeting moment Otto considered carrying Verity up to the boats. He eased down the coverlet and put his ear to her chest to see if her heart was still beating – which it was. She didn't move, though, not so much as the flutter of an eyelid, and when he gave her a none-too-gentle shake – 'Verity, Verity, can you hear me?' – she did not respond.

There is a point at which devotion becomes folly but where that point lay Otto had no notion. Whether he loved Verity Buskin Millar or whether he did not was a matter of no account now. He couldn't leave her to die alone.

He waited by the bed, holding her lifeless hand.

At length, the slope became so bad that the milk glass and pill box slid from the bedside stand. Verity's dresses on the open rail swayed outward as if they were trying to fly away. Perfume bottles and cream jars toppled from the dressing table.

The rake of the room was so acute that Otto could no longer stand upright. He scrambled on to the bed. He gripped the carved bed-head with both hands. He dug his heels into the eiderdown, felt it slither and slip away from him and, far off at first, caught the clatter of the doors in the alleyway as they flew open.

The stateroom stank of Halcyon Rose from the broken perfume bottle, but he could smell the sea too, or thought he could. He prayed that his nieces were safe; the children safe, that everyone he cared about had got safe away. He suffered one last spasm of fear and a terrible, terrible urge to throw himself to the floor and crawl away, for none of it was as it should be, tender and sad, soft and sad and dignified.

Verity rolled against him, an arm flung out. For an instant he thought she'd come round, that she knew he was there and was reaching out to him. Hanging on to the bed-head he trapped her hips with his knees. He looked down into her wide open eyes, empty of all expression now, all trace of life. Then the bed slid, grating, across the room and pitched him into a corner by the wardrobe where he lay quite still among the debris until the sea came rushing in.

'Cavendish,' Teddy Norris said, 'I thought you'd gone ages ago.'

'Doesn't look like it, does it?' Clive said. 'Where's Anna?'

'Last seen landing in somebody's lap in lifeboat number four,' Teddy said. 'Howard dumped her overboard.'

'Kicking and screaming, no doubt. She wouldn't want to leave you.'

'How well you know my wife,' Howard said. 'At least she's been taken care of and someone else can worry about her now. I gather Julie and the children . . .'

'Safe away,' Clive said. 'I do believe the band's stopped playing? Not that I mind much. Never was keen on "Land of Hope and Glory". Is there any hope of getting off on one of the collapsibles?'

'You know more about that than I do,' Howard said. 'God knows, you made enough drawings of this tub.'

'Top of the officers' quarters, I think,' Clive said. 'Two of them. Stupid place to put boats, I always thought.'

'What the hell is that?' said Howard, turning. 'Oh, it's the mob from steerage making a break for it. Dear God, what hope have they now? Poor devils.'

They were clinging grimly to the rail at the top the stairs when the sea surged over the bridge and the rake of the deck increased, nosing down towards the bow. A wave rolled lazily along the boat deck. The stern rose in ponderous response. From directly above them, one man, and then another, jumped from the roof of the officers' quarters clear into the sea and, looking up, they saw the prow of a collapsible tip and the boat crash upside down not far from the base of the funnel.

They were still slithering and clambering up the plane of the deck to reach it when the water engulfed them.

'Too late now,' Teddy shouted and, vaulting the rail, disappeared.

'What about it, old son?' Clive said. 'Now or never. The suction will do for us otherwise and we won't stand any chance.'

'You first,' Howard said.

'No, we'll go together.'

'Suits me,' Howard shouted and, holding hands with his one and only friend, cocked his legs over the rail and dropped, flailing, into the icy sea.

38

It was a strange journey, beautiful as a dream in its way. Later, Walter would claim he remembered it all quite vividly, but Julie doubted it. He had cuddled into her, a blanket around him, and had slept by fits and starts through the darkest hours when lanterns had pricked the night like fallen stars and other boats had joined them. She had been too far away to watch the ship go down, removed from the full horror of it, too far off to hear the pitiful cries of those in the water or pick out human shapes clinging to the upended stern. At least she didn't have that picture to haunt her in years to come.

She sat near the bow of the lifeboat with Maisie and the children. It was cold but otherwise comfortable; not too crowded. She didn't doubt that they would all be rescued; Clive too. She fretted about Anna, though, Anna and Howard, Anna and Teddy and, most of all, Uncle Otto whom she'd last seen leading Verity away from the balustrade above the lounge. It would be no easy thing to cope with Verity drunk, Julie told herself, but if anyone could do it her dear old uncle could. She conjured up an image of Verity, still tipsy, singing a music-hall song to amuse the passengers in whatever boat she happened to be in and, as a false dawn glinted in the east, fancied she could hear little snatches of

Verity's song drifting across the water from somewhere not far off.

The quiet sea, the twinkling stars, the splash of oars, voices from other lifeboats echoing across the water like conversations in a darkened room; she had no idea how long they'd been adrift.

Her head was down, chin resting on Walter's cheek, when a crewman behind her in the bow called out, 'What's that?' and, shipping his oar, got to his feet.

Julie roused herself and looked round.

Far off on the line of the horizon she made out a faint flash of light, not glinting or shimmering but roving like a searchlight, then, as everyone in the boat fell silent, heard what she thought was the boom of a gun.

'Cannon, that's a bloomin' cannon,' the crewman in the bow declared, 'or my name's not McGinty.'

'Or a rocket, perhaps,' a female passenger suggested. 'Keep watching.'

With Fran secure in the crook of her arm, Maisie leaned on the gunwale and peered past the crewman's knees. Minutes passed, silent minutes. Walter stirred under the blanket and whimpered a little.

'I think I see another light,' said Maisie.

'By gum, it is,' the crewman said. 'Watch, watch for two in line.'

Walter shook off the blanket and stuck out his head. He uttered no sound, asked no questions but clung to Julie like a limpet and, as if he understood what was going on and what it signified, peered into the darkness too.

'I see them,' shouted an officer from the tiller platform. 'It's a ship and she's bearing down fast by the look of it.'

No one cheered and no one cried. It was a little too soon for optimism.

'Whose maid is this?' someone demanded when Anna tumbled into the lifeboat. 'Is she one of yours, Mrs Scully?'

'No,' Maude answered tartly. 'It's my friend, Anna Buskin.'

They had been dropping down the side of the ship by that time, passing lighted staterooms and open portholes with water gushing through them.

Anna was clad in the evening gown she'd worn to dinner. If she'd been wearing one of the old-style corsets that had recently gone out of fashion she might have suffered less damage but her corset was light and shaped to her waist and had afforded no protection when she struck the gunwale.

A sailor clambered down a rope and dropped into the boat. He was followed by several other men, not sailors. Anna heard someone shout, 'Pull away. Pull away,' and everyone who could find an oar, men and women, began rowing.

Barrels, boxes and steamer chairs rained down into the sea from the *Titanic*. Anna crouched at Maude's knee, gasping as pain ripped through her. Maude barked angrily at some woman unseen while a man seated close did his best to placate her. Anna looked up at a sky filled with brilliant stars, a million stars glittering like diamonds and, coughing, found blood in her mouth.

'Help me,' she said. 'Please, help me.'

They were still close to the ship. Anna watched it plunge rapidly towards the bow, the funnels tilt and crumble. The bow went under. All the lights went out. The stern rose against the starlit sky, hung there, upright, for what seemed like an eternity then vanished too, leaving the sea appallingly empty.

Hat gone, chin resting on Anna's cheek, Maude muttered prayers in a language Anna didn't understand; Jewish prayers for the dead and dying, perhaps, while all around in the icy water the dying cried out to be saved.

The officer in charge shouted, 'Pull for your lives or the suction will have us.' But there was no suction, only a wave, a single slapping wave that rocked the lifeboat wildly for an instant and passed on. Arguments broke out again. Anna saw a hand and naked arm snake over the gunwale, followed by a coarse-featured face, a face she would never forget, but before she could react it slipped away, arm and hand slithering lazily from the gunwale like weed from a rock.

Conscious of no sound save the whistle of air in her lungs, Anna crept into the space Maude made for her and drew up her knees to contain the pain.

She clenched her teeth to stop them chattering and with Maude's arms around her and Maude's coat over her shoulders, told herself that she mustn't fall asleep, that for Howard's sake – or Teddy's – she must survive.

Emily had been taken under the wing of a burly Italian, someone or other's valet, whom she'd met in the servants' dining room on the big ship and who had shared space with her in the lifeboat. Now she was all alone – or professed to be – he had offered himself up as her protector. In other circumstances Maisie might have been amused by the speed with which Emily nabbed a patron but with lifeboats still arriving her haste seemed mean and insensitive. Maisie was quite relieved when Emily, a borrowed shawl over her shoulders and the valet's arm about her waist, vanished downstairs into the third-class saloon where, Maisie gathered, half the Italian nation was waiting to question her about her ordeal.

Walter and Fran had been wide-awake when the lifeboat had come alongside the *Carpathia*, which, to Walter's disgust, had only one funnel. He'd gone up in a cradle, roped like a prisoner. Fran, wailing all the way, had made her ascent in a canvas bag with only her head sticking out. Maisie, who had boarded first, had been waiting on deck to help unpack the toddler who, once safe in Nanny's arms, had soon stopped crying. A steward had given her a cup of hot cocoa that she'd shared with Fran while Walter, holding a seaman's hand, had watched his mother clamber up from the lifeboat.

'Oh, God! Thank God!' Julie said and, to Walter's chagrin, hoisted him up and waggled him above her head as if he were still a baby. Then, curiously composed, she provided the purser with her name and cabin number and, beckoning Maisie to keep up, joined the crowd round a steward who was handing out telegraph forms. Kneeling on the deck, she scribbled a message to her papa to inform him that she and the children were safe.

Then they were shown downstairs to the first-class saloon where sandwiches and coffee were being served and blankets and warm clothing, donated by the *Carpathia*'s passengers, were laid out for those who had need of them. Doctors were on hand and the worst victims of the cold were escorted to cabins to be treated. Leaving the children in Maisie's care, Julie returned to the deck to join the other wives in their anxious vigil.

Maisie found places at a table and fed Fran and Walter milky porridge sweetened with syrup. There was nothing much in her mind save a mixture of relief and anxiety until she looked across the saloon and saw two dark-haired little girls, bewildered, lost and alone, being comforted by a stewardess and then, abruptly, the magnitude of the night's events struck home.

Following her gaze, Walter leaned an elbow on the table and whispered, 'Nanny, do you think they'd like to play with me?'

'No, dear,' Maisie said, as evenly as possible. 'Somehow I don't think they would.'

'Never mind,' Walter said. 'I expect Daddy will be here soon.'

The sea that stretched to the skyline was no longer vast and empty. It was filled with field ice dotted with floating bergs tinted pink by the morning sun. The fresh breeze had taken on an Arctic bite but Julie was unaware of the bitter cold as she watched the lifeboats nose through the ice and come alongside.

In one crowded boat was Maude, Maude but no Max. Looking down, Julie saw her sister huddled in a heap in the stern, so weak that two sailors had to shin down to fasten her into a cradle and, hanging on ropes, guide the cradle up to the deck where two doctors, one of them Italian, waited to receive it.

Out among the ice floes another lifeboat appeared and, even as Julie hesitated, another, but beyond them nothing, nothing but ice and bergs and a sky as raw as an unprimed canvas. She turned reluctantly from the rail and crossed the deck. The doctors were bending over Anna who was barely conscious.

Julie eased through the crowd.

'I'm her sister,' she said. 'Is she going to be all right?'

The Italian doctor spread his hands but the English doctor, kneeling by the cradle, looked up. 'Does she have a husband?'

'Yes.'

'Is he on board?'

'No.'

The doctor rose and signalled to the stewards who lifted the cradle and headed for the stairs.

'Who is she?' the doctor said. 'And who are you?'

'I'm Mrs Cavendish. My sister is Mrs Buskin. Is it just the cold?'

'No,' the doctor said. 'I suspect she has an injury. I'm trying to find a cabin for her. Once I've examined her I'll know more. Are you – are you alone?'

'My children are with my maid downstairs.'

'Good,' he said. 'Good,' but, Julie noticed, he didn't ask about her husband.

He said, 'You may accompany us, if you wish. It might comfort your sister to have you there.' He was a small sandy-haired man, not yet middle-aged. He wore no over-coat, hat or scarf and his hands shook a little with the cold. He blew on his fingers and tucked them into the cut of his waistcoat.

'All right, Mrs Cavendish. I'll send someone to fetch you if—'

'No,' Julie said. 'I'll come.'

★

The cabin was small and plainly furnished. It belonged to two Spanish gentlemen, cousins, who were returning to Gibraltar after visiting relatives in New York. The room smelled of strong tobacco and bay rum hair tonic. On the dressing table were two framed photographs, family portraits, and hanging from a hook on the wall a crucifix on a silver chain. The Spanish gentlemen had been among the first of the *Carpathia*'s passengers to volunteer their cabin and, putting pride aside, had decamped to the first-class dining room to help serve hot drinks to the frozen souls who had been rescued from the clutches of the sea.

Both beds had been turned down, sheets and pillowcases changed and fresh towels hung on the rack by the washbasin. The stewards transferred Anna from the cradle to one of the beds and went away.

It was warm in the little cabin. Julie felt her ears tingle and her fingers throb as she stooped over her sister and, on the doctor's instruction, carefully removed Anna's dress and bodice. Anna moaned and opened her eyes.

'I thought it might be you,' she said. 'What – what ship is this?'

'The *Carpathia*.'

'Are the children safe?'

'Yes, they're here.'

'Any – anyone else?'

'No, not yet,' said Julie.

'Oh, God!' Anna gasped and, leaning forward, clutched Julie's arm. 'Oh, God! I'm cold. I'm so cold.'

The doctor touched Julie's shoulder. She eased Anna against the pillows and watched him apply the cup of the stethoscope to her sister's chest then gently turn her on to her side and deftly peel away her underclothes to expose a long blue-black bruise that ran from hip to breast.

'Ribs,' the doctor said. 'Lie quite still, Mrs Buskin. I'm going to find something to ease the pain while I examine you. I'll only be a few minutes.'

He left the bedside and, drawing Julie with him, moved to the door.

He spoke in a practised whisper. 'Even if the ribs are only cracked I suspect they may have ruptured a wall of the lung. If the ribs are broken, however, a perforation of the pleura is much more likely. I'm not really equipped to tap off any large accumulations of fluid that may occur but I'll do my best, if it comes to it. In the interim, I'll give her an opiate and strap the side. Is she robust?'

'Yes, she's healthy,' Julie said.

'I'm sure we can keep her stable until we reach a hospital.' He went out into the passageway. 'Do you have relatives or friends in New York?'

'I – I don't know,' Julie said.

'You don't know?' the doctor said and then, 'Ah, yes, I see.'

'Doctor,' Julie said, 'is the ship moving?'

'I do believe it is.'

'What does that mean?'

'It means' – he paused – 'all the lifeboats are accounted for.'

Julie said, 'Now we're going back to pick up survivors?'

'Yes, of course,' the doctor said, giving nothing away.

Julia swallowed hard. 'The truth, please; will there *be* any survivors?'

'Frankly, Mrs Cavendish,' the doctor said, 'I doubt it.'

★

Hours of working an oar in the lifeboat that had plucked him from the sea had failed to bring warmth to his frozen limbs. He was still flapping away at the oar when dawn leaked over the horizon, other lifeboats became visible and not long after that a steamship appeared in the far distance. He summoned the last of his energy then, and, obeying to the letter the orders of the Quartermaster at the tiller, bent to the oar like a galley slave, while the boat, filled to capacity, wallowed through a sea of broken ice and around bergs as big as bungalows.

Clearing the ice field at last, they negotiated a stretch of choppy water and made a long sweep round to the steamship's sheltered port side. By then all he could think of was his need to empty his bladder and the embarrassment it would cause if he were caught short with so many women around.

It was a small ship, puny-looking compared to *Titanic,* but at least it was still above the waterline, still afloat. He released the oar, saw it knuckle against *Carpathia*'s hull and, popping from the rowlock, splash over the side and float swiftly away. He was at a loss to understand the outbreak of cheering by passengers in the lifeboat and from spectators on the deck above. To take his mind off his discomfort, he scanned the rail for familiar faces – Julie or Anna – but saw neither one of them, only Max Scully's wife, Maude, and her Jewish friend in the bandit hat, who, like a host of other harassed women, were calling down to him and waving and were, thank God, all too easy to ignore.

He did his bit because it was expected of him. He helped nervous matrons on to the ladder or into the swaying chair, handed up the boat's one child – a solemn boy of eight or ten – to a seaman who carried him up the ladder like a sack of oats.

Passengers up top squawked like seagulls. Crewmen reached out eager hands to haul the younger women on board while he, standing rigid and desperate amidships, waited like the gentleman he was until the Quartermaster gave him a signal and he threw himself on the ladder, swarmed up it, scrambled on to the deck and, grabbing a steward by the arm, hissed, 'Lavatory, lavatory. Quick.'

The steward took him by the arm, rushed him along the deck and down a short flight of uncarpeted stairs and, with a shove to send him on his way, catapulted him into the gents with a cry of 'There you go, sir.'

Seated, relieved, on the unfamiliar pedestal, he cupped his head in his hands and, rocking forward, let out a groan that turned involuntarily into a sob. And then he was sobbing, sobbing unrestrainedly until the steward knocked on the cubicle door and asked if he was all right.

'Fine,' he said. 'Yes, thank you, I'm fine now.'

'Dry clothes in the locker at the end of the alley. Hot drinks in the dining saloon. I take it, sir, you are first-class.'

'What?' he said. 'Oh! Yes, first-class through and through.' Then, drying his eyes with the heel of his hand, he went out to face the world again.

The oily medicine in the wine glass tasted sweet and bitter at one and the same time. She was so eager for relief she might have emptied the entire glass if the doctor had allowed it. He held the glass carefully to her lips and, with Julie supporting her head, drew it away after she'd taken three small sips.

At first the padding strapped tightly round her middle had done nothing to contain her pain and, indeed, only seemed to compound it. She was very disappointed in the doctor. He had fed her three sips of laudanum before he'd examined her and two more before he'd applied the strapping, which had taken rather a long time. He had lifted her breasts to fit the padding round her and trim it off and she'd waited for him to say something complimentary about her figure but, of course, he was far too professional to do so with Julie in the room.

The second dose of laudanum had been more effective than the first. When the third dose trickled over her throat she knew she had found her saviour.

At last she could draw breath without pain cutting her in half and when she coughed the skirling bagpipe noise in her chest was reduced to not much more than a coy little whistle. She was cold, though, still cold and, with pain easing by the minute, found her irritation with her sister rising at approximately the same rate.

'Where are they?' she heard herself say. 'Why aren't they here?'

All sorts of strange people had been popping in and out: a stewardess carrying bandages, scissors and a basin, a sallow-skinned man with moustaches like Uncle Otto's who, she gathered, was also a doctor; another man, dark-skinned too, who had gruffly apologised for intruding and, without even looking at her, had fished something from the wardrobe and gone whisking out again. There had been all sorts of odd noises, too, odd voices in the passageway. When she closed her eyes it was almost as if she were still half asleep in the Dutch-style stateroom on *Titanic*, drifting not on a tide of morphine but of expectation.

She was well aware what had happened: that *Titanic* had gone down.

She could recall with perfect clarity the events of the evening and the early part of the night, but everything now was vague. She couldn't understand why the photographs in the amber frames on the bed-stand weren't of Otto and Verity, of Papa or Howard, or even Julie and the children; that one, yes, the peaceful garden scene Clive had photographed with the big box camera he'd bought with money from the sale of a painting. She peered at the photographs, blurred by icy light from the porthole above the bed, while Julie tucked two soft blankets over her and a quilt that reeked of Turkish tobacco.

Fighting against the weight of the quilt, plucking at it with her cold fingers, she said petulantly. 'Well, where is he? Doesn't anyone care about me?'

She heard Julie say, 'Tell her, tell her, damn it, and be done with it.'

'Tell me what?' she said. 'What is it? What's wrong?'

Looking up from the pillow she saw Julie, haggard and white-lipped, leaning on the doctor's arm, heard the doctor say something she couldn't quite catch, saw Julie turn away and, to Anna's annoyance, the sandy-haired doctor darting after her, leaving her, his patient, to fend for herself for a while.

She listened to the soft little whistle in her lungs, steady and rhythmic as a ship's engines, a tiny engine in her chest, valves and pistons beating regularly. She was warmer now, quite comfortable really, now the pain had abated. Howard would surely come in his own good time and when he did she would give him a piece of her mind for dumping her overboard; in fact, she would never let him forget it, though she might, in time, forgive him.

She closed her eyes, prepared to let the morphine draw her down into sleep.

She heard the door open, felt the weight of someone's forearm indent the pillow beside her ear. She felt breath on her cheek and lips brush her brow.

Corduroy and knitted wool, a faint smell of paint and turpentine; she struggled to open her eyes.

'Howard,' she said sleepily, 'is that you?'

'No, Anna,' Teddy said. 'It's me.'

JESSICA STIRLING

A Corner of the Heart

Susan Hooper may be a docker's daughter, but when her secretarial skills land her in the midst of London's literary sophisticates she can hold her own. Until she encounters Mercer Hughes. She finds herself falling reluctantly in love with the handsome literary agent with the notorious reputation and the shady past.

Soon Susan is mixing in circles where pimps and gangsters rub shoulders with wealthy fascist sympathisers in support of the war in Spain. Her idealistic brother and father seem a world away, and even her old friend, newspaperman Danny Cahill, is shocked.

But Susan has not forgotten them. As the threat of world war grows she realizes she must choose between the family she still cares about and a lover who will not let her go.

HODDER

JESSICA STIRLING

The Paradise Waltz

Christine Summers is a modern girl. It's 1932, and the pretty schoolteacher has no intention of sacrificing her independence to marry anyone, least of all Charley Noonan, the rough-tongued young farmer who has pursued her for years.

When she meets lonely widower Alan Kelso, however, the mood, the music and the man all seem to slip into place and Christine finds herself falling in love.

But Alan has also caught the eye of pony breeder Beatty McCall. Passionate, experienced and unscrupulous, Beatty wants him for herself and is willing to offer him more than Christine can ever hope to match.

Sometimes, though, all it takes is just one dance to change your life forever.

HODDER

JESSICA STIRLING

One True Love

Susanne Thorne is an orphan of means, one reason why Bette Hollander carries the young English girl off to her home in far-away Scotland.

Bette would be more than happy for Susanne to fall in love with her handsome, headstrong son Louis, for marriage to the little heiress would repay old debts and restore the Hollander family's fortunes.

But love cannot be delivered to order and as Susanne grows up and proves to have a mind of her own, Bette's plans for a match made in heaven seem fated to end in disaster.

HODDER